LORD JIM

LORD JIM

A Tale

BY

JOSEPH CONRAD

"It is certain my Conviction gains infinitely, the
moment another soul will believe in it."—NOVALIS.

POCKET EDITION

WILLIAM BLACKWOOD & SONS LTD.
EDINBURGH AND LONDON
MCMXXXI

TO

MR AND MRS G. F. W. HOPE

With grateful affection

after

many years of friendship.

LORD JIM.

CHAPTER I.

HE was an inch, perhaps two, under six feet, power-fully built, and he advanced straight at you with a slight stoop of the shoulders, head forward, and a fixed from-under stare which made you think of a charging bull. His voice was deep, loud, and his manner displayed a kind of dogged self-assertion which had nothing aggressive in it. It seemed a necessity, and it was directed apparently as much at himself as at anybody else. He was spotlessly neat, apparelled in immaculate white from shoes to hat, and in the various Eastern ports where he got his living as ship-chandler's water-clerk he was very popular.

A water-clerk need not pass an examination in anything under the sun, but he must have Ability in the abstract and demonstrate it practically. His work consists in racing under sail, steam, or oars against other water-clerks for any ship about to anchor, greeting her captain cheerily, forcing upon him a card—the business card of the ship-chandler—

and on his first visit on shore piloting him firmly but
without ostentation to a vast, cavern-like shop which
is full of things that are eaten and drunk on board
ship ; where you can get everything to make her
seaworthy and beautiful, from a set of chain-hooks
for her cable to a book of gold-leaf for the carvings
of her stern ; and where her commander is received
like a brother by a ship-chandler he has never seen
before. There is a cool parlour, easy-chairs, bottles,
cigars, writing implements, a copy of harbour regu-
lations, and a warmth of welcome that melts the salt
of a three months' passage out of a seaman's heart.
The connection thus begun is kept up, as long as
the ship remains in harbour, by the daily visits of
the water-clerk. To the captain he is faithful like
a friend and attentive like a son, with the patience
of Job, the unselfish devotion of a woman, and the
jollity of a boon companion. Later on the bill is
sent in. It is a beautiful and humane occupation.
Therefore good water-clerks are scarce. When a
water-clerk who possesses Ability in the abstract has
also the advantage of having been brought up to the
sea, he is worth to his employer a lot of money and
some humouring. Jim had always good wages and
as much humouring as would have bought the
fidelity of a fiend. Nevertheless, with black ingrati-
tude he would throw up the job suddenly and depart.
To his employers the reasons he gave were obviously
inadequate. They said " Confounded fool ! " as soon
as his back was turned. This was their criticism on
his exquisite sensibility.

To the white men in the waterside business and to
the captains of ships he was just Jim—nothing more.
He had, of course, another name, but he was anxious
that it should not be pronounced. His incognito,

which had as many holes as a sieve, was not meant to hide a personality but a fact. When the fact broke through the incognito he would leave suddenly the seaport where he happened to be at the time and go to another—generally farther east. He kept to seaports because he was a seaman in exile from the sea, and had Ability in the abstract, which is good for no other work but that of a water-clerk. He retreated in good order towards the rising sun, and the fact followed him casually but inevitably. Thus in the course of years he was known successively in Bombay, in Calcutta, in Rangoon, in Penang, in Batavia—and in each of these halting-places was just Jim the water-clerk. Afterwards, when his keen perception of the Intolerable drove him away for good from seaports and white men, even into the virgin forest, the Malays of the jungle village, where he had elected to conceal his deplorable faculty, added a word to the monosyllable of his incognito. They called him Tuan Jim : as one might say—Lord Jim.

Originally he came from a parsonage. Many commanders of fine merchant-ships come from these abodes of piety and peace. Jim's father possessed such certain knowledge of the Unknowable as made for the righteousness of people in cottages without disturbing the ease of mind of those whom an unerring Providence enables to live in mansions. The little church on a hill had the mossy greyness of a rock seen through a ragged screen of leaves. It had stood there for centuries, but the trees around probably remembered the laying of the first stone. Below, the red front of the rectory gleamed with a warm tint in the midst of grass-plots, flower-beds, and fir-trees, with an orchard at the back, a paved stable-yard to the left, and the sloping glass of greenhouses tacked along a wall of bricks. The living had belonged to the family for generations ; but Jim was one of five sons, and when after a course of light holiday literature his vocation for the sea had declared itself, he was sent at once to a " training-ship for officers of the mercantile marine."

He learned there a little trigonometry and how to cross top-gallant yards. He was generally liked. He had the third place in navigation and pulled stroke in the first cutter. Having a steady head with an excellent physique, he was very smart aloft. His station was in the fore-top, and often from there he looked down, with the contempt of a man destined to shine in the midst of dangers, at the peaceful multitude of roofs cut in two by the brown tide of the stream, while scattered on the outskirts of the surrounding plain the factory chimneys rose perpendicular against a grimy sky, each slender like a pencil, and belching out smoke like a volcano. He could see the big ships departing, the broad-beamed ferries constantly on the move, the little boats floating far below his feet, with the hazy splendour of the sea in the distance, and the hope of a stirring life in the world of adventure.

On the lower deck in the babel of two hundred voices he would forget himself, and beforehand live in his mind the sea-life of light literature. He saw himself saving people from sinking ships, cutting away masts in a hurricane, swimming through a surf with a line ; or as a lonely castaway, barefooted and half naked, walking on uncovered reefs in search of shellfish to stave off starvation. He confronted savages on tropical shores, quelled mutinies on the high seas, and in a small boat upon the ocean kept up the hearts of despairing men—always an example of devotion to duty, and as unflinching as a hero in a book.

"Something's up. Come along."

He leaped to his feet. The boys were streaming up the ladders. Above could be heard a great scurrying about and shouting, and when he got through the hatchway he stood still—as if confounded.

It was the dusk of a winter's day. The gale had freshened since noon, stopping the traffic on the river, and now blew with the strength of a hurricane in fitful bursts that boomed like salvoes of great guns firing over the ocean. The rain slanted in sheets that flicked and subsided, and between whiles Jim had threatening glimpses of the tumbling tide, the small craft jumbled and tossing along the shore, the motionless buildings in the driving mist, the broad ferry-boats pitching ponderously at anchor, the vast landing-stages heaving up and down and smothered in sprays. The next gust seemed to blow all this away. The air was full of flying water. There was a fierce purpose in the gale, a furious earnestness in the screech of the wind, in the brutal tumult of earth and sky, that seemed directed at him, and made him hold his breath in awe. He stood still. It seemed to him he was whirled around.

He was jostled. "Man the cutter!" Boys rushed past him. A coaster running in for shelter had crashed through a schooner at anchor, and one of the ship's instructors had seen the accident. A mob of boys clambered on the rails, clustered round the davits. "Collision. Just ahead of us.

Mr Symons saw it." A push made him stagger against the mizzen-mast, and he caught hold of a rope. The old training-ship chained to her moorings quivered all over, bowing gently head to wind, and with her scanty rigging humming in a deep bass the breathless song of her youth at sea. "Lower away !" He saw the boat, manned, drop swiftly below the rail, and rushed after her. He heard a splash. "Let go ; clear the falls !" He leaned over. The river alongside seethed in frothy streaks. The cutter could be seen in the falling darkness under the spell of tide and wind, that for a moment held her bound, and tossing abreast of the ship. A yelling voice in her reached him faintly : "Keep stroke, you young whelps, if you want to save anybody ! Keep stroke !" And suddenly she lifted high her bow, and, leaping with raised oars over a wave, broke the spell cast upon her by the wind and tide.

Jim felt his shoulder gripped firmly. "Too late, youngster." The captain of the ship laid a restraining hand on that boy, who seemed on the point of leaping overboard, and Jim looked up with the pain of conscious defeat in his eyes. The captain smiled sympathetically. "Better luck next time. This will teach you to be smart."

A shrill cheer greeted the cutter. She came dancing back half full of water, and with two exhausted men washing about on her bottom boards. The tumult and the menace of wind and sea now appeared very contemptible to Jim, increasing the regret of his awe at their inefficient menace. Now he knew what to think of it. It seemed to him he cared nothing for the gale. He could affront greater perils. He would do so—better than anybody. Not a particle of fear was left. Nevertheless he brooded apart that evening while the bowman of the cutter—a boy with a face like a girl's and big grey eyes—was the hero of the lower deck. Eager questioners crowded round him. He narrated : " I just saw his head bobbing, and I dashed my boat-hook in the water. It caught in his breeches and I nearly went overboard, as I thought I would, only old Symons let go the tiller and grabbed my legs—the boat nearly swamped. Old Symons is a fine old chap. I don't mind a bit him being grumpy with us. He swore at me all the time he held my leg, but that was only his way of telling me to stick to the boat-hook. Old Symons is awfully excitable—isn't he ? No—not the little fair chap— the other, the big one with a beard. When we pulled him in he groaned, ' Oh, my leg ! oh, my leg ! ' and turned up his eyes. Fancy such a big chap fainting like a girl. Would any of you fellows faint for a jab with a boat-hook ?—I wouldn't. It went into his leg so far." He showed the boat-hook, which he had carried below for the purpose, and produced a sensation. " No, silly ! It was not his flesh that held him—his breeches did. Lots of blood, of course."

Jim thought it a pitiful display of vanity. The gale had ministered to a heroism as spurious as its own pretence of terror. He felt angry with the brutal tumult of earth and sky for taking him unawares and checking unfairly a generous readiness for narrow escapes. Otherwise he was rather glad he had not gone into the cutter, since a lower achievement had served the turn. He had enlarged his knowledge more than those who had done the work. When all men flinched, then—he felt sure—

he alone would know how to deal with the spurious menace of wind and seas. He knew what to think of it. Seen dispassionately, it seemed contemptible. He could detect no trace of emotion in himself, and the final effect of a staggering event was that, unnoticed and apart from the noisy crowd of boys, he exulted with fresh certitude in his avidity for adventure, and in a sense of many-sided courage.

CHAPTER II.

AFTER two years of training he went to sea, and entering the regions so well known to his imagination, found them strangely barren of adventure. He made many voyages. He knew the magic monotony of existence between sky and water : he had to bear the criticism of men, the exactions of the sea, and the prosaic severity of the daily task that gives bread— but whose only reward is in the perfect love of the work. This reward eluded him. Yet he could not go back, because there is nothing more enticing, disenchanting, and enslaving than the life at sea. Besides, his prospects were good. He was gentlemanly, steady, tractable, with a thorough knowledge of his duties ; and in time, when yet very young, he became chief mate of a fine ship, without ever having been tested by those events of the sea that show in the light of day the inner worth of a man, the edge of his temper, and the fibre of his stuff ; that reveal the quality of his resistance and the secret truth of his pretences, not only to others but also to himself.

Only once in all that time he had again the glimpse of the earnestness in the anger of the sea. That truth is not so often made apparent as people might think. There are many shades in the danger of adventures and gales, and it is only now and then that there appears on the face of facts a sinister violence of intention—that indefinable something which forces it upon the mind and the heart of a man, that this complication of accidents or these elemental furies are coming at him with a purpose of malice, with a strength beyond control, with an unbridled cruelty that means to tear out of him his hope and his fear, the pain of his fatigue and his longing for rest : which means to smash, to destroy, to annihilate all he had seen, known, loved, enjoyed, or hated ; all that is priceless and necessary—the sunshine, the memories, the future,—which means to sweep the whole precious world utterly away from his sight by the simple and appalling act of taking his life.

Jim, disabled by a falling spar at the beginning of a week of which his Scottish captain used to say afterwards, " Man ! it's a pairfect meeracle to me how she lived through it ! " spent many days stretched on his back, dazed, battered, hopeless, and tormented as if at the bottom of an abyss of unrest. He did not care what the end would be, and in his lucid moments overvalued his indifference. The danger, when not seen, has the imperfect vagueness of human thought. The fear grows shadowy ; and Imagination, the enemy of men, the father of all terrors, unstimulated, sinks to rest in the dulness of exhausted emotion. Jim saw nothing but the disorder of his tossed cabin. He lay there battened down in the midst of a small devastation, and felt secretly glad he had not to go on deck. But now and again an uncontrollable rush of anguish would grip him bodily, make him gasp and writhe under the blankets, and then the unintelligent brutality of an existence liable to the agony of such sensations filled him with a despairing desire to escape at any cost. Then fine weather returned, and he thought no more about it.

His lameness, however, persisted, and when the ship arrived at an Eastern port he had to go to the hospital. His recovery was slow, and he was left behind.

There were only two other patients in the white men's ward : the purser of a gunboat, who had broken his leg falling down a hatchway ; and a kind of railway contractor from a neighbouring province, afflicted by some mysterious tropical disease, who held the doctor for an ass, and indulged in secret debaucheries of patent medicine which his Tamil servant used to smuggle in with unwearied devotion. They told each other the story of their lives, played cards a little, or, yawning and in pyjamas, lounged through the day in easy-chairs without saying a word. The hospital stood on a hill, and a gentle breeze entering through the windows, always flung wide open, brought into the bare room the softness of the sky, the languor of the earth, the bewitching breath of the Eastern waters. There were perfumes in it, suggestions of infinite repose, the gift of endless dreams. Jim looked every day over the thickets of gardens, beyond the roofs of the town, over the fronds of palms growing on the shore, at that roadstead which is a thoroughfare to the East,—at the road-stead dotted by garlanded islets, lighted by festal sunshine, its ships like toys, its brilliant activity resembling a holiday pageant, with the eternal serenity of the Eastern sky overhead and the smiling peace of the Eastern seas possessing the space as far as the horizon.

Directly he could walk without a stick, he descended into the town to look for some opportunity to get home. Nothing offered just then, and, while waiting, he associated naturally with the men of his calling in the port. These were of two kinds. Some, very few and seen there but seldom, led mysterious lives, had preserved an undefaced energy with the temper of buccaneers and the eyes of dreamers. They appeared to live in a crazy maze of plans, hopes, dangers, enterprises, ahead of civilisation, in the dark places of the sea ; and their death was the only event of their fantastic existence that seemed to have a reasonable certitude of achievement. The majority were men who, like himself, thrown there by some accident, had remained as officers of country ships. They had now a horror of the home service, with its harder conditions, severer view of duty, and the hazard of stormy oceans. They were attuned to the eternal peace of Eastern sky and sea. They loved short passages, good deck-chairs, large native crews, and the distinction of being white. They shuddered at the thought of hard work, and led precariously easy lives, always on the verge of dismissal, always on the verge of engagement, serving Chinamen, Arabs, half-castes— would have served the devil himself had he made it easy enough. They talked everlastingly of turns of luck : how So-and-so got charge of a boat on the coast of China—a soft thing ; how this one had an easy billet in Japan somewhere, and that one was doing well in the Siamese navy ; and in all they said—in their actions, in their looks, in their persons—could be detected the soft spot, the place of decay, the determination to lounge safely through existence.

To Jim that gossiping crowd, viewed as seamen, seemed at first more unsubstantial than so many shadows. But at length he found a fascination in the sight of those men, in their appearance of doing so well on such a small allowance of danger and toil. In time, beside the original disdain there grew up slowly another sentiment ; and suddenly, giving up the idea of going home, he took a berth as chief mate of the *Patna*.

The *Patna* was a local steamer as old as the hills, lean like a greyhound, and eaten up with rust worse than a condemned water-tank. She was owned by a Chinaman, chartered by an Arab, and commanded by a sort of renegade New South Wales German, very anxious to curse publicly his native country, but who, apparently on the strength of Bismarck's victorious policy, brutalised all those he was not afraid of, and wore a " blood-and-iron " air, combined with a purple nose and a red moustache. After she had been painted outside and whitewashed inside, eight hundred pilgrims (more or less) were driven on board of her as she lay with steam up alongside a wooden jetty.

They streamed aboard over three gangways, they streamed in urged by faith and the hope of paradise, they streamed in with a continuous tramp and shuffle of bare feet, without a word, a murmur, or a look back ; and when clear of confining rails spread on all sides over the deck, flowed forward and aft, overflowed down the yawning hatchways, filled the inner recesses of the ship—like water filling a cistern, like water flowing into crevices and crannies, like water rising silently even with the rim. Eight hundred men and women with faith and hopes, with affections and memories, they had collected there, coming from north and south and from the outskirts of the East, after treading the jungle paths, descending the rivers, coasting in praus along the shallows, crossing in small canoes from island to island, passing through suffering, meeting strange sights, beset by strange fears, upheld by one desire. They came from solitary huts in the wilderness, from populous campongs, from villages by the sea. At the call of an idea they had left their forests, their clearings, the protection of their rulers, their prosperity, their poverty, the surroundings of their youth and the graves of their fathers. They came covered with dust, with sweat, with grime, with rags—the strong men at the head of family parties, the lean old men pressing forward without hope of return ; young boys with fearless eyes glancing curiously, shy little girls with tumbled long hair ; the timid women muffled up and clasping to their breasts, wrapped in loose ends of soiled head-cloths, their sleeping babies, the unconscious pilgrims of an exacting belief.

" Look at dese cattle," said the German skipper to his new chief mate.

An Arab, the leader of that pious voyage, came last. He walked slowly aboard, handsome and grave in his white gown and large turban. A string of servants followed, loaded with his luggage ; the *Patna* cast off and backed away from the wharf.

She was headed between two small islets, crossed obliquely the anchoring-ground of sailing-ships, swung through half a circle in the shadow of a hill, then ranged close to a ledge of foaming reefs. The Arab, standing up aft, recited aloud the prayer of travellers by sea. He invoked the favour of the Most High upon that journey, implored His blessing on men's toil and on the secret purposes of their hearts ; the steamer pounded in the dusk the calm water of the Strait ; and far astern of the pilgrim ship a screw-pile lighthouse, planted by unbelievers on a treacherous shoal, seemed to wink at her its eye of flame, as if in derision of her errand of faith.

She cleared the Straits, crossed the bay, continued on her way through the " One-degree " passage. She held on straight for the Red Sea under a serene sky, under a sky scorching and unclouded, enveloped in a fulgor of sunshine that killed all thought, oppressed the heart, withered all impulses of strength and energy. And under the sinister splendour of that sky the sea, blue and profound, remained still, without a stir, without a ripple, without a wrinkle—viscous, stagnant, dead. The *Patna*, with a slight hiss, passed over that plain luminous and smooth, unrolled a black ribbon of smoke across the sky, left behind her on the water a white ribbon of foam that vanished at once, like the phantom of a track drawn upon a lifeless sea by the phantom of a steamer.

Every morning the sun, as if keeping pace in his revolutions with the progress of the pilgrimage, emerged with a silent burst of light exactly at the same distance astern of the ship, caught up with her at noon, pouring the concentrated fire of his rays on the pious purposes of the men, glided past on his descent, and sank mysteriously into the sea evening after evening, preserving the same distance ahead of her advancing bows. The five whites on board lived amidships, isolated from the human cargo. The awnings covered the deck with a white roof from stem to stern, and a faint hum, a low murmur of sad voices, alone revealed the presence of a crowd of people upon the great blaze of the ocean. Such were the days, still, hot, heavy, disappearing one by one into the past, as if falling into an abyss for ever open in the wake of the ship ; and the ship, lonely under a wisp of smoke, held on her steadfast way black and smouldering in a luminous immensity, as if scorched by a flame flicked at her from a heaven without pity.

The nights descended on her like a benediction.

CHAPTER III.

A MARVELLOUS stillness pervaded the world, and the stars, together with the serenity of their rays, seemed to shed upon the earth the assurance of everlasting security. The young moon recurved, and shining low in the west, was like a slender shaving thrown up from a bar of gold, and the Arabian Sea, smooth and cool to the eye like a sheet of ice, extended its perfect level to the perfect circle of a dark horizon. The propeller turned without a check, as though its beat had been part of the scheme of a safe universe ; and on each side of the *Patna* two deep folds of water, permanent and sombre on the unwrinkled shimmer, enclosed within their straight and diverging ridges a few white swirls of foam bursting in a low hiss, a few wavelets, a few ripples, a few undulations that, left behind, agitated the surface of the sea for an instant after the passage of the ship, subsided splashing gently, calmed down at last into the circular stillness of water and sky with the black speck of the moving hull remaining everlastingly in its centre.

Jim on the bridge was penetrated by the great certitude of unbounded safety and peace that could be read on the silent aspect of nature like the certitude of fostering love upon the placid tenderness of a mother's face. Below the roof of awnings, surrendered to the wisdom of white men and to their courage, trusting the power of their unbelief and the iron shell of their fire-ship, the pilgrims of an exacting faith slept on mats, on blankets, on bare planks, on every deck, in all the dark corners, wrapped in dyed cloths, muffled in soiled rags, with their heads resting on small bundles, with their faces pressed to bent forearms : the men, the women, the children ; the old with the young, the decrepit with the lusty—all equal before sleep, death's brother.

A draught of air, fanned from forward by the speed of the ship, passed steadily through the long gloom between the high bulwarks, swept over the rows of prone bodies ; a few dim flames in globe-lamps were hung short here and there under the ridge-poles, and in the blurred circles of light thrown down and trembling slightly to the unceasing vibration of the ship appeared a chin upturned, two closed eyelids, a dark hand with silver rings, a meagre limb draped in a torn covering, a head bent back, a naked foot, a throat bared and stretched as if offering itself to the knife. The well-to-do had made for their families shelters with heavy boxes and dusty mats ; the poor reposed side by side with all they had on earth tied up in a rag under their heads ; the lone old men slept, with drawn-up legs, upon their prayer-carpets, with their hands over their ears and one elbow on each side of the face : a father, his shoulders up and his knees under his forehead, dozed dejectedly by a boy who slept on his back with tousled hair and one arm commandingly extended ; a woman covered from head to foot, like a corpse, with a piece of white sheeting, had a naked child in the hollow of each arm ; the Arab's belongings, piled right aft, made a heavy mound of broken outlines, with a cargo-lamp swung above, and a great confusion of vague forms behind : gleams of paunchy brass pots, the foot-rest of a deck-chair, blades of spears, the straight scabbard of an old sword leaning against a heap of pillows, the spout of a tin coffee-pot. The patent log on the taffrail periodically rang a single tinkling stroke for every mile traversed on an errand of faith. Above the mass of sleepers a faint and patient sigh at times floated, the exhalation of a troubled dream ; and short metallic clangs bursting out suddenly in the depths of the ship, the harsh scrape of a shovel, the violent slam of a furnace-door, exploded brutally, as if the men handling the mysterious things below had their breasts full of fierce anger : while the slim high hull of the steamer went on evenly ahead, without a sway of her bare masts, cleaving continuously the great calm of the waters under the inaccessible serenity of the sky.

Jim paced athwart, and his footsteps in the vast silence were loud to his own ears, as if echoed by the

watchful stars : his eyes roaming about the line of
the horizon, seemed to gaze hungrily into the unattainable, and did not see the shadow of the coming
event. The only shadow on the sea was the shadow
of the black smoke pouring heavily from the funnel
its immense streamer, whose end was constantly
dissolving in the air. Two Malays, silent and almost
motionless, steered, one on each side of the wheel,
whose brass rim shone fragmentarily in the oval of
light thrown out by the binnacle. Now and then
a hand, with black fingers alternately letting go and
catching hold of revolving spokes, appeared in the
illumined part ; the links of wheel-chains ground
heavily in the grooves of the barrel. Jim would
glance at the compass, would glance around the
unattainable horizon, would stretch himself till his
joints cracked, with a leisurely twist of the body,
in the very excess of wellbeing ; and, as if made
audacious by the invincible aspect of the peace,
he felt he cared for nothing that could happen
to him to the end of his days. From time to time
he glanced idly at a chart pegged out with four
drawing-pins on a low three-legged table abaft
the steering-gear case. The sheet of paper por-
traying the depths of the sea presented a shiny
surface under the light of a bull's-eye lamp lashed
to a stanchion, a surface as level and smooth as the
glimmering surface of the waters. Parallel rulers
with a pair of dividers reposed on it ; the ship's
position at last noon was marked with a small
black cross, and the straight pencil-line drawn firmly
as far as Perim figured the course of the ship—the
path of souls towards the holy place, the promise
of salvation, the reward of eternal life—while the
pencil with its sharp end touching the Somali coast

lay round and still like a naked ship's spar floating in the pool of a sheltered dock. " How steady she goes," thought Jim with wonder, with something like gratitude for this high peace of sea and sky. At such times his thoughts would be full of valorous deeds : he loved these dreams and the success of his imaginary achievements. They were the best parts of life, its secret truth, its hidden reality. They had a gorgeous virility, the charm of vagueness, they passed before him with a heroic tread ; they carried his soul away with them and made it drunk with the divine philtre of an unbounded confidence in itself. There was nothing he could not face. He was so pleased with the idea that he smiled, keeping perfunctorily his eyes ahead ; and when he happened to glance back he saw the white streak of the wake drawn as straight by the ship's keel upon the sea as the black line drawn by the pencil upon the chart.

The ash-buckets racketed, clanking up and down the stoke-hold ventilators, and this tin-pot clatter warned him the end of his watch was near. He sighed with content, with regret as well at having to part from that serenity which fostered the adventurous freedom of his thoughts. He was a little sleepy too, and felt a pleasurable languor running through every limb as though all the blood in his body had turned to warm milk. His skipper had come up noiselessly, in pyjamas and with his sleeping-jacket flung wide open. Red of face, only half awake, the left eye partly closed, the right staring stupid and glassy, he hung his big head over the chart and scratched his ribs sleepily. There was something obscene in the sight of his naked flesh. His bared breast glistened soft and greasy as though he had sweated out his fat in his sleep. He pronounced a professional remark in a voice harsh and dead, resembling the rasping sound of a wood-file on the edge of a plank ; the fold of his double chin hung like a bag triced up close under the hinge of his jaw. Jim started, and his answer was full of deference ; but the odious and fleshy figure, as though seen for the first time in a revealing moment, fixed itself in his memory for ever as the incarnation of everything vile and base that lurks in the world we love : in our own hearts we trust for our salvation, in the men that surround us, in the sights that fill out eyes, in the sounds that fill our ears, and in the air that fills our lungs.

The thin gold shaving of the moon floating slowly downwards had lost itself on the darkened surface of the waters, and the eternity beyond the sky seemed to come down nearer to the earth, with the augmented glitter of the stars, with the more profound sombreness in the lustre of the half-transparent dome covering the flat disc of an opaque sea. The ship moved so smoothly that her onward motion was imperceptible to the senses of men, as though she had been a crowded planet speeding through the dark spaces of ether behind the swarm of suns, in the appalling and calm solitudes awaiting the breath of future creations. " Hot is no name for it down below," said a voice.

Jim smiled without looking round. The skipper presented an unmoved breadth of back : it was the renegade's trick to appear pointedly unaware of your existence unless it suited his purpose to turn at you with a devouring glare before he let loose a torrent of foamy, abusive jargon that came like a gush from a sewer. Now he emitted only a sulky grunt ; the second engineer at the head of the bridge-ladder,

kneading with damp palms a dirty sweat-rag, unabashed, continued the tale of his complaints. The
sailors had a good time of it up here, and what was
the use of them in the world he would be blowed if
he could see. The poor devils of engineers had to
get the ship along anyhow, and they could very
well do the rest too; by gosh they—— "Shut
up!" growled the German stolidly. "Oh yes!
Shut up—and when anything goes wrong you fly to
us, don't you?" went on the other. He was more
than half cooked, he expected; but anyway, now,
he did not mind how much he sinned, because these
last three days he had passed through a fine course
of training for the place where the bad boys go when
they die—b'gosh, he had—besides being made jolly
well deaf by the blasted racket below. The durned,
compound, surface-condensing, rotten scrap-heap
rattled and banged down there like an old deck-
winch, only more so; and what made him risk his
life every night and day that God made amongst
the refuse of a breaking-up yard flying round at
fifty-seven revolutions, was more than *he* could tell.
He must have been born reckless, b'gosh. He
. . . "Where did you get drink?" inquired the
German, very savage, but motionless in the light
of the binnacle, like a clumsy effigy of a man cut
out of a block of fat. Jim went on smiling at the
retreating horizon; his heart was full of generous
impulses, and his thought was contemplating his
own superiority. "Drink!" repeated the engineer
with amiable scorn: he was hanging on with both
hands to the rail, a shadowy figure with flexible
legs. "Not from you, captain. You're far too
mean, b'gosh. You would let a good man die sooner
than give him a drop of shnaps. That's what

you Germans call economy. Penny wise, pound
foolish." He became sentimental. The chief had
given him a four-finger nip about ten o'clock—
" only one, s'elp me ! "—good old chief ; but as to
getting the old fraud out of his bunk—a five-ton
crane couldn't do it. Not it. Not to-night anyhow.
He was sleeping sweetly like a little child, with a
bottle of prime brandy under his pillow. From the
thick throat of the commander of the *Patna* came
a low rumble, on which the sound of the word
schwein fluttered high and low like a capricious
feather in a faint stir of air. He and the chief
engineer had been cronies for a good few years—
serving the same jovial, crafty, old Chinaman, with
horn-rimmed goggles and strings of red silk plaited
into the venerable grey hairs of his pigtail. The
quay-side opinion in the *Patna's* home-port was
that these two in the way of brazen peculation
" had done together pretty well everything you can
think of." Outwardly they were badly matched :
one dull-eyed, malevolent, and of soft fleshy curves ;
the other lean, all hollows, with a head long and
bony like the head of an old horse, with sunken
cheeks, with sunken temples, with an indifferent
glazed glance of sunken eyes. He had been stranded
out East somewhere—in Canton, in Shanghai, or
perhaps in Yokohama ; he probably did not care to
remember himself the exact locality, nor yet the
cause of his shipwreck. He had been, in mercy to
his youth, kicked quietly out of his ship twenty
years ago or more, and it might have been so much
worse for him that the memory of the episode had
in it hardly a trace of misfortune. Then, steam
navigation expanding in these seas and men of his
craft being scarce at first, he had " got on " after

a sort. He was eager to let strangers know in a dismal mumble that he was "an old stager out here." When he moved a skeleton seemed to sway loose in his clothes ; his walk was mere wandering, and he was given to wander thus around the engine-room skylight, smoking, without relish, doctored tobacco in a brass bowl at the end of a cherrywood stem four feet long, with the imbecile gravity of a thinker evolving a system of philosophy from the hazy glimpse of a truth. He was usually anything but free with his private store of liquor ; but on that night he had departed from his principles, so that his second, a weak-headed child of Wapping, what with the unexpectedness of the treat and the strength of the stuff, had become very happy, cheeky, and talkative. The fury of the New South Wales German was extreme ; he puffed like an exhaust-pipe, and Jim, faintly amused by the scene, was impatient for the time when he could get below : the last ten minutes of the watch were irritating like a gun that hangs fire ; those men did not belong to the world of heroic adventure ; they weren't bad chaps though. Even the skipper himself . . . His gorge rose at the mass of panting flesh from which issued gurgling mutters, a cloudy trickle of filthy expressions ; but he was too pleasurably languid to dislike actively this or any other thing. The quality of these men did not matter ; he rubbed shoulders with them, but they could not touch him ; he shared the air they breathed, but he was different. . . . Would the skipper go for the engineer ? . . . The life was easy, and he was too sure of himself—too sure of himself to. . . . The line dividing his meditation from a surreptitious doze on his feet was thinner than a thread in a spider's web.

The second engineer was coming by easy transitions to the consideration of his finances and of his courage.

"Who's drunk? I? No, no, captain! That won't do. You ought to know by this time the chief ain't free-hearted enough to make a sparrow drunk, b'gosh. I've never been the worse for liquor in my life; the stuff ain't made yet that would make *me* drunk. I could drink liquid fire against your whisky peg for peg, b'gosh, and keep as cool as a cucumber. If I thought I was drunk I would jump overboard—do away with myself, b'gosh. I would! Straight! And I won't go off the bridge. Where do you expect me to take the air on a night like this, eh? On deck amongst that vermin down there? Likely—ain't it! And I am not afraid of anything you can do."

The German lifted two heavy fists to heaven and shook them a little without a word.

"I don't know what fear is," pursued the engineer, with the enthusiasm of sincere conviction. "I am not afraid of doing all the bloomin' work in this rotten hooker, b'gosh! And a jolly good thing for you that there are some of us about the world that aren't afraid of their lives, or where would you be— you and this old thing here with her plates like brown paper—brown paper, s'elp me? It's all very fine for you—you get a power of pieces out of her one way and another; but what about me—what do I get? A measly hundred and fifty dollars a-month and find yourself. I wish to ask you respectfully —respectfully, mind—who wouldn't chuck a dratted job like this? 'Tain't safe, s'elp me, it ain't! Only I am one of them fearless fellows . . ."

He let go the rail and made ample gestures as if

demonstrating in the air the shape and extent of his valour ; his thin voice darted in prolonged squeaks upon the sea, he tiptoed back and forth for the better emphasis of utterance, and suddenly pitched down head-first as though he had been clubbed from behind. He said " Damn ! " as he tumbled ; an instant of silence followed upon his screeching : Jim and the skipper staggered forward by common accord, and catching themselves up, stood very stiff and still gazing, amazed, at the undisturbed level of the sea. Then they looked upwards at the stars.

What had happened ? The wheezy thump of the engines went on. Had the earth been checked in her course ? They could not understand ; and suddenly the calm sea, the sky without a cloud, appeared formidably insecure in their immobility, as it poised on the brow of yawning destruction. The engineer rebounded vertically full length and collapsed again into a vague heap. This heap said " What's that ? " in the muffled accents of profound grief. A faint noise as of thunder, of thunder infinitely remote, less than a sound, hardly more than a vibration, passed slowly, and the ship quivered in response, as if the thunder had growled deep down in the water. The eyes of the two Malays at the wheel glittered towards the white men, but their dark hands remained closed on the spokes. The sharp hull driving on its way seemed to rise a few inches in succession through its whole length, as though it had become pliable, and settled down again rigidly to its work of cleaving the smooth surface of the sea. Its quivering stopped, and the faint noise of thunder ceased all at once, as though the ship had steamed across a narrow belt of vibrating water and of humming air.

CHAPTER IV.

A MONTH or so afterwards, when Jim, in answer
to pointed questions, tried to tell honestly the truth
of this experience, he said, speaking of the ship:
"She went over whatever it was as easy as a snake
crawling over a stick." The illustration was good:
the questions were aiming at facts, and the official
Inquiry was being held in the police court of an
Eastern port. He stood elevated in the witness-box,
with burning cheeks in a cool lofty room: the big
framework of punkahs moved gently to and fro high
above his head, and from below many eyes were
looking at him out of dark faces, out of white faces,
out of red faces, out of faces attentive, spellbound,
as if all these people sitting in orderly rows upon
narrow benches had been enslaved by the fascination
of his voice. It was very loud, it rang startling in
his own ears, it was the only sound audible in the
world, for the terribly distinct questions that extorted his answers seemed to shape themselves in
anguish and pain within his breast,—came to him
poignant and silent like the terrible questioning of
one's conscience. Outside the court the sun blazed—
within was the wind of great punkahs that made
you shiver, the shame that made you burn, the
attentive eyes whose glance stabbed. The face of
the presiding magistrate, clean shaved and im-
passible, looked at him deadly pale between the red
faces of the two nautical assessors. The light of a
broad window under the ceiling fell from above on
the heads and shoulders of the three men, and they
were fiercely distinct in the half-light of the big

court-room where the audience seemed composed of
staring shadows. They wanted facts. Facts! They
demanded facts from him, as if facts could explain
anything!

"After you had concluded you had collided with
something floating awash, say a water-logged wreck,
you were ordered by your captain to go forward and
ascertain if there was any damage done. Did you
think it likely from the force of the blow?" asked
the assessor sitting to the left. He had a thin
horseshoe beard, salient cheek-bones, and with both
elbows on the desk clasped his rugged hands before
his face, looking at Jim with thoughtful blue eyes;
the other, a heavy, scornful man, thrown back in his
seat, his left arm extended full length, drummed
delicately with his finger-tips on a blotting-pad: in
the middle the magistrate upright in the roomy
arm-chair, his head inclined slightly on the shoulder,
had his arms crossed on his breast and a few flowers
in a glass vase by the side of his inkstand.

"I did not," said Jim. "I was told to call no one
and to make no noise for fear of creating a panic.
I thought the precaution reasonable. I took one
of the lamps that were hung under the awnings
and went forward. After opening the forepeak
hatch I heard splashing in there. I lowered then
the lamp the whole drift of its lanyard, and saw
that the forepeak was more than half full of water
already. I knew then there must be a big hole
below the water-line." He paused.

"Yes," said the big assessor, with a dreamy smile
at the blotting-pad; his fingers played incessantly,
touching the paper without noise.

"I did not think of danger just then. I might
have been a little startled: all this happened in such

a quiet way and so very suddenly. I knew there
was no other bulkhead in the ship but the collision
bulkhead separating the forepeak from the forehold.
I went back to tell the captain. I came upon the
second engineer getting up at the foot of the bridge-
ladder : he seemed dazed, and told me he thought
his left arm was broken ; he had slipped on the top
step when getting down while I was forward. He
exclaimed, 'My God ! That rotten bulkhead 'll give
way in a minute, and the damned thing will go
down under us like a lump of lead.' He pushed me
away with his right arm and ran before me up the
ladder, shouting as he climbed. His left arm hung
by his side. I followed up in time to see the captain
rush at him and knock him down flat on his back.
He did not strike him again : he stood bending over
him and speaking angrily but quite low. I fancy he
was asking him why the devil he didn't go and stop
the engines, instead of making a row about it on
deck. I heard him say, 'Get up ! Run, fly !' He
swore also. The engineer slid down the starboard
ladder and bolted round the skylight to the engine-
room companion which was on the port-side. He
moaned as he ran. . . .''

He spoke slowly ; he remembered swiftly and with
extreme vividness ; he could have reproduced like an
echo the moaning of the engineer for the better information of these men who wanted facts. After his
first feeling of revolt he had come round to the view
that only a meticulous precision of statement would
bring out the true horror behind the appalling face
of things. The facts those men were so eager to
know had been visible, tangible, open to the senses,
occupying their place in space and time, requiring
for their existence a fourteen-hundred-ton steamer

and twenty-seven minutes by the watch ; they made a whole that had features, shades of expression, a complicated aspect that could be remembered by the eye, and something else besides, something invisible, a directing spirit of perdition that dwelt within, like a malevolent soul in a detestable body. He was anxious to make this clear. This had not been a common affair, everything in it had been of the utmost importance, and fortunately he remembered everything. He wanted to go on talking for truth's sake, perhaps for his own sake also ; and while his utterance was deliberate, his mind positively flew round and round the serried circle of facts that had surged up all about him to cut him off from the rest of his kind : it was like a creature that, finding itself imprisoned within an enclosure of high stakes, dashes round and round, distracted in the night, trying to find a weak spot, a crevice, a place to scale, some opening through which it may squeeze itself and escape. This awful activity of mind made him hesitate at times in his speech. . . .

" The captain kept on moving here and there on the bridge ; he seemed calm enough, only he stumbled several times ; and once as I stood speaking to him he walked right into me as though he had been stone-blind. He made no definite answer to what I had to tell. He mumbled to himself ; all I heard of it were a few words that sounded like ' confounded steam ! ' and ' infernal steam ! '—something about steam. I thought . . ."

He was becoming irrelevant ; a question to the point cut short his speech, like a pang of pain, and he felt extremely discouraged and weary. He was coming to that, he was coming to that—and now, checked brutally, he had to answer by yes or no. He answered truthfully by a curt " Yes, I did " ; and fair of face, big of frame, with young, gloomy eyes, he held his shoulders upright above the box while his soul writhed within him. He was made to answer another question so much to the point and so useless, then waited again. His mouth was tastelessly dry, as though he had been eating dust, then salt and bitter as after a drink of sea-water. He wiped his damp forehead, passed his tongue over parched lips, felt a shiver run down his back. The big assessor had dropped his eyelids, and drummed on without a sound, careless and mournful ; the eyes of the other above the sunburnt, clasped fingers seemed to glow with kindliness ; the magistrate had swayed forward ; his pale face hovered near the flowers, and then dropping sideways over the arm of his chair, he rested his temple in the palm of his hand. The wind of the punkahs eddied down on the heads, on the dark-faced natives wound about in voluminous draperies, on the Europeans sitting together very hot and in drill suits that seemed to fit them as close as their skins, and holding their round pith hats on their knees ; while gliding along the walls the court peons, buttoned tight in long white coats, flitted rapidly to and fro, running on bare toes, red - sashed, red turban on head, as noiseless as ghosts, and on the alert like so many retrievers.

Jim's eyes, wandering in the intervals of his answers, rested upon a white man who sat apart from the others, with his face worn and clouded, but with quiet eyes that glanced straight, interested and clear. Jim answered another question and was tempted to cry out, " What's the good of this, what's the good!" He tapped with his foot slightly, bit his lip, and looked away over the heads. He met the eyes of the white man. The glance directed at him was not the fascinated stare of the others. It was an act of intelligent volition. Jim between two questions forgot himself so far as to find leisure for a thought. This fellow—ran the thought—looks at me as though he could see somebody or something past my shoulder. He had come across that man before—in the street perhaps. He was positive he had never spoken to him. For days, for many days, he had spoken to no one, but had held silent, incoherent, and endless converse with himself, like a prisoner alone in his cell or like a wayfarer lost in a wilderness. At present he was answering questions that did not matter though they had a purpose, but he doubted whether he would ever again speak out as long as he lived. The sound of his own truthful statements confirmed his deliberate opinion that speech was of no use to him any longer. That man there seemed to be aware of his hopeless difficulty. Jim looked at him, then turned away resolutely, as after a final parting.

And later on, many times, in distant parts of the world, Marlow showed himself willing to remember Jim, to remember him at length, in detail and audibly.

Perhaps it would be after dinner, on a verandah draped in motionless foliage and crowned with flowers, in the deep dusk speckled by fiery cigar-ends. The elongated bulk of each cane-chair harboured a silent listener. Now and then a small red glow would move abruptly, and expanding light up the fingers of a languid hand, part of a face in profound repose, or flash a crimson gleam into a pair of pen-

sive eyes overshadowed by a fragment of an un-
ruffled forehead : and with the very first word
uttered Marlow's body, extended at rest in the seat,
would become very still, as though his spirit had
winged its way back into the lapse of time and were
speaking through his lips from the past.

CHAPTER V.

" OH yes. I attended the inquiry," he would say,
" and to this day I haven't left off wondering why
I went. I am willing to believe each of us has
a guardian angel, if you fellows will concede to
me that each of us has a familiar devil as well.
I want you to own up, because I don't like to feel
exceptional in any way, and I know I have him—
the devil, I mean. I haven't seen him, of course,
but I go upon circumstantial evidence. He is
there right enough, and, being malicious, he lets
me in for that kind of thing. What kind of thing,
you ask ? Why, the inquiry thing, the yellow-
dog thing—you wouldn't think a mangy, native
tyke would be allowed to trip up people in the
verandah of a magistrate's court, would you ?—
the kind of thing that by devious, unexpected,
truly diabolical ways causes me to run up against
men with soft spots, with hard spots, with hidden
plague spots, by Jove ! and loosens their tongues
at the sight of me for their infernal confidences ;
as though, forsooth, I had no confidences to make
to myself, as though—God help me !—I didn't

have enough confidential information about myself
to harrow my own soul till the end of my appointed
time. And what I have done to be thus favoured
I want to know. I declare I am as full of my own
concerns as the next man, and I have as much
memory as the average pilgrim in this valley, so
you see I am not particularly fit to be a receptacle
of confessions. Then why ? Can't tell—unless it
be to make time pass away after dinner. Charley,
my dear chap, your dinner was extremely good,
and in consequence these men here look upon a
quiet rubber as a tumultuous occupation. They
wallow in your good chairs and think to themselves,
' Hang exertion. Let that Marlow talk.'

"Talk ! So be it. And it's easy enough to talk
of Master Jim, after a good spread, two hundred
feet above the sea-level, with a box of decent cigars
handy, on a blessed evening of freshness and starlight that would make the best of us forget we
are only on sufferance here and got to pick our
way in cross lights, watching every precious minute
and every irremediable step, trusting we shall
manage yet to go out decently in the end—but
not so sure of it after all—and with dashed little
help to expect from those we touch elbows with
right and left. Of course there are men here and
there to whom the whole of life is like an after-
dinner hour with a cigar ; easy, pleasant, empty,
perhaps enlivened by some fable of strife to be
forgotten before the end is told—before the end is
told—even if there happens to be any end to it.

"My eyes met his for the first time at that inquiry.
You must know that everybody connected in any
way with the sea was there, because the affair had
been notorious for days, ever since that mysterious

cable message came from Aden to start us all cackling.
I say mysterious, because it was so in a sense though
it contained a naked fact, about as naked and ugly
as a fact can well be. The whole waterside talked
of nothing else. First thing in the morning as I
was dressing in my state-room, I would hear through
the bulkhead my Parsee Dubash jabbering about the
Patna with the steward, while he drank a cup of
tea, by favour, in the pantry. No sooner on shore
I would meet some acquaintance, and the first
remark would be, ' Did you ever hear of anything
to beat this ? ' and according to his kind the man
would smile cynically, or look sad, or let out a swear
or two. Complete strangers would accost each other
familiarly, just for the sake of easing their minds on
the subject : every confounded loafer in the town
came in for a harvest of drinks over this affair : you
heard of it in the harbour office, at every ship-
broker's, at your agent's, from whites, from natives,
from half-castes, from the very boatmen squatting
half-naked on the stone steps as you went up—by
Jove ! There was some indignation, not a few jokes,
and no end of discussions as to what had become
of them, you know. This went on for a couple of
weeks or more, and the opinion that whatever was
mysterious in this affair would turn out to be tragic
as well, began to prevail, when one fine morning, as
I was standing in the shade by the steps of the
harbour office, I perceived four men walking towards
me along the quay. I wondered for a while where
that queer lot had sprung from, and suddenly, I
may say, I shouted to myself, ' Here they are ! '

" There they were, sure enough, three of them as
large as life, and one much larger of girth than any
living man has a right to be, just landed with a good

breakfast inside of them from an outward bound
Dale Line steamer that had come in about an hour
after sunrise. There could be no mistake ; I spotted
the jolly skipper of the *Patna* at the first glance : the
fattest man in the whole blessed tropical belt clear
round that good old earth of ours. Moreover, nine
months or so before, I had come across him in
Samarang. His steamer was loading in the Roads,
and he was abusing the tyrannical institutions of the
German empire, and soaking himself in beer all day
long and day after day in De Jongh's back-shop,
till De Jongh, who charged a guilder for every bottle
without as much as the quiver of an eyelid, would
beckon me aside, and, with his little leathery face
all puckered up, declare confidentially, ' Business is
business, but this man, captain, he make me very
sick. Tfui ! '

"I was looking at him from the shade. He was
hurrying on a little in advance, and the sunlight
beating on him brought out his bulk in a startling
way. He made me think of a trained baby elephant
walking on hind-legs. He was extravagantly gorgeous too—got up in a soiled sleeping suit, bright
green and deep orange vertical stripes, with a pair
of ragged straw slippers on his bare feet, and somebody's cast-off pith hat, very dirty and two sizes too
small for him, tied up with a manilla rope-yarn on
the top of his big head. You understand a man
like that hasn't the ghost of a chance when it comes
to borrowing clothes. Very well. On he came in
hot haste, without a look right or left, passed within
three feet of me, and in the innocence of his heart
went on pelting up-stairs into the harbour-office to
make his deposition, or report, or whatever you like
to call it.

" It appears he addressed himself in the first instance to the principal shipping-master. Archie Ruthvel had just come in, and, as his story goes, was about to begin his arduous day by giving a dressing-down to his chief clerk. Some of you might have known him—an obliging little Portuguese half-caste with a miserably skinny neck, and always on the hop to get something from the shipmasters in the way of eatables—a piece of salt pork, a bag of biscuits, a few potatoes, or what not. One voyage, I recollect, I tipped him a live sheep out of the remnant of my sea-stock : not that I wanted him to do anything for me—he couldn't, you know—but because his child-like belief in the sacred right to perquisites quite touched my heart. It was so strong as to be almost beautiful. The race—the two races rather—and the climate . . . However, never mind. I know where I have a friend for life.

" Well, Ruthvel says he was giving him a severe lecture—on official morality, I suppose—when he heard a kind of subdued commotion at his back, and turning his head he saw, in his own words, something round and enormous, resembling a sixteen-hundred-weight sugar-hogshead wrapped in striped flannel-ette, up-ended in the middle of the large floor space in the office. He declares he was so taken aback that for quite an appreciable time he did not realise the thing was alive, and sat still wondering for what purpose and by what means that object had been transported in front of his desk. The archway from the anteroom was crowded with punkah-pullers, sweepers, police peons, the coxswain and crew of the harbour steam-launch, all craning their necks and almost climbing on each other's backs. Quite a riot. By that time the fellow had managed to tug and jerk his hat clear of his head, and advanced with slight bows at Ruthvel, who told me the sight was so discomposing that for some time he listened, quite unable to make out what that apparition wanted. It spoke in a voice harsh and lugubrious but intrepid, and little by little it dawned upon Archie that this was a development of the *Patna* case. He says that as soon as he understood who it was before him he felt quite unwell,—Archie is so sympathetic and easily upset,—but pulled himself together and shouted 'Stop! I can't listen to you. You must go to the Master Attendant. I can't possibly listen to you. Captain Elliot is the man you want to see. This way, this way.' He jumped up, ran round that long counter, pulled, shoved: the other let him, surprised but obedient at first, and only at the door of the private office some sort of animal instinct made him hang back and snort like a frightened bullock. 'Look here! what's up? Let go! Look here!' Archie flung open the door without knocking. 'The master of the *Patna*, sir,' he shouts. 'Go in, captain.' He saw the old man lift his head from some writing so sharp that his nose-nippers fell off, banged the door to, and fled to his desk, where he had some papers waiting for his signature: but he says the row that burst out in there was so awful that he couldn't collect his senses sufficiently to remember the spelling of his own name. Archie's the most sensitive shipping-master in the two hemispheres. He declares he felt as though he had thrown a man to a hungry lion. No doubt the noise was great. I heard it down below, and I have every reason to believe it was heard clear across the Esplanade as far as the band-stand. Old father Elliot had a great stock of words and could shout—and didn't

mind who he shouted at either. He would have
shouted at the Viceroy himself. As he used to tell
me : 'I am as high as I can get ; my pension is
safe. I've a few pounds laid by, and if they don't
like my notions of duty I would just as soon go home
as not. I am an old man, and I have always spoken
my mind. All I care for now is to see my girls
married before I die.' He was a little crazy on that
point. His three daughters were awfully nice,
though they resembled him amazingly, and on the
mornings he woke up with a gloomy view of their
matrimonial prospects the office would read it in his
eye and tremble, because, they said, he was sure
to have somebody for breakfast. However, that
morning he did not eat the renegade, but, if I may
be allowed to carry on the metaphor, chewed him
up very small, so to speak, and—ah ! ejected him
again.

" Thus in a very few moments I saw his monstrous
bulk descend in haste and stand still on the outer
steps. He had stopped close to me for the purpose
of profound meditation : his large purple cheeks
quivered. He was biting his thumb, and after a
while noticed me with a sidelong vexed look. The
other three chaps that had landed with him made
a little group waiting at some distance. There
was a sallow-faced, mean little chap with his arm
in a sling, and a long individual in a blue flannel
coat, as dry as a chip and no stouter than a broomstick, with drooping grey moustaches, who looked
about him with an air of jaunty imbecility. The
third was an upstanding, broad-shouldered youth,
with his hands in his pockets, turning his back on
the other two who appeared to be talking together
earnestly. He stared across the empty Esplanade.

A ramshackle gharry, all dust and venetian blinds, pulled up short opposite the group, and the driver, throwing up his right foot over his knee, gave himself up to the critical examination of his toes. The young chap, making no movement, not even stirring his head, just stared into the sunshine. This was my first view of Jim. He looked as unconcerned and unapproachable as only the young can look. There he stood, clean-limbed, clean-faced, firm on his feet, as promising a boy as the sun ever shone on; and, looking at him, knowing all he knew and a little more too, I was as angry as though I had detected him trying to get something out of me by false pretences. He had no business to look so sound. I thought to myself—well, if this sort can go wrong like that . . . and I felt as though I could fling down my hat and dance on it from sheer mortification, as I once saw the skipper of an Italian barque do because his duffer of a mate got into a mess with his anchors when making a flying moor in a roadstead full of ships. I asked myself, seeing him there apparently so much at ease—is he silly? is he callous? He seemed ready to start whistling a tune. And note, I did not care a rap about the behaviour of the other two. Their persons somehow fitted the tale that was public property, and was going to be the subject of an official inquiry. 'That old mad rogue up-stairs called me a hound,' said the captain of the *Patna*. I can't tell whether he recognised me—I rather think he did; but at any rate our glances met. He glared—I smiled; hound was the very mildest epithet that had reached me through the open window. 'Did he?' I said from some strange inability to hold my tongue. He nodded, bit his

thumb again, swore under his breath : then lifting
his head and looking at me with sullen and passionate impudence—'Bah ! the Pacific is big, my
friendt. You damned Englishmen can do your
worst ; I know where there's plenty room for a
man like me: I am well aguaindt in Apia, in
Honolulu, in . . .' He paused reflectively, while
without effort I could depict to myself the sort of
people he was 'aguaindt' with in those places. I
won't make a secret of it that I had been 'aguaindt'
with not a few of that sort myself. There are times
when a man must act as though life were equally
sweet in any company. I've known such a time,
and, what's more, I shan't now pretend to pull a
long face over my necessity, because a good many
of that bad company from want of moral—moral
—what shall I say ?—posture, or from some other
equally profound cause, were twice as instructive
and twenty times more amusing than the usual
respectable thief of commerce you fellows ask to
sit at your table without any real necessity—from
habit, from cowardice, from good-nature, from a
hundred sneaking and inadequate reasons.

" ' You Englishmen are all rogues,' went on my
patriotic Flensborg or Stettin Australian. I really
don't recollect now what decent little port on the
shores of the Baltic was defiled by being the nest of
that precious bird. 'What are you to shout ? Eh ?
You tell me ? You no better than other people, and
that old rogue he make Gottam fuss with me.' His
thick carcass trembled on its legs that were like a
pair of pillars ; it trembled from head to foot.
'That's what you English always make—make a
tam' fuss—for any little thing, because I was not
born in your tam' country. Take away my certi-

ficate. Take it. I don't want the certificate. A
man like me don't want your verfluchte certificate.
I shpit on it.' He spat. 'I vill an Amerigan citizen
begome,' he cried, fretting and fuming and shuffling
his feet as if to free his ankles from some invisible
and mysterious grasp that would not let him get
away from that spot. He made himself so warm
that the top of his bullet head positively smoked.
Nothing mysterious prevented me from going away :
curiosity is the most obvious of sentiments, and it
held me there to see the effect of a full information
upon that young fellow who, hands in pockets, and
turning his back upon the sidewalk, gazed across the
grass plots of the Esplanade at the yellow portico of
the Malabar Hotel with the air of a man about to go
for a walk as soon as his friend is ready. That's how
he looked, and it was odious. I waited to see him
overwhelmed, confounded, pierced through and
through, squirming like an impaled beetle—and I
was half-afraid to see it too—if you understand what
I mean. Nothing more awful than to watch a man
who has been found out, not in a crime but in a more
than criminal weakness. The commonest sort of
fortitude prevents us from becoming criminals in a
legal sense ; it is from weakness unknown, but
perhaps suspected, as in some parts of the world you
suspect a deadly snake in every bush,—from weakness
that may lie hidden, watched or unwatched, prayed
against or manfully scorned, repressed or maybe
ignored more than half a lifetime, not one of us is
safe. We are snared into doing things for which
we get called names, and things for which we get
hanged, and yet the spirit may well survive,—survive the condemnation, survive the halter, by Jove !
And there are things—they look small enough some-

times too—by which some of us are totally and completely undone. I watched the youngster there. I liked his appearance ; I knew his appearance ; he came from the right place ; he was one of us. He stood there for all the parentage of his kind, for men and women by no means clever or amusing, but whose very existence is based upon honest faith, and upon the instinct of courage. I don't mean military courage, or civil courage, or any special kind of courage. I mean just that inborn ability to look temptations straight in the face,—a readiness unintellectual enough, goodness knows, but without a pose,—a power of resistance, don't you see, ungracious if you like, but priceless—an unthinking and blessed stiffness before the outward and inward terrors, before the might of nature and the seductive corruption of men—backed by a faith invulnerable to the strength of facts, to the contagion of example, to the solicitation of ideas. Hang ideas ! They are tramps, vagabonds, knocking at the backdoor of your mind, each taking a little of your substance, each carrying away some crumb of that belief in a few simple notions you must cling to if you want to live decently and would like to die easy !

" This has nothing to do with Jim, directly ; only he was outwardly so typical of that good stupid kind we like to feel marching right and left of us in life, of the kind that is not disturbed by the vagaries of intelligence and the perversions of—of nerves, let us say. He was the kind of fellow you would, on the strength of his looks, leave in charge of the deck —figuratively and professionally speaking. I say I would, and I ought to know. Haven't I turned out youngsters enough in my time, for the service of the

Red Rag, to the craft of the sea, to the craft whose
whole secret could be expressed in one short sentence,
and yet must be driven afresh every day into young
heads till it becomes the component part of every
waking thought—till it is present in every dream
of their young sleep! The sea has been good to
me, but when I remember all these boys that passed
through my hands, some grown up now and some
drowned by this time, but all good stuff for the sea,
I don't think I have done badly by it either. Were
I to go home to-morrow, I bet that before two days
passed over my head some sunburnt young chief
mate would overtake me at some dock gateway
or other, and a fresh deep voice speaking above
my hat would ask: 'Don't you remember me, sir?
Why! little So-and-so. Such and such a ship. It
was my first voyage.' And I would remember a
bewildered little shaver, no higher than the back
of this chair, with a mother and perhaps a big
sister on the quay, very quiet but too upset to
wave their handkerchiefs at the ship that glides
out gently between the pier-heads: or perhaps some
decent middle-aged father who had come early with
his boy to see him off, and stays all the morning,
because he is interested in the windlass apparently,
and stays too long, and has got to scramble ashore
at last with no time at all to say good-bye. The
mud pilot on the poop sings out to me in a drawl,
'Hold her with the check line for a moment, Mister
Mate. There's a gentleman wants to get ashore.
. . . Up with you, sir. Nearly got carried off to
Talcahuano, didn't you? Now's your time; easy
does it. . . . All right. Slack away again forward
there.' The tugs, smoking like the pit of perdition,
get hold and churn the old river into fury; the

gentleman ashore is dusting his knees—the benevolent steward has shied his umbrella after him. All very proper. He has offered his bit of sacrifice to the sea, and now he may go home pretending he thinks nothing of it ; and the willing little victim shall be very sea-sick before next morning. By-and-by, when he has learned all the little mysteries and the one great secret of the craft, he shall be fit to live or die as the sea may decree ; and the man who had taken a hand in this fool game, in which the sea wins every toss, will be pleased to have his back slapped by a heavy young hand, and to hear a cheery sea-puppy voice : 'Do you remember me, sir ? The little So-and-so.'

"I tell you this is good ; it tells you that once in your life at least you had gone the right way to work. I have been thus slapped, and I have winced, for the slap was heavy, and I have glowed all day long and gone to bed feeling less lonely in the world by virtue of that hearty thump. Don't I remember the little So-and-so's ! I tell you I ought to know the right kind of looks. I would have trusted the deck to that youngster on the strength of a single glance, and gone to sleep with both eyes—and, by Jove ! it wouldn't have been safe. There are depths of horror in that thought. He looked as genuine as a new sovereign, but there was some infernal alloy in his metal. How much ? The least thing—the least drop of something rare and accursed ; the least drop !—but he made you—standing there with his don't-care-hang air—he made you wonder whether perchance he were nothing more rare than brass.

"I couldn't believe it. I tell you I wanted to see him squirm for the honour of the craft. The other two no-account chaps spotted their captain, and began to move slowly towards us. They chatted together as they strolled, and I did not care any more than if they had not been visible to the naked eye. They grinned at each other—might have been exchanging jokes, for all I know. I saw that with one of them it was a case of a broken arm ; and as to the long individual with grey moustaches he was the chief engineer, and in various ways a pretty notorious personality. They were nobodies. They approached. The skipper gazed in an inanimate way between his feet : he seemed to be swollen to an unnatural size by some awful disease, by the mysterious action of an unknown poison. He lifted his head, saw the two before him waiting, opened his mouth with an extraordinary, sneering contortion of his puffed face—to speak to them, I suppose—and then a thought seemed to strike him. His thick, purplish lips came together without a sound, he went off in a resolute waddle to the gharry and began to jerk at the door-handle with such a blind brutality of impatience that I expected to see the whole concern overturned on its side, pony and all. The driver, shaken out of his meditation over the sole of his foot, displayed at once all the signs of intense terror, and held with both hands, looking round from his box at this vast carcass forcing its way into his conveyance. The little machine shook and rocked tumultuously, and the crimson nape of that lowered neck, the size of these straining thighs, the immense heaving of that dingy, striped green-and-orange back, the whole burrowing effort of that gaudy and sordid mass, troubled one's sense of probability with a droll and fearsome effect, like one of those grotesque and distinct visions that scare and fascinate one in a fever. He disappeared. I

half expected the roof to split in two, the little
box on wheels to burst open in the manner of a
ripe cotton-pod—but it only sank with a click of
flattened springs, and suddenly one venetian blind
rattled down. His shoulders reappeared, jammed in
the small opening ; his head hung out, distended and
tossing like a captive balloon, perspiring, furious,
spluttering. He reached for the gharry-wallah with
vicious flourishes of a fist as dumpy and red as a
lump of raw meat. He roared at him to be off, to
go on. Where ? Into the Pacific, perhaps. The
driver lashed ; the pony snorted, reared once, and
darted off at a gallop. Where ? To Apia ? to
Honolulu ? He had 6000 miles of tropical belt to
disport himself in, and I did not hear the precise
address. A snorting pony snatched him into
' ewigkeit ' in the twinkling of an eye, and I never
saw him again ; and, what's more, I don't know of
anybody that ever had a glimpse of him after he
departed from my knowledge sitting inside a ramshackle little gharry that fled round the corner in a
white smother of dust. He departed, disappeared,
vanished, absconded ; and absurdly enough it looked
as though he had taken that gharry with him, for
never again did I come across a sorrel pony with a
slit ear and a lackadaisical Tamil driver afflicted by a
sore foot. The Pacific is indeed big ; but whether
he found a place for a display of his talents in it or
not, the fact remains he had flown into space like a
witch on a broomstick. The little chap with his arm
in a sling started to run after the carriage, bleating,
' Captain ! I say, Captain ! I sa-a-ay ! '—but after
a few steps stopped short, hung his head, and walked
back slowly. At the sharp rattle of the wheels
the young fellow spun round where he stood. He

made no other movement, no gesture, no sign, and
remained facing in the new direction after the
gharry had swung out of sight.

"All this happened in much less time than it
takes to tell, since I am trying to interpret for
you into slow speech the instantaneous effect of
visual impressions. Next moment the half-caste
clerk, sent by Archie to look a little after the poor
castaways of the *Patna*, came upon the scene.
He ran out eager and bareheaded, looking right
and left, and very full of his mission. It was doomed
to be a failure as far as the principal person was
concerned, but he approached the others with fussy
importance, and, almost immediately, found himself involved in a violent altercation with the chap
that carried his arm in a sling, and who turned
out to be extremely anxious for a row. He wasn't
going to be ordered about—'not he, b'gosh.' He
wouldn't be terrified with a pack of lies by a cocky
half-bred little quill-driver. He was not going to
be bullied by 'no object of that sort,' if the story
were true 'ever so'! He bawled his wish, his desire,
his determination to go to bed. 'If you weren't a
God-forsaken Portuguee,' I heard him yell, 'you
would know that the hospital is the right place for
me.' He pushed the fist of his sound arm under
the other's nose; a crowd began to collect; the
half-caste, flustered, but doing his best to appear
dignified, tried to explain his intentions. I went
away without waiting to see the end.

"But it so happened that I had a man in the
hospital at the time, and going there to see about
him the day before the opening of the Inquiry, I
saw in the white men's ward that little chap tossing on his back, with his arm in splints, and quite

light-headed. To my great surprise the other
one, the long individual with drooping white moustaches, had also found his way there. I remembered I had seen him slinking away during the
quarrel, in a half prance, half shuffle, and trying
very hard not to look scared. He was no stranger
to the port, it seems, and in his distress was able
to make tracks straight for Mariani's billiard-room
and grog-shop near the bazaar. That unspeakable
vagabond, Mariani, who had known the man and
had ministered to his vices in one or two other
places, kissed the ground, in a manner of speaking,
before him, and shut him up with a supply of
bottles in an up-stairs room of his infamous hovel.
It appears he was under some hazy apprehension
as to his personal safety, and wished to be concealed. However, Mariani told me a long time
after (when he came on board one day to dun
my steward for the price of some cigars) that he
would have done more for him without asking any
questions, from gratitude for some unholy favour
received very many years ago—as far as I could
make out. He thumped twice his brawny chest,
rolled enormous black and white eyes glistening
with tears : 'Antonio never forget—Antonio never
forget ! ' What was the precise nature of the
immoral obligation I never learned, but be it what
it may, he had every facility given him to remain
under lock and key, with a chair, a table, a mattress
in a corner, and a litter of fallen plaster on the
floor, in an irrational state of funk, and keeping
up his pecker with such tonics as Mariani dispensed.
This lasted till the evening of the third day, when,
after letting out a few horrible screams, he found
himself compelled to seek safety in flight from

a legion of centipedes. He burst the door open, made one leap for dear life down the crazy little stairway, landed bodily on Mariani's stomach, picked himself up, and bolted like a rabbit into the streets. The police plucked him off a garbage-heap in the early morning. At first he had a notion they were carrying him off to be hanged, and fought for liberty like a hero, but when I sat down by his bed he had been very quiet for two days. His lean bronzed head, with white moustaches, looked fine and calm on the pillow, like the head of a war-worn soldier with a child-like soul, had it not been for a hint of spectral alarm that lurked in the blank glitter of his glance, resembling a nondescript form of a terror crouching silently behind a pane of glass. He was so extremely calm, that I began to indulge in the eccentric hope of hearing something explanatory of the famous affair from his point of view. Why I longed to go grubbing into the deplorable details of an occurrence which, after all, concerned me no more than as a member of an obscure body of men held together by a community of inglorious toil and by fidelity to a certain standard of conduct, I can't explain. You may call it an unhealthy curiosity if you like ; but I have a distinct notion I wished to find something. Perhaps, unconsciously, I hoped I would find that something, some profound and redeeming cause, some merciful explanation, some convincing shadow of an excuse. I see well enough now that I hoped for the impossible—for the laying of what is the most obstinate ghost of man's creation, of the uneasy doubt uprising like a mist, secret and gnawing like a worm, and more chilling than the certitude of death—the doubt of the sovereign power en-

throned in a fixed standard of conduct. It is the
hardest thing to stumble against; it is the thing
that breeds yelling panics and good little quiet
villainies ; it's the true shadow of calamity. Did I
believe in a miracle? and why did I desire it so
ardently? Was it for my own sake that I wished
to find some shadow of an excuse for that young
fellow whom I had never seen before, but whose
appearance alone added a touch of personal concern to the thoughts suggested by the knowledge
of his weakness—made it a thing of mystery and
terror—like a hint of a destructive fate ready for
us all whose youth—in its day—had resembled his
youth? I fear that such was the secret motive of
my prying. I was, and no mistake, looking for
a miracle. The only thing that at this distance
of time strikes me as miraculous is the extent of
my imbecility. I positively hoped to obtain from
that battered and shady invalid some exorcism
against the ghost of doubt. I must have been
pretty desperate too, for, without loss of time,
after a few indifferent and friendly sentences which
he answered with languid readiness, just as any
decent sick man would do, I produced the word
Patna wrapped up in a delicate question as in a
wisp of floss silk. I was delicate selfishly ; I did
not want to startle him ; I had no solicitude for
him ; I was not furious with him and sorry for
him : his experience was of no importance, his
redemption would have had no point for me. He
had grown old in minor iniquities, and could no
longer inspire aversion or pity. He repeated *Patna?*
interrogatively, seemed to make a short effort of
memory, and said : ' Quite right. I am an old
stager out here. I saw her go down.' I made

ready to vent my indignation at such a stupid lie, when he added smoothly, 'She was full of reptiles.'

"This made me pause. What did he mean? The unsteady phantom of terror behind his glassy eyes seemed to stand still and look into mine wistfully. 'They turned me out of my bunk in the middle watch to look at her sinking,' he pursued in a reflective tone. His voice sounded alarmingly strong all at once. I was sorry for my folly. There was no snowy-winged coiff of a nursing sister to be seen flitting in the perspective of the ward; but away in the middle of a long row of empty iron bedsteads an accident case from some ship in the Roads sat up brown and gaunt with a white bandage set rakishly on the forehead. Suddenly my interesting invalid shot out an arm thin like a tentacle and clawed my shoulder. 'Only my eyes were good enough to see. I am famous for my eyesight. That's why they called me, I expect. None of them was quick enough to see her go, but they saw that she was gone right enough, and sang out together— like this.' . . . A wolfish howl searched the very recesses of my soul. 'Oh! make 'im dry up,' whined the accident case irritably. 'You don't believe me, I suppose, went on the other, with an air of ineffable conceit. 'I tell you there are no such eyes as mine this side of the Persian Gulf. Look under the bed.'

"Of course I stooped instantly. I defy anybody not to have done so. 'What can you see?' he asked. 'Nothing,' I said, feeling awfully ashamed of myself. He scrutinised my face with wild and withering contempt. 'Just so,' he said, 'but if I were to look I could see—there's no eyes like mine,

I tell you.' Again he clawed, pulling at me downwards in his eagerness to relieve himself by a confidential communication. 'Millions of pink toads.
There's no eyes like mine. Millions of pink toads.
It's worse than seeing a ship sink. I could look
at sinking ships and smoke my pipe all day long.
Why don't they give me back my pipe? I would
get a smoke while I watched these toads. The ship
was full of them. They've got to be watched, you
know.' He winked facetiously. The perspiration
dripped on him off my head, my drill coat clung
to my wet back : the afternoon breeze swept impetuously over the row of bedsteads, the stiff folds
of curtains stirred perpendicularly, rattling on brass
rods, the covers of empty beds blew about noiselessly
near the bare floor all along the line, and I shivered
to the very marrow. The soft wind of the tropics
played in that naked ward as bleak as a winter's
gale in an old barn at home. 'Don't you let him
start his hollering, mister,' hailed from afar the
accident case in a distressed angry shout that came
ringing between the walls like a quavering call
down a tunnel. The clawing hand hauled at my
shoulders ; he leered at me knowingly. 'The ship
was full of them, you know, and we had to clear
out on the strict Q.T.,' he whispered with extreme
rapidity. 'All pink. All pink—as big as mastiffs,
with an eye on the top of the head and claws all
round their ugly mouths. Ough ! Ough ! ' Quick
jerks as of galvanic shocks disclosed under the flat
coverlet the outlines of meagre and agitated legs ;
he let go my shoulder and reached after something
in the air ; his body trembled tensely like a released
harp-string ; and while I looked down, the spectral
horror in him broke through his glassy gaze. In-

stantly his face of an old soldier, with its noble and
calm outlines, became decomposed before my eyes by
the corruption of stealthy cunning, of an abominable
caution and of desperate fear. He restrained a cry
—'Ssh; what are they doing now down there?' he
asked, pointing to the floor with fantastic precau-
tions of voice and gesture, whose meaning, borne
upon my mind in a lurid flash, made me very sick
of my cleverness. 'They are all asleep,' I answered,
watching him narrowly. That was it. That's what
he wanted to hear; these were the exact words that
could calm him. He drew a long breath. 'Ssh!
Quiet, steady. I am an old stager out here. I
know them brutes. Bash in the head of the first
that stirs. There's too many of them, and she
won't swim more than ten minutes.' He panted
again. 'Hurry up,' he yelled suddenly, and went
on in a steady scream: 'They are all awake—
millions of them. They are trampling on me!
Wait! Oh, wait! I'll smash them in heaps like
flies. Wait for me! Help! H-e-elp!' An inter-
minable and sustained howl completed my discom-
fiture. I saw in the distance the accident case raise
deplorably both his hands to his bandaged head;
a dresser, aproned to the chin, showed himself in
the vista of the ward, as if seen in the small end of a
telescope. I confessed myself fairly routed, and
without more ado, stepping out through one of the
long windows, escaped into the outside gallery. The
howl pursued me like a vengeance. I turned into a
deserted landing, and suddenly all became very still
and quiet around me, and I descended the bare and
shiny staircase in a silence that enabled me to
compose my distracted thoughts. Down below I
met one of the resident surgeons who was crossing

the courtyard and stopped me. 'Been to see your
man, Captain? I think we may let him go to-morrow.
These fools have no notion of taking care of themselves, though. I say, we've got the chief engineer
of that pilgrim ship here. A curious case. D.T.'s of
the worst kind. He has been drinking hard in that
Greek's or Italian's grog-shop for three days. What
can you expect? Four bottles of that kind of
brandy a-day, I am told. Wonderful, if true.
Sheeted with boiler-iron inside, I should think. The
head, ah! the head, of course, gone, but the curious
part is there's some sort of method in his raving.
I am trying to find out. Most unusual—that thread
of logic in such a delirium. Traditionally he ought
to see snakes, but he doesn't. Good old tradition's
at a discount nowadays. Eh! His—er—visions are
batrachian. Ha! ha! No, seriously, I never
remember being so interested in a case of jim-jams
before. He ought to be dead, don't you know, after
such a festive experiment. Oh! he is a tough
object. Four-and-twenty years of the tropics too.
You ought really to take a peep at him. Noble-
looking old boozer. Most extraordinary man I ever
met—medically, of course. Won't you?'

"I had been all along exhibiting the usual polite
signs of interest, but now assuming an air of regret
I murmured of want of time, and shook hands in a
hurry. 'I say,' he cried after me, 'he can't attend
that inquiry. Is his evidence material, you think?'

"'Not in the least,' I called back from the gateway."

CHAPTER VI.

"The authorities were evidently of the same opinion. The inquiry was not adjourned. It was held on the appointed day to satisfy the law, and it was well attended because of its human interest no doubt. There was no incertitude as to facts— as to the one material fact, I mean. How the *Patna* came by her hurt it was impossible to find out ; the court did not expect to find out ; and in the whole audience there was not a man who cared. Yet, as I've told you, all the sailors in the port attended, and the waterside business was fully represented. Whether they knew it or not, the interest that drew them there was purely psychological,—the expectation of some essential disclosure as to the strength, the power, the horror, of human emotions. Naturally nothing of the kind could be disclosed. The examination of the only man able and willing to face it was beating futilely round the well-known fact, and the play of questions upon it was as instructive as the tapping with a hammer on an iron box, were the object to find out what's inside. However, an official inquiry could not be any other thing. Its object was not the fundamental why, but the superficial how, of this affair.

"The young chap could have told them, and, though that very thing was the thing that interested the audience, the questions put to him necessarily led him away from what to me, for instance, would have been the only truth worth knowing. You can't expect the constituted authorities to inquire into the state of a man's soul—or is it

only of his liver? Their business was to come
down upon the consequences, and frankly, a casual
police magistrate and two nautical assessors are
not much good for anything else. I don't mean to
imply these fellows were stupid. The magistrate
was very patient. One of the assessors was a
sailing-ship skipper with a reddish beard, and of a
pious disposition. Brierly was the other. Big
Brierly. Some of you must have heard of Big
Brierly—the captain of the crack ship of the Blue
Star line. That's the man.

"He seemed consumedly bored by the honour
thrust upon him. He had never in his life made
a mistake, never had an accident, never a mishap,
never a check in his steady rise, and he seemed to
be one of these lucky fellows who know nothing of
indecision, much less of self-mistrust. At thirty-two
he had one of the best commands going in the
Eastern trade—and, what's more, he thought a lot
of what he had. There was nothing like it in the
world, and I suppose if you had asked him point-
blank he would have confessed that in his opinion
there was not such another commander. The choice
had fallen upon the right man. The rest of mankind
that did not command the sixteen-knot steel steamer
Ossa were rather poor creatures. He had saved
lives at sea, had rescued ships in distress, had a
gold chronometer presented to him by the under-
writers, and a pair of binoculars with a suitable
inscription from some foreign Government, in com-
memoration of these services. He was acutely
aware of his merits and of his rewards. I liked him
well enough, though some I know—meek, friendly
men at that—couldn't stand him at any price. I
haven't the slightest doubt he considered himself

vastly my superior—indeed, had you been Emperor
of East and West, you could not have ignored
your inferiority in his presence—but I couldn't get
up any real sentiment of offence. He did not
despise me for anything I could help, for anything
I was—don't you know ? I was a negligeable
quantity simply because I was not *the* fortunate
man of the earth, not Montague Brierly in command of the *Ossa*, not the owner of an inscribed
gold chronometer and of silver-mounted binoculars
testifying to the excellence of my seamanship and
to my indomitable pluck ; not possessed of an acute
sense of my merits and of my rewards, besides the
love and worship of a black retriever, the most
wonderful of its kind—for never was such a man
loved thus by such a dog. No doubt, to have all
this forced upon you was exasperating enough ; but
when I reflected that I was associated in these fatal
disadvantages with twelve hundred millions of other
more or less human beings, I found I could bear my
share of his good-natured and contemptuous pity for
the sake of something indefinite and attractive in
the man. I have never defined to myself this
attraction, but there were moments when I envied
him. The sting of life could do no more to his
complacent soul than the scratch of a pin to the
smooth face of a rock. This was enviable. As I
looked at him, flanking on one side the unassuming
pale-faced magistrate who presided at the inquiry,
his self-satisfaction presented to me and to the
world a surface as hard as granite. He committed
suicide very soon after.

" No wonder Jim's case bored him, and while I
thought with something akin to fear of the immensity of his contempt for the young man under

examination, he was probably holding silent inquiry into his own case. The verdict must have been of unmitigated guilt, and he took the secret of the evidence with him in that leap into the sea. If I understand anything of men, the matter was no doubt of the gravest import, one of those trifles that awaken ideas—start into life some thought with which a man unused to such a companionship finds it impossible to live. I am in a position to know that it wasn't money, and it wasn't drink, and it wasn't woman. He jumped overboard at sea barely a week after the end of the inquiry, and less than three days after leaving port on his outward passage; as though on that exact spot in the midst of waters he had suddenly perceived the gates of the other world flung open wide for his reception.

"Yet it was not a sudden impulse. His grey-headed mate, a first-rate sailor and a nice old chap with strangers, but in his relations with his commander the surliest chief-officer I've ever seen, would tell the story with tears in his eyes. It appears that when he came on deck in the morning Brierly had been writing in the chart-room. 'It was ten minutes to four,' he said, 'and the middle watch was not relieved yet of course. He heard my voice on the bridge speaking to the second mate, and called me in. I was loth to go, and that's the truth, Captain Marlow,—I couldn't stand poor Captain Brierly, I tell you with shame; we never know what a man is made of. He had been promoted over too many heads, not counting my own, and he had a damnable trick of making you feel small, nothing but by the way he said "Good morning." I never addressed him, sir, but on matters of duty, and then it was as much as I could do to keep a civil tongue in my head.' (He flattered himself there. I often wondered how Brierly could put up with his manners for more than half a voyage.) ' I've a wife and children,' he went on, ' and I had been ten years in the Company, always expecting the next command—more fool I. Says he, just like this : "Come in here, Mr Jones," in that swagger voice of his—"Come in here, Mr Jones." In I went. "We'll lay down her position," says he, stooping over the chart, a pair of dividers in hand. By the standing orders, the officer going off duty would have done that at the end of his watch. However, I said nothing, and looked on while he marked off the ship's position with a tiny cross and wrote the date and the time. I can see him this moment writing his neat figures : seventeen, eight, four A.M. The year would be written in red ink at the top of the chart. He never used his charts more than a year, Captain Brierly didn't. I've the chart now. When he had done he stands looking down at the mark he had made and smiling to himself, then looks up at me. "Thirty-two miles more as she goes," says he, "and then we shall be clear, and you may alter the course twenty degrees to the southward."

" ' We were passing to the north of the Hector Bank that voyage. I said, "All right, sir," wondering what he was fussing about, since I had to call him before altering the course anyhow. Just then eight bells were struck : we came out on the bridge, and the second mate before going off mentions in the usual way—"Seventy-one on the log." Captain Brierly looks at the compass and then all round. It was dark and clear, and all the stars were out as plain as on a frosty night in high latitudes.

Suddenly he says with a sort of a little sigh : "I am going aft, and shall set the log at zero for you myself, so that there can be no mistake. Thirty-two miles more on this course and then you are safe. Let's see—the correction on the log is six per cent additive ; say, then, thirty by the dial to run, and you may come twenty degrees to starboard at once. No use losing any distance—is there ? " I had never heard him talk so much at a stretch, and to no purpose as it seemed to me. I said nothing. He went down the ladder, and the dog, that was always at his heels whenever he moved, night or day, followed, sliding nose first, after him. I heard his boot-heels tap, tap on the after-deck, then he stopped and spoke to the dog—" Go back, Rover. On the bridge, boy ! Go on—get." Then he calls out to me from the dark, " Shut that dog up in the chart-room, Mr Jones—will you ? "

" ' This was the last time I heard his voice, Captain Marlow. These are the last words he spoke in the hearing of any living human being, sir.' At this point the old chap's voice got quite unsteady. ' He was afraid the poor brute would jump after him, don't you see ? ' he pursued with a quaver. ' Yes, Captain Marlow. He set the log for me ; he—would you believe it ?—he put a drop of oil in it too. There was the oil-feeder where he left it near by. The boatswain's mate got the hose along aft to wash down at half-past five ; by-and-by he knocks off and runs up on the bridge,— " Will you please come aft, Mr Jones," he says. " There's a funny thing. I don't like to touch it." It was Captain Brierly's gold chronometer watch carefully hung under the rail by its chain.

" ' As soon as my eyes fell on it something struck

me, and I knew, sir. My legs got soft under me.
It was as if I had seen him go over; and I could
tell how far behind he was left too. The taffrail-
log marked eighteen miles and three-quarters, and
four iron belaying-pins were missing round the
mainmast. Put them in his pockets to help him
down, I suppose; but, Lord! what's four iron pins
to a powerful man like Captain Brierly. Maybe his
confidence in himself was just shook a bit at the
last. That's the only sign of fluster he gave in his
whole life, I should think; but I am ready to answer
for him, that once over he did not try to swim a
stroke, the same as he would have had pluck enough
to keep up all day long on the bare chance had he
fallen overboard accidentally. Yes, sir. He was
second to none—if he said so himself, as I heard him
once. He had written two letters in the middle
watch, one to the Company and the other to me.
He gave me a lot of instructions as to the passage—
I had been in the trade before he was out of his time
—and no end of hints as to my conduct with our
people in Shanghai, so that I should keep the command of the *Ossa*. He wrote like a father would to
a favourite son, Captain Marlow, and I was five-and-
twenty years his senior and had tasted salt water
before he was fairly breeched. In his letter to the
owners—it was left open for me to see—he said that
he had always done his duty by them—up to that
moment—and even now he was not betraying their
confidence, since he was leaving the ship to as com-
petent a seaman as could be found—meaning me,
sir, meaning me! He told them that if the last act
of his life didn't take away all his credit with them,
they would give weight to my faithful service and to
his warm recommendation, when about to fill the

vacancy made by his death. And much more like
this, sir. I couldn't believe my eyes. It made me
feel queer all over,' went on the old chap, in great
perturbation, and squashing something in the corner
of his eye with the end of a thumb as broad as a
spatula. 'You would think, sir, he had jumped
overboard only to give an unlucky man a last show
to get on. What with the shock of him going in
this awful rash way, and thinking myself a made
man by that chance, I was nearly off my chump for
a week. But no fear. The captain of the *Pelion*
was shifted into the *Ossa*—came aboard in Shanghai
—a little popinjay, sir, in a grey check suit, with his
hair parted in the middle. "Aw—I am—aw—your
new captain, Mister—Mister—aw—Jones." He was
drowned in scent—fairly stunk with it, Captain
Marlow. I daresay it was the look I gave him that
made him stammer. He mumbled something about
my natural disappointment—I had better know at
once that his chief officer got the promotion to the
Pelion—he had nothing to do with it, of course—
supposed the office knew best—sorry. . . . Says I,
"Don't you mind old Jones, sir ; dam' his soul, he's
used to it." I could see directly I had shocked his
delicate ear, and while we sat at our first tiffin
together he began to find fault in a nasty manner
with this and that in the ship. I never heard such
a voice out of a Punch and Judy show. I set my
teeth hard, and glued my eyes to my plate, and held
my peace as long as I could ; but at last I had to
say something : up he jumps tiptoeing, ruffling all
his pretty plumes, like a little fighting cock. "You'll
find you have a different person to deal with than
the late Captain Brierly." "I've found it," says I,
very glum, but pretending to be mighty busy with

my steak. "You are an old ruffian, Mr—aw—
Jones; and what's more, you are known for an old
ruffian in the employ," he squeaks at me. The
damned bottle-washers stood about listening with
their mouths stretched from ear to ear. "I may
be a hard case," answers I, "but I ain't so far
gone as to put up with the sight of you sitting in
Captain Brierly's chair." With that I lay down my
knife and fork. "You would like to sit in it yourself—that's where the shoe pinches," he sneers. I
left the saloon, got my rags together, and was on
the quay with all my dunnage about my feet before
the stevedores had turned to again. Yes. Adrift—
on shore—after ten years' service—and with a poor
woman and four children six thousand miles off
depending on my half-pay for every mouthful they
ate. Yes, sir! I chucked it rather than hear
Captain Brierly abused. He left me his night-
glasses—here they are; and he wished me to take
care of the dog—here he is. Hallo, Rover, poor
boy. Where's the captain, Rover?' The dog looked
up at us with mournful yellow eyes, gave one desolate bark, and crept under the table.

"All this was taking place, more than two years
afterwards, on board that nautical ruin the *Fire-
Queen* this Jones had got charge of—quite by a
funny accident, too—from Matherson—mad Matherson they generally called him—the same who used
to hang out in Haï-phong, you know, before the
occupation days. The old chap snuffled on—

"'Ay, sir, Captain Brierly will be remembered
here, if there's no other place on earth. I wrote
fully to his father and did not get a word in reply—
neither Thank you, nor Go to the devil!—nothing!
Perhaps they did not want to know.'

"The sight of that watery-eyed old Jones mopping his bald head with a red cotton handkerchief, the sorrowing yelp of the dog, the squalor of that fly-blown cuddy which was the only shrine of his memory, threw a veil of inexpressibly mean pathos over Brierly's remembered figure, the posthumous revenge of fate for that belief in his own splendour which had almost cheated his life of its legitimate terrors. Almost! Perhaps wholly. Who can tell what flattering view he had induced himself to take of his own suicide?

"'Why did he commit the rash act, Captain Marlow—can you think?' asked Jones, pressing his palms together. 'Why? It beats me! Why?' He slapped his low and wrinkled forehead. 'If he had been poor and old and in debt—and never a show—or else mad. But he wasn't of the kind that goes mad, not he. You trust me. What a mate don't know about his skipper isn't worth knowing. Young, healthy, well off, no cares. . . . I sit here sometimes thinking, thinking, till my head fairly begins to buzz. There was some reason.'

"'You may depend on it, Captain Jones,' said I, 'it wasn't anything that would have disturbed much either of us two,' I said; and then, as if a light had been flashed into the muddle of his brain, poor old Jones found a last word of amazing profundity. He blew his nose, nodding at me dolefully: 'Ay, ay! neither you nor I, sir, had ever thought so much of ourselves.'

"Of course the recollection of my last conversation with Brierly is tinged with the knowledge of his end that followed so close upon it. I spoke with him for the last time during the progress of the inquiry. It was after the first adjournment, and he

came up with me in the street. He was in a state
of irritation, which I noticed with surprise, his usual
behaviour when he condescended to converse being
perfectly cool, with a trace of amused tolerance, as
if the existence of his interlocutor had been a rather
good joke. 'They caught me for that inquiry, you
see,' he began, and for a while enlarged complain-
ingly upon the inconveniences of daily attendance
in court. 'And goodness knows how long it will
last. Three days, I suppose.' I heard him out in
silence ; in my then opinion it was a way as good
as another of putting on side. 'What's the use of
it ? It is the stupidest set out you can imagine,'
he pursued hotly. I remarked that there was no
option. He interrupted me with a sort of pent-up
violence. 'I feel like a fool all the time.' I looked
up at him. This was going very far—for Brierly—
when talking of Brierly. He stopped short, and
seizing the lapel of my coat, gave it a slight tug.
'Why are we tormenting that young chap ? ' he
asked. This question chimed in so well to the
tolling of a certain thought of mine that, with the
image of the absconding renegade in my eye, I
answered at once, 'Hanged if I know, unless it be
that he lets you.' I was astonished to see him fall
into line, so to speak, with that utterance, which
ought to have been tolerably cryptic. He said
angrily, 'Why, yes. Can't he see that wretched
skipper of his has cleared out ? What does he
expect to happen ? Nothing can save him. He's
done for.' We walked on in silence a few steps.
'Why eat all that dirt ? ' he exclaimed, with an
oriental energy of expression—about the only sort
of energy you can find a trace of east of the fiftieth
meridian. I wondered greatly at the direction of

his thoughts, but now I strongly suspect it was strictly in character : at bottom poor Brierly must have been thinking of himself. I pointed out to him that the skipper of the *Patna* was known to have feathered his nest pretty well, and could procure almost anywhere the means of getting away. With Jim it was otherwise : the Government was keeping him in the Sailors' Home for the time being, and probably he hadn't a penny in his pocket to bless himself with. It costs some money to run away. 'Does it ? Not always,' he said, with a bitter laugh, and to some further remark of mine— 'Well, then, let him creep twenty feet underground and stay there ! By heavens ! *I* would.' I don't know why his tone provoked me, and I said, ' There is a kind of courage in facing it out as he does, knowing very well that if he went away nobody would trouble to run after him.' 'Courage be hanged ! ' growled Brierly. 'That sort of courage is of no use to keep a man straight, and I don't care a snap for such courage. If you were to say it was a kind of cowardice now—of softness. I tell you what, I will put up two hundred rupees if you put up another hundred and undertake to make the beggar clear out early to-morrow morning. The fellow's a gentleman if he ain't fit to be touched— he will understand. He must ! This infernal publicity is too shocking : there he sits while all these confounded natives, serangs, lascars, quartermasters, are giving evidence that's enough to burn a man to ashes with shame. This is abominable. Why, Marlow, don't you think, don't you feel, that this is abominable ; don't you now—come—as a seaman ? If he went away all this would stop at once.' Brierly said these words with a most unusual animation,

and made as if to reach after his pocket-book.
I restrained him, and declared coldly that the
cowardice of these four men did not seem to me
a matter of such great importance. 'And you
call yourself a seaman, I suppose,' he pronounced
angrily. I said that's what I called myself, and I
hoped I was too. He heard me out, and made a
gesture with his big arm that seemed to deprive me
of my individuality, to push me away into the crowd.
'The worst of it,' he said, 'is that all you fellows
have no sense of dignity ; you don't think enough
of what you are supposed to be.'

" We had been walking slowly meantime, and now
stopped opposite the harbour office, in sight of the
very spot from which the immense captain of the
Patna had vanished as utterly as a tiny feather
blown away in a hurricane. I smiled. Brierly
went on : ' This is a disgrace. We've got all kinds
amongst us—some anointed scoundrels in the lot ;
but, hang it, we must preserve professional decency
or we become no better than so many tinkers going
about loose. We are trusted. Do you understand ?
—trusted ! Frankly, I don't care a snap for all the
pilgrims that ever came out of Asia, but a decent
man would not have behaved like this to a full
cargo of old rags in bales. We aren't an organised
body of men, and the only thing that holds us
together is just the name for that kind of decency.
Such an affair destroys one's confidence. A man
may go pretty near through his whole sea-life
without any call to show a stiff upper lip. But
when the call comes. . . . Aha ! . . . If I . . .'

" He broke off, and in a changed tone, ' I'll give
you two hundred rupees now, Marlow, and you just
talk to that chap. Confound him ! I wish he had

never come out here. Fact is, I rather think some
of my people know his. The old man's a parson,
and I remember now I met him once when staying
with my cousin in Essex last year. If I am not
mistaken, the old chap seemed rather to fancy his
sailor son. Horrible. I can't do it myself—but
you. . . .'

"Thus, apropos of Jim, I had a glimpse of the
real Brierly a few days before he committed his
reality and his sham together to the keeping of
the sea. Of course I declined to meddle. The tone
of this last ' but you ' (poor Brierly couldn't help it),
that seemed to imply I was no more noticeable than
an insect, caused me to look at the proposal with
indignation, and on account of that provocation,
or for some other reason, I became positive in my
mind that the inquiry was a severe punishment to
that Jim, and that his facing it—practically of
his own freewill—was a redeeming feature in his
abominable case. I hadn't been so sure of it before.
Brierly went off in a huff. At the time his state
of mind was more of a mystery to me than it is
now.

"Next day, coming into court late, I sat by
myself. Of course I could not forget the conversation I had with Brierly, and now I had them both
under my eyes. The demeanour of one suggested
gloomy impudence and of the other a contemptuous
boredom ; yet one attitude might not have been
truer than the other, and I was aware that one was
not true. Brierly was not bored—he was exasperated ; and if so, then Jim might not have been
impudent. According to my theory he was not. I
imagined he was hopeless. Then it was that our
glances met. They met, and the look he gave me

was discouraging of any intention I might have had to speak to him. Upon either hypothesis—insolence or despair—I felt I could be of no use to him. This was the second day of the proceedings. Very soon after that exchange of glances the inquiry was adjourned again to the next day. The white men began to troop out at once. Jim had been told to stand down some time before, and was able to leave amongst the first. I saw his broad shoulders and his head outlined in the light of the door, and while I made my way slowly out talking with some one— some stranger who had addressed me casually—I could see him from within the court-room resting both elbows on the balustrade of the verandah and turning his back on the small stream of people trickling down the few steps. There was a murmur of voices and a shuffle of boots.

"The next case was that of assault and battery committed upon a money-lender, I believe ; and the defendant—a venerable villager with a straight white beard—sat on a mat just outside the door with his sons, daughters, sons-in-law, their wives, and, I should think, half the population of his village besides, squatting or standing around him. A slim dark woman, with part of her back and one black shoulder bared, and with a thin gold ring in her nose, suddenly began to talk in a high-pitched, shrewish tone. The man with me instinctively looked up at her. We were then just through the door, passing behind Jim's burly back.

"Whether those villagers had brought the yellow dog with them, I don't know. Anyhow, a dog was there, weaving himself in and out amongst people's legs in that mute stealthy way native dogs have, and my companion stumbled over him. The dog leaped away without a sound; the man, raising his voice a little, said with a slow laugh, 'Look at that wretched cur,' and directly afterwards we became separated by a lot of people pushing in. I stood back for a moment against the wall while the stranger managed to get down the steps and disappeared. I saw Jim spin round. He made a step forward and barred my way. We were alone; he glared at me with an air of stubborn resolution. I became aware I was being held up, so to speak, as if in a wood. The verandah was empty by then, the noise and movement in court had ceased: a great silence fell upon the building, in which, somewhere far within, an oriental voice began to whine abjectly. The dog, in the very act of trying to sneak in at the door, sat down hurriedly to hunt for fleas.

"'Did you speak to me?' asked Jim very low, and bending forward, not so much towards me but at me, if you know what I mean. I said 'No' at once. Something in the sound of that quiet tone of his warned me to be on my defence. I watched him. It was very much like a meeting in a wood, only more uncertain in its issue, since he could possibly want neither my money nor my life—nothing that I could simply give up or defend with a clear conscience. 'You say you didn't,' he said, very sombre. 'But I heard.' 'Some mistake,' I protested, utterly at a loss, and never taking my eyes off him. To watch his face was like watching a darkening sky before a clap of thunder, shade upon shade imperceptibly coming on, the gloom growing mysteriously intense in the calm of maturing violence.

"'As far as I know, I haven't opened my lips

in your hearing,' I affirmed with perfect truth. I was getting a little angry, too, at the absurdity of this encounter. It strikes me now I have never in my life been so near a beating—I mean it literally ; a beating with fists. I suppose I had some hazy prescience of that eventuality being in the air. Not that he was actively threatening me. On the contrary, he was strangely passive—don't you know ? but he was lowering, and, though not exceptionally big, he looked generally fit to demolish a wall. The most reassuring symptom I noticed was a kind of slow and ponderous hesitation, which I took as a tribute to the evident sincerity of my manner and of my tone. We faced each other. In the court the assault case was proceeding. I caught the words : 'Well—buffalo—stick—in the greatness of my fear. . . .'

" ' What did you mean by staring at me all the morning ? ' said Jim at last. He looked up and looked down again. ' Did you expect us all to sit with downcast eyes out of regard for your suscepti-bilities ? ' I retorted sharply. I was not going to submit meekly to any of his nonsense. He raised his eyes again, and this time continued to look me straight in the face. ' No. That's all right,' he pronounced with an air of deliberating with himself upon the truth of this statement—' that's all right. I am going through with that. Only '—and there he spoke a little faster—' I won't let any man call me names outside this court. There was a fellow with you. You spoke to him—oh yes—I know ; 'tis all very fine. You spoke to him, but you meant me to hear. . . .'

" I assured him he was under some extraordinary delusion. I had no conception how it came about.

'You thought I would be afraid to resent this,' he
said, with just a faint tinge of bitterness. I was
interested enough to discern the slightest shades of
expression, but I was not in the least enlightened ;
yet I don't know what in these words, or perhaps
just the intonation of that phrase, induced me
suddenly to make all possible allowances for him. I
ceased to be annoyed at my unexpected predicament.
It was some mistake on his part ; he was blun-
dering, and I had an intuition that the blunder
was of an odious, of an unfortunate nature. I was
anxious to end this scene on grounds of decency,
just as one is anxious to cut short some unprovoked
and abominable confidence. The funniest part was,
that in the midst of all these considerations of the
higher order I was conscious of a certain trepida-
tion as to the possibility—nay, likelihood—of this
encounter ending in some disreputable brawl which
could not possibly be explained, and would make
me ridiculous. I did not hanker after a three days'
celebrity as the man who got a black eye or something of the sort from the mate of the *Patna*. He,
in all probability, did not care what he did, or at
any rate would be fully justified in his own eyes. It
took no magician to see he was amazingly angry
about something, for all his quiet and even torpid
demeanour. I don't deny I was extremely desirous
to pacify him at all costs, had I only known what
to do. But I didn't know, as you may well imagine.
It was a blackness without a single gleam. We
confronted each other in silence. He hung fire for
about fifteen seconds, then made a step nearer, and
I made ready to ward off a blow, though I don't
think I moved a muscle. 'If you were as big as two
men and as strong as six,' he said very softly, ' I

would tell you what I think of you. You . . .'
'Stop!' I exclaimed. This checked him for a
second. 'Before you tell me what you think of me,'
I went on quickly, 'will you kindly tell me what it is
I've said or done?' During the pause that ensued
he surveyed me with indignation, while I made
supernatural efforts of memory, in which I was
hindered by the oriental voice within the court-room
expostulating with impassioned volubility against a
charge of falsehood. Then we spoke almost together.
'I will soon show you I am not,' he said, in a tone
suggestive of a crisis. 'I declare I don't know,' I
protested earnestly at the same time. He tried to
crush me by the scorn of his glance. 'Now that
you see I am not afraid you try to crawl out of
it,' he said. 'Who's a cur now—hey?' Then, at
last, I understood.

"He had been scanning my features as though
looking for a place where he would plant his fist.
'I will allow no man,' . . . he mumbled threaten-
ingly. It was, indeed, a hideous mistake; he had
given himself away utterly. I can't give you an
idea how shocked I was. I suppose he saw some
reflection of my feelings in my face, because his
expression changed just a little. 'Good God!' I
stammered, 'you don't think I . . .' 'But I am
sure I've heard,' he persisted, raising his voice for
the first time since the beginning of this deplorable scene. Then with a shade of disdain he added,
'It wasn't you, then? Very well; I'll find the
other.' 'Don't be a fool,' I cried in exasperation;
'it wasn't that at all.' 'I've heard,' he said again
with an unshaken and sombre perseverance.

"There may be those who could have laughed at
his pertinacity. I didn't. Oh, I didn't! There had

never been a man so mercilessly shown up by his
own natural impulse. A single word had stripped
him of his discretion—of that discretion which is
more necessary to the decencies of our inner being
than clothing is to the decorum of our body. 'Don't
be a fool,' I repeated. 'But the other man said it,
you don't deny that?' he pronounced distinctly, and
looking in my face without flinching. 'No, I don't
deny,' said I, returning his gaze. At last his eyes
followed downwards the direction of my pointing
finger. He appeared at first uncomprehending, then
confounded, and at last amazed and scared as though
a dog had been a monster and he had never seen a
dog before. 'Nobody dreamt of insulting you,' I
said.

"He contemplated the wretched animal, that
moved no more than an effigy: it sat with ears
pricked and its sharp muzzle pointed into the doorway, and suddenly snapped at a fly like a piece of
mechanism.

"I looked at him. The red of his fair sunburnt
complexion deepened suddenly under the down of
his cheeks, invaded his forehead, spread to the roots
of his curly hair. His ears became intensely crimson, and even the clear blue of his eyes was darkened
many shades by the rush of blood to his head. His
lips pouted a little, trembling as though he had been
on the point of bursting into tears. I perceived
he was incapable of pronouncing a word from the
excess of his humiliation. From disappointment too
—who knows? Perhaps he looked forward to that
hammering he was going to give me for rehabilita-
tion, for appeasement? Who can tell what relief
he expected from this chance of a row? He was
naïve enough to expect anything; but he had given

himself away for nothing in this case. He had been
frank with himself—let alone with me—in the wild
hope of arriving in that way at some effective
refutation, and the stars had been ironically unpro-
pitious. He made an inarticulate noise in his throat
like a man imperfectly stunned by a blow on the
head. It was pitiful.

"I didn't catch up again with him till well outside
the gate. I had even to trot a bit at the last, but
when, out of breath at his elbow, I taxed him with
running away, he said, 'Never!' and at once turned
at bay. I explained I never meant to say he was
running away from *me*. 'From no man—from not
a single man on earth,' he affirmed with a stubborn
mien. I forbore to point out the one obvious exception which would hold good for the bravest of
us; I thought he would find out by himself very
soon. He looked at me patiently while I was thinking of something to say, but I could find nothing on
the spur of the moment, and he began to walk on.
I kept up, and anxious not to lose him, I said
hurriedly that I couldn't think of leaving him under
a false impression of my—of my—I stammered. The
stupidity of the phrase appalled me while I was trying to finish it, but the power of sentences has
nothing to do with their sense or the logic of their
construction. My idiotic mumble seemed to please
him. He cut it short by saying, with courteous
placidity that argued an immense power of self-
control or else a wonderful elasticity of spirits—
'Altogether my mistake.' I marvelled greatly at
this expression : he might have been alluding to
some trifling occurrence. Hadn't he understood its
deplorable meaning? 'You may well forgive me,'
he continued, and went on a little moodily, 'All

these staring people in court seemed such fools that
—that it might have been as I supposed.'

"This opened suddenly a new view of him to
my wonder. I looked at him curiously and met
his unabashed and impenetrable eyes. 'I can't
put up with this kind of thing,' he said, very simply,
'and I don't mean to. In court it's different;
I've got to stand that—and I can do it too.'

"I don't pretend I understood him. The views
he let me have of himself were like those glimpses
through the shifting rents in a thick fog—bits of
vivid and vanishing detail, giving no connected idea
of the general aspect of a country. They fed one's
curiosity without satisfying it; they were no good
for purposes of orientation. Upon the whole he was
misleading. That's how I summed him up to myself
after he left me late in the evening. I had been
staying at the Malabar House for a few days, and
on my pressing invitation he dined with me there."

———————

CHAPTER VII.

"An outward-bound mail-boat had come in that
afternoon, and the big dining-room of the hotel was
more than half full of people with a hundred pounds
round-the-world tickets in their pockets. There were
married couples looking domesticated and bored with
each other in the midst of their travels; there were
small parties and large parties, and lone individuals
dining solemnly or feasting boisterously, but all
thinking, conversing, joking, or scowling as was their

wont at home ; and just as intelligently receptive of new impressions as their trunks upstairs. Henceforth they would be labelled as having passed through this and that place, and so would be their luggage. They would cherish this distinction of their persons, and preserve the gummed tickets on their portmanteaus as documentary evidence, as the only permanent trace of their improving enterprise. The dark-faced servants tripped without noise over the vast and polished floor ; now and then a girl's laugh would be heard, as innocent and empty as her mind, or, in a sudden hush of crockery, a few words in an affected drawl from some wit embroidering for the benefit of a grinning tableful the last funny story of shipboard scandal. Two nomadic old maids, dressed up to kill, worked acrimoniously through the bill of fare, whispering to each other with faded lips, wooden-faced and bizarre, like two sumptuous scarecrows. A little wine opened Jim's heart and loosened his tongue. His appetite was good, too, I noticed. He seemed to have buried somewhere the opening episode of our acquaintance. It was like a thing of which there would be no more question in this world. And all the time I had before me these blue, boyish eyes looking straight into mine, this young face, these capable shoulders, the open bronzed forehead with a white line under the roots of clustering fair hair, this appearance appealing at sight to all my sympathies : this frank aspect, the artless smile, the youthful seriousness. He was of the right sort ; he was one of us. He talked soberly, with a sort of composed unreserve, and with a quiet bearing that might have been the outcome of manly self-control, of impudence, of callousness, of a colossal unconsciousness, of a gigantic deception. Who can tell! From our tone we might have been discussing a third person, a football match, last year's weather. My mind floated in a sea of conjectures till the turn of the conversation enabled me, without being offensive, to remark that, upon the whole, this inquiry must have been pretty trying to him. He darted his arm across the tablecloth, and clutching my hand by the side of my plate, glared fixedly. I *was* startled. 'It must be awfully hard,' I stammered, confused by this display of speechless feeling. 'It is—hell,' he burst out in a muffled voice.

"This movement and these words caused two well-groomed male globe-trotters at a neighbouring table to look up in alarm from their iced pudding. I rose, and we passed into the front gallery for coffee and cigars.

"On little octagon tables candles burned in glass globes; clumps of stiff-leaved plants separated sets of cosy wicker chairs; and between the pairs of columns, whose reddish shafts caught in a long row the sheen from the tall windows, the night, glittering and sombre, seemed to hang like a splendid drapery. The riding lights of ships winked afar like setting stars, and the hills across the roadstead resembled rounded black masses of arrested thunder-clouds.

"'I couldn't clear out,' Jim began. 'The skipper did—that's all very well for him. I couldn't, and I wouldn't. They all got out of it in one way or another, but it wouldn't do for me.'

"I listened with concentrated attention, not daring to stir in my chair; I wanted to know—and to this day I don't know, I can only guess. He would be confident and depressed all in the same breath, as if some conviction of innate blamelessness had

checked the truth writhing within him at every
turn. He began by saying, in the tone in which
a man would admit his inability to jump a twenty-
foot wall, that he could never go home now; and
this declaration recalled to my mind what Brierly
had said, 'that the old parson in Essex seemed to
fancy his sailor son not a little.'

"I can't tell you whether Jim knew he was
especially 'fancied,' but the tone of his references
to 'my Dad' was calculated to give me a notion
that the good old rural dean was about the finest
man that ever had been worried by the cares of
a large family since the beginning of the world.
This, though never stated, was implied with an
anxiety that there should be no mistake about
it, which was really very true and charming, but
added a poignant sense of lives far off to the other
elements of the story. 'He has seen it all in the
home papers by this time,' said Jim. 'I can never
face the poor old chap.' I did not dare to lift my eyes
at this till I heard him add, 'I could never explain.
He wouldn't understand.' Then I looked up.
He was smoking reflectively, and after a moment,
rousing himself, began to talk again. He discovered
at once a desire that I should not confound him
with his partners in—in crime, let us call it. He
was not one of them; he was altogether of another
sort. I gave no sign of dissent. I had no intention,
for the sake of barren truth, to rob him of the
smallest particle of any saving grace that would
come in his way. I didn't know how much of it
he believed himself. I didn't know what he was
playing up to—if he was playing up to anything
at all—and I suspect he did not know either;
for it is my belief no man ever understands quite

his own artful dodges to escape from the grim
shadow of self-knowledge. I made no sound all
the time he was wondering what he had better do
after 'that stupid inquiry was over.'

"Apparently he shared Brierly's contemptuous
opinion of these proceedings ordained by law. He
would not know where to turn, he confessed, clearly
thinking aloud rather than talking to me. Certificate gone, career broken, no money to get away,
no work that he could obtain as far as he could
see. At home he could perhaps get something;
but it meant going to his people for help, and that
he would not do. He saw nothing for it but ship
before the mast—could get perhaps a quartermaster's billet in some steamer. Would do for
a quartermaster. . . . 'Do you think you would?'
I asked pitilessly. He jumped up, and going to
the stone balustrade looked out into the night. In
a moment he was back, towering above my chair
with his youthful face clouded yet by the pain of
a conquered emotion. He had understood very
well I did not doubt his ability to steer a ship.
In a voice that quavered a bit he asked me, 'Why
did I say that? I had been "no end kind" to
him. I had not even laughed at him when'—
here he began to mumble—'that mistake, you know
—made a confounded ass of myself.' I broke in
by saying rather warmly that for me such a mistake was not a matter to laugh at. He sat down
and drank deliberately some coffee, emptying the
small cup to the last drop. 'That does not mean
I admit for a moment the cap fitted,' he declared
distinctly. 'No?' I said. 'No,' he affirmed with
quiet decision. 'Do you know what *you* would
have done? Do you? And you don't think your-

self' . . . he gulped something . . . 'you don't think yourself a—a—cur?'

"And with this—upon my honour!—he looked up at me inquisitively. It was a question it appears—a *bonâ-fide* question! However, he didn't wait for an answer. Before I could recover he went on, with his eyes straight before him, as if reading off something written on the body of the night. 'It is all in being ready. I wasn't; not—not then. I don't want to excuse myself; but I would like to explain—I would like somebody to understand—somebody—one person at least! You! Why not you?'

"It was solemn, and a little ridiculous too, as they always are, those struggles of an individual trying to save from the fire his idea of what his moral identity should be, this precious notion of a convention, only one of the rules of the game, nothing more, but all the same so terribly effective by its assumption of unlimited power over natural instincts, by the awful penalties of its failure. He began his story quietly enough. On board that Dale Line steamer that had picked up these four floating in a boat upon the discreet sunset glow of the sea, they had been after the first day looked askance upon. The fat skipper told some story, the others had been silent, and at first it had been accepted. You don't cross-examine poor castaways you had the good luck to save, if not from cruel death, then at least from cruel suffering. Afterwards, with time to think it over, it might have struck the officers of the *Avondale* that there was 'something fishy' in the affair; but of course they would keep their doubts to themselves. They had picked up the captain, the mate, and two engineers of the steamer *Patna* sunk at sea, and that, very properly, was enough for them. I did not ask Jim about the nature of his feelings during the ten days he spent on board. From the way he narrated that part I was at liberty to infer he was partly stunned by the discovery he had made—the discovery about himself—and no doubt was at work trying to explain it away to the only man who was capable of appreciating all its tremendous magnitude. You must understand he did not try to minimise its importance. Of that I am sure ; and therein lies his distinction. As to what sensations he experienced when he got ashore and heard the unforeseen conclusion of the tale in which he had taken such a pitiful part, he told me nothing of them, and it is difficult to imagine. " I wonder whether he felt the ground cut from under his feet ? I wonder ? But no doubt he managed to get a fresh foothold very soon. He was ashore a whole fortnight waiting in the Sailors' Home, and as there were six or seven men staying there at the time, I had heard of him a little. Their languid opinion seemed to be that, in addition to his other shortcomings, he was a sulky brute. He had passed these days on the verandah, buried in a long chair, and coming out of his place of sepulture only at meal-times or late at night, when he wandered on the quays all by himself, detached from his surroundings, irresolute and silent, like a ghost without a home to haunt. ' I don't think I've spoken three words to a living soul in all that time,' he said, making me very sorry for him ; and directly he added, ' One of these fellows would have been sure to blurt out something I had made up my mind not to put up with, and I didn't

want a row. No! Not then. I was too—too . . .
I had no heart for it.' 'So that bulkhead held
out after all,' I remarked cheerfully. 'Yes,' he
murmured, 'it held. And yet I swear to you I
felt it bulge under my hand.' 'It's extraordinary
what strains old iron will stand sometimes,' I said.
Thrown back in his seat, his legs stiffly out and
arms hanging down, he nodded slightly several
times. You could not conceive a sadder spectacle.
Suddenly he lifted his head; he sat up; he slapped
his thigh. 'Ah! what a chance missed! My God!
what a chance missed!' he blazed out, but the
ring of the last 'missed' resembled a cry wrung
out by pain.

"He was silent again with a still, far-away
look of fierce yearning after that missed distinction,
with his nostrils for an instant dilated, sniffing the
intoxicating breath of that wasted opportunity. If
you think I was either surprised or shocked you
do me an injustice in more ways than one! Ah,
he was an imaginative beggar! He would give
himself away; he would give himself up. I could
see in his glance darted into the night all his inner
being carried on, projected headlong into the fanciful realm of recklessly heroic aspirations. He had
no leisure to regret what he had lost, he was so
wholly and naturally concerned for what he had
failed to obtain. He was very far away from me
who watched him across three feet of space. With
every instant he was penetrating deeper into the
impossible world of romantic achievements. He got
to the heart of it at last! A strange look of beatitude
overspread his features, his eyes sparkled in the
light of the candle burning between us; he positively
smiled! He had penetrated to the very heart—to

the very heart. It was an ecstatic smile that your faces—or mine either—will never wear, my dear boys. I whisked him back by saying, 'If you had stuck to the ship, you mean!'

"He turned upon me, his eyes suddenly amazed and full of pain, with a bewildered, startled, suffering face, as though he had tumbled down from a star. Neither you nor I will ever look like this on any man. He shuddered profoundly, as if a cold finger-tip had touched his heart. Last of all he sighed.

"I was not in a merciful mood. He provoked one by his contradictory indiscretions. 'It is unfortunate you didn't know beforehand!' I said with every unkind intention; but the perfidious shaft fell harmless—dropped at his feet like a spent arrow, as it were, and he did not think of picking it up. Perhaps he had not even seen it. Presently, lolling at ease, he said, 'Dash it all! I tell you it bulged. I was holding up my lamp along the angle-iron in the lower deck when a flake of rust as big as the palm of my hand fell off the plate, all of itself.' He passed his hand over his forehead. 'The thing stirred and jumped off like something alive while I was looking at it.' 'That made you feel pretty bad,' I observed casually. 'Do you suppose,' he said, 'that I was thinking of myself, with a hundred and sixty people at my back, all fast asleep in that fore-'tween-deck alone—and more of them aft; more on the deck—sleeping—knowing nothing about it—three times as many as there were boats for, even if there had been time? I expected to see the iron open out as I stood there and the rush of water going over them as they lay. . . . What could I do—what?'

" I can easily picture him to myself in the peopled gloom of the cavernous place, with the light of the globe-lamp falling on a small portion of the bulk-head that had the weight of the ocean on the other side, and the breathing of unconscious sleepers in his ears. I can see him glaring at the iron, startled by the falling rust, overburdened by the knowledge of an imminent death. This, I gathered, was the second time he had been sent forward by that skipper of his, who, I rather think, wanted to keep him away from the bridge. He told me that his first impulse was to shout and straight away make all those people leap out of sleep into terror ; but such an overwhelming sense of his helplessness came over him that he was not able to produce a sound. This is, I suppose, what people mean by the tongue cleaving to the roof of the mouth. ' Too dry,' was the concise expression he used in reference to this state. Without a sound, then, he scrambled out on deck through the number one hatch. A wind-sail rigged down there swung against him acci-dentally, and he remembered that the light touch of the canvas on his face nearly knocked him off the hatchway ladder.

" He confessed that his knees wobbled a good deal as he stood on the foredeck looking at another sleeping crowd. The engines having been stopped by that time, the steam was blowing off. Its deep rumble made the whole night vibrate like a bass string. The ship trembled to it.

" He saw here and there a head lifted off a mat, a vague form uprise in sitting posture, listen sleepily for a moment, sink down again into the billowy con-fusion of boxes, steam-winches, ventilators. He was aware all these people did not know enough to take intelligent notice of that strange noise. The ship of iron, the men with white faces, all the sights, all the sounds, everything on board to that ignorant and pious multitude was strange alike, and as trustworthy as it would for ever remain incomprehensible. It occurred to him that the fact was fortunate. The idea of it was simply terrible.

" You must remember he believed, as any other man would have done in his place, that the ship would go down at any moment ; the bulging, rust-eaten plates that kept back the ocean, fatally must give way, all at once like an undermined dam, and let in a sudden and overwhelming flood. He stood still looking at these recumbent bodies, a doomed man aware of his fate, surveying the silent company of the dead. They *were* dead ! Nothing could save them ! There were boats enough for half of them perhaps, but there was no time. No time ! No time ! It did not seem worth while to open his lips, to stir hand or foot. Before he could shout three words, or make three steps, he would be floundering in a sea whitened awfully by the desperate struggles of human beings, clamorous with the distress of cries for help. There was no help. He imagined what would happen perfectly ; he went through it all motionless by the hatchway with the lamp in his hand,—he went through it to the very last harrowing detail. I think he went through it again while he was telling me these things he could not tell the court.

" ' I saw as clearly as I see you now that there was nothing I could do. It seemed to take all life out of my limbs. I thought I might just as well stand where I was and wait. I did not think I had many seconds . . .' Suddenly the steam ceased blowing off. The noise, he remarked, had been distracting, but the silence at once became intolerably oppressive.

" ' I thought I would choke before I got drowned,' he said.

" He protested he did not think of saving himself. The only distinct thought formed, vanishing, and reforming in his brain, was : eight hundred people and seven boats ; eight hundred people and seven boats.

" ' Somebody was speaking aloud inside my head,' he said a little wildly. ' Eight hundred people and seven boats—and no time ! Just think of it.' He leaned towards me across the little table, and I tried to avoid his stare. ' Do you think I was afraid of death ? ' he asked in a voice very fierce and low. He brought down his open hand with a bang that made the coffee-cups dance. ' I am ready to swear I was not—I was not. . . . By God—no ! ' He hitched himself upright and crossed his arms ; his chin fell on his breast.

" The soft clashes of crockery reached us faintly through the high windows. There was a burst of voices, and several men came out in high good-humour into the gallery. They were exchanging jocular reminiscences of the donkeys in Cairo. A pale anxious youth stepping softly on long legs was being chaffed by a strutting and rubicund globe-trotter about his purchases in the bazaar. ' No, really—do you think I've been done to that extent ? ' he inquired very earnest and deliberate. The band moved away, dropping into chairs as they went ; matches flared, illuminating for a second faces without the ghost of an expression and the flat glaze of white shirt-fronts ; the hum of many conversations

animated with the ardour of feasting sounded to
me absurd and infinitely remote.

"'Some of the crew were sleeping on the number
one hatch within reach of my arm,' began Jim
again.

"You must know they kept Kalashee watch in
that ship, all hands sleeping through the night, and
only the reliefs of quartermasters and look-out men
being called. He was tempted to grip and shake the
shoulder of the nearest lascar, but he didn't. Something held his arm down along his sides. He was
not afraid—oh no ! only he just couldn't—that's all.
He was not afraid of death perhaps, but I'll tell you
what, he was afraid of the emergency. His confounded imagination had evoked for him all the
horrors of panic, the trampling rush, the pitiful
screams, boats swamped—all the appalling in-
cidents of a disaster at sea he had ever heard of. He
might have been resigned to die, but I suspect he
wanted to die without added terrors, quietly, in a
sort of peaceful trance. A certain readiness to perish
is not so very rare, but it is seldom that you meet
men whose souls, steeled in the impenetrable armour
of resolution, are ready to fight a losing battle to
the last, the desire of peace waxes stronger as hope
declines, till at last it conquers the very desire of
life. Which of us here has not observed this, or
maybe experienced something of that feeling in his
own person—this extreme weariness of emotions, the
vanity of effort, the yearning for rest ? Those
striving with unreasonable forces know it well,—
the shipwrecked castaways in boats, wanderers lost
in a desert, men battling against the unthinking
might of nature, or the stupid brutality of crowds."

CHAPTER VIII.

" How long he stood stock-still by the hatch expecting every moment to feel the ship dip under
his feet and the rush of water take him at the
back and toss him like a chip, I cannot say. Not
very long—two minutes perhaps. A couple of men
he could not make out began to converse drowsily,
and also, he could not tell where, he detected a
curious noise of shuffling feet. Above these faint
sounds there was that awful stillness preceding a
catastrophe, that trying silence of the moment
before the crash ; then it came into his head that
perhaps he would have time to rush along and cut
all the lanyards of the gripes, so that the boats
would float off as the ship went down.

" The *Patna* had a long bridge, and all the boats
were up there, four on one side and three on the
other—the smallest of them on the port-side and
nearly abreast of the steering gear. He assured
me, with evident anxiety to be believed, that he had
been most careful to keep them ready for instant
service. He knew his duty. I daresay he was a
good enough mate as far as that went. ' I always
believed in being prepared for the worst,' he commented, staring anxiously in my face. I nodded
my approval of the sound principle, averting my
eyes before the subtle unsoundness of the man.

" He started unsteadily to run. He had to step
over legs, avoid stumbling against the heads. Suddenly some one caught hold of his coat from below,
and a distressed voice spoke under his elbow. The
light of the lamp he carried in his right hand fell

upon an upturned dark face whose eyes entreated him together with the voice. He had picked up enough of the language to understand the word water, repeated several times in a tone of insistence, of prayer, almost of despair. He gave a jerk to get away, and felt an arm embrace his leg.

" ' The beggar clung to me like a drowning man,' he said impressively. ' Water, water ! What water did he mean ? What did he know ? As calmly as I could I ordered him to let go. He was stopping me, time was pressing, other men began to stir ; I wanted time—time to cut the boats adrift. He got hold of my hand now, and I felt that he would begin to shout. It flashed upon me it was enough to start a panic, and I hauled off with my free arm and slung the lamp in his face. The glass jingled, the light went out, but the blow made him let go, and I ran off—I wanted to get at the boats ; I wanted to get at the boats. He leaped after me from behind. I turned on him. He would not keep quiet ; he tried to shout ; I had half throttled him before I made out what he wanted. He wanted some water— water to drink ; they were on strict allowance, you know, and he had with him a young boy I had noticed several times. His child was sick—and thirsty. He had caught sight of me as I passed by, and was begging for a little water. That's all. We were under the bridge, in the dark. He kept on snatching at my wrists ; there was no getting rid of him. I dashed into my berth, grabbed my water-bottle, and thrust it into his hands. He vanished. I didn't find out till then how much I was in want of a drink myself.' He leaned on one elbow with a hand over his eyes.

" I felt a creepy sensation all down my backbone ;

there was something peculiar in all this. The fingers
of the hand that shaded his brow trembled slightly.
He broke the short silence.

" ' These things happen only once to a man and
. . . Ah ! well ! When I got on the bridge at last
the beggars were getting one of the boats off the
chocks. A boat ! I was running up the ladder
when a heavy blow fell on my shoulder, just missing my head. It didn't stop me, and the chief
engineer—they had got him out of his bunk by
then—raised the boat-stretcher again. Somehow I
had no mind to be surprised at anything. All this
seemed natural—and awful—and awful. I dodged
that miserable maniac, lifted him off the deck as
though he had been a little child, and he started
whispering in my arms : " Don't ! don't ! I thought
you were one of them niggers." I flung him away, he
skidded along the bridge and knocked the legs from
under the little chap—the second. The skipper,
busy about the boat, looked round and came at me
head down, growling like a wild beast. I flinched
no more than a stone. I was as solid standing there
as this,' he tapped lightly with his knuckles the wall
beside his chair. ' It was as though I had heard it
all, seen it all, gone through it all twenty times
already. I wasn't afraid of them. I drew back
my fist and he stopped short, muttering—

" ' " Ah ! it's you. Lend a hand quick."

" ' That's what he said. Quick ! As if anybody
could be quick enough. Aren't you going to do
something,' I asked. ' " Yes. Clear out," he snarled
over his shoulder.

" ' I don't think I understood then what he meant.
The other two had picked themselves up by that
time, and they rushed together to the boat. They

D

tramped, they wheezed, they shoved, they cursed
the boat, the ship, each other—cursed me. All in
mutters. I didn't move, I didn't speak. I watched
the slant of the ship. She was as still as if landed
on the blocks in a dry dock—only she was like this.'
He held up his hand, palm under, the tips of the
fingers inclined downwards. 'Like this,' he repeated.
' I could see the line of the horizon before me, as clear
as a bell, above her stem-head ; I could see the water
far off there black and sparkling, and still—still as a
pond, deadly still, more still than ever sea was before
—more still than I could bear to look at. Have you
watched a ship floating head down, checked in sinking by a sheet of old iron too rotten to stand being
shored up. Have you ? Oh yes, shored up ? I
thought of that—I thought of every mortal thing ;
but can you shore up a bulkhead in five minutes
—or in fifty for that matter ? Where was I going
to get men that would go down below ? And
the timber—the timber ! Would you have had
the courage to swing the maul for the first blow
if you had seen that bulkhead ? Don't say you
would : you had not seen it ; nobody would.
Hang it—to do a thing like that you must believe
there is a chance, one in a thousand, at least, some
ghost of a chance ; and you would not have believed.
Nobody would have believed. You think me a cur
for standing there, but what would you have done ?
What ! You can't tell—nobody can tell. One must
have time to turn round. What would you have me
do ? Where was the kindness in making crazy with
fright all those people I could not save single-handed
—that nothing could save ? Look here ! As true
as I sit on this chair before you . . .'

   "He drew quick breaths at every few words and

shot quick glances at my face, as though in his
anguish he were watchful of the effect. He was
not speaking to me, he was only speaking before
me, in a dispute with an invisible personality, an
antagonistic and inseparable partner of his existence
—another possessor of his soul. These were issues
beyond the competency of a court of inquiry : it
was a subtle and momentous quarrel as to the true
essence of life, and did not want a judge. He
wanted an ally, a helper, an accomplice. I felt the
risk I ran of being circumvented, blinded, decoyed,
bullied, perhaps, into taking a definite part in a
dispute impossible of decision if one had to be fair
to all the phantoms in possession—to the reputable
that had its claims and to the disreputable that had
its exigencies. I can't explain to you who haven't
seen him and who hear his words only at second
hand the mixed nature of my feelings. It seemed
to me I was being made to comprehend the Inconceivable—and I know of nothing to compare with
the discomfort of such a sensation. I was made to
look at the convention that lurks in all truth and
on the essential sincerity of falsehood. He appealed
to all sides at once,—to the side turned perpetually
to the light of day, and to that side of us which,
like the other hemisphere of the moon, exists
stealthily in perpetual darkness, with only a fearful
ashy light falling at times on the edge. He swayed
me. I own to it, I own up. The occasion was
obscure, insignificant—what you will : a lost youngster, one in a million—but then he was one of us ;
an incident as completely devoid of importance as
the flooding of an ant-heap, and yet the mystery of
his attitude got hold of me as though he had been
an individual in the forefront of his kind, as if the

obscure truth involved were momentous enough to
affect mankind's conception of itself. . . ."

Marlow paused to put new life into his expiring
cheroot, seemed to forget all about the story, and
abruptly began again.

"My fault of course. One has no business really
to get interested. It's a weakness of mine. His
was of another kind. My weakness consists in not
having a discriminating eye for the incidental—for
the externals,—no eye for the hod of the rag-picker
or the fine linen of the next man. Next man—
that's it. I have met so many men," he pursued,
with momentary sadness—"met them too with a
certain—certain—impact, let us say ; like this fellow,
for instance—and in each case all I could see was
merely the human being. A confounded demo-
cratic quality of vision which may be better than
total blindness, but has been of no advantage to me
—I can assure you. Men expect one to take into
account their fine linen. But I never could get up
any enthusiasm about these things. Oh ! It's a
failing ; it's a failing ; and then comes a soft evening ; a lot of men too indolent for whist—and a
story. . . ."

He paused again to wait for an encouraging
remark, perhaps, but nobody spoke ; only the host,
as if reluctantly performing a duty, murmured—

"You are so subtle, Marlow."

"Who ? I ? " said Marlow in a low voice. "Oh
no ! But *he* was ; and try as I may for the success
of this yarn I am missing innumerable shades—they
were so fine, so difficult to render in colourless words.
Because he complicated matters by being so simple,
too—the simplest poor devil ! . . . By Jove ! he
was amazing. There he sat telling me that just as

I saw him before my eyes he wouldn't be afraid to face anything—and believing in it too. I tell you it was fabulously innocent and it was enormous, enormous! I watched him covertly, just as though I had suspected him of an intention to take a jolly good rise out of me. He was confident that, on the square, 'on the square, mind!' there was nothing he couldn't meet. Ever since he had been 'so high'—'quite a little chap,' he had been preparing himself for all the difficulties that can beset one on land and water. He confessed proudly to this kind of foresight. He had been elaborating dangers and defences, expecting the worst, rehearsing his best. He must have led a most exalted existence. Can you fancy it? A succession of adventures, so much glory, such a victorious progress! and the deep sense of his sagacity crowning every day of his inner life. He forgot himself; his eyes shone; and with every word my heart, searched by the light of his absurdity, was growing heavier in my breast. I had no mind to laugh, and lest I should smile I made for myself a stolid face. He gave signs of irritation.

"'It is always the unexpected that happens,' I said in a propitiatory tone. My obtuseness provoked him into a contemptuous 'Pshaw!' I suppose he meant that the unexpected couldn't touch him; nothing less than the unconceivable itself could get over his perfect state of preparation. He had been taken unawares—and he whispered to himself a malediction upon the waters and the firmament, upon the ship, upon the men. Everything had betrayed him! He had been tricked into that sort of high-minded resignation which prevented him lifting as much as his little finger, while these others who had a very clear perception of the

actual necessity were tumbling against each other
and sweating desperately over that boat business.
Something had gone wrong there at the last moment.
It appears that in their flurry they had contrived
in some mysterious way to get the sliding bolt of
the foremost boat-chock jammed tight, and forthwith had gone out of the remnants of their minds
over the deadly nature of that accident. It must
have been a pretty sight, the fierce industry of
these beggars toiling on a motionless ship that
floated quietly in the silence of a world asleep,
fighting against time for the freeing of that boat,
grovelling on all-fours, standing up in despair,
tugging, pushing, snarling at each other venom-
ously, ready to kill, ready to weep, and only kept
from flying at each other's throats by the fear of
death that stood silent behind them like an inflexible
and cold-eyed taskmaster. Oh yes! It must have
been a pretty sight. He saw it all, he could talk
about it with scorn and bitterness ; he had a minute
knowledge of it by means of some sixth sense, I
conclude, because he swore to me he had remained
apart without a glance at them and at the boat—
without one single glance. And I believe him. I
should think he was too busy watching the threatening slant of the ship, the suspended menace discovered in the midst of the most perfect security
—fascinated by the sword hanging by a hair over
his imaginative head.

"Nothing in the world moved before his eyes,
and he could depict to himself without hindrance
the sudden swing upwards of the dark skyline, the
sudden tilt up of the vast plain of the sea, the swift
still rise, the brutal fling, the grasp of the abyss,
the struggle without hope, the starlight closing over

his head for ever like the vault of a tomb—the revolt
of his young life—the black end. He could! By
Jove! who couldn't? And you must remember he
was a finished artist in that peculiar way, he was
a gifted poor devil with the faculty of swift and
forestalling vision. The sights it showed him had
turned him into cold stone from the soles of his
feet to the nape of his neck; but there was a hot
dance of thoughts in his head, a dance of lame,
blind, mute thoughts—a whirl of awful cripples.
Didn't I tell you he confessed himself before me as
though I had the power to bind and to loose. He
burrowed deep, deep, in the hope of my absolution,
which would have been of no good to him. This
was one of these cases which no solemn deception
can palliate, where no man can help; where his
very Maker seems to abandon a sinner to his own
devices.

"He stood on the starboard side of the bridge, as
far as he could get from the struggle for the boat,
which went on with the agitation of madness and
the stealthiness of a conspiracy. The two Malays
had meantime remained holding to the wheel. Just
picture to yourselves the actors in that, thank God!
unique, episode of the sea, four beside themselves
with fierce and secret exertions, and three looking
on in complete immobility, above the awnings covering the profound ignorance of hundreds of human
beings, with their weariness, with their dreams, with
their hopes, arrested, held by an invisible hand
on the brink of annihilation. For that they were
so, makes no doubt to me · given the state of the
ship, this was the deadliest possible description of
accident that could happen. These beggars by
the boat had every reason to go distracted with

funk. Frankly, had I been there, I would not have given as much as a counterfeit farthing for the ship's chance to keep above water to the end of each successive second. And still she floated! These sleeping pilgrims were destined to accomplish their whole pilgrimage to the bitterness of some other end. It was as if the Omnipotence whose mercy they confessed had needed their humble testimony on earth for a while longer, and had looked down to make a sign, 'Thou shalt not!' to the ocean. Their escape would trouble me as a prodigiously inexplicable event, did I not know how tough old iron can be—as tough sometimes as the spirit of some men we meet now and then, worn to a shadow and breasting the weight of life. Not the least wonder of these twenty minutes, to my mind, is the behaviour of the two helmsmen. They were amongst the native batch of all sorts brought over from Aden to give evidence at the inquiry. One of them, labouring under intense bashfulness, was very young, and with his smooth, yellow, cheery countenance looked even younger than he was. I remember perfectly Brierly asking him, through the interpreter, what he thought of it at the time, and the interpreter, after a short colloquy, turning to the court with an important air—

" 'He says he thought nothing.'

"The other with patient blinking eyes, a blue cotton handkerchief, faded with much washing, bound with a smart twist over a lot of grey wisps, his face shrunk into grim hollows, his brown skin made darker by a mesh of wrinkles, explained that he had a knowledge of some evil thing befalling the ship, but there had been no order; he could not remember an order; why should he leave the helm?

To some further questions he jerked back his spare shoulders, and declared it never came into his mind then that the white men were about to leave the ship through fear of death. He did not believe it now. There might have been secret reasons. He wagged his old chin knowingly. Aha! secret reasons. He was a man of great experience, and he wanted *that* white Tuan to know—he turned towards Brierly, who didn't raise his head—that he had acquired a knowledge of many things by serving white men on the sea for a great number of years—and, suddenly, with shaky excitement he poured upon our spell-bound attention a lot of queer-sounding names, names of dead-and-gone skippers, names of forgotten country ships, names of familiar and distorted sound, as if the hand of dumb time had been at work on them for ages. They stopped him at last. A silence fell upon the court,—a silence that remained unbroken for at least a minute, and passed gently into a deep murmur. This episode was *the* sensation of the second day's proceedings—affecting all the audience, affecting everybody except Jim, who was sitting moodily at the end of the first bench, and never looked up at this extraordinary and damning witness that seemed possessed of some mysterious theory of defence.

"So these two lascars stuck to the helm of that ship without steerage-way, where death would have found them if such had been their destiny. The whites did not give them half a glance, had probably forgotten their existence. Assuredly Jim did not remember it. He remembered he could do nothing; he could do nothing, now he was alone. There was nothing to do but to sink with the ship. No use making a disturbance about it. Was there? He waited upstanding, without a sound, stiffened in the idea of some sort of heroic discretion. The first engineer ran cautiously across the bridge to tug at his sleeve.

" ' Come and help! For God's sake, come and help ! '

" He ran back to the boat on the points of his toes, and returned directly to worry at his sleeve, begging and cursing at the same time.

" ' I believe he would have kissed my hands,' said Jim savagely, ' and, next moment, he starts foaming and whispering in my face, " If I had the time I would like to crack your skull for you." I pushed him away. Suddenly he caught hold of me round the neck. Damn him! I hit him. I hit out without looking. " Won't you save your own life—you infernal coward," he sobs. Coward! He called me an infernal coward! Ha! ha! ha! ha! He called me—ha! ha! ha! . . .'

" He had thrown himself back and was shaking with laughter. I had never in my life heard anything so bitter as that noise. It fell like a blight on all the merriment about donkeys, pyramids, bazaars, or what not. Along the whole dim length of the gallery the voices dropped, the pale blotches of faces turned our way with one accord, and the silence became so profound that the clear tinkle of a teaspoon falling on the tesselated floor of the verandah rang out like a tiny and silvery scream.

" ' You mustn't laugh like this, with all these people about,' I remonstrated. ' It isn't nice for them, you know.'

" He gave no sign of having heard at first, but after a while with a stare that, missing me altogether, seemed to probe the heart of some awful vision, he muttered carelessly—'Oh! they'll think I am drunk.'

"And after that you would have thought from his appearance he would never make a sound again. But—no fear! He could no more stop telling now than he could have stopped living by the mere exertion of his will."

CHAPTER IX.

"'I was saying to myself, "Sink—curse you! Sink!"' These were the words with which he began again. He wanted it over. He was severely left alone, and he formulated in his head this address to the ship in a tone of imprecation, while at the same time he enjoyed the privilege of witnessing scenes—as far as I can judge—of low comedy. They were still at that bolt. The skipper was ordering. 'Get under and try to lift;' and the others naturally shirked. You understand that to be squeezed flat under the keel of a boat wasn't a desirable position to be caught in if the ship went down suddenly. 'Why don't you—you the strongest?' whined the little engineer. 'Gott-for-dam! I am too thick,' spluttered the skipper in despair. It was funny enough to make angels weep. They stood idle for a moment, and suddenly the chief engineer rushed again at Jim.

"'Come and help, man! Are you mad to throw your only chance away? Come and help, man! Man! Look there—look!'

"And at last Jim looked astern where the other pointed with maniacal insistence. He saw a silent black squall which had eaten up already one-third of the sky. You know how these squalls come up there about that time of the year. First you see a darkening of the horizon—no more; then a cloud rises opaque like a wall. A straight edge of vapour lined with sickly whitish gleams flies up from the south-west, swallowing the stars in whole constellations; its shadow flies over the waters, and confounds sea and sky into one abyss of obscurity. And all is still. No thunder, no wind, no sound; not a flicker of lightning. Then in the tenebrous immensity a livid arch appears; a swell or two like undulations of the very darkness run past, and, suddenly, wind and rain strike together with a peculiar impetuosity as if they had burst through something solid. Such a cloud had come up while they weren't looking. They had just noticed it, and were perfectly justified in surmising that if in absolute stillness there was some chance for the ship to keep afloat a few minutes longer, the least disturbance of the sea would make an end of her instantly. Her first nod to the swell that precedes the burst of such a squall would be also her last, would become a plunge, would, so to speak, be prolonged into a long dive, down, down to the bottom. Hence, these new capers of their fright, these new antics in which they displayed their extreme aversion to die.

"'It was black, black,' pursued Jim with moody steadiness. 'It had sneaked upon us from behind. The infernal thing! I suppose there had been at the back of my head some hope yet. I don't know. But that was all over anyhow. It maddened me to see myself caught like this. I was angry, as though

I had been trapped. I *was* trapped! The night was
hot, too, I remember. Not a breath of air.'

"He remembered so well that, gasping in the
chair, he seemed to sweat and choke before my eyes.
No doubt it maddened him; it knocked him over
afresh—in a manner of speaking—but it made him
also remember that important purpose which had
sent him rushing on that bridge only to slip clean
out of his mind. He had intended to cut the life-
boats clear of the ship. He whipped out his knife
and went to work slashing as though he had seen
nothing, had heard nothing, had known of no one
on board. They thought him hopelessly wrong-
headed and crazy, but dared not protest noisily
against this useless loss of time. When he had done
he returned to the very same spot from which he
had started. The chief was there, ready with a
clutch at him to whisper close to his head, scathingly,
as though he wanted to bite his ear—

"'You silly fool! do you think you'll get the
ghost of a show when all that lot of brutes is in the
water? Why, they will batter your head for you
from these boats.'

"He wrung his hands, ignored, at Jim's elbow.
The skipper kept up a nervous shuffle in one place
and mumbled, 'Hammer! hammer! Mein Gott!
Get a hammer.'

"The little engineer whimpered like a child, but,
broken arm and all, he turned out the least craven
of the lot as it seems, and, actually, mustered enough
pluck to run an errand to the engine-room. No
trifle it must be owned in fairness to him. Jim told
me he darted desperate looks like a cornered man,
gave one low wail, and dashed off. He was back
instantly clambering, hammer in hand, and without

a pause flung himself at the bolt. The others gave up Jim at once and ran off to assist. He heard the tap, tap of the hammer, the sound of the released chock falling over. The boat was clear. Only then he turned to look—only then. But he kept his distance—he kept his distance. He wanted me to know he had kept his distance; that there was nothing in common between him and these men—who had the hammer. Nothing whatever. It is more than probable he thought himself cut off from them by a space that could not be traversed, by an obstacle that could not be overcome, by a chasm without bottom. He was as far as he could get from them—the whole breadth of the ship.

" His feet were glued to that remote spot and his eyes to their indistinct group bowed together and swaying strangely in the common torment of fear. A hand-lamp lashed to a stanchion above a little table rigged up on the bridge—the *Patna* had no chart-room amidships—threw a light on their labouring shoulders, on their arched and bobbing backs. They pushed at the bow of the boat; they pushed out into the night; they pushed, and would no more look back at him. They had given him up as if indeed he had been too far, too hopelessly separated from themselves, to be worth an appealing word, a glance, or a sign. They had no leisure to look back upon his passive heroism, to feel the sting of his abstention. The boat was heavy; they pushed at the bow with no breath to spare for an encouraging word : but the turmoil of terror that had scattered their self-command like chaff before the wind, converted their desperate exertions into a bit of fooling, upon my word, fit for knockabout clowns in a farce. They pushed with their hands, with their heads, they pushed for dear life with all the weight of their bodies, they pushed with all the might of their souls—only no sooner had they succeeded in canting the stem clear of the davit than they would leave off like one man and start a wild scramble into her. As a natural consequence the boat would swing in abruptly, driving them back, helpless and jostling against each other. They would stand non-plussed for a while, exchanging in fierce whispers all the infamous names they could call to mind, and go at it again. Three times this occurred. He described it to me with morose thoughtfulness. He hadn't lost a single movement of that comic business. ' I loathed them. I hated them. I had to look at all that,' he said without emphasis, turning upon me a sombrely watchful glance. ' Was ever there any one so shamefully tried ! '

" He took his head in his hands for a moment, like a man driven to distraction by some unspeakable outrage. These were things he could not explain to the court—and not even to me ; but I would have been little fitted for the reception of his confidences had I not been able at times to understand the pauses between the words. In this assault upon his fortitude there was the jeering intention of a spiteful and vile vengeance ; there was an element of bur-lesque in his ordeal—a degradation of funny grimaces in the approach of death or dishonour.

" He related facts which I have not forgotten, but at this distance of time I couldn't recall his very words : I only remember that he managed wonder-fully to convey the brooding rancour of his mind into the bare recital of events. Twice, he told me, he shut his eyes in the certitude that the end was upon him already, and twice he had to open them again. Each time he noted the darkening of the great stillness. The shadow of the silent cloud had fallen upon the ship from the zenith, and seemed to have extinguished every sound of her teeming life. He could no longer hear the voices under the awnings. He told me that each time he closed his eyes a flash of thought showed him that crowd of bodies, laid out for death, as plain as daylight. When he opened them, it was to see the dim struggle of four men fighting like mad with a stubborn boat. 'They would fall back before it time after time, stand swearing at each other, and suddenly make another rush in a bunch. . . . Enough to make you die laughing,' he commented with downcast eyes; then raising them for a moment to my face with a dismal smile, ' I ought to have a merry life of it, by God! for I shall see that funny sight a good many times yet before I die.' His eyes fell again. ' See and hear. . . . See and hear,' he repeated twice, at long intervals, filled by vacant staring.

" He roused himself.

" ' I made up my mind to keep my eyes shut,' he said, ' and I couldn't. I couldn't, and I don't care who knows it. Let them go through that kind of thing before they talk. Just let them—and do better —that's all. The second time my eyelids flew open and my mouth too. I had felt the ship move. She just dipped her bows—and lifted them gently—and slow! everlastingly slow; and ever so little. She hadn't done that much for days. The cloud had raced ahead, and this first swell seemed to travel upon a sea of lead. There was no life in that stir. It managed, though, to knock over something in my head. What would you have done? You are sure of yourself—aren't you? What would you do if you felt now—this minute—the house here move, just move a little under your chair. Leap ! By heavens ! you would take one spring from where you sit and land in that clump of bushes yonder.'

" He flung his arm out at the night beyond the stone balustrade. I held my peace. He looked at me very steadily, very severe. There could be no mistake : I was being bullied now, and it behoved me to make no sign lest by a gesture or a word I should be drawn into a fatal admission about myself which would have had some bearing on the case. I was not disposed to take any risk of that sort. Don't forget I had him before me, and really he was too much like one of us not to be dangerous. But if you want to know I don't mind telling you that I did, with a rapid glance, estimate the distance to the mass of denser blackness in the middle of the grass plot before the verandah. He exaggerated. I would have landed short by several feet—and that's the only thing of which I am fairly certain.

" The last moment had come, as he thought, and he did not move. His feet remained glued to the planks if his thoughts were knocking about loose in his head. It was at this moment too that he saw one of the men around the boat step backwards suddenly, clutch at the air with raised arms, totter and collapse. He didn't exactly fall, he only slid gently into a sitting posture, all hunched up, and with his shoulders propped against the side of the engine-room skylight. ' That was the donkey-man. A haggard, white-faced chap with a ragged moustache. Acted third engineer,' he explained.

" ' Dead,' I said. We had heard something of that in court.

" ' So they say,' he pronounced with sombre in-

difference. 'Of course I never knew. Weak heart.
The man had been complaining of being out of sorts
for some time before. Excitement. Over-exertion.
Devil only knows. Ha! ha! ha! It was easy to
see he did not want to die either. Droll, isn't it?
May I be shot if he hadn't been fooled into killing
himself! Fooled—neither more nor less. Fooled
into it, by heavens! just as I . . . Ah! If he had
only kept still; if he had only told them to go to
the devil when they came to rush him out of his bunk
because the ship was sinking! If he had only stood
by with his hands in his pockets and called them
names!'

"He got up, shook his fist, glared at me, and sat
down.

"'A chance missed, eh?' I murmured.

"'Why don't you laugh?' he said. 'A joke
hatched in hell. Weak heart! . . . I wish sometimes mine had been.'

"This irritated me. 'Do you?' I exclaimed with
deep-rooted irony. 'Yes! Can't you understand,'
he cried. 'I don't know what more you could wish
for,' I said angrily. He gave me an utterly uncomprehending glance. This shaft had also gone wide
of the mark, and he was not the man to bother about
stray arrows. Upon my word, he was too unsuspect-
ing; he was not fair game. I was glad that my
missile had been thrown away,—that he had not
even heard the twang of the bow.

"Of course he could not know at the time the man
was dead. The next minute—his last on board—
was crowded with a tumult of events and sensations
which beat about him like the sea upon a rock. I
use the simile advisedly, because from his relation I
am forced to believe he had preserved through it all

a strange illusion of passiveness, as though he had not acted but had suffered himself to be handled by the infernal powers who had selected him for the victim of their practical joke. The first thing that came to him was the grinding surge of the heavy davits swinging out at last—a jar which seemed to enter his body from the deck through the soles of his feet, and travel up his spine to the crown of his head. Then, the squall being very near now, another and a heavier swell lifted the passive hull in a threatening heave that checked his breath, while his brain and his heart together were pierced as with daggers by panic-stricken screams. ' Let go ! For God's sake, let go ! Let go ! She's going.' Following upon that the boat-falls ripped through the blocks, and a lot of men began to talk in startled tones under the awnings. ' When these beggars did break out, their yelps were enough to wake the dead,' he said. Next, after the splashing shock of the boat literally dropped in the water, came the hollow noises of stamping and tumbling in her, mingled with confused shouts : ' Unhook ! Unhook ! Shove ! Unhook ! Shove for you life ! Here's the squall down on us. . . .' He heard, high above his head, the faint muttering of the wind ; he heard below his feet a cry of pain. A lost voice alongside started cursing a swivel hook. The ship began to buzz fore and aft like a disturbed hive, and, as quietly as he was telling me of all this —because just then he was very quiet in attitude, in face, in voice—he went on to say without the slightest warning as it were, ' I stumbled over his legs.'

" This was the first I heard of his having moved at all. I could not restrain a grunt of surprise. Something had started him off at last, but of the exact moment, of the cause that tore him out of his immobility, he knew no more than the uprooted tree knows of the wind that laid it low. All this had come to him : the sounds, the sights, the legs of the dead man—by Jove ! The infernal joke was being crammed devilishly down his throat, but—look you—he was not going to admit of any sort of swallowing motion in his gullet. It's extraordinary how he could cast upon you the spirit of his illusion. I listened as if to a tale of black magic at work upon a corpse.

" ' He went over sideways, very gently, and this is the last thing I remember seeing on board,' he continued. ' I did not care what he did. It looked as though he were picking himself up : I thought he was picking himself up, of course : I expected him to bolt past me over the rail and drop into the boat after the others. I could hear them knocking about down there, and a voice as if crying up a shaft called out " George." Then three voices together raised a yell. They came to me separately : one bleated, another screamed, one howled. Ough ! '

" He shivered a little, and I beheld him rise slowly as if a steady hand from above had been pulling him out of the chair by his hair. Up, slowly—to his full height, and when his knees had locked stiff the hand let him go, and he swayed a little on his feet. There was a suggestion of awful stillness in his face, in his movements, in his very voice when he said ' They shouted '—and involuntarily I pricked up my ears for the ghost of that shout that would be heard directly through the false effect of silence. ' There were eight hundred people in that ship,' he said, impaling me to the back of my seat with an awful blank stare. ' Eight hundred living people, and they were yelling after the one dead man to come down and be saved. "Jump, George! Jump! Oh, jump!" I stood by with my hand on the davit. I was very quiet. It had come over pitch dark. You could see neither sky nor sea. I heard the boat alongside go bump, bump, and not another sound down there for a while, but the ship under me was full of talking noises. Suddenly the skipper howled "Mein Gott! The squall! The squall! Shove off!" With the first hiss of rain, and the first gust of wind, they screamed, "Jump, George! We'll catch you! Jump!" The ship began a slow plunge; the rain swept over her like a broken sea; my cap flew off my head; my breath was driven back into my throat. I heard as if I had been on the top of a tower another wild screech, "Geo-o-o-orge! Oh, jump!" She was going down, down, head first under me. . . .'

"He raised his hand deliberately to his face, and made picking motions with his fingers as though he had been bothered with cobwebs, and afterwards he looked into the open palm for quite half a second before he blurted out—

"'I had jumped . . .' He checked himself, averted his gaze. . . . 'It seems,' he added.

"His clear blue eyes turned to me with a piteous stare, and looking at him standing before me, dumfounded and hurt, I was oppressed by a sad sense of resigned wisdom, mingled with the amused and profound pity of an old man helpless before a childish disaster.

"'Looks like it,' I muttered.

"'I knew nothing about it till I looked up,' he explained hastily. And that's possible too. You had to listen to him as you would to a small boy in trouble. He didn't know. It had happened some-

how. It would never happen again. He had landed
partly on somebody and fallen across a thwart. He
felt as though all his ribs on his left side must be
broken ; then he rolled over, and saw vaguely the
ship he had deserted uprising above him, with the
red side-light glowing large in the rain like a fire on
the brow of a hill seen through a mist. ‘ She seemed
higher than a wall ; she loomed like a cliff over the
boat, . . . I wished I could die,’ he cried. ‘ There
was no going back. It was as if I had jumped into
a well—into an everlasting deep hole. . . .’ ”

CHAPTER X.

“ HE locked his fingers together and tore them
apart. Nothing could be more true : he had indeed
jumped into an everlasting deep hole. He had
tumbled from a height he could never scale again.
By that time the boat had gone driving forward
past the bows. It was too dark just then for them
to see each other, and, moreover, they were blinded
and half drowned with rain. He told me it was
like being swept by a flood through a cavern. They
turned their backs to the squall ; the skipper, it
seems, got an oar over the stern to keep the boat
before it, and for two or three minutes the end of
the world had come through a deluge in a pitchy
blackness. The sea hissed ‘ like twenty thousand
kettles.’ That’s his simile, not mine. I fancy there
was not much wind after the first gust ; and he
himself had admitted at the inquiry that the sea

never got up that night to any extent. He crouched
down in the bows and stole a furtive glance back.
He saw just one yellow gleam of the mast-head light
high up and blurred like a last star ready to dis-
solve. 'It terrified me to see it still there,' he said.
That's what he said. What terrified him was the
thought that the drowning was not over yet. No
doubt he wanted to be done with that abomination
as quickly as possible. Nobody in the boat made a
sound. In the dark she seemed to fly, but of course
she could not have had much way. Then the
shower swept ahead, and the great, distracting,
hissing noise followed the rain into distance and died
out. There was nothing to be heard then but the
slight wash about the boat's sides. Somebody's
teeth were chattering violently. A hand touched
his back. A faint voice said, 'You there?' Another
cried out shakily, 'She's gone!' and they all stood
up together to look astern. They saw no lights.
All was black. A thin cold drizzle was driving into
their faces. The boat lurched slightly. The teeth
chattered faster, stopped, and began again twice
before the man could master his shiver sufficiently to
say, 'Ju-ju-st in ti-ti-me. . . . Brrrr.' He recognised the voice of the chief engineer saying surlily,
'I saw her go down. I happened to turn my head.'
The wind had dropped almost completely.

"They watched in the dark with their heads half
turned to windward as if expecting to hear cries.
At first he was thankful the night had covered up
the scene before his eyes, and then to know of it and
yet to have seen and heard nothing appeared somehow the culminating-point of an awful misfortune.
'Strange isn't it?' he murmured. interrupting
himself in his disjointed narrative.

"It did not seem so strange to me. He must have had an unconscious conviction that the reality could not be half as bad, not half as anguishing, appalling, and vengeful as the created terror of his imagination. I believe that, in this first moment, his heart was wrung with all the suffering, that his soul knew the accumulated savour of all the fear, all the horror, all the despair of eight hundred human beings pounced upon in the night by a sudden and violent death, else why should he have said, 'It seemed to me that I must jump out of that accursed boat and swim back to see—half a mile—more—any distance—to the very spot . . .'? Why this impulse? Do you see the significance? Why back to the very spot? Why not drown alongside—if he meant drowning—why back to the very spot, to see—as if his imagination had to be soothed by the assurance that all was over before death could bring relief? I defy any one of you to offer another explanation. It was one of those bizarre and exciting glimpses through the fog. It was an extraordinary disclosure. He let it out as the most natural thing one could say. He fought down that impulse and then he became conscious of the silence. He mentioned this to me. A silence of the sea, of the sky, merged into one indefinite immensity still as death around these saved, palpitating lives. 'You might have heard a pin drop in the boat,' he said with a queer contraction of his lips, like a man trying to master his sensibilities while relating some extremely moving fact. A silence! God alone, who had willed him as he was, knows what he made of it in his heart. 'I didn't think any spot on earth could be so still,' he said. 'You couldn't distinguish the sea from the sky; there was nothing to see and nothing to hear. Not a glimmer, not a shape, not a sound. You could have believed that every bit of dry land had gone to the bottom ; that every man on earth but I and these beggars in the boat had got drowned.' He leaned over the table with his knuckles propped amongst coffee-cups, liqueur-glasses, cigar-ends. ' I seemed to believe it. Everything was gone and—all was over . . .' he fetched a deep sigh . . . ' with me.' "

Marlow sat up abruptly and flung away his cheroot with force. It made a darting red trail like a toy rocket fired through the drapery of creepers. Nobody stirred.

"Hey, what do you think of it ? " he cried with sudden animation. " Wasn't he true to himself, wasn't he ? His saved life was over for want of ground under his feet, for want of sights for his eyes, for want of voices in his ears. Annihilation—hey ! And all the time it was only a clouded sky, a sea that did not break, the air that did not stir. Only a night ; only a silence.

" It lasted for a while, and then they were suddenly and unanimously moved to make a noise over their escape. ' I knew from the first she would go.' ' Not a minute too soon.' ' A narrow squeak, b'gosh !' He said nothing, but the breeze that had dropped came back, a gentle draught freshened steadily, and the sea joined its murmuring voice to this talkative reaction succeeding the dumb moments of awe. She was gone ! She was gone ! Not a doubt of it. Nobody could have helped. They repeated the same words over and over again as though they couldn't stop themselves. Never doubted she would go. The lights were gone. No mistake. The lights were gone. Couldn't expect anything else. She had to go. . . . He noticed that they talked as though they had left behind them nothing but an empty ship. They concluded she would not have been long when she once started. It seemed to cause them some sort of satisfaction. They assured each other that she couldn't have been long about it—'Just shot down like a flat-iron.' The chief engineer declared that the mast-head light at the moment of sinking seemed to drop 'like a lighted match you throw down.' At this the second laughed hysterically. 'I am g-g-glad, I am gla-a-a-d.' His teeth went on 'like an electric rattle,' said Jim, 'and all at once he began to cry. He wept and blubbered like a child, catching his breath and sobbing "Oh dear! oh dear! oh dear!" He would be quiet for a while and start suddenly, "Oh, my poor arm! oh, my poor a-a-a-arm!" I felt I could knock him down. Some of them sat in the stern-sheets. I could just make out their shapes. Voices came to me, mumble, mumble, grunt, grunt. All this seemed very hard to bear. I was cold too. And I could do nothing. I thought that if I moved I would have to go over the side and— . . .'

"His hand groped stealthily, came in contact with a liqueur-glass, and was withdrawn suddenly as if it had touched a red-hot coal. I pushed the bottle slightly. 'Won't you have some more?' I asked. He looked at me angrily. 'Don't you think I can tell you what there is to tell without screwing myself up?' he asked. The squad of globe-trotters had gone to bed. We were alone but for a vague white form erect in the shadow, that, being looked at, cringed forward, hesitated, backed away silently. It was getting late, but I did not hurry my guest.

"In the midst of his forlorn state he heard his

companions begin to abuse some one. 'What kept
you from jumping, you lunatic?' said a scolding
voice. The chief engineer left the stern-sheets, and
could be heard clambering forward as if with hostile
intentions against 'the greatest idiot that ever was.'
The skipper shouted with rasping effort offensive
epithets from where he sat at the oar. He lifted
his head at that uproar, and heard the name 'George,'
while a hand in the dark struck him on the breast.
'What have you got to say for yourself, you fool?'
queried somebody, with a sort of virtuous fury.
'They were after me,' he said. 'They were abusing
me—abusing me . . . by the name of George.'

"He paused to stare, tried to smile, turned his
eyes away and went on. 'That little second puts
his head right under my nose, "Why, it's that
blasted mate!" "What!" howls the skipper from
the other end of the boat. "No!" shrieks the
chief. And he too stooped to look at my face.'

"The wind had left the boat suddenly. The rain
began to fall again, and the soft, uninterrupted, a
little mysterious sound with which the sea receives a
shower arose on all sides in the night. 'They were
too taken aback to say anything more at first,' he
narrated steadily, 'and what could I have to say to
them?' He faltered for a moment, and made an
effort to go on. 'They called me horrible names.'
His voice, sinking to a whisper, now and then would
leap up suddenly, hardened by the passion of scorn,
as though he had been talking of secret abominations.
'Never mind what they called me,' he said grimly.
'I could hear hate in their voices. A good thing too.
They could not forgive me for being in that boat.
They hated it. It made them mad. . . .' He
laughed short. . . . 'But it kept me from—Look!

I was sitting with my arms crossed, on the gun-wale! . . .' He perched himself smartly on the edge of the table and crossed his arms. . . . 'Like this—see? One little tilt backwards and I would have been gone—after the others. One little tilt—the least bit—the least bit.' He frowned, and tapping his forehead with the tip of his middle finger, 'It was there all the time,' he said impressively. 'All the time—that notion. And the rain—cold, thick, cold as melted snow—colder—on my thin cotton clothes—I'll never be so cold again in my life, I know. And the sky was black too—all black. Not a star, not a light anywhere. Nothing outside that confounded boat and those two yapping before me like a couple of mean mongrels at a tree'd thief. Yap! yap! What you doing here? You're a fine sort! Too much of a bloomin' gentleman to put his hand to it. Come out of your trance, did you? To sneak in? Did you? Yap! yap! You ain't fit to live! Yap! yap! Two of them together trying to out-bark each other. The other would bay from the stern through the rain—couldn't see him—couldn't make out—some of his filthy jargon. Yap! yap! Bow-ow-ow-ow-ow! Yap! yap! It was sweet to hear them; it kept me alive—I tell you. It has saved my life. At it they went, as if trying to drive me overboard with the noise! . . . I wonder you had pluck enough to jump. You ain't wanted here. If I had known who it was, I would have tipped you over—you skunk. What have you done with the other? Where did you get the pluck to jump—you coward? What's to prevent us three from firing you overboard? . . . They were out of breath; the shower passed away upon the sea. Then nothing. There was nothing round the boat, not even a sound. Wanted to see me overboard, did they? Upon my soul! I think they would have had their wish if they had only kept quiet. Fire me overboard! Would they? "Try," I said. "I would for twopence." "Too good for you," they screeched together. It was so dark that it was only when one or the other of them moved that I was quite sure of seeing him. By heavens! I only wish they had tried.'

"I couldn't help exclaiming, 'What an extra-ordinary affair!'

"'Not bad—eh?' he said, as if in some sort astounded. 'They pretended to think I had done away with that donkey-man for some reason or other. Why should I? And how the devil was I to know? Didn't I get somehow into that boat? into that boat—I . . .' The muscles round his lips contracted into an unconscious grimace that tore through the mask of his usual expression—something violent, short-lived and illuminating like a twist of lightning that admits the eye for an instant into the secret convolutions of a cloud. 'I did. I was plainly there with them—wasn't I? Isn't it awful a man should be driven to do a thing like that—and be responsible? What did I know about their George they were howling after? I remembered I had seen him curled up on the deck. "Murdering coward!" the chief kept on calling me. He didn't seem able to remember any other two words. I didn't care, only his noise began to worry me. "Shut up," I said. At that he collected himself for a confounded screech. "You killed him. You killed him." "No," I shouted, "but I will kill you directly." I jumped up, and he fell backwards over a thwart with an awful loud thump. I don't know why. Too dark.

Tried to step back, I suppose. I stood still facing aft, and the wretched little second began to whine, " You ain't going to hit a chap with a broken arm— and you call yourself a gentleman, too." I heard a heavy tramp—one—two—and wheezy grunting. The other beast was coming at me, clattering his oar over the stern. I saw him moving, big, big—as you see a man in a mist, in a dream. " Come on," I cried. I would have tumbled him over like a bale of shakings. He stopped, muttered to himself, and went back. Perhaps he had heard the wind. I didn't. It was the last heavy gust we had. He went back to his oar. I was sorry. I would have tried to—to . . .'

" He opened and closed his curved fingers, and his hands had an eager and cruel flutter. ' Steady, steady,' I murmured.

" ' Eh ? What ? I am not excited,' he remonstrated, awfully hurt, and with a convulsive jerk of his elbow knocked over the cognac-bottle. I started forward, scraping my chair. He bounced off the table as if a mine had been exploded behind his back, and half turned before he alighted, crouching on his feet to show me a startled pair of eyes and a face white about the nostrils. A look of intense annoyance succeeded. ' Awfully sorry. How clumsy of me ! ' he mumbled, very vexed, while the pungent odour of spilt alcohol enveloped us suddenly with an atmosphere of a low drinking-bout in the cool, pure darkness of the night. The lights had been put out in the dining-hall ; our candle glimmered solitary in the long gallery, and the columns had turned black from pediment to capital. On the vivid stars the high corner of the Harbour Office stood out distinct across the Esplanade, as though the sombre pile had glided nearer to see and hear.

"He assumed an air of indifference.

"'I daresay I am less calm now than I was then. I was ready for anything. These were trifles. . . .'

"'You had a lively time of it in that boat,' I remarked.

"'I was ready,' he repeated. 'After the ship's lights had gone, anything might have happened in that boat—anything in the world—and the world no wiser. I felt this, and I was pleased. It was just dark enough too. We were like men walled up quick in a roomy grave. No concern with anything on earth. Nobody to pass an opinion. Nothing mattered.' For the third time during this conversation he laughed harshly, but there was no one about to suspect him of being only drunk. 'No fear, no law, no sounds, no eyes—not even our own, till—till sunrise at least.'

"I was struck by the suggestive truth of his words. There is something peculiar in a small boat upon the wide sea. Over the lives borne from under the shadow of death there seems to fall the shadow of madness. When your ship fails you, your whole world seems to fail you; the world that made you, restrained you, taken care of you. It is as if the souls of men floating on an abyss and in touch with immensity had been set free for any excess of heroism, absurdity, or abomination. Of course, as with belief, thought, love, hate, conviction, or even the visual aspect of material things, there are as many ship-wrecks as there are men, and in this one there was something abject which made the isolation more complete,—there was a villainy of circumstances that cut these men off more completely from the rest of mankind, whose ideal of conduct had never under-gone the trial of a fiendish and appalling joke. They

were exasperated with him for being a half-hearted
shirker : he focussed on them his hate of the whole
thing ; he would have liked to take a signal revenge
for the abhorrent opportunity they had put in his
way. Trust a boat on the high seas to bring out the
Irrational that lurks at the bottom of every thought,
sentiment, sensation, emotion. It was part of the
burlesque meanness pervading that particular disaster at sea that they did not come to blows. It was
all threats, all a terribly effective feint, a sham from
beginning to end, planned by the tremendous disdain
of the Dark Powers whose real terrors, always on
the verge of triumph, are perpetually foiled by the
steadfastness of men. I asked, after waiting for a
while, ' Well, what happened ? ' A futile question.
I knew too much already to hope for the grace of
a single uplifting touch, for the favour of hinted
madness, of shadowed horror. ' Nothing,' he said.
' I meant business, but they meant noise only.
Nothing happened.'

"And the rising sun found him just as he had
jumped up first in the bows of the boat. What a
persistence of readiness ! He had been holding the
tiller in his hand, too, all the night. They had
dropped the rudder overboard while attempting to
ship it, and I suppose the tiller got kicked forward
somehow while they were rushing up and down that
boat trying to do all sorts of things at once so as to
get clear of the side. It was a long heavy piece of
hard wood, and apparently he had been clutching it
for six hours or so. If you don't call that being
ready ! Can you imagine him, silent and on his feet
half the night, his face to the gusts of rain, staring at
sombre forms, watchful of vague movements, straining his ears to catch rare low murmurs in the stern-

sheets! Firmness of courage or effort of fear?
What do you think? And the endurance is undeniable too. Six hours more or less on the defensive;
six hours of alert immobility while the boat drove
slowly or floated arrested according to the caprice
of the wind; while the sea, calmed, slept at last;
while the clouds passed above his head; while the
sky from an immensity lustreless and black, diminished to a sombre and lustrous vault, scintillated
with a greater brilliance, faded to the east, paled at
the zenith; while the dark shapes blotting the low
stars astern got outlines, relief; became shoulders,
heads, faces, features,—confronted him with dreary
stares, had dishevelled hair, torn clothes, blinked
red eyelids at the white dawn. 'They looked as
though they had been knocking about drunk in
gutters for a week,' he described graphically; and
then he muttered something about the sunrise being
of a kind that foretells a calm day. You know that
sailor habit of referring to the weather in every
connection. And on my side his few mumbled words
were enough to make me see the lower limb of the
sun clearing the line of the horizon, the tremble of a
vast ripple running over all the visible expanse of
the sea, as if the waters had shuddered, giving birth
to the globe of light, while the last puff of the breeze
would stir the air in a sigh of relief.

"'They sat in the stern shoulder to shoulder, with
the skipper in the middle, like three dirty owls, and
stared at me,' I heard him say with an intention of
hate that distilled a corrosive virtue into the commonplace words like a drop of powerful poison falling into a glass of water; but my thoughts dwelt
upon that sunrise. I could imagine under the
pellucid emptiness of the sky these four men im-

prisoned in the solitude of the sea, the lonely sun, regardless of the speck of life, ascending the clear curve of the heaven as if to gaze ardently from a greater height at his own splendour reflected in the still ocean. 'They called out to me from aft,' said Jim, 'as though we had been chums together. I heard them. They were begging me to be sensible and drop that "blooming piece of wood." Why *would* I carry on so? They hadn't done me any harm—had they? There had been no harm. . . . No harm!'

" His face crimsoned as though he could not get rid of the air in his lungs.

" ' No harm!' he burst out. 'I leave it to you. You can understand. Can't you? You see it— don't you? No harm! Good God! What more could they have done? Oh yes, I know very well— I jumped. Certainly. I jumped! I told you I jumped; but I tell you they were too much for any man. It was their doing as plainly as if they had reached up with a boat-hook and pulled me over. Can't you see it? You must see it. Come. Speak —straight out.'

" His uneasy eyes fastened upon mine, questioned, begged, challenged, entreated. For the life of me I couldn't help murmuring, 'You've been tried.' ' More than is fair,' he caught up swiftly. ' I wasn't given half a chance—with a gang like that. And now they were friendly—oh, so damnably friendly! Chums, shipmates. All in the same boat. Make the best of it. They hadn't meant anything. They didn't care a hang for George. George had gone back to his berth for something at the last moment and got caught. The man was a manifest fool. Very sad, of course. . . . Their eyes looked at me;

their lips moved ; they wagged their heads at the
other end of the boat—three of them ; they beckoned
—to me. Why not ? Hadn't I jumped ? I said
nothing. There are no words for the sort of things
I wanted to say. If I had opened my lips just then
I would have simply howled like an animal. I was
asking myself when I would wake up. They urged
me aloud to come aft and hear quietly what the
skipper had to say. We were sure to be picked
up before the evening—right in the track of all the
Canal traffic ; there was smoke to the north-west
now.

" ' It gave me an awful shock to see this faint,
faint blur, this low trail of brown mist through
which you could see the boundary of sea and sky.
I called out to them that I could hear very well
where I was. The skipper started swearing, as
hoarse as a crow. He wasn't going to talk at the
top of his voice for *my* accommodation. " Are you
afraid they will hear you on shore ? " I asked. He
glared as if he would have liked to claw me to pieces.
The chief engineer advised him to humour me. He
said I wasn't right in my head yet. The other rose
astern, like a thick pillar of flesh—and talked—
talked. . . .'

" Jim remained thoughtful. ' Well ? ' I said.
' What did I care what story they agreed to make
up ? ' he cried recklessly. ' They could tell what
they jolly well liked. It was their business. I
knew the story. Nothing they could make people
believe could alter it for me. I let him talk, argue
—talk, argue. He went on and on and on. Suddenly I felt my legs give way under me. I was
sick, tired—tired to death. I let fall the tiller,
turned my back on them, and sat down on the

foremost thwart. I had enough. They called to
me to know if I understood—wasn't it true, every
word of it? It was true, by God! after their
fashion. I did not turn my head. I heard them
palavering together. "The silly ass won't say anything." "Oh, he understands well enough." "Let
him be; he will be all right." "What can he do?"
What could I do! Weren't we all in the same boat.
I tried to be deaf. The smoke had disappeared to
the northward. It was a dead calm. They had a
drink from the water-breaker, and I drank too.
Afterwards they made a great business of spreading
the boat-sail over the gunwales. Would I keep a
look-out? They crept under, out of my sight, thank
God! I felt weary, weary, done up, as if I hadn't
had one hour's sleep since the day I was born. I
couldn't see the water for the glitter of the sunshine.
From time to time one of them would creep out,
stand up to take a look all round, and get under
again. I could hear spells of snoring below the
sail. Some of them could sleep. One of them at
least. I couldn't! All was light, light, and the
boat seemed to be falling through it. Now and
then I would feel quite surprised to find myself
sitting on a thwart. . . .'

"He began to walk with measured steps to and
fro before my chair, one hand in his trousers-pocket,
his head bent thoughtfully, and his right arm at
long intervals raised for a gesture that seemed to
put out of his way an invisible intruder.

"'I suppose you think I was going mad,' he began
in a changed tone. 'And well you may, if you
remember I had lost my cap. The sun crept all the
way from east to west over my bare head, but that
day I could not come to any harm, I suppose.

The sun could not make me mad. . . .' His right arm put aside the idea of madness. . . . 'Neither could it kill me. . . .' Again his arm repulsed a shadow. . . . '*That* rested with me.'

" 'Did it ? ' I said, inexpressibly amazed at this new turn, and I looked at him with the same sort of feeling I might be fairly conceived to experience had he, after spinning round on his heel, presented an altogether new face.

" 'I didn't get brain fever, I did not drop dead either,' he went on. 'I didn't bother myself at all about the sun over my head. I was thinking as coolly as any man that ever sat thinking in the shade. That greasy beast of a skipper poked his big cropped head from under the canvas and screwed his fishy eyes up at me. "Donnerwetter! you will die," he growled, and drew in like a turtle. I had seen him. I had heard him. He didn't interrupt me. I was thinking just then that I wouldn't.'

" He tried to sound my thought with an attentive glance dropped on me in passing. 'Do you mean to say you had been deliberating with yourself whether you would die ? ' I asked in as impenetrable a tone as I could command. He nodded without stopping. ' Yes, it had come to that as I sat there alone,' he said. He passed on a few steps to the imaginary end of his beat, and when he flung round to come back both his hands were thrust deep into his pockets. He stopped short in front of my chair and looked down. 'Don't you believe it ? ' he inquired with tense curiosity. I was moved to make a solemn declaration of my readiness to believe implicitly anything he thought fit to tell me."

CHAPTER XI.

"He heard me out with his head on one side, and I had another glimpse through a rent in the mist in which he moved and had his being. The dim candle spluttered within the ball of glass, and that was all I had to see him by; at his back was the dark night with the clear stars, whose distant glitter disposed in retreating planes lured the eye into the depths of a greater darkness; and yet a mysterious light seemed to show me his boyish head, as if in that moment the youth within him had, for a moment, gleamed and expired. 'You are an awful good sort to listen like this,' he said. 'It does me good. You don't know what it is to me. You don't' . . . words seemed to fail him. It was a distinct glimpse. He was a youngster of the sort you like to see about you; of the sort you like to imagine yourself to have been; of the sort whose appearance claims the fellowship of these illusions you had thought gone out, extinct, cold, and which, as if rekindled at the approach of another flame, give a flutter deep, deep down somewhere, give a flutter of light . . . of heat! . . . Yes; I had a glimpse of him then, . . . and it was not the last of that kind. . . . 'You don't know what it is for a fellow in my position to be believed—make a clean breast of it to an elder man. It is so difficult—so awfully unfair—so hard to understand.'

"The mists were closing again. I don't know how old I appeared to him—and how much wise? Not half as old as I felt just then; not half as uselessly wise as I knew myself to be. Surely in no other craft as in that of the sea do the hearts of those already launched to sink or swim go out so much to the youth on the brink, looking with shining eyes upon that glitter of the vast surface which is only a reflection of his own glances full of fire. There is such magnificent vagueness in the expectations that had driven each of us to sea, such a glorious indefiniteness, such a beautiful greed of adventures that are their own and only reward! What we get —well, we won't talk of that; but can one of us restrain a smile? In no other kind of life is the illusion more wide of reality—in no other is the beginning *all* illusion—the disenchantment more swift—the subjugation more complete. Hadn't we all commenced with the same desire, ended with the same knowledge, carried the memory of the same cherished glamour through the sordid days of imprecation? What wonder that when some heavy prod gets home the bond is found to be close; that besides the fellowship of the craft there is felt the strength of a wider feeling—the feeling that binds a man to a child. He was there before me, believing that age and wisdom can find a remedy against the pain of truth, giving me a glimpse of himself as a young fellow in a scrape that is the very devil of a scrape, the sort of scrape greybeards wag at solemnly while they hide a smile. And he had been deliberating upon death—confound him! He had found *that* to meditate about because he thought he had saved his life, while all its glamour had gone with the ship in the night. What more natural! It was tragic enough and funny enough in all conscience to call aloud for compassion, and in what was I better than the rest of us to refuse him my pity. And even as I looked at him the mists rolled into the rent, and his voice spoke—

" ' I was so lost, you know. It was the sort of thing one does not expect to happen to one. It was not like a fight, for instance.'

" ' It was not,' I admitted. He appeared changed, as if he had suddenly matured.

" ' One couldn't be sure,' he muttered.

" ' Ah ! You were not sure,' I said, and was placated by the sound of a faint sigh that passed between us like the flight of a bird in the night.

" ' Well, I wasn't,' he said courageously. ' It was something like that wretched story they made up. It was not a lie—but it wasn't truth all the same. It was something. . . . One knows a downright lie. There was not the thickness of a sheet of paper between the right and the wrong of this affair.'

" ' How much more did you want ? ' I asked ; but I think I spoke so low that he did not catch what I said. He had advanced his argument as though life had been a network of paths separated by chasms. His voice sounded reasonable.

" ' Suppose I had not—I mean to say, suppose I had stuck to the ship ? Well. How much longer ? Say a minute—half a minute. Come. In thirty seconds, as it seemed certain then, I would have been overboard ; and do you think I would not have laid hold of the first thing that came in my way—oar, life-buoy, grating—anything. Wouldn't you ? '

" '. ' And be saved,' I interjected.

" ' I would have meant to be,' he retorted. ' And that's more than I meant when I ' . . . he shivered as if about to swallow some nauseous drug . . .

'jumped,' he pronounced with a convulsive effort,
whose stress, as if propagated by the waves of the
air, made my body stir a little in the chair. He
fixed me with lowering eyes. 'Don't you believe
me ? ' he cried. 'I swear ! . . . Confound it !
You got me here to talk, and . . . You must ! . . .
You said you would believe.' 'Of course I do,' I
protested, in a matter-of-fact tone which produced a
calming effect. 'Forgive me,' he said. 'Of course I
wouldn't have talked to you about all this if you
had not been a gentleman. I ought to have known
. . . I am—I am—a gentleman too . . .' 'Yes,
yes,' I said hastily. He was looking me squarely in
the face, and withdrew his gaze slowly. 'Now you
understand why I didn't after all . . . didn't go
out in that way. I wasn't going to be frightened at
what I had done. And, anyhow, if I had stuck to
the ship I would have done my best to be saved.
Men have been known to float for hours—in the
open sea—and be picked up not much the worse for
it. I might have lasted it out better than many
others. There's nothing the matter with *my* heart.'
He withdrew his right fist from his pocket, and the
blow he struck on his chest resounded like a muffled
detonation in the night.

"'No,' I said. He meditated, with his legs
slightly apart and his chin sunk. 'A hair's-breadth,'
he muttered. 'Not the breadth of a hair between
this and that. And at the time . . .'

"'It is difficult to see a hair at midnight,' I put
in, a little viciously I fear. Don't you see what I
mean by the solidarity of the craft ? I was aggrieved
against him, as though he had cheated me—me !—of
a splendid opportunity to keep up the illusion of my
beginnings, as though he had robbed our common

life of the last spark of its glamour. 'And so you cleared out—at once.'

" ' Jumped,' he corrected me incisively. 'Jumped —mind ! ' he repeated, and I wondered at the evident but obscure intention. 'Well, yes ! Perhaps I could not see then. But I had plenty of time and any amount of light in that boat. And I could think too. Nobody would know, of course, but this did not make it any easier for me. You've got to believe that too. I did not want all this talk. . . . No . . . Yes . . . I won't lie . . . I wanted it : it is the very thing I wanted—there. Do you think you or anybody could have made me if I . . . I am—I am not afraid to tell. And I wasn't afraid to think either. I looked it in the face. I wasn't going to run away. At first—at night, if it hadn't been for these fellows I might have . . . No ! by heavens ! I was not going to give them that satisfaction. They had done enough. They made up a story, and believed it for all I know. But I knew the truth, and I would live it down—alone, with myself. I wasn't going to give in to such a beastly unfair thing. What did it prove after all ? I was confoundedly cut up. Sick of life—to tell you the truth ; but what would have been the good to shirk it—in—in—that way ? That was not the way. I believe—I believe it would have—it would have ended—nothing.'

" He had been walking up and down, but with the last word he turned short at me.

" ' What do *you* believe ? ' he asked with violence. A pause ensued, and suddenly I felt myself overcome by a profound and hopeless fatigue, as though his voice had startled me out of a dream of wandering through empty spaces whose im-

mensity had harassed my soul and exhausted my
body.

"'. . . Would have ended nothing,' he muttered
over me obstinately, after a little while. 'No! the
proper thing was to face it out—alone before myself
—wait for another chance—find out . . .'"

CHAPTER XII.

"ALL around everything was still as far as the ear
could reach. The mist of his feelings shifted between
us, as if disturbed by his struggles, and in the rifts
of the immaterial veil he would appear to my staring
eyes distinct of form and pregnant with vague appeal
like a symbolic figure in a picture. The chill air of
the night seemed to lie on my limbs as heavy as a
slab of marble.

"'I see,' I murmured, more to prove to myself
that I could break my state of numbness than for
any other reason.

"'The *Avondale* picked us up just before sunset,'
he remarked moodily. 'Steamed right straight for
us. We had only to sit and wait.'

"After a long interval, he said, 'They told their
story.' And again there was that oppressive silence.
'Then only I knew what it was I had made up my
mind to,' he added.

"'You said nothing,' I whispered.

"'What could I say?' he asked, in the same low
tone. . . . 'Shock slight. Stopped the ship. Ascertained the damage. Took measures to get the

boats out without creating a panic. As the first
boat was lowered ship went down in a squall. Sank
like lead. . . . What could be more clear ' . . . he
hung his head . . . 'and more awful ? ' His lips
quivered while he looked straight into my eyes. ' I
had jumped—hadn't I ? ' he asked dismayed.
' That's what I had to live down. The story didn't
matter.' . . . He clasped his hands for an instant,
glanced right and left into the gloom : ' It was like
cheating the dead,' he stammered.

" ' And there were no dead,' I said.

" He went away from me at this. That is the
only way I can describe it. In a moment I saw his
back close to the balustrade. He stood there for
some time, as if admiring the purity and the peace
of the night. Some flowering-shrub in the garden
below spread its powerful scent through the damp
air. He returned to me with hasty steps.

" ' And that did not matter,' he said, as stubbornly
as you please.

" ' Perhaps not,' I admitted. I began to have a
notion he was too much for me. After all, what
did I know ?

" ' Dead or not dead, I could not get clear,' he
said. ' I had to live ; hadn't I ? '

" ' Well, yes—if you take it in that way,' I
mumbled.

" ' I was glad of course,' he threw out carelessly,
with his mind fixed on something else. ' The exposure,' he pronounced slowly, and lifted his head.
' Do you know what was my first thought when I
heard ? I was relieved. I was relieved to learn that
those shouts—did I tell you I had heard shouts ?
No ? Well, I did. Shouts for help, . . . blown
along with the drizzle. Imagination, I suppose.

And yet I can hardly . . . How stupid. . . . The others did not. I asked them afterwards. They all said No. No? And I was hearing them even then! I might have known—but I didn't think—I only listened. Very faint screams—day after day. Then that little half-caste chap here came up and spoke to me. "The *Patna* . . . French gunboat . . . towed successfully to Aden . . . Investigation . . . Marine Office . . . Sailor's Home . . . arrangements made for your board and lodging!" I walked along with him, and I enjoyed the silence. So there had been no shouting. Imagination. I had to believe him. I could hear nothing any more. I wonder how long I could have stood it. It was getting worse, too . . . I mean—louder.'

"He fell into thought.

"'And I had heard nothing! Well—so be it. But the lights! The lights did go! We did not see them. They were not there. If they had been, I would have swam back—I would have gone back and shouted alongside—I would have begged them to take me on board. . . . I would have had my chance. . . . You doubt me? . . . How do you know how I felt? . . . What right have you to doubt? . . . I very nearly did it as it was—do you understand?' His voice fell. 'There was not a glimmer—not a glimmer,' he protested mournfully. 'Don't you understand that if there had been, you would not have seen me here? You see me—and you doubt.'

"I shook my head negatively. This question of the lights being lost sight of when the boat could not have been more than a quarter of a mile from the ship was a matter for much discussion. Jim stuck to it that there was nothing to be seen after the first shower had cleared away ; and the others had affirmed the same thing to the officers of the *Avondale*. Of course people shook their heads and smiled. One old skipper who sat near me in court tickled my ear with his white beard to murmur, ' Of course they would lie.' As a matter of fact nobody lied ; not even the chief engineer with his story of the mast-head light dropping like a match you throw down. Not consciously, at least. A man with his liver in such a state might very well have seen a floating spark in the corner of his eye when stealing a hurried glance over his shoulder. They had seen no light of any sort though they were well within range, and they could only explain this in one way : the ship had gone down. It was obvious and comforting. The foreseen fact coming so swiftly had justified their haste. No wonder they did not cast about for any other explanation. Yet the true one was very simple, and as soon as Brierly suggested it the court ceased to bother about the question. If you remember, the ship had been stopped, and was lying with her head on the course steered through the night, with her stern canted high and her bows brought low down in the water through the filling of the fore-compartment. Being thus out of trim, when the squall struck her a little on the quarter, she swung head to wind as sharply as though she had been at anchor. By this change in her position all her lights were in a very few moments shut off from the boat to leeward. It may very well be that, had they been seen, they would have had the effect of a mute appeal—that their glimmer lost in the darkness of the cloud would have had the mysterious power of the human glance that can awaken the feelings of remorse and pity.

It would have said, 'I am here—still here' . . . and what more can the eye of the most forsaken of human beings say ? But she turned her back on them as if in disdain of their fate : she had swung round, burdened, to glare stubbornly at the new danger of the open sea which she so strangely survived to end her days in a breaking-up yard, as if it had been her recorded fate to die obscurely under the blows of many hammers. What were the various ends their destiny provided for the pilgrims I am unable to say ; but the immediate future brought, at about nine o'clock next morning, a French gunboat homeward bound from Réunion. The report of her commander was public property. He had swept a little out of his course to ascertain what was the matter with that steamer floating dangerously by the head upon a still and hazy sea. There was an ensign, union down, flying at her main gaff (the serang had the sense to make a signal of distress at daylight) ; but the cooks were preparing the food in the cooking-boxes forward as usual. The decks were packed as close as a sheep-pen : there were people perched all along the rails, jammed on the bridge in a solid mass ; hundreds of eyes stared, and not a sound was heard when the gunboat ranged abreast, as if all that multitude of lips had been sealed by a spell.

"The Frenchman hailed, could get no intelligible reply, and after ascertaining through his binoculars that the crowd on deck did not look plague-stricken, decided to send a boat. Two officers came on board, listened to the serang, tried to talk with the Arab, couldn't make head or tail of it : but of course the nature of the emergency was obvious enough. They were also very much struck by discovering a white

man, dead and curled up peacefully on the bridge.
'*Fort intrigués par ce cadavre*,' as I was informed
a long time after by an elderly French lieutenant
whom I came across one afternoon in Sydney, by
the merest chance, in a sort of café, and who remembered the affair perfectly. Indeed this affair, I may
notice in passing, had an extraordinary power of
defying the shortness of memories and the length
of time : it seemed to live, with a sort of uncanny
vitality, in the minds of men, on the tips of their
tongues. I've had the questionable pleasure of
meeting it often, years afterwards, thousands of
miles away, emerging from the remotest possible
talk, coming to the surface of the most distant
allusions. Has it not turned up to-night between
us ? And J am the only seaman here. I am the
only one to whom it is a memory. And yet it has
made its way out ! But if two men who, unknown
to each other, knew of this affair met accidentally
on any spot of this earth, the thing would pop up
between them as sure as fate, before they parted.
I had never seen that Frenchman before, and at
the end of an hour we had done with each other
for life : he did not seem particularly talkative
either ; he was a quiet, massive chap in a creased
uniform, sitting drowsily over a tumbler half full
of some dark liquid. His shoulder-straps were a
bit tarnished, his clean-shaved cheeks were large
and sallow ; he looked like a man who would be
given to taking snuff—don't you know ? I won't
say he did ; but the habit would have fitted that
kind of man. It all began by his handing me a
number of 'Home News,' which I didn't want,
across the marble table. I said 'Merci.' We ex-
changed a few apparently innocent remarks, and

suddenly, before I knew how it had come about, we
were in the midst of it, and he was telling me how
much they had been 'intrigued by that corpse.' It
turned out he had been one of the boarding officers.

"In the establishment where we sat one could get
a variety of foreign drinks which were kept for the
visiting naval officers, and he took a sip of the
dark medical-looking stuff, which probably was
nothing more nasty than *cassis à l'eau*, and glancing
with one eye into the tumbler, shook his head
slightly. '*Impossible de comprendre—vous concevez*,'
he said, with a curious mixture of unconcern and
thoughtfulness. I could very easily conceive how
impossible it had been for them to understand.
Nobody in the gunboat knew enough English to
get hold of the story as told by the serang. There
was a good deal of noise, too, round the two officers.
'They crowded upon us. There was a circle round
that dead man (*autour de ce mort*),' he described.
'One had to attend to the most pressing. These
people were beginning to agitate themselves—*Parbleu!* A mob like that—don't you see?' he interjected with philosophic indulgence. As to the
bulkhead, he had advised his commander that the
safest thing was to leave it alone, it was so villainous
to look at. They got two hawsers on board promptly
(*en toute hâte*) and took the *Patna* in tow—stern
foremost at that—which, under the circumstances,
was not so foolish, since the rudder was too much
out of the water to be of any great use for steering,
and this manœuvre eased the strain on the bulkhead, whose state, he expounded with stolid glibness,
demanded the greatest care (*éxigeait les plus grands
ménagements*). I could not help thinking that my
new acquaintance must have had a voice in most

of these arrangements : he looked a reliable officer, no longer very active, and he was seamanlike too, in a way, though as he sat there, with his thick fingers clasped lightly on his stomach, he reminded you of one of those snuffy, quiet village priests, into whose ears are poured the sins, the sufferings, the remorse of peasant generations, on whose faces the placid and simple expression is like a veil thrown over the mystery of pain and distress. He ought to have had a threadbare black *soutane* buttoned smoothly up to his ample chin, instead of a frock-coat with shoulder-straps and brass buttons. His broad bosom heaved regularly while he went on telling me that it had been the very devil of a job, as doubtless (*sans doute*) I could figure to myself in my quality of a seaman (*en votre qualité de marin*). At the end of the period he inclined his body slightly towards me, and, pursing his shaved lips, allowed the air to escape with a gentle hiss. ' Luckily,' he continued, ' the sea was level like this table, and there was no more wind than there is here.' . . . The place struck me as indeed intolerably stuffy, and very hot ; my face burned as though I had been young enough to be embarrassed and blushing. They had directed their course, he pursued, to the nearest English port ' *naturellement*,' where their responsibility ceased, ' *Dieu merci.*' . . . He blew out his flat cheeks a little. . . . ' Because, mind you (*notez bien*), all the time of towing we had two quartermasters stationed with axes by the hawsers, to cut us clear of our tow in case she . . .' He fluttered downwards his heavy eyelids, making his meaning as plain as possible. . . . ' What would you ! One does what one can (*on fait ce qu'on peut*),' and for a moment he managed to invest his ponderous immobility with an air of resignation. 'Two quartermasters—thirty hours—always there. Two!' he repeated, lifting up his right hand a little, and exhibiting two fingers. This was absolutely the first gesture I saw him make. It gave me the opportunity to 'note' a starred scar on the back of his hand—effect of a gunshot clearly; and, as if my sight had been made more acute by this discovery, I perceived also the seam of an old wound, beginning a little below the temple and going out of sight under the short grey hair at the side of his head—the graze of a spear or the cut of a sabre. He clasped his hands on his stomach again. 'I remained on board that, that—my memory is going (*s'en va*). *Ah! Patt-nà. C'est bien ça. Patt-nà. Merci.* It is droll how one forgets. I stayed on that ship thirty hours. . . .'

"'You did!' I exclaimed. Still gazing at his hands, he pursed his lips a little, but this time made no hissing sound. 'It was judged proper,' he said, lifting his eyebrows dispassionately, 'that one of the officers should remain to keep an eye open (*pour ouvrir l'œil*)' . . . he sighed idly . . . 'and for communicating by signals with the towing ship—do you see—and so on. For the rest, it was my opinion too. We made our boats ready to drop over—and I also on that ship took measures. . . . *Enfin!* One has done one's possible. It was a delicate position. Thirty hours. They prepared me some food. As for the wine—go and whistle for it—not a drop.' In some extraordinary way, without any marked change in his inert attitude and in the placid expression of his face, he managed to convey the idea of profound disgust. 'I—you know—when it comes to eating without my glass of wine—I am nowhere.'

" I was afraid he would enlarge upon the grievance, for though he didn't stir a limb or twitch a feature, he made one aware how much he was irritated by the recollection. But he seemed to forget all about it. They delivered their charge to the ' port author-ities,' as he expressed it. He was struck by the calmness with which it had been received. ' One might have thought they had such a droll find (*drôle de trouvaille*) brought them every day. You are extraordinary—you others,' he commented, with his back propped against the wall, and looking himself as incapable of an emotional display as a sack of meal. There happened to be a man-of-war and an Indian Marine steamer in the harbour at the time, and he did not conceal his admiration of the efficient manner in which the boats of these two ships cleared the *Patna* of her passengers. Indeed his torpid demeanour concealed nothing : it had that mysterious, almost miraculous, power of producing striking effects by means impossible of detection which is the last word of the highest art. ' Twenty-five minutes—watch in hand—twenty-five, no more.' . . . He unclasped and clasped again his fingers without removing his hands from his stomach, and made it infinitely more effective than if he had thrown up his arms to heaven in amaze-ment. . . . 'All that lot (*tout ce monde*) on shore—with their little affairs—nobody left but a guard of seamen (*marine de l'État*) and that interesting corpse (*cet intéressant cadavre*). Twenty-five min-utes.' . . . With downcast eyes and his head tilted slightly on one side he seemed to roll knowingly on his tongue the savour of a smart bit of work.

He persuaded one without any further demonstration that his approval was eminently worth having,
and resuming his hardly interrupted immobility,
he went on to inform me that, being under orders
to make the best of their way to Toulon, they left
in two hours' time, ' so that (*de sorte que*) there are
many things in this incident of my life (*dans cet
épisode de ma vie*) which have remained obscure.' "

CHAPTER XIII.

" AFTER these words, and without a change of
attitude, he, so to speak, submitted himself passively
to a state of silence. I kept him company ; and
suddenly, but not abruptly, as if the appointed time
had arrived for his moderate and husky voice to
come out of his immobility, he pronounced, ' *Mon
Dieu !* how the time passes ! ' Nothing could have
been more commonplace than this remark ; but its
utterance coincided for me with a moment of vision.
It's extraordinary how we go through life with eyes
half shut, with dull ears, with dormant thoughts.
Perhaps it's just as well ; and it may be that it is
this very dulness that makes life to the incalculable
majority so supportable and so welcome. Nevertheless, there can be but few of us who had never known
one of these rare moments of awakening when we
see, hear, understand ever so much—everything—in
a flash—before we fall back again into our agreeable
somnolence. I raised my eyes when he spoke, and I
saw him as though I had never seen him before. I

saw his chin sunk on his breast, the clumsy folds of his coat, his clasped hands, his motionless pose, so curiously suggestive of his having been simply left there. Time had passed indeed: it had overtaken him and gone ahead. It had left him hopelessly behind with a few poor gifts: the iron-grey hair, the heavy fatigue of the tanned face, two scars, a pair of tarnished shoulder-straps; one of those steady, reliable men who are the raw material of great reputations, one of those uncounted lives that are buried without drums and trumpets under the foundations of monumental successes. 'I am now third lieutenant of the *Victorieuse*' (she was the flagship of the French Pacific squadron at the time), he said, detaching his shoulders from the wall a couple of inches to introduce himself. I bowed slightly on my side of the table, and told him I commanded a merchant vessel at present anchored in Rushcutters' Bay. He had 'remarked' her,—a pretty little craft. He was very civil about it in his impassive way. I even fancy he went the length of tilting his head in compliment as he repeated, breathing visibly the while, 'Ah, yes. A little craft painted black—very pretty—very pretty (*très coquet*).' After a time he twisted his body slowly to face the glass door on our right. 'A dull town (*Triste ville*),' he observed, staring into the street. It was a brilliant day; a southerly buster was raging, and we could see the passers-by, men and women, buffeted by the wind on the side-walks, the sunlit fronts of the houses across the road blurred by the tall whirls of dust. 'I descended on shore,' he said, 'to stretch my legs a little, but . . .' He didn't finish, and sank into the depths of his repose. 'Pray—tell me,' he began,

coming up ponderously, 'what was there at the
bottom of this affair—precisely (*au juste*) ? It is
curious. That dead man, for instance—and so
on.

"'There were living men too,' I said ; 'much
more curious.'

"'No doubt, no doubt,' he agreed half audibly,
then, as if after mature consideration, murmured,
'Evidently.' I made no difficulty in communicating
to him what had interested me most in this affair.
It seemed as though he had a right to know :
hadn't he spent thirty hours on board the *Patna*
—had he not taken the succession, so to speak,
had he not done 'his possible' ? He listened to
me, looking more priest-like than ever, and with
what—probably on account of his downcast eyes—
had the appearance of devout concentration. Once
or twice he elevated his eyebrows (but without
raising his eyelids), as one would say 'The devil !'
Once he calmly exclaimed, 'Ah, bah !' under
his breath, and when I had finished he pursed his
lips in a deliberate way and emitted a sort of sorrow-
ful whistle.

"In any one else it might have been an evidence
of boredom, a sign of indifference ; but he, in his
occult way, managed to make his immobility appear profoundly responsive, and as full of valuable
thoughts as an egg is of meat. What he said at
last was nothing more than a 'very interesting,'
pronounced politely, and not much above a whisper.
Before I got over my disappointment he added, but
as if speaking to himself, 'That's it. That *is* it.'
His chin seemed to sink lower on his breast, his
body to weigh heavier on his seat. I was about
to ask him what he meant when a sort of pre-

paratory tremor passed over his whole person, as a faint ripple may be seen upon stagnant water even before the wind is felt. 'And so that poor young man ran away along with the others,' he said, with grave tranquillity.

"I don't know what made me smile: it is the only genuine smile of mine I can remember in connection with Jim's affair. But somehow this simple statement of the matter sounded funny in French. . . . '*S'est enfui avec les autres*,' had said the lieutenant. And suddenly I began to admire the discrimination of the man. He had made out the point at once: he did get hold of the only thing I cared about. I felt as though I were taking professional opinion on the case. His imperturbable and mature calmness was that of an expert in possession of the facts, and to whom one's perplexities are mere child's-play. 'Ah! The young, the young,' he said indulgently. 'And after all, one does not die of it.' 'Die of what?' I asked swiftly. 'Of being afraid.' He elucidated his meaning and sipped his drink.

"I perceived that the three last fingers of his wounded hand were stiff and could not move independently of each other, so that he took up his tumbler with an ungainly clutch. 'One is always afraid. One may talk, but . . .' He put down the glass awkwardly. . . . 'The fear, the fear—look you—it is always there.' . . . He touched his breast near a brass button, on the very spot where Jim had given a thump to his own when protesting that there was nothing the matter with his heart. I suppose I made some sign of dissent, because he insisted, 'Yes! yes! One talks, one talks; this is all very fine; but at the end of the reckoning one is

no cleverer than the next man—and no more brave.
Brave ! This is always to be seen. I have rolled my
hump (*roulé ma bosse*),' he said, using the slang
expression with imperturbable seriousness, ' in all
parts of the world ; I have known brave men—
famous ones ! *Allez !* ' . . . He drank carelessly.
. . . ' Brave—you conceive—in the Service—one
has got to be—the trade demands it (*le métier veux
ça*). Is it not so ? ' he appealed to me reasonably.
' *Eh bien !* Each of them—I say each of them, if he
were an honest man—*bien entendu*—would confess
that there is a point—there is a point—for the best
of us—there is somewhere a point when you let go
everything (*vous lachez tout*). And you have got to
live with that truth—do you see ? Given a certain
combination of circumstances, fear is sure to come.
Abominable funk (*un trac épouvantable*). And even
for those who do not believe this truth there is fear
all the same—the fear of themselves. Absolutely so.
Trust me. Yes. Yes. . . . At my age one knows
what one is talking about—*que diable !* ' . . . He
had delivered himself of all this as immovably as
though he had been the mouthpiece of abstract
wisdom, but at this point he heightened the effect
of detachment by beginning to twirl his thumbs
slowly. ' It's evident—*parbleu !* ' he continued ;
' for, make up your mind as much as you like, even
a simple headache or a fit of indigestion (*un dérange-
ment d'estomac*) is enough to . . . Take me, for
instance—I have made my proofs. *Eh bien !* I,
who am speaking to you, once . . .'

" He drained his glass and returned to his twirling.
' No, no ; one does not die of it,' he pronounced
finally, and when I found he did not mean to proceed
with the personal anecdote, I was extremely dis-

appointed ; the more so as it was not the sort of story, you know, one could very well press him for. I sat silent, and he too, as if nothing could please him better. Even his thumbs were still now. Suddenly his lips began to move. 'That is so,' he resumed placidly. 'Man is born a coward (*L'homme est né poltron*). It is a difficulty—*parbleu !* It would be too easy otherwise. But habit—habit—necessity —do you see ?—the eye of others—*voilà*. One puts up with it. And then the example of others who are no better than yourself, and yet make good countenance. . . .'

" His voice ceased.

" 'That young man—you will observe—had none of these inducements—at least at the moment,' I remarked.

" He raised his eyebrows forgivingly : 'I don't say ; I don't say. The young man in question might have had the best dispositions—the best dispositions,' he repeated, wheezing a little.

" 'I am glad to see you taking a lenient view,' I said. 'His own feeling in the matter was—ah !— hopeful, and . . .'

" The shuffle of his feet under the table interrupted me. He drew up his heavy eyelids. Drew up, I say—no other expression can describe the steady deliberation of the act—and at last was disclosed completely to me. I was confronted by two narrow grey circlets, like two tiny steel rings around the profound blackness of the pupils. The sharp glance, coming from that massive body, gave a notion of extreme efficiency, like a razor-edge on a battle-axe. 'Pardon,' he said punctiliously. His right hand went up, and he swayed forward. 'Allow me . . . I contended that one may get on knowing very well that one's courage does not come of itself (*ne vient pas tout seul*). There's nothing much in that to get upset about. One truth the more ought not to make life impossible. . . . But the honour—the honour, monsieur ! . . . The honour . . . that is real—that is ! And what life may be worth when ' . . . he got on his feet with a ponderous impetuosity, as a startled ox might scramble up from the grass . . . ' when the honour is gone—*ah ça ! par exemple*—I can offer no opinion. I can offer no opinion—because— monsieur—I know nothing of it.'

"I had risen too, and, trying to throw infinite politeness into our attitudes, we faced each other mutely, like two china dogs on a mantelpiece. Hang the fellow ! he had pricked the bubble. The blight of futility that lies in wait for men's speeches had fallen upon our conversation, and made it a thing of empty sounds. 'Very well,' I said, with a disconcerted smile ; 'but couldn't it reduce itself to not being found out ? ' He made as if to retort readily, but when he spoke he had changed his mind. 'This, monsieur, is too fine for me—much above me—I don't think about it.' He bowed heavily over his cap, which he held before him by the peak, between the thumb and the forefinger of his wounded hand. I bowed too. We bowed together : we scraped our feet at each other with much ceremony, while a dirty specimen of a waiter looked on critically, as though he had paid for the performance. 'Serviteur,' said the Frenchman. Another scrape. 'Monsieur ' . . . 'Monsieur.' . . . The glass door swung behind his burly back. I saw the southerly buster get hold of him and drive him down wind with his hand to his head, his shoulders braced, and the tails of his coat blown hard against his legs.

"I sat down again alone and discouraged—discouraged about Jim's case. If you wonder that after more than three years it had preserved its actuality, you must know that I had seen him only very lately. I had come straight from Samarang, where I had loaded a cargo for Sydney: an utterly uninteresting bit of business,—what Charley here would call one of my rational transactions—and in Samarang I had seen something of Jim. He was then working for De Jongh, on my recommendation. Water-clerk. 'My representative afloat,' as De Jongh called him. You can't imagine a mode of life more barren of consolation, less capable of being invested with a spark of glamour—unless it be the business of an insurance canvasser. Little Bob Stanton—Charley here knew him well—had gone through that experience. The same who got drowned afterwards trying to save a lady's-maid in the *Sephora* disaster. A case of collision on a hazy morning off the Spanish coast—you may remember. All the passengers had been packed tidily into the boats and shoved clear of the ship, when Bob sheered alongside again and scrambled back on deck to fetch that girl. How she had been left behind I can't make out; anyhow, she had gone completely crazy—wouldn't leave the ship —held to the rail like grim death. The wrestling-match could be seen plainly from the boats; but poor Bob was the shortest chief mate in the merchant service, and the woman stood five feet ten in her shoes and was as strong as a horse, I've been told. So it went on, pull devil, pull baker, the wretched girl screaming all the time, and Bob letting out a yell now and then to warn his boat to keep well clear of the ship. One of the hands told me, hiding a smile at the recollection, ' It was for all the world, sir, like a naughty youngster fighting with his mother.' The same old chap said that ' At the last we could see that Mr Stanton had given up hauling at the gal, and just stood by looking at her, watchful like. We thought afterwards he must 've been reckoning that, maybe, the rush of water would tear her away from the rail by-and-by and give him a show to save her. We daren't come alongside for our life ; and after a bit the old ship went down all on a sudden with a lurch to starboard—plop. The suck in was something awful. We never saw anything alive or dead come up.' Poor Bob's spell of shore-life had been one of the complications of a love affair, I believe. He fondly hoped he had done with the sea for ever, and made sure he had got hold of all the bliss on earth, but it came to canvassing in the end. Some cousin of his in Liverpool put him up to it. He used to tell us his experiences in that line. He made us laugh till we cried, and, not altogether displeased at the effect, undersized and bearded to the waist like a gnome, he would tiptoe amongst us and say, ' It's all very well for you beggars to laugh, but my immortal soul was shrivelled down to the size of a parched pea after a week of that work.' I don't know how Jim's soul accommodated itself to the new conditions of his life—I was kept too busy in getting him something to do that would keep body and soul together—but I am pretty certain his adventurous fancy was suffering all the pangs of starvation. It had certainly nothing to feed upon in this new calling. It was distressing

to see him at it, though he tackled it with a stubborn
serenity for which I must give him full credit. I
kept my eye on his shabby plodding with a sort
of notion that it was a punishment for the heroics
of his fancy—an expiation for his craving after
more glamour than he could carry. He had loved
too well to imagine himself a glorious racehorse,
and now he was condemned to toil without honour
like a costermonger's donkey. He did it very
well. He shut himself in, put his head down, said
never a word. Very well; very well indeed—
except for certain fantastic and violent outbreaks,
on the deplorable occasions when the irrepressible
Patna case cropped up. Unfortunately that scandal
of the Eastern seas would not die out. And this
is the reason why I could never feel I had done
with Jim for good.

"I sat thinking of him after the French lieutenant
had left, not, however, in connection with De Jongh's
cool and gloomy backshop, where we had hurriedly
shaken hands not very long ago, but as I had seen
him years before in the last flickers of the candle,
alone with me in the long gallery of the Malabar
House, with the chill and the darkness of the night
at his back. The respectable sword of his country's
law was suspended over his head. To-morrow—or
was it to-day? (midnight had slipped by long before
we parted)—the marble-faced police magistrate,
after distributing fines and terms of imprisonment
in the assault-and-battery case, would take up the
awful weapon and smite his bowed neck. Our com-
munion in the night was uncommonly like a last vigil
with a condemned man. He was guilty too. He was
guilty—as I had told myself repeatedly, guilty and
done for; nevertheless, I wished to spare him the

mere detail of a formal execution. I don't pretend to explain the reasons of my desire—I don't think I could ; but if you haven't got a sort of notion by this time, then I must have been very obscure in my narrative, or you too sleepy to seize upon the sense of my words. I don't defend my morality. There was no morality in the impulse which induced me to lay before him Brierly's plan of evasion—I may call it— in all its primitive simplicity. There were the rupees —absolutely ready in my pocket and very much at his service. Oh ! a loan ; a loan of course—and if an introduction to a man (in Rangoon) who could put some work in his way. . . . Why ! with the greatest pleasure. I had pen, ink, and paper in my room on the first floor. And even while I was speaking I was impatient to begin the letter : day, month, year, 2.30 A.M. . . . for the sake of our old friendship I ask you to put some work in the way of Mr James So-and-so, in whom, &c., &c. . . . I was even ready to write in that strain about him. If he had not enlisted my sympathies he had done better for himself—he had gone to the very fount and origin of that sentiment, he had reached the secret sensibility of my egoism. I am concealing nothing from you, because were I to do so my action would appear more unintelligible than any man's action has the right to be, and—in the second place—to-morrow you shall forget my sincerity along with the other lessons of the past. In this transaction, to speak grossly and precisely, I was the irreproachable man ; but the subtle intentions of my immorality were defeated by the moral simplicity of the criminal. No doubt he was selfish too, but his selfishness had a higher origin, a more lofty aim. I discovered that, say what I would, he was eager to go through

the ceremony of execution ; and I didn't say much,
for I felt that in argument his youth would tell
against me heavily : he believed where I had already
ceased to doubt. There was something fine in the
wildness of his unexpressed, hardly formulated hope.
'Clear out ! Couldn't think of it,' he said, with a
shake of the head. 'I make you an offer for which
I neither demand nor expect any sort of gratitude,'
I said ; 'you shall repay the money when convenient, and . . .' 'Awfully good of you,' he
muttered without looking up. I watched him
narrowly : the future must have appeared horribly
uncertain to him ; but he did not falter, as though
indeed there had been nothing wrong with his
heart. I felt angry—not for the first time that night.
'The whole wretched business,' I said, 'is bitter
enough, I should think, for a man of your kind . . .'
'It is, it is,' he whispered twice, with his eyes fixed
on the floor. It was heart-rending. He towered
above the light, and I could see the down on his
cheek, the colour mantling warm under the smooth
skin of his face. Believe me or not, I say it was
outrageously heart-rending. It provoked me to
brutality. 'Yes,' I said ; 'and allow me to confess
that I am totally unable to imagine what advantage
you can expect from this licking of the dregs.'
'Advantage !' he murmured out of his stillness. 'I
am dashed if I do,' I said, enraged. 'I've been trying
to tell you all there is in it,' he went on slowly,
as if meditating something unanswerable. 'But
after all, it is *my* trouble.' I opened my mouth to retort, and discovered suddenly that I'd lost all confidence in myself ; and it was as if he too had given
me up, for he mumbled like a man thinking half
aloud. 'Went away . . . went into hospitals . . .

Not one of them would face it. . . . They ! . . .'
He moved his hand slightly to imply disdain. 'But
I've got to get over this thing, and I mustn't
shirk any of it or . . . I won't shirk any of it.' He
was silent. He gazed as though he had been haunted.
His unconscious face reflected the passing expressions
of scorn, of despair, of resolution,—reflected them in
turn, as a magic mirror would reflect the gliding
passage of unearthly shapes. He lived surrounded
by deceitful ghosts, by austere shades. 'Oh ! nonsense, my dear fellow,' I began. He had a movement of impatience. 'You don't seem to understand,' he said incisively ; then looking at me
without a wink, 'I may have jumped, but I don't
run away.' 'I meant no offence,' I said ; and added
stupidly, 'Better men than you have found it expedient to run, at times.' He coloured all over,
while in my confusion I half-choked myself with
my own tongue. 'Perhaps so,' he said at last ;
'I am not good enough ; I can't afford it. I am
bound to fight this thing down—I am fighting it
now.' I got out of my chair and felt stiff all over.
The silence was embarrassing, and to put an end
to it I imagined nothing better but to remark, 'I
had no idea it was so late,' in an airy tone. . . .
'I daresay you have had enough of this,' he said
brusquely : 'and to tell you the truth '—he began
to look round for his hat—' so have I.'

"Well ! he had refused this unique offer. He
had struck aside my helping hand ; he was ready
to go now, and beyond the balustrade the night
seemed to wait for him very still, as though he
had been marked down for its prey. I heard his
voice. 'Ah ! here it is.' He had found his hat.
For a few seconds we hung in the wind. 'What

will you do after—after . . .' I asked very low.
'Go to the dogs as likely as not,' he answered in
a gruff mutter. I had recovered my wits in a
measure, and judged best to take it lightly. 'Pray
remember,' I said, 'that I should like very much
to see you again before you go.' 'I don't know
what's to prevent you. The damned thing won't
make me invisible,' he said with intense bitterness,
—'no such luck.' And then at the moment of
taking leave he treated me to a ghastly muddle of
dubious stammers and movements, to an awful display of hesitations. God forgive him—me! He
had taken it into his fanciful head that I was likely
to make some difficulty as to shaking hands. It
was too awful for words. I believe I shouted suddenly at him as you would bellow to a man you
saw about to walk over a cliff; I remember our
voices being raised, the appearance of a miserable
grin on his face, a crushing clutch on my hand, a
nervous laugh. The candle spluttered out, and the
thing was over at last, with a groan that floated
up to me in the dark. He got himself away somehow. The night swallowed his form. He was a
horrible bungler. Horrible. I heard the quick
crunch-crunch of the gravel under his boots. He
was running. Absolutely running, with nowhere
to go to. And he was not yet four-and-twenty.''

CHAPTER XIV.

" I SLEPT little, hurried over my breakfast, and after a slight hesitation gave up my early morning visit to my ship. It was really very wrong of me, because, though my chief mate was an excellent man all round, he was the victim of such black imaginings that if he did not get a letter from his wife at the expected time he would go quite distracted with rage and jealousy, lose all grip on the work, quarrel with all hands, and either weep in his cabin or develop such a ferocity of temper as all but drove the crew to the verge of mutiny. The thing had always seemed inexplicable to me : they had been married thirteen years ; I had a glimpse of her once, and, honestly, I couldn't conceive a man abandoned enough to plunge into sin for the sake of such an unattractive person. I don't know whether I have not done wrong by refraining from putting that view before poor Selvin : the man made a little hell on earth for himself, and I also suffered indirectly, but some sort of, no doubt, false delicacy prevented me. The marital relations of seamen would make an interesting subject, and I could tell you instances. . . . However, this is not the place, nor the time, and we are concerned with Jim—who was unmarried. If his imaginative conscience or his pride ; if all the extravagant ghosts and austere shades that were the disastrous familiars of his youth would not let him run away from the block, I, who of course can't be suspected of such familiars, was irresistibly impelled to go and see his head roll off. I wended

my way towards the court. I didn't hope to be
very much impressed or edified, or interested or
even frightened—though, as long as there is any
life before one, a jolly good fright now and then
is a salutary discipline. But neither did I expect
to be so awfully depressed. The bitterness of
his punishment was in its chill and mean atmosphere. The real significance of crime is in its being
a breach of faith with the community of mankind,
and from that point of view he was no mean traitor,
but his execution was a hole-and-corner affair.
There was no high scaffolding, no scarlet cloth
(did they have scarlet cloth on Tower Hill ? They
should have had), no awe-stricken multitude to be
horrified at his guilt and be moved to tears at his
fate—no air of sombre retribution. There was, as
I walked along, the clear sunshine, a brilliance too
passionate to be consoling, the streets full of jumbled
bits of colour like a damaged kaleidoscope : yellow,
green, blue, dazzling white, the brown nudity of an
undraped shoulder, a bullock-cart with a red canopy,
a company of native infantry in a drab body with
dark heads marching in dusty laced boots, a native
policeman in a sombre uniform of scanty cut and
belted in patent leather, who looked up at me with
orientally pitiful eyes as though his migrating spirit
were suffering exceedingly from that unforeseen—
what d'ye call 'em ?—avatar—incarnation. Under
the shade of a lonely tree in the courtyard, the
villagers connected with the assault case sat in a
picturesque group, looking like a chromo-lithograph
of a camp in a book of Eastern travel. One missed
the obligatory thread of smoke in the foreground
and the pack-animals grazing. A blank yellow
wall rose behind overtopping the tree, reflecting the

glare. The court-room was sombre, seemed more vast. High up in the dim space the punkahs were swaying short to and fro, to and fro. Here and there a draped figure, dwarfed by the bare walls, remained without stirring amongst the rows of empty benches, as if absorbed in pious meditation. The plaintiff, who had been beaten, an obese chocolate-coloured man with shaved head, one fat breast bare and a bright yellow caste-mark above the bridge of his nose, sat in pompous immobility : only his eyes glittered, rolling in the gloom, and the nostrils dilated and collapsed violently as he breathed. Brierly dropped into his seat looking done up, as though he had spent the night in sprinting on a cinder-track. The pious sailing-ship skipper appeared excited and made uneasy movements, as if restraining with difficulty an impulse to stand up and exhort us earnestly to prayer and repentance. The head of the magistrate, delicately pale under the neatly arranged hair, resembled the head of a hopeless invalid after he had been washed and brushed and propped up in bed. He moved aside the vase of flowers—a bunch of purple with a few pink blossoms on long stalks—and seizing in both hands a long sheet of bluish paper, ran his eye over it, propped his forearms on the edge of the desk, and began to read aloud in an even, distinct, and careless voice.

" By Jove ! For all my foolishness about scaffolds and heads rolling off—I assure you it was infinitely worse than a beheading. A heavy sense of finality brooded over all this, unrelieved by the hope of rest and safety following the fall of the axe. These proceedings had all the cold vengefulness of a death-sentence, and the cruelty of a sentence of exile.

This is how I looked at it that morning—and even now I seem to see an undeniable vestige of truth in that exaggerated view of a common occurrence. You may imagine how strongly I felt this at the time. Perhaps it is for that reason that I could not bring myself to admit the finality. The thing was always with me, I was always eager to take opinion on it, as though it had not been practically settled : individual opinion—international opinion— by Jove ! That Frenchman's, for instance. His own country's pronouncement was uttered in the passionless and definite phraseology a machine would use, if machines could speak. The head of the magistrate was half hidden by the paper, his brow was like alabaster.

" There were several questions before the Court. The first as to whether the ship was in every respect fit and seaworthy for the voyage. The Court found she was not. The next point, I remember, was, whether up to the time of the accident the ship had been navigated with proper and seamanlike care. They said Yes to that, goodness knows why, and then they declared that there was no evidence to show the exact cause of the accident. A floating derelict probably. I myself remember that a Norwegian barque bound out with a cargo of pitch-pine had been given up as missing about that time, and it was just the sort of craft that would capsize in a squall and float bottom up for months—a kind of maritime ghoul on the prowl to kill ships in the dark. Such wandering corpses are common enough in the North Atlantic, which is haunted by all the terrors of the sea,—fogs, icebergs, dead ships bent upon mischief, and long sinister gales that fasten upon one like a vampire till all the strength and the spirit and even hope are gone, and one feels like the empty shell of a man. But there—in those seas—the incident was rare enough to resemble a special arrangement of a malevolent providence, which, unless it had for its object the killing of a donkeyman and the bringing of worse than death upon Jim, appeared an utterly aimless piece of devilry. This view occurring to me took off my attention. For a time I was aware of the magistrate's voice as a sound merely; but in a moment it shaped itself into distinct words . . . 'in utter disregard of their plain duty,' it said. The next sentence escaped me somehow, and then . . . 'abandoning in the moment of danger the lives and property confided to their charge' . . . went on the voice evenly, and stopped. A pair of eyes under the white forehead shot darkly a glance above the edge of the paper. I looked for Jim hurriedly, as though I had expected him to disappear. He was very still—but he was there. He sat pink and fair and extremely attentive. 'Therefore, . . .' began the voice emphatically. He stared with parted lips, hanging upon the words of the man behind the desk. These came out into the stillness wafted on the wind made by the punkahs, and I, watching for their effect upon him, caught only the fragments of official language. . . . 'The Court . . . Gustav So-and-so master . . . native of Germany, . . . James So-and-so . . . mate . . . certificates cancelled.' A silence fell. The magistrate had dropped the paper, and, leaning sideways on the arm of his chair, began to talk with Brierly easily. People started to move out; others were pushing in, and I also made for the door. Outside I stood still, and when Jim passed me on his way to the gate,

I caught at his arm and detained him. The look he gave discomposed me as though I had been responsible for his state : he looked at me as if I had been the embodied evil of life. 'It's all over,' I stammered. 'Yes,' he said thickly. 'And now let no man . . .' He jerked his arm out of my grasp. I watched his back as he went away. It was a long street, and he remained in sight for some time. He walked rather slow, and straddling his legs a little, as if he had found it difficult to keep a straight line. Just before I lost him I fancied he staggered a bit.

"'Man overboard,' said a deep voice behind me. Turning round, I saw a fellow I knew slightly, a West Australian ; Chester was his name. He, too, had been looking after Jim. He was a man with an immense girth of chest, a rugged, clean-shaved face of mahogany colour, and two blunt tufts of iron-grey, thick, wiry hairs on his upper lip. He had been pearler, wrecker, trader, whaler too, I believe ; in his own words—anything and everything a man may be at sea, but a pirate. The Pacific, north and south, was his proper hunting-ground ; but he had wandered so far afield looking for a cheap steamer to buy. Lately he had discovered—so he said—a guano island somewhere, but its approaches were dangerous, and the anchorage, such as it was, could not be considered safe, to say the least of it. 'As good as a gold-mine,' he would exclaim. 'Right bang in the middle of the Walpole Reefs, and if it's true enough that you can get no holding-ground anywhere in less than forty fathom, then what of that ? There are the hurricanes, too. But it's a first-rate thing. As good as a gold-mine—better ! Yet there's not a fool of them that will see it. I can't get a skipper or a shipowner to go near the place. So I made up

my mind to cart the blessed stuff myself.' . . . This
was what he required a steamer for, and I knew he
was just then negotiating enthusiastically with a
Parsee firm for an old, brig-rigged, sea-anachronism
of ninety horse-power. We had met and spoken
together several times. He looked knowingly after
Jim. 'Takes it to heart?' he asked scornfully.
'Very much,' I said. 'Then he's no good,' he
opined. 'What's all the to-do about? A bit of ass's
skin. That never yet made a man. You must see
things exactly as they are—if you don't, you may
just as well give in at once. You will never do
anything in this world. Look at me. I made it a
practice never to take anything to heart.' 'Yes,' I
said, 'you see things as they are.' 'I wish I could
see my partner coming along, that's what I wish
to see,' he said. 'Know my partner? Old Robinson. Yes; *the* Robinson. Don't *you* know? The
notorious Robinson. The man who smuggled more
opium and bagged more seals in his time than any
loose Johnny now alive. They say he used to board
the sealing-schooners up Alaska way when the fog
was so thick that the Lord God, He alone, could tell
one man from another. Holy-Terror Robinson.
That's the man. He is with me in that guano thing.
The best chance he ever came across in his life.' He
put his lips to my ear. 'Cannibal?—well, they used
to give him the name years and years ago. You
remember the story? A shipwreck on the west side
of Stewart Island; that's right; seven of them got
ashore, and it seems they did not get on very well
together. Some men are too cantankerous for anything—don't know how to make the best of a bad
job—don't see things as they are—as they *are*, my
boy! And then what's the consequence? Obvious!

F 2

Trouble, trouble; as likely as not a knock on the
head; and serve 'em right too. That sort is the
most useful when it's dead. The story goes that a
boat of Her Majesty's ship *Wolverine* found him
kneeling on the kelp, naked as the day he was born,
and chanting some psalm-tune or other; light
snow was falling at the time. He waited till the boat
was an oar's length from the shore, and then up and
away. They chased him for an hour up and down
the boulders, till a marine flung a stone that took
him behind the ear providentially and knocked him
senseless. Alone? Of course. But that's like that
tale of sealing-schooners; the Lord God knows the
right and the wrong of that story. The cutter did
not investigate much. They wrapped him in a
boat-cloak and took him off as quick as they could,
with a dark night coming on, the weather threatening,
and the ship firing recall guns every five minutes.
Three weeks afterwards he was as well as ever. He
didn't allow any fuss that was made on shore to
upset him; he just shut his lips tight, and let people
screech. It was bad enough to have lost his ship,
and all he was worth besides, without paying attention to the hard names they called him. That's
the man for me.' He lifted his arm for a signal
to some one down the street. 'He's got a little
money, so I had to let him into my thing. Had to!
It would have been sinful to throw away such a
find, and I was cleaned out myself. It cut me to
the quick, but I could see the matter just as it was,
and if I *must* share—thinks I—with any man, then
give me Robinson. I left him at breakfast in the
hotel to come to court, because I've an idea. . . .
Ah! Good morning, Captain Robinson. . . . Friend
of mine, Captain Robinson.'

" An emaciated patriarch in a suit of white drill, a solah topi with a green-lined rim on a head trembling with age, joined us after crossing the street in a trotting shuffle, and stood propped with both hands on the handle of an umbrella. A white beard with amber streaks hung lumpily down to his waist. He blinked his creased eyelids at me in a bewildered way. 'How do you do? how do you do?' he piped amiably, and tottered. 'A little deaf,' said Chester aside. 'Did you drag him over six thousand miles to get a cheap steamer?' I asked. 'I would have taken him twice round the world as soon as look at him,' said Chester with immense energy. 'The steamer will be the making of us, my lad. Is it my fault that every skipper and shipowner in the whole of blessed Australasia turns out a blamed fool? Once I talked for three hours to a man in Auckland. "Send a ship," I said, "send a ship. I'll give you half of the first cargo for yourself, free gratis for nothing—just to make a good start." Says he, " I wouldn't do it if there was no other place on earth to send a ship to." Perfect ass, of course. Rocks, currents, no anchorage, sheer cliff to lay to, no insurance company would take the risk, didn't see how he could get loaded under three years. Ass! I nearly went on my knees to him. " But look at the thing as it is," says I. " Damn rocks and hurricanes. Look at it as it is. There's guano there, Queensland sugar-planters would fight for—fight for on the quay, I tell you." . . . What can you do with a fool? . . . " That's one of your little jokes, Chester," he says. . . . Joke! I could have wept. Ask Captain Robinson here. . . . And there was another shipowning fellow—a fat chap in a white waistcoat in Wellington, who seemed to think I was

up to some swindle or other. "I don't know what
sort of fool you're looking for," he says, " but I am
busy just now. Good morning." I longed to take
him in my two hands and smash him through the
window of his own office. But I didn't. I was as
mild as a curate. "Think of it," says I. "*Do*
think it over. I'll call to-morrow." He grunted
something about being "out all day." On the stairs
I felt ready to beat my head against the wall from
vexation. Captain Robinson here can tell you. It
was awful to think of all that lovely stuff lying waste
under the sun—stuff that would send the sugar-cane
shooting sky-high. The making of Queensland!
The making of Queensland! And in Brisbane,
where I went to have a last try, they gave me the
name of a lunatic. Idiots! The only sensible man
I came across was the cabman who drove me about.
A broken-down swell he was, I fancy. Hey! Captain
Robinson? You remember I told you about my
cabby in Brisbane—don't you? The chap had a
wonderful eye for things. He saw it all in a jiffy.
It was a real pleasure to talk with him. One evening
after a devil of a day amongst shipowners I felt so
bad that, says I, "I must get drunk. Come along;
I must get drunk, or I'll go mad." "I am your
man," he says; "go ahead." I don't know what I
would have done without him. Hey! Captain
Robinson.'

"He poked the ribs of his partner. 'He! he!
he!' laughed the Ancient, looked aimlessly down the
street, then peered at me doubtfully with sad, dim
pupils. . . . 'He! he! he!' . . . He leaned
heavier on the umbrella, and dropped his gaze on
the ground. I needn't tell you I had tried to get
away several times, but Chester had foiled every

attempt by simply catching hold of my coat. 'One minute. I've a notion.' 'What's your infernal notion?' I exploded at last. 'If you think I am going in with you . . .' 'No, no, my boy. Too late, if you wanted ever so much. We've got a steamer.' 'You've got the ghost of a steamer,' I said. 'Good enough for a start—there's no superior nonsense about us. Is there, Captain Robinson?' 'No! no! no!' croaked the old man without lifting his eyes, and the senile tremble of his head became almost fierce with determination. 'I understand you know that young chap,' said Chester, with a nod at the street from which Jim had disappeared long ago. 'He's been having grub with you in the Malabar last night—so I was told.'

"I said that was true, and after remarking that he too liked to live well and in style, only that, for the present, he had to be saving of every penny— 'none too many for the business! Isn't that so, Captain Robinson?'—he squared his shoulders and stroked his dumpy moustache, while the notorious Robinson, coughing at his side, clung more than ever to the handle of the umbrella, and seemed ready to subside passively into a heap of old bones. 'You see, the old chap has all the money,' whispered Chester confidentially. 'I've been cleaned out trying to engineer the dratted thing. But wait a bit, wait a bit. The good time is coming.' . . . He seemed suddenly astonished at the signs of impatience I gave. 'Oh, crakee!' he cried; 'I am telling you of the biggest thing that ever was, and you . . .' 'I have an appointment,' I pleaded mildly. 'What of that?' he asked with genuine surprise; 'let it wait.' 'That's exactly what I am doing now,' I remarked; 'hadn't you better tell me

what it is you want?' 'Buy twenty hotels like
that,' he growled to himself; 'and every joker
boarding in them too—twenty times over.' He
lifted his head smartly. 'I want that young chap.'
'I don't understand,' I said. 'He's no good, is he?'
said Chester crisply. 'I know nothing about it,' I
protested. 'Why, you told me yourself he was taking
it to heart,' argued Chester. 'Well, in my opinion
a chap who . . . Anyhow, he can't be much good;
but then you see I am on the look-out for somebody,
and I've just got a thing that will suit him. I'll
give him a job on my island.' He nodded signifi-
cantly. 'I'm going to dump forty coolies there—if
I've to steal 'em. Somebody must work the stuff.
Oh! I mean to act square: wooden shed, corru-
gated-iron roof—I know a man in Hobart who will
take my bill at six months for the materials. I do.
Honour bright. Then there's the water-supply. I'll
have to fly round and get somebody to trust me for
half-a-dozen second-hand iron tanks. Catch rain-
water, hey? Let him take charge. Make him
supreme boss over the coolies. Good idea, isn't it?
What do you say?' 'There are whole years when
not a drop of rain falls on Walpole,' I said, too
amazed to laugh. He bit his lip and seemed bothered.
'Oh, well, I will fix up something for them—or land
a supply. Hang it all! That's not the question.'

"I said nothing. I had a rapid vision of Jim
perched on a shadowless rock, up to his knees in
guano, with the screams of sea-birds in his ears, the
incandescent ball of the sun above his head; the
empty sky and the empty ocean all a-quiver, sim-
mering together in the heat as far as the eye could
reach. 'I wouldn't advise my worst enemy . . .' I
began. 'What's the matter with you?' cried

Chester ; 'I mean to give him a good screw—that is, as soon as the thing is set going, of course. It's as easy as falling off a log. Simply nothing to do ; two six-shooters in his belt . . . Surely he wouldn't be afraid of anything forty coolies could do—with two six-shooters and he the only armed man too ! It's much better than it looks. I want you to help me to talk him over.' 'No !' I shouted. Old Robinson lifted his bleared eyes dismally for a moment, Chester looked at me with infinite contempt. 'So you wouldn't advise him ? ' he uttered slowly. 'Certainly not,' I answered, as indignant as though he had requested me to help murder somebody ; 'moreover, I am sure he wouldn't. He is badly cut up, but he isn't mad as far as I know.' 'He is no earthly good for anything,' Chester mused aloud. 'He would just have done for me. If you only could see a thing as it is, you would see it's the very thing for him. And besides . . . Why ! it's the most splendid, sure chance . . .' He got angry suddenly. 'I must have a man. There ! . . .' He stamped his foot and smiled unpleasantly. 'Anyhow, I could guarantee the island wouldn't sink under him—and I believe he is a bit particular on that point.' 'Good morning,' I said curtly. He looked at me as though I had been an incomprehensible fool. . . . 'Must be moving, Captain Robinson,' he yelled suddenly into the old man's ear. 'These Parsee Johnnies are waiting for us to clinch the bargain.' He took his partner under the arm with a firm grip, swung him round, and, unexpectedly, leered at me over his shoulder. 'I was trying to do him a kindness,' he asserted, with an air and tone that made my blood boil. 'Thank you for nothing—in his name,' I rejoined. 'Oh ! you are devilish smart,' he sneered; ' but you are like the rest of them. Too much in the clouds. See what *you* will do with him.' ' I don't know that I want to do anything with him.' ' Don't you ? ' he spluttered; his grey moustache bristled with anger, and by his side the notorious Robinson, propped on the umbrella, stood with his back to me, as patient and still as a worn-out cab-horse. ' I haven't found a guano island,' I said. ' It's my belief you wouldn't know one if you were led right up to it by the hand,' he riposted quickly; ' and in this world you've got to see a thing first, before you can make use of it. Got to see it through and through at that, neither more nor less.' ' And get others to see it too,' I insinuated with a glance at the bowed back by his side. Chester snorted at me. ' His eyes are right enough—don't you worry. He ain't a puppy.' ' Oh dear, no ! ' I said. ' Come along, Captain Robinson,' he shouted, with a sort of bullying deference under the rim of the old man's hat; the Holy Terror gave a submissive little jump. The ghost of a steamer was waiting for them, Fortune on that fair isle ! They made a curious pair of Argonauts. Chester strode on leisurely, well set up, portly, and of conquering mien; the other, long, wasted, drooping, and hooked to his arm, shuffled his withered shanks with desperate haste."

CHAPTER XV.

"I DID not start in search of Jim at once, only because I had really an appointment which I could not neglect. Then, as ill-luck would have it, in my agent's office I was fastened upon by a fellow fresh from Madagascar with a little scheme for a wonderful piece of business. It had something to do with cattle and cartridges and a Prince Ravonalo something; but the pivot of the whole affair was the stupidity of some admiral—Admiral Pierre, I think. Everything turned on that, and the chap couldn't find words strong enough to express his confidence. He had globular eyes starting out of his head with a fishy glitter, bumps on his forehead, and wore his long hair brushed back without a parting. He had a favourite phrase which he kept on repeating triumphantly, 'The minimum of risk with the maximum of profit is my motto. What?' He made my head ache, spoiled my tiffin, but got his own out of me all right; and as soon as I had shaken him off, I made straight for the water-side. I caught sight of Jim leaning over the parapet of the quay. Three native boatmen quarrelling over five annas were making an awful row at his elbow. He didn't hear me come up, but spun round as if the slight contact of my finger had released a catch. 'I was looking,' he stammered. I don't remember what I said, not much anyhow, but he made no difficulty in following me to the hotel.

"He followed me as manageable as a little child, with an obedient air, with no sort of manifestation, rather as though he had been waiting for me there to come along and carry him off. I need not have been so surprised as I was at his tractability. On all the round earth, which to some seems so big and that others affect to consider as rather smaller than a mustard-seed, he had no place where he could—what shall I say?—where he could withdraw. That's it! Withdraw—be alone with his loneliness. He walked by my side very calm, glancing here and there, and once turned his head to look after a Sidiboy fireman in a cutaway coat and yellowish trousers, whose black face had silky gleams like a lump of anthracite coal. I doubt, however, whether he saw anything, or even remained all the time aware of my companionship, because if I had not edged him to the left here, or pulled him to the right there, I believe he would have gone straight before him in any direction till stopped by a wall or some other obstacle. I steered him into my bedroom, and sat down at once to write letters. This was the only place in the world (unless, perhaps, the Walpole Reef—but that was not so handy) where he could have it out with himself without being bothered by the rest of the universe. The damned thing—as he had expressed it—had not made him invisible, but I behaved exactly as though he were. No sooner in my chair I bent over my writing-desk like a medieval scribe, and, but for the movement of the hand holding the pen, remained anxiously quiet. I can't say I was frightened ; but I certainly kept as still as if there had been something dangerous in the room, that at the first hint of a movement on my part would be provoked to pounce upon me. There was not much in the room —you know how these bedrooms are—a sort of four-poster bedstead under a mosquito-net, two or three chairs, the table I was writing at, a bare floor.

A glass door opened on an upstairs verandah, and
he stood with his face to it, having a hard time
with all possible privacy. Dusk fell; I lit a candle
with the greatest economy of movement and as
much prudence as though it were an illegal proceeding. There is no doubt that he had a very
hard time of it, and so had I, even to the point, I
must own, of wishing him to the devil, or on Walpole
Reef at least. It occurred to me once or twice
that, after all, Chester was, perhaps, the man to
deal effectively with such a disaster. That strange
idealist had found a practical use for it at once—
unerringly, as it were. It was enough to make one
suspect that, maybe, he really could see the true
aspect of things that appeared mysterious or utterly
hopeless to less imaginative persons. I wrote and
wrote; I liquidated all the arrears of my correspon-
dence, and then went on writing to people who had
no reason whatever to expect from me a gossipy
letter about nothing at all. At times I stole a sidelong glance. He was rooted to the spot, but convulsive shudders ran down his back; his shoulders
would heave suddenly. He was fighting, he was
fighting—mostly for his breath, as it seemed. The
massive shadows, cast all one way from the straight
flame of the candle, seemed possessed of gloomy
consciousness; the immobility of the furniture had
to my furtive eye an air of attention. I was becoming
fanciful in the midst of my industrious scribbling;
and though, when the scratching of my pen stopped
for a moment, there was complete silence and stillness in the room, I suffered from that profound
disturbance and confusion of thought which is caused
by a violent and menacing uproar—of a heavy gale at
sea, for instance. Some of you may know what I

mean,—that mingled anxiety, distress, and irritation
with a sort of craven feeling creeping in—not pleasant
to acknowledge, but which gives a quite special
merit to one's endurance. I don't claim any merit
for standing the stress of Jim's emotions; I could
take refuge in the letters; I could have written to
strangers if necessary. Suddenly, as I was taking
up a fresh sheet of notepaper, I heard a low sound,
the first sound that, since we had been shut up
together, had come to my ears in the dim stillness of
the room. I remained with my head down, with my
hand arrested. Those who had kept vigil by a sick-
bed have heard such faint sounds in the stillness of
the night watches, sounds wrung from a racked body,
from a weary soul. He pushed the glass door with
such force that all the panes rang : he stepped out,
and I held my breath, straining my ears without
knowing what else I expected to hear. He was
really taking too much to heart an empty formality
which to Chester's rigorous criticism seemed unworthy
the notice of a man who could see things as they
were. An empty formality ; a piece of parchment.
Well, well. As to an inaccessible guano deposit, that
was another story altogether. One could intellig-
ibly break one's heart over that. A feeble burst of
many voices mingled with the tinkle of silver and
glass floated up from the dining-room below ; through
the open door the outer edge of the light from my
candle fell on his back faintly ; beyond all was black ;
he stood on the brink of a vast obscurity, like a
lonely figure by the shore of a sombre and hopeless
ocean. There was the Walpole Reef in it—to be
sure—a speck in the dark void, a straw for the
drowning man. My compassion for him took the
shape of the thought that I wouldn't have liked his

people to see him at that moment. I found it trying myself. His back was no longer shaken by his gasps; he stood straight as an arrow, faintly visible and still; and the meaning of this stillness sank to the bottom of my soul like lead into the water, and made it so heavy that for a second I wished heartily that the only course left open for me were to pay for his funeral. Even the law had done with him. To bury him would have been such an easy kindness! It would have been so much in accordance with the wisdom of life, which consists in putting out of sight all the reminders of our folly, of our weakness, of our mortality; all that makes against our efficiency— the memory of our failures, the hints of our undying fears, the bodies of our dead friends. Perhaps he did take it too much to heart. And if so then— Chester's offer. . . . At this point I took up a fresh sheet and began to write resolutely. There was nothing but myself between him and the dark ocean. I had a sense of responsibility. If I spoke, would that motionless and suffering youth leap into the obscurity—clutch at the straw? I found out how difficult it may be sometimes to make a sound. There is a weird power in a spoken word. And why the devil not? I was asking myself persistently while I drove on with my writing. All at once, on the blank page, under the very point of the pen, the two figures of Chester and his antique partner, very distinct and complete, would dodge into view with stride and gestures, as if reproduced in the field of some optical toy. I would watch them for a while. No! They were too fantasmal and extravagant to enter into any one's fate. And a word carries far— very far—deals destruction through time as the bullets go flying through space. I said nothing; and he, out there with his back to the light, as if bound and gagged by all the invisible foes of man, made no stir and made no sound."

CHAPTER XVI.

"The time was coming when I should see him loved, trusted, admired, with a legend of strength and prowess forming round his name as though he had been the stuff of a hero. It's true—I assure you ; as true as I'm sitting here talking about him in vain. He, on his side, had that faculty of beholding at a hint the face of his desire and the shape of his dream, without which the earth would know no lover and no adventurer. He captured much honour and an Arcadian happiness (I won't say anything about innocence) in the bush, and it was as good to him as the honour and the Arcadian happiness of the streets to another man. Felicity, felicity—how shall I say it ?—is quaffed out of a golden cup in every latitude : the flavour is with you—with you alone, and you can make it as intoxicating as you please. He was of the sort that would drink deep, as you may guess from what went before. I found him, if not exactly intoxicated, then at least flushed with the elixir at his lips. He had not obtained it at once. There had been, as you know, a period of probation amongst infernal ship-chandlers, during which he had suffered and I had worried about— about—my trust—you may call it. I don't know that I am completely reassured now, after beholding

him in all his brilliance. That was my last view of
him—in a strong light, dominating, and yet in complete accord with his surroundings—with the life of
the forests and with the life of men. I own that
I was impressed, but I must admit to myself that
after all this is not the lasting impression. He was
protected by his isolation, alone of his own superior
kind, in close touch with nature, that keeps faith on
such easy terms with her lovers. But I cannot fix
before my eye the image of his safety. I shall
always remember him as seen through the open
door of my room, taking, perhaps, too much to
heart the mere consequences of his failure. I am
pleased, of course, that some good—and even some
splendour—came out of my endeavours ; but at
times it seems to me it would have been better for
my peace of mind if I had not stood between him
and Chester's confoundedly generous offer. I wonder
what his exuberant imagination would have made of
Walpole islet—that most hopelessly forsaken crumb
of dry land on the face of the waters. It is not
likely I would ever have heard, for, I must tell you,
that Chester, after calling at some Australian port
to patch up his brig-rigged sea-anachronism, steamed
out into the Pacific with a crew of twenty-two hands
all told, and the only news having a possible bearing
upon the mystery of his fate was the news of a
hurricane which is supposed to have swept in its
course over the Walpole shoals, a month or so afterwards. Not a vestige of the Argonauts ever turned
up ; not a sound came out of the waste. Finis !
The Pacific is the most discreet of live, hot-tempered
oceans : the chilly Antarctic can keep a secret too,
but more in the manner of a grave.

" And there is a sense of blessed finality in such

discretion, which is what we all more or less sincerely
are ready to admit—for what else is it that makes
the idea of death supportable? End! Finis! the
potent word that exorcises from the house of life the
haunting shadow of fate. This is what—notwithstanding the testimony of my eyes and his own
earnest assurances—I miss when I look back upon
Jim's success. While there's life there is hope, truly;
but there is fear too. I don't mean to say that I
regret my action, nor will I pretend that I can't
sleep o' nights in consequence; still the idea obtrudes
itself that he made so much of his disgrace while it
is the guilt alone that matters. He was not—if I
may say so—clear to me. He was not clear. And
there is a suspicion he was not clear to himself either.
There were his fine sensibilities, his fine feelings, his
fine longings—a sort of sublimated, idealised selfishness. He was—if you allow me to say so—very
fine; very fine—and very unfortunate. A little
coarser nature would not have borne the strain;
it would have had to come to terms with itself—
with a sigh, with a grunt, or even with a guffaw;
a still coarser one would have remained invulnerably
ignorant and completely uninteresting.

"But he was too interesting or too unfortunate
to be thrown to the dogs, or even to Chester. I
felt this while I sat with my face over the paper
and he fought and gasped, struggling for his breath
in that terribly stealthy way, in my room; I felt it
when he rushed out on the verandah as if to fling
himself over—and didn't; I felt it more and more
all the time he remained outside, faintly lighted on
the background of night, as if standing on the shore
of a sombre and hopeless sea.

"An abrupt heavy rumble made me lift my head.

The noise seemed to roll away, and suddenly a searching and violent glare fell on the blind face of the night. The sustained and dazzling flickers seemed to last for an unconscionable time. The growl of the thunder increased steadily while I looked at him, distinct and black, planted solidly upon the shores of a sea of light. At the moment of greatest brilliance the darkness leaped back with a culminating crash, and he vanished before my dazzled eyes as utterly as though he had been blown to atoms. A blustering sigh passed ; furious hands seemed to tear at the shrubs, shake the tops of the trees below, slam doors, break window-panes all along the front of the building. He stepped in, closing the door behind him, and found me bending over the table : my sudden anxiety as to what he would say was very great, and akin to a fright. 'May I have a cigarette ? ' he asked. I gave a push to the box without raising my head. 'I want—want—tobacco,' he muttered. I became extremely buoyant. 'Just a moment,' I grunted pleasantly. He took a few steps here and there. 'That's over,' I heard him say. A single distant clap of thunder came from the sea like a gun of distress. 'The monsoon breaks up early this year,' he remarked conversationally, somewhere behind me. This encouraged me to turn round, which I did as soon as I had finished addressing the last envelope. He was smoking greedily in the middle of the room, and though he heard the stir I made, he remained with his back to me for a time.

" ' Come—I carried it off pretty well,' he said, wheeling suddenly. 'Something's paid off—not much. I wonder what's to come.' His face did not show any emotion, only it appeared a little

darkened and swollen, as though he had been hold
ing his breath. He smiled reluctantly as it were
and went on while I gazed up at him mutely. . . .
' Thank you, though—your room—jolly convenient—
for a chap—badly hipped.' . . . The rain pattered
and swished in the garden ; a water-pipe (it must have
had a hole in it) performed just outside the window
a parody of blubbering woe with funny sobs and
gurgling lamentations, interrupted by jerky spasms o
silence. . . . 'A bit of shelter,' he mumbled and ceased

"A flash of faded lightning darted in through
the black framework of the windows and ebbed ou
without any noise. I was thinking how I had bes
approach him (I did not want to be flung off again
when he gave a little laugh. 'No better than a
vagabond now' . . . the end of the cigarette
smouldered between his fingers . . . 'without a
single—single,' he pronounced slowly ; and ' ye
. . .' He paused ; the rain fell with redoubled
violence. 'Some day one's bound to come upon
some sort of chance to get it all back again. Must !
he whispered distinctly, glaring at my boots.

"I did not even know what it was he wished
so much to regain, what it was he had so terribly
missed. It might have been so much that it was
impossible to say. A piece of ass's skin, according
to Chester. . . . He looked up at me inquisitively
' Perhaps. If life's long enough,' I muttered through
my teeth with unreasonable animosity. 'Don't
reckon too much on it.'

"'Jove ! I feel as if nothing could ever touch
me,' he said in a tone of sombre conviction. 'I
this business couldn't knock me over, then there's
no fear of there being not enough time to—climb
out, and . . .' He looked upwards.

" It struck me that it is from such as he that the great army of waifs and strays is recruited, the army that marches down, down into all the gutters of the earth. As soon as he left my room, that ' bit of shelter,' he would take his place in the ranks, and begin the journey toward the bottomless pit. I at least had no illusions ; but it was I, too, who a moment ago had been so sure of the power of words, and now was afraid to speak, in the same way one dares not move for fear of losing a slippery hold. It is when we try to grapple with another man's intimate need that we perceive how incomprehensible, wavering, and misty are the beings that share with us the sight of the stars and the warmth of the sun. It is as if loneliness were a hard and absolute condition of existence ; the envelope of flesh and blood on which our eyes are fixed melts before the outstretched hand, and there remains only the capricious, unconsolable, and elusive spirit that no eye can follow, no hand can grasp. It was the fear of losing him that kept me silent, for it was borne upon me suddenly and with unaccountable force that should I let him slip away into the darkness I would never forgive myself.

" ' Well. Thanks—once more. You've been—er —uncommonly—really there's no word to . . . Uncommonly ! I don't know why, I am sure. I am afraid I don't feel as grateful as I would if the whole thing hadn't been so brutally sprung on me. Because at bottom . . . you, yourself . . .' He stuttered.

" ' Possibly,' I struck in. He frowned.

" ' All the same, one is responsible.' He watched me like a hawk.

" ' And that's true, too,' I said.

" ' Well. I've gone with it to the end, and I don't intend to let any man cast it in my teeth without—without—resenting it.' He clenched his fist.

" ' There's yourself,' I said with a smile—mirthless enough, God knows—but he looked at me menacingly. ' That's my business,' he said. An air of indomitable resolution came and went upon his face like a vain and passing shadow. Next moment he looked a dear good boy in trouble as before. He flung away the cigarette. ' Good-bye,' he said, with the sudden haste of a man who had lingered too long in view of a pressing bit of work waiting for him ; and then for a second or so he made not the slightest movement. The downpour fell with the heavy uninterrupted rush of a sweeping flood, with a sound of unchecked overwhelming fury that called to one's mind the images of collapsing bridges, of uprooted trees, of undermined mountains. No man could breast the colossal and headlong stream that seemed to break and swirl against the dim stillness in which we were precariously sheltered as if on an island. The perforated pipe gurgled, choked, spat, and splashed in odious ridicule of a swimmer fighting for his life. ' It is raining,' I remonstrated, ' and I . . .' ' Rain or shine,' he began brusquely, checked himself, and walked to the window. ' Perfect deluge,' he muttered after a while : he leaned his forehead on the glass. ' It's dark, too.'

" ' Yes, it is very dark,' I said.

" He pivoted on his heels, crossed the room, and had actually opened the door leading into the corridor before I leaped up from my chair. ' Wait,' I cried, ' l want you to . . .' ' I can't dine with you again to-night,' he flung at me, with one leg

out of the room already. 'I haven't the slightest
intention to ask you,' I shouted. At this he drew
back his foot, but remained mistrustfully in the very
doorway. I lost no time in entreating him earnestly
not to be absurd; to come in and shut the door."

CHAPTER XVII.

"HE came in at last; but I believe it was mostly
the rain that did it; it was falling just then with a
devastating violence which quieted down gradually
while we talked. His manner was very sober and
set; his bearing was that of a naturally taciturn
man possessed by an idea. My talk was of the
material aspect of his position; it had the sole
aim of saving him from the degradation, ruin, and
despair that out there close so swiftly upon a friend-
less, homeless man; I pleaded with him to accept
my help; I argued reasonably: and every time I
looked up at that absorbed smooth face, so grave
and youthful, I had a disturbing sense of being
no help but rather an obstacle to some mysterious,
inexplicable, impalpable striving of his wounded
spirit.

"'I suppose you intend to eat and drink and to
sleep under shelter in the usual way,' I remember
saying with irritation. 'You say you won't touch
the money that is due to you.' . . . He came as
near as his sort can to making a gesture of horror.
(There were three weeks and five days' pay owing
him as mate of the *Patna*.) 'Well, that's too little

to matter anyhow ; but what will you do to-morrow ?
Where will you turn ? You must live . . .' 'That
isn't the thing,' was the comment that escaped
him under his breath. I ignored it, and went on
combating what I assumed to be the scruples of
an exaggerated delicacy. 'On every conceivable
ground,' I concluded, 'you must let me help you.'
'You can't,' he said very simply and gently, and
holding fast to some deep idea which I could detect
shimmering like a pool of water in the dark, but
which I despaired of ever approaching near enough
to fathom. I surveyed his well-proportioned bulk
'At any rate,' I said, 'I am able to help what I
can see of you. I don't pretend to do more.' He
shook his head sceptically without looking at me.
I got very warm. 'But I can,' I insisted. 'I can
do even more. I *am* doing more. I am trusting
you . . .' 'The money . . .' he began. 'Upon
my word you deserve being told to go to the devil,'
I cried, forcing the note of indignation. He was
startled, smiled, and I pressed my attack home.
'It isn't a question of money at all. You are too
superficial,' I said (and at the same time I was
thinking to myself : Well, here goes ! And perhaps
he is, after all). 'Look at the letter I want you to
take. I am writing to a man of whom I've never
asked a favour, and I am writing about you in terms
that one only ventures to use when speaking of
an intimate friend. I make myself unreservedly
responsible for you. That's what I am doing.
And really if you will only reflect a little what that
means . . .'

"He lifted his head. The rain had passed away ;
only the water-pipe went on shedding tears with
an absurd drip, drip outside the window. It was

very quiet in the room, whose shadows huddled together in corners, away from the still flame of the candle flaring upright in the shape of a dagger; his face after a while seemed suffused by a reflection of a soft light as if the dawn had broken already.

" ' Jove ! ' he gasped out. ' It is noble of you ! '

" Had he suddenly put out his tongue at me in derision, I could not have felt more humiliated. I thought to myself—Serve me right for a sneaking humbug. . . . His eyes shone straight into my face, but I perceived it was not a mocking brightness. All at once he sprang into jerky agitation, like one of these flat wooden figures that are worked by a string. His arms went up, then came down with a slap. He became another man altogether. ' And I had never seen,' he shouted ; then suddenly bit his lip and frowned. ' What a bally ass I've been,' he said very slow in an awed tone. . . . ' You are a brick,' he cried next in a muffled voice. He snatched my hand as though he had just then seen it for the first time, and dropped it at once. ' Why ! this is what I—you—I . . .' he stammered, and then with a return of his old stolid, I may say mulish, manner he began heavily, ' I would be a brute now if I . . .' and then his voice seemed to break. ' That's all right,' I said. I was almost alarmed by this display of feeling, through which pierced a strange elation. I had pulled the string accidentally, as it were ; I did not fully understand the working of the toy. ' I must go now,' he said. ' Jove ! You *have* helped me. Can't sit still. The very thing . . .' He looked at me with puzzled admiration. ' The very thing . . .'

" Of course it was the thing. It was ten to one that I had saved him from starvation—of that

peculiar sort that is almost invariably associated
with drink. This was all. I had not a single illusion
on that score, but looking at him, I allowed myself
to wonder at the nature of the one he had, within
the last three minutes, so evidently taken unto his
bosom. I had forced into his hand the means to
carry on decently the serious business of life, to
get food, drink, and shelter of the customary kind,
while his wounded spirit, like a bird with a broken
wing, might hop and flutter into some hole, to die
quietly of inanition there. This is what I had
thrust upon him : a definitely small thing ; and—
behold !—by the manner of its reception it loomed
in the dim light of the candle like a big, indistinct,
perhaps a dangerous shadow. ' You don't mind me
not saying anything appropriate,' he burst out.
' There isn't anything one could say. Last night
already you have done me no end of good. Listening
to me—you know. I give you my word I've thought
more than once the top of my head would fly
off . . .' He darted—positively darted—here and
there, rammed his hands into his pockets, jerked
them out again, flung his cap on his head. I had
no idea it was in him to be so airily brisk. I thought
of a dry leaf imprisoned in an eddy of wind, while
a mysterious apprehension, a load of indefinite
doubt, weighed me down in my chair. He stood
stock-still, as if struck motionless by a discovery.
' You have given me confidence,' he declared soberly.
' Oh ! for God's sake, my dear fellow—don't ! ' I
entreated, as though he had hurt me. ' All right.
I'll shut up now and henceforth. Can't prevent me
thinking though . . . Never mind ! . . . I'll show
yet . . .' He went to the door in a hurry, paused
with his head down, and came back, stepping

deliberately. 'I always thought that if a fellow could begin with a clean slate. . . . And now you . . . in a measure . . . yes . . . clean slate.' I waved my hand, and he marched out without looking back; the sound of his footfalls died out gradually behind the closed door—the unhesitating tread of a man walking in broad daylight.

"But as to me, left alone with the solitary candle, I remained strangely unenlightened. I was no longer young enough to behold at every turn the magnificence that besets our insignificant footsteps in good and in evil. I smiled to think that, after all, it was yet he, of us two, who had the light. And I felt sad. A clean slate, did he say? As if the initial word of each our destiny were not graven in imperishable characters upon the face of a rock."

CHAPTER XVIII.

"Six months afterwards my friend (he was a cynical, more than middle-aged bachelor, with a reputation for eccentricity, and owned a rice-mill) wrote to me, and judging, from the warmth of my recommendation, that I would like to hear, enlarged a little upon Jim's perfections. These were apparently of a quiet and effective sort. 'Not having been able so far to find more in my heart than a resigned toleration for any individual of my kind, I have lived till now alone in a house that even in this steaming climate could be considered as too big for one man. I have had him to live with me for some time past. It seems I haven't made a mistake.' It seemed to me on reading this letter that my friend had found in his heart more than tolerance for Jim,—that there were the beginnings of active liking. Of course he stated his grounds in a characteristic way. For one thing, Jim kept his freshness in the climate. Had he been a girl—my friend wrote—one could have said he was blooming—blooming modestly—like a violet, not like some of these blatant tropical flowers. He had been in the house for six weeks, and had not as yet attempted to slap him on the back, or address him as 'old boy,' or try to make him feel a superannuated fossil. He had nothing of the exasperating young man's chatter. He was good-tempered, had not much to say for himself, was not clever by any means, thank goodness—wrote my friend. It appeared, however, that Jim was clever enough to be quietly appreciative of his wit, while, on the other hand, he amused him by his naïveness. 'The dew is yet on him, and since I had the bright idea of giving him a room in the house and having him at meals I feel less withered myself. The other day he took it into his head to cross the room with no other purpose but to open a door for me ; and I felt more in touch with mankind than I had been for years. Ridiculous, isn't it ? Of course I guess there is something—some awful little scrape—which you know all about—but if I am sure that it is terribly heinous, I fancy one could manage to forgive it. For my part, I declare I am unable to imagine him guilty of anything much worse than robbing an orchard. *Is it* much worse ? Perhaps you ought to have told me ; but it is such a long time since we both turned saints that you may have forgotten

we too had sinned in our time? It may be that
some day I shall have to ask you, and then I shall
expect to be told. I don't care to question him
myself till I have some idea what it is. Moreover,
it's too soon as yet. Let him open the door a few
times more for me. . . .' Thus my friend. I
was trebly pleased—at Jim's shaping so well, at the
tone of the letter, at my own cleverness. Evidently
I had known what I was doing. I had read characters
aright, and so on. And what if something unexpected
and wonderful were to come of it? That evening,
reposing in a deck-chair under the shade of my own
poop awning (it was in Hong-Kong harbour), I laid
on Jim's behalf the first stone of a castle in Spain.

"I made a trip to the northward, and when I
returned I found another letter from my friend
waiting for me. It was the first envelope I tore
open. 'There are no spoons missing, as far as I
know,' ran the first line; 'I haven't been interested
enough to inquire. He is gone, leaving on the
breakfast-table a formal little note of apology,
which is either silly or heartless. Probably both
—and it's all one to me. Allow me to say, lest
you should have some more mysterious young men
in reserve, that I have shut up shop, definitely
and for ever. This is the last eccentricity I shall
be guilty of. Do not imagine for a moment that
I care a hang; but he is very much regretted at
tennis-parties, and for my own sake I've told a
plausible lie at the club. . . .' I flung the letter
aside and started looking through the batch on my
table, till I came upon Jim's handwriting. Would
you believe it? One chance in a hundred! But it is
always that hundredth chance! That little second
engineer of the *Patna* had turned up in a more or

less destitute state and got a temporary job of looking after the machinery of the mill. 'I couldn't stand the familiarity of the little beast,' Jim wrote from a seaport seven hundred miles south of the place where he should have been in clover. 'I am now for the time with Egström & Blake, ship-chandlers, as their—well—runner, to call the thing by its right name. For reference I gave them your name, which they know of course, and if you could write a word in my favour it would be a permanent employment.' I was utterly crushed under the ruins of my castle, but of course I wrote as desired. Before the end of the year my new charter took me that way, and I had an opportunity of seeing him.

"He was still with Egström & Blake, and we met in what they called 'our parlour' opening out of the store. He had that moment come in from boarding a ship, and confronted me head down, ready for a tussle. 'What have you got to say for yourself?' I began as soon as we had shaken hands. 'What I wrote you—nothing more,' he said stubbornly. 'Did the fellow blab—or what?' I asked. He looked up at me with a troubled smile. 'Oh no! He didn't. He made it a kind of confidential business between us. He was most damnably mysterious whenever I came over to the mill; he would wink at me in a respectful manner—as much as to say we know what we know. Infernally fawning and familiar—and that sort of thing . . .' He threw himself into a chair and stared down his legs. 'One day we happened to be alone and the fellow had the cheek to say, "Well, Mr James"— I was called Mr James there as if I had been the son—" here we are together once more. This is better than the old ship—ain't it?" ' . . . Wasn't

it appalling, eh? I looked at him, and he put on
a knowing air. "Don't you be uneasy, sir," he
says. "I know a gentleman when I see one, and
I know how a gentleman feels. I hope, though,
you will be keeping me on this job. I had a hard
time of it too, along of that rotten old *Patna* racket."
Jove! It was awful. I don't know what I should
have said or done if I had not just then heard Mr
Denver calling me in the passage. It was tiffin-time,
and we walked together across the yard and through
the garden to the bungalow. He began to chaff
me in his kindly way . . . I believe he liked me . . .'

"Jim was silent for a while.

"'I know he liked me. That's what made it so
hard. Such a splendid man! . . . That morning
he slipped his hand under my arm. . . . He, too,
was familiar with me.' He burst into a short laugh,
and dropped his chin on his breast. 'Pah! When
I remembered how that mean little beast had been
talking to me,' he began suddenly in a vibrating
voice, 'I couldn't bear to think of myself . . . I
suppose you know . . .' I nodded. . . . 'More
like a father,' he cried; his voice sank. 'I would
have had to tell him. I couldn't let it go on—
could I?' 'Well?' I murmured, after waiting a
while. 'I preferred to go,' he said slowly; 'this
thing must be buried.'

"We could hear in the shop Blake upbraiding
Egström in an abusive, strained voice. They had
been associated for many years, and every day
from the moment the doors were opened to the
last minute before closing, Blake, a little man with
sleek, jetty hair and unhappy, beady eyes, could
be heard rowing his partner incessantly with a sort
of scathing and plaintive fury. The sound of that

everlasting scolding was part of the place like the other fixtures ; even strangers would very soon come to disregard it completely unless it be perhaps to mutter ' Nuisance,' or to get up suddenly and shut the door of the ' parlour.' Egström himself, a raw-boned, heavy Scandinavian, with a busy manner and immense blonde whiskers, went on directing his people, checking parcels, making out bills or writing letters at a stand-up desk in the shop, and comported himself in that clatter exactly as though he had been stone-deaf. Now and again he would emit a bothered perfunctory ' Sssh,' which neither produced nor was expected to produce the slightest effect. ' They are very decent to me here,' said Jim. ' Blake's a little cad, but Egström's all right.' He stood up quickly, and walking with measured steps to a tripod telescope standing in the window and pointed at the roadstead, he applied his eye to it. ' There's that ship which had been becalmed outside all the morning has got a breeze now and is coming in,' he remarked patiently ; ' I must go and board.' We shook hands in silence, and he turned to go. ' Jim ! ' I cried. He looked round with his hand on the lock. ' You—you have thrown away something like a fortune.' He came back to me all the way from the door. ' Such a splendid old chap,' he said. ' How could I ? .How could I ? ' His lips twitched. ' Here it does not matter.' ' Oh ! you—you——' I began, and had to cast about for a suitable word, but before I became aware that there was no name that would just do, he was gone. I heard outside Egström's deep gentle voice saying cheerily, ' That's the *Sarah W. Granger*, Jimmy. You must manage to be first aboard ; ' and directly Blake struck in, screaming after the manner of an outraged cockatoo, 'Tell the captain we've got some of his mail here. That'll fetch him. D'ye hear, Mister What's-your-name?' And there was Jim answering Egström with something boyish in his tone. 'All right. I'll make a race of it.' He seemed to take refuge in the boat-sailing part of that sorry business.

"I did not see him again that trip, but on my next (I had a six months' charter) I went up to the store. Ten yards away from the door Blake's scolding met my ears, and when I came in he gave me a glance of utter wretchedness; Egström, all smiles, advanced, extending a large bony hand. 'Glad to see you, Captain. . . . Sssh. . . . Been thinking you were about due back here. What did you say, sir? . . . Sssh. . . . Oh! him! He has left us. Come into the parlour.' . . . After the slam of the door Blake's strained voice became faint, as the voice of one scolding desperately in a wilderness. . . . 'Put us to a great inconvenience, too. Used us badly—I must say . . .' 'Where's he gone to? Do you know?' I asked. 'No. It's no use asking either,' said Egström, standing be-whiskered and obliging before me with his arms hanging down his sides clumsily, and a thin silver watch-chain looped very low on a rucked-up blue serge waistcoat. 'A man like that don't go any-where in particular.' I was too concerned at the news to ask for the explanation of that pronounce-ment, and he went on. 'He left—let's see—the very day a steamer with returning pilgrims from the Red Sea put in here with two blades of her propeller gone. Three weeks ago now.' 'Wasn't there something said about the *Patna* case?' I asked, fearing the worst. He gave a start, and looked at me as if I had been a sorcerer. 'Why, yes! How do you know? Some of them were talking about it here. There was a captain or two, the manager of Vanlo's engineering shop at the harbour, two or three others, and myself. Jim was in here too, having a sandwich and a glass of beer; when we are busy—you see, captain—there's no time for a proper tiffin. He was standing by this table eating sandwiches, and the rest of us were round the telescope watching that steamer come in; and by-and-by Vanlo's manager began to talk about the chief of the *Patna;* he had done some repairs for him once, and from that he went on to tell us what an old ruin she was, and the money that had been made out of her. He came to mention her last voyage, and then we all struck in. Some said one thing and some another—not much—what you or any other man might say; and there was some laughing. Captain O'Brien of the *Sarah W. Granger,* a large, noisy old man with a stick—he was sitting listening to us in this arm-chair here—he let drive suddenly with his stick at the floor, and roars out, "Skunks!" . . . Made us all jump. Vanlo's manager winks at us and asks, "What's the matter, Captain O'Brien?" "Matter! matter!" the old man began to shout; "what are you Injuns laughing at? It's no laughing matter. It's a disgrace to human natur'—that's what it is. I would despise being seen in the same room with one of those men. Yes, sir!" He seemed to catch my eye like, and I had to speak out of civility. "Skunks!" says I, "of course, Captain O'Brien, and I wouldn't care to have them here myself, so you're quite safe in this room, Captain O'Brien. Have a little something cool to drink."

" Dam' your drink, Egström," says he, with a twinkle in his eye ; " when I want a drink I will shout for it. I am going to quit. It stinks here now." At this all the others burst out laughing, and out they go after the old man. And then, sir, that blasted Jim he puts down the sandwich he had in his hand and walks round the table to me ; there was his glass of beer poured out quite full. " I am off," he says—just like this. " It isn't half-past one yet," says I ; " you might snatch a smoke first." I thought he meant it was time for him to go down to his work. When I understood what he was up to, my arms fell—so ! Can't get a man like that every day, you know, sir ; a regular devil for sailing a boat : ready to go out miles to sea to meet ships in any sort of weather. More than once a captain would come in here full of it, and the first thing he would say would be, " That's a reckless sort of a lunatic you've got for water-clerk, Egström. I was feeling my way in at daylight under short canvas when there comes flying out of the mist right under my forefoot a boat half under water, sprays going over the mast-head, two frightened niggers on the bottom boards, a yelling fiend at the tiller. Hey ! hey ! Ship ahoy ! ahoy ! Captain ! Hey ! hey ! Egström & Blake's man first to speak to you ! Hey ! hey ! Egström & Blake ! Hallo ! hey ! whoop ! Kick the niggers—out reefs—a squall on at the time—shoots ahead whooping and yelling to me to make sail and he would give me a lead in—more like a demon than a man. Never saw a boat handled like that in all my life. Couldn't have been drunk—was he ? Such a quiet, soft-spoken chap too—blush like a girl when he came on board. . . ." I tell you, Captain Marlow,

nobody had a chance against us with a strange
ship when Jim was out. The other ship-chandlers
just kept their old customers, and . . .'

"Egström appeared overcome with emotion.

"'Why, sir—it seemed as though he wouldn't
mind going a hundred miles out to sea in an old
shoe to nab a ship for the firm. If the business
had been his own and all to make yet, he couldn't
have done more in that way. And now . . . all
at once . . . like this! Thinks I to myself: "Oho!
a rise in the screw—that's the trouble—is it? All
right," says I, "no need of all that fuss with me,
Jimmy. Just mention your figure. Anything in
reason." He looks at me as if he wanted to swallow
something that stuck in his throat. "I can't stop
with you." "What's that blooming joke?" I asks.
He shakes his head, and I could see in his eye he
was as good as gone already, sir. So I turned to
him and slanged him till all was blue. "What is it
you're running away from?" I asks. "Who has
been getting at you? What scared you? You
haven't as much sense as a rat; they don't clear
out from a good ship. Where do you expect to
get a better berth?—you this and you that." I
made him look sick, I can tell you. "This business
ain't going to sink," says I. He gave a big jump.
"Good-bye," he says, nodding at me like a lord;
"you ain't half a bad chap, Egström. I give you
my word that if you knew my reasons you wouldn't
care to keep me." "That's the biggest lie you ever
told in your life," says I; "I know my own mind."
He made me so mad that I had to laugh. "Can't
you really stop long enough to drink this glass of
beer here, you funny beggar, you?" I don't know
what came over him; he didn't seem able to find

the door ; something comical, I can tell you, captain. I drank the beer myself. "Well, if you're in such a hurry, here's luck to you in your own drink," says I ; "only, you mark my words, if you keep up this game you'll very soon find that the earth ain't big enough to hold you—that's all." He gave me one black look, and out he rushed with a face fit to scare little children.'

"Egström snorted bitterly, and combed one auburn whisker with knotty fingers. 'Haven't been able to get a man that was any good since. It's nothing but worry, worry, worry in business. And where might you have come across him, captain, if it's fair to ask ? '

"' He was the mate of the *Patna* that voyage,' I said, feeling that I owed some explanation. For a time Egström remained very still, with his fingers plunged in the hair at the side of his face, and then exploded. 'And who the devil cares about that ? ' 'I daresay no one,' I began . . . 'And what the devil is he—anyhow—for to go on like this ? ' He stuffed suddenly his left whisker into his mouth and stood amazed. 'Jee ! ' he exclaimed, 'I told him the earth wouldn't be big enough to hold his caper.' "

CHAPTER XIX.

" I HAVE told you these two episodes at length to show his manner of dealing with himself under the new conditions of his life. There were many others

of the sort, more than I could count on the fingers of
my two hands. They were all equally tinged by a
high-minded absurdity of intention which made their
futility profound and touching. To fling away your
daily bread so as to get your hands free for a grapple
with a ghost may be an act of prosaic heroism. Men
had done it before (though we who have lived know
full well that it is not the haunted soul but the
hungry body that makes an outcast), and men who
had eaten and meant to eat every day had applauded
the creditable folly. He was indeed unfortunate, for
all his recklessness could not carry him out from
under the shadow. There was always a doubt of
his courage. The truth seems to be that it is impossible to lay the ghost of a fact. You can face
it or shirk it—and I have come across a man or two
who could wink at their familiar shades. Obviously
Jim was not of the winking sort; but what I could
never make up my mind about was whether his line
of conduct amounted to shirking his ghost or to
facing him out.

"I strained my mental eyesight only to discover
that, as with the complexion of all our actions, the
shade of difference was so delicate that it was impossible to say. It might have been flight and it
might have been a mode of combat. To the common
mind he became known as a rolling stone, because
this was the funniest part: he did after a time
become perfectly known, and even notorious, within
the circle of his wanderings (which had a diameter
of, say, three thousand miles), in the same way as
an eccentric character is known to a whole country-
side. For instance, in Bankok, where he found
employment with Yucker Brothers, charterers and
teak merchants, it was almost pathetic to see him

go about in sunshine hugging his secret, which
was known to the very up-country logs on the river.
Schomberg, the keeper of the hotel where he boarded,
a hirsute Alsatian of manly bearing and an irrepressible retailer of all the scandalous gossip of the place,
would, with both elbows on the table, impart an
adorned version of the story to any guest who cared
to imbibe knowledge along with the more costly
liquors. 'And, mind you, the nicest fellow you could
meet,' would be his generous conclusion; 'quite
superior.' It says a lot for the casual crowd that
frequented Schomberg's establishment that Jim
managed to hang out in Bankok for a whole six
months. I remarked that people, perfect strangers,
took to him as one takes to a nice child. His manner
was reserved, but it was as though his personal
appearance, his hair, his eyes, his smile, made friends
for him wherever he went. And, of course, he was
no fool. I heard Siegmund Yucker (native of Swit-
zerland), a gentle creature ravaged by a cruel
dyspepsia, and so frightfully lame that his head
swung through a quarter of a circle at every step he
took, declare appreciatively that for one so young he
was ' of great gabasidy,' as though it had been a mere
question of cubic contents. 'Why not send him up
country?' I suggested anxiously. (Yucker Brothers
had concessions and teak forests in the interior.)
'If he has capacity, as you say, he will soon get hold
of the work. And physically he is very fit. His
health is always excellent.' 'Ach! It's a great
ting in dis goundry to be vree vrom tispep-shia,'
sighed poor Yucker enviously, casting a stealthy
glance at the pit of his ruined stomach. I left him
drumming pensively on his desk and muttering,
' Es ist ein idee. Es ist ein idee.' Unfortunately,

that very evening an unpleasant affair took place
in the hotel.

"I don't know that I blame Jim very much,
but it was a truly regrettable incident. It belonged to the lamentable species of bar-room scuffles,
and the other party to it was a cross-eyed Dane
of sorts whose visiting-card recited under his mis-
begotten name : first lieutenant in the Royal
Siamese Navy. The fellow, of course, was utterly
hopeless at billiards, but did not like to be beaten,
I suppose. He had had enough to drink to turn
nasty after the sixth game, and made some scornful
remark at Jim's expense. Most of the people there
didn't hear what was said, and those who had heard
seemed to have had all precise recollection scared
out of them by the appalling nature of the consequences that immediately ensued. It was very
lucky for the Dane that he could swim, because the
room opened on a verandah and the Menam flowed
below very wide and black. A boat-load of Chinamen, bound, as likely as not, on some thieving
expedition, fished out the officer of the King of Siam,
and Jim turned up at about midnight on board my
ship without a hat. 'Everybody in the room seemed
to know,' he said, gasping yet from the contest, as
it were. He was rather sorry, on general principles,
for what had happened, though in this case there
had been, he said, ' no option.' But what dismayed
him was to find the nature of his burden as well
known to everybody as though he had gone about
all that time carrying it on his shoulders. Naturally
after this he couldn't remain in the place. He
was universally condemned for the brutal violence,
so unbecoming a man in his delicate position ; some
maintained he had been disgracefully drunk at the

time ; others criticised his want of tact. Even
Schomberg was very much annoyed. ' He is a very
nice young man,' he said argumentatively to me,
' but the lieutenant is a first-rate fellow too. He
dines every night at my *table d'hôte*, you know.
And there's a billiard-cue broken. I can't allow
that. First thing this morning I went over with
my apologies to the lieutenant, and I think I've
made it all right for myself ; but only think, captain,
if everybody started such games ! Why, the man
might have been drowned ! And here I can't run
out into the next street and buy a new cue. I've
got to write to Europe for them. No, no ! A
temper like that won't do ! ' . . . He was extremely
sore on the subject.

" This was the worst incident of all in his—his
retreat. Nobody could deplore it more than myself ;
for if, as somebody said hearing him mentioned, ' Oh
yes ! I know. He has knocked about a good deal
out here,' yet he had somehow avoided being battered
and chipped in the process. This last affair, however,
made me seriously uneasy, because if his exquisite
sensibilities were to go the length of involving him
in pot-house shindies, he would lose his name of an
inoffensive, if aggravating, fool, and acquire that of
a common loafer. For all my confidence in him I
could not help reflecting that in such cases from the
name to the thing itself is but a step. I suppose
you will understand that by that time I could not
think of washing my hands of him. I took him
away from Bankok in my ship, and we had a longish
passage. It was pitiful to see how he shrank within
himself. A seaman, even if a mere passenger, takes
an interest in a ship, and looks at the sea-life around
him with the critical enjoyment of a painter, for

instance, looking at another man's work. In every
sense of the expression he is ' on deck ' ; but my Jim,
for the most part, skulked down below as though he
had been a stowaway. He infected me so that I
avoided speaking on professional matters, such as
would suggest themselves naturally to two sailors
during a passage. For whole days we did not
exchange a word ; I felt extremely unwilling to
give orders to my officers in his presence. Often,
when alone with him on deck or in the cabin, we
didn't know what to do with our eyes.

" I placed him with De Jongh, as you know, glad
enough to dispose of him in any way, yet persuaded
that his position was now growing intolerable. He
had lost some of that elasticity which had enabled
him to rebound back into his uncompromising position after every overthrow. One day, coming ashore,
I saw him standing on the quay ; the water of the
roadstead and the sea in the offing made one smooth
ascending plane, and the outermost ships at anchor
seemed to ride motionless in the sky. He was waiting
for his boat, which was being loaded at our feet
with packages of small stores for some vessel ready
to leave. After exchanging greetings, we remained
silent—side by side. ' Jove ! ' he said suddenly,
' this is killing work.'

" He smiled at me ; I must say he generally could
manage a smile. I made no reply. I knew very
well he was not alluding to his duties ; he had an
easy time of it with De Jongh. Nevertheless, as
soon as he had spoken I became completely convinced
that the work was killing. I did not even look at
him. ' Would you like,' said I, ' to leave this part
of the world altogether ; try California or the West
Coast ? I'll see what I can do . . .' He interrupted

me a little scornfully. 'What difference would it make?' . . . I felt at once convinced that he was right. It would make no difference; it was not relief he wanted; I seemed to perceive dimly that what he wanted, what he was, as it were, waiting for, was something not easy to define—something in the nature of an opportunity. I had given him many opportunities, but they had been merely opportunities to earn his bread. Yet what more could any man do? The position struck me as hopeless, and poor Brierly's saying recurred to me, 'Let him creep twenty feet underground and stay there.' Better that, I thought, than this waiting above ground for the impossible. Yet one could not be sure even of that. There and then, before his boat was three oars' lengths away from the quay, I had made up my mind to go and consult Stein in the evening.

"This Stein was a wealthy and respected merchant. His 'house' (because it was a house, Stein & Co., and there was some sort of partner who, as Stein said, 'looked after the Moluccas') had a large inter-island business, with a lot of trading posts established in the most out-of-the-way places for collecting the produce. His wealth and his respectability were not exactly the reasons why I was anxious to seek his advice. I desired to confide my difficulty to him because he was one of the most trustworthy men I had ever known. The gentle light of a simple, unwearied, as if were, and intelligent good-nature illumined his long hairless face. It had deep downward folds, and was pale as of a man who had always led a sedentary life—which was indeed very far from being the case. His hair was thin, and brushed back from a massive and lofty forehead.

One fancied that at twenty he must have looked
very much like what he was now at threescore. It
was a student's face ; only the eyebrows nearly all
white, thick and bushy, together with the resolute
searching glance that came from under them, were
not in accord with his, I may say, learned appearance.
He was tall and loose-jointed ; his slight stoop,
together with an innocent smile, made him appear
benevolently ready to lend you his ear ; his long arms
with pale big hands had rare deliberate gestures of a
pointing out, demonstrating kind. I speak of him at
length, because under this exterior, and in conjunc-
tion with an upright and indulgent nature, this man
possessed an intrepidity of spirit and a physical
courage that could have been called reckless had it
not been like a natural function of the body—say
good digestion, for instance—completely unconscious of itself. It is sometimes said of a man that
he carries his life in his hand. Such a saying would
have been inadequate if applied to him ; during the
early part of his existence in the East he had been
playing ball with it. All this was in the past, but I
knew the story of his life and the origin of his
fortune. He was also a naturalist of some distinction,
or perhaps I should say a learned collector. Ento-
mology was his special study. His collection of
Buprestidæ and *Longicorns*—beetles all—horrible
miniature monsters, looking malevolent in death
and immobility, and his cabinet of butterflies,
beautiful and hovering under the glass of cases on
lifeless wings, had spread his fame far over the earth.
The name of this merchant, adventurer, sometime
adviser of a Malay sultan (to whom he never alluded
otherwise than as ' my poor Mohammed Bonso '),
had, on account of a few bushels of dead insects,

become known to learned persons in Europe, who could have had no conception, and certainly would not have cared to know anything, of his life or character. I, who knew, considered him an eminently suitable person to receive my confidences about Jim's difficulties as well as my own."

CHAPTER XX.

"LATE in the evening I entered his study, after traversing an imposing but empty dining-room very dimly lit. The house was silent. I was preceded by an elderly grim Javanese servant in a sort of livery of white jacket and yellow sarong, who, after throwing the door open, exclaimed low, 'O master!' and stepping aside, vanished in a mysterious way as though he had been a ghost only momentarily embodied for that particular service. Stein turned round with the chair, and in the same movement his spectacles seemed to get pushed up on his forehead. He welcomed me in his quiet and humorous voice. Only one corner of the vast room, the corner in which stood his writing-desk, was strongly lighted by a shaded reading-lamp, and the rest of the spacious apartment melted into shapeless gloom like a cavern. Narrow shelves filled with dark boxes of uniform shape and colour ran round the walls, not from floor to ceiling, but in a sombre belt about four feet broad. Catacombs of beetles. Wooden tablets were hung above at irregular intervals. The light reached one of them, and the word *Coleoptera* written in gold

letters glittered mysteriously upon a vast dimness.
The glass cases containing the collection of butterflies were ranged in three long rows upon slender-
legged little tables. One of these cases had been
removed from its place and stood on the desk, which
was bestrewn with oblong slips of paper blackened
with minute handwriting.

" ' So you see me—so,' he said. His hand hovered
over the case where a butterfly in solitary grandeur
spread out dark bronze wings, seven inches or more
across, with exquisite white veinings and a gorgeous
border of yellow spots. ' Only one specimen like
this they have in *your* London, and then—no more.
To my small native town this my collection I shall
bequeath. Something of me. The best.'

" He bent forward in the chair and gazed intently,
his chin over the front of the case. I stood at his
back. ' Marvellous,' he whispered, and seemed to
forget my presence. His history was curious. He
had been born in Bavaria, and when a youth of
twenty-two had taken an active part in the revolu-
tionary movement of 1848. Heavily compromised,
he managed to make his escape, and at first found a
refuge with a poor republican watchmaker in Trieste.
From there he made his way to Tripoli with a stock
of cheap watches to hawk about,—not a very great
opening truly, but it turned out lucky enough, because it was there he came upon a Dutch traveller—
a rather famous man, I believe, but I don't remember
his name. It was that naturalist who, engaging him
as a sort of assistant, took him to the East. They
travelled in the Archipelago together and separately,
collecting insects and birds, for four years or more.
Then the naturalist went home, and Stein, having no
home to go to, remained with an old trader he had

come across in his journeys in the interior of Celebes—
if Celebes may be said to have an interior. This old
Scotsman, the only white man allowed to reside in
the country at the time, was a privileged friend of
the chief ruler of Wajo States, who was a woman.
I often heard Stein relate how that chap, who was
slightly paralysed on one side, had introduced him
to the native court a short time before another
stroke carried him off. He was a heavy man with a
patriarchal white beard, and of imposing stature.
He came into the council-hall where all the rajahs,
pangerans, and headmen were assembled, with the
queen, a fat wrinkled woman (very free in her
speech, Stein said), reclining on a high couch under
a canopy. He dragged his leg, thumping with his
stick, and grasped Stein's arm, leading him right
up to the couch. 'Look, queen, and you rajahs,
this is my son,' he proclaimed in a stentorian voice.
'I have traded with your fathers, and when I die
he shall trade with you and your sons.'

"By means of this simple formality Stein inherited
the Scotsman's privileged position and all his stock-
in-trade, together with a fortified house on the banks
of the only navigable river in the country. Shortly
afterwards the old queen, who was so free in her
speech, died, and the country became disturbed by
various pretenders to the throne. Stein joined the
party of a younger son, the one of whom thirty
years later he never spoke otherwise but as 'my poor
Mohammed Bonzo.' They both became the heroes
of innumerable exploits; they had wonderful adventures, and once stood a siege in the Scotsman's
house for a month, with only a score of followers
against a whole army. I believe the natives talk of
that war to this day. Meantime, it seems, Stein

never failed to annex on his own account every
butterfly or beetle he could lay hands on. After
some eight years of war, negotiations, false truces,
sudden outbreaks, reconciliation, treachery, and so
on, and just as peace seemed at last permanently
established, his 'poor Mohammed Bonzo' was
assassinated at the gate of his own royal residence
while dismounting in the highest spirits on his
return from a successful deer-hunt. This event
rendered Stein's position extremely insecure, but
he would have stayed perhaps had it not been
that a short time afterwards he lost Mohammed's
sister (' my dear wife the princess,' he used to say
solemnly), by whom he had had a daughter—mother
and child both dying within three days of each
other from some infectious fever. He left the
country, which this cruel loss had made unbearable
to him. Thus ended the first and adventurous part
of his existence. What followed was so different
that, but for the reality of sorrow which remained
with him, this strange past must have resembled a
dream. He had a little money ; he started life
afresh, and in the course of years acquired a con-
siderable fortune. At first he had travelled a good
deal amongst the islands, but age had stolen upon
him, and of late he seldom left his spacious house
three miles out of town, with an extensive garden,
and surrounded by stables, offices, and bamboo
cottages for his servants and dependants, of whom he
had many. He drove in his buggy every morning to
town, where he had an office with white and Chinese
clerks. He owned a small fleet of schooners and
native craft, and dealt in island produce on a large
scale. For the rest he lived solitary, but not mis-
anthropic, with his books and his collection, classing

and arranging specimens, corresponding with ento-
mologists in Europe, writing up a descriptive
catalogue of his treasures. Such was the history of
the man whom I had come to consult upon Jim's
case without any definite hope. Simply to hear
what he would have to say would have been a relief.
I was very anxious, but I respected the intense,
almost passionate, absorption with which he looked
at a butterfly, as though on the bronze sheen of these
frail wings, in the white tracings, in the gorgeous
markings, he could see other things, an image of
something as perishable and defying destruction as
these delicate and lifeless tissues displaying a splendour unmarred by death.

" ' Marvellous ! ' he repeated, looking up at me.
' Look ! The beauty—but that is nothing—look
at the accuracy, the harmony. And so fragile !
And so strong ! And so exact ! This is Nature—
the balance of colossal forces. Every star is so—
and every blade of grass stands *so*—and the mighty
Kosmos in perfect equilibrium produces—this. This
wonder ; this masterpiece of Nature—the great
artist.'

" ' Never heard an entomologist go on like this,' I
observed cheerfully. ' Masterpiece ! And what of
man ? '

" ' Man is amazing, but he is not a masterpiece,'
he said, keeping his eyes fixed on the glass case.
' Perhaps the artist was a little mad. Eh ? What
do you think ? Sometimes it seems to me that man
is come where he is not wanted, where there is no
place for him ; for if not, why should he want
all the place ? Why should he run about here and
there making a great noise about himself, talking
about the stars, disturbing the blades of grass ? . . .'

" ' Catching butterflies,' I chimed in.

" He smiled, threw himself back in his chair, and stretched his legs. ' Sit down,' he said. ' I captured this rare specimen myself one very fine morning. And I had a very big emotion. You don't know what it is for a collector to capture such a rare specimen. You can't know.'

" I smiled at my ease in a rocking-chair. His eyes seemed to look far beyond the wall at which they stared ; and he narrated how, one night, a messenger arrived from his ' poor Mohammed,' requiring his presence at the ' residenz '—as he called it—which was distant some nine or ten miles by a bridle-path over a cultivated plain, with patches of forest here and there. Early in the morning he started from his fortified house, after embracing his little Emma, and leaving the ' princess,' his wife, in command. He described how she came with him as far as the gate, walking with one hand on the neck of his horse ; she had on a white jacket, gold pins in her hair, and a brown leather belt over her left shoulder with a revolver in it. ' She talked as women will talk,' he said, ' telling me to be careful, and to try to get back before dark, and what a great wickedness it was for me to go alone. We were at war, and the country was not safe ; my men were putting up bullet-proof shutters to the house and loading their rifles, and she begged me to have no fear for her. She could defend the house against anybody till I returned. And I laughed with pleasure a little. I liked to see her so brave and young and strong. I too was young then. At the gate she caught hold of my hand and gave it one squeeze and fell back. I made my horse stand still outside till I heard the bars of the gate put up behind me. There was a great enemy of mine, a great noble—and a great rascal too—roaming with a band in the neighbourhood. I cantered for four or five miles ; there had been rain in the night, but the mists had gone up, up— and the face of the earth was clean ; it lay smiling to me, so fresh and innocent—like a little child. Suddenly somebody fires a volley—twenty shots at least it seemed to me. I hear bullets sing in my ear, and my hat jumps to the back of my head. It was a little intrigue, you understand. They got my poor Mohammed to send for me and then laid that ambush. I see it all in a minute, and I think—— This wants a little management. My pony snort, jump, and stand, and I fall slowly forward with my head on his mane. He begins to walk, and with one eye I could see over his neck a faint cloud of smoke hanging in front of a clump of bamboos to my left. I think—— Aha ! my friends, why you not wait long enough before you shoot ? This is not yet *gelungen*. Oh no ! I get hold of my revolver with my right hand—quiet—quiet. After all, there were only seven of these rascals. They get up from the grass and start running with their sarongs tucked up, waving spears above their heads, and yelling to each other to look out and catch the horse, because I was dead. I let them come as close as the door here, and then bang, bang, bang—take aim each time too. One more shot I fire at a man's back, but I miss. Too far already. And then I sit alone on my horse with the clean earth smiling at me, and there are the bodies of three men lying on the ground. One was curled up like a dog, another on his back had an arm over his eyes as if to keep off the sun, and the third man he draws up his leg very slowly and makes it with one kick straight again. I watch

him very carefully from my horse, but there is no
more—*bleibt ganz ruhig*—keep still, so. And as I
looked at his face for some sign of life I observed
something like a faint shadow pass over his forehead.
It was the shadow of this butterfly. Look at the
form of the wing. This species fly high with a
strong flight. I raised my eyes and I saw him
fluttering away. I think—— Can it be possible?
And then I lost him. I dismounted and went on
very slow, leading my horse and holding my revolver
with one hand and my eyes darting up and down
and right and left, everywhere! At last I saw him
sitting on a small heap of dirt ten feet away. At
once my heart began to beat quick. I let go my
horse, keep my revolver in one hand, and with the
other snatch my soft felt hat off my head. One step.
Steady. Another step. Flop! I got him! When I
got up I shook like a leaf with excitement, and when
I opened these beautiful wings and made sure what
a rare and so extraordinary perfect specimen I had,
my head went round and my legs became so weak
with emotion that I had to sit on the ground. I had
greatly desired to possess myself of a specimen of
that species when collecting for the professor. I
took long journeys and underwent great privations;
I had dreamed of him in my sleep, and here suddenly
I had him in my fingers—for myself! In the words
of the poet ' (he pronounced it ' boet ')—

> ' " So halt' ich's endlich denn in meinen Händen,
> Und nenn' es in gewissem Sinne mein." '

He gave to the last word the emphasis of a suddenly
lowered voice, and withdrew his eyes slowly from
my face. He began to charge a long-stemmed pipe

usily and in silence, then, pausing with his thumb
n the orifice of the bowl, looked again at me
ignificantly.

"'Yes, my good friend. On that day I had
othing to desire; I had greatly annoyed my
rincipal enemy; I was young, strong; I had
riendship; I had the love' (he said 'lof') 'of
woman, a child I had, to make my heart very full—
nd even what I had once dreamed in my sleep had
ome into my hand too!'

"He struck a match, which flared violently. His
houghtful placid face twitched once.

"'Friend, wife, child,' he said slowly, gazing at
he small flame—'phoo!' The match was blown
ut. He sighed and turned again to the glass case.
The frail and beautiful wings quivered faintly, as
f his breath had for an instant called back to life
hat gorgeous object of his dreams.

"'The work,' he began suddenly, pointing to the
cattered slips, and in his usual gentle and cheery
one, 'is making great progress. I have been this
are specimen describing. . . . Na! And what is
our good news?'

"'To tell you the truth, Stein,' I said with an
ffort that surprised me, 'I came here to describe
specimen. . . .'

"'Butterfly?' he asked, with an unbelieving and
umorous eagerness.

"'Nothing so perfect,' I answered, feeling sud-
enly dispirited with all sorts of doubts. 'A man!'

"'Ach so!' he murmured, and his smiling
ountenance, turned to me, became grave. Then
fter looking at me for a while he said slowly,
Well—I am a man too.'

"Here you have him as he was; he knew how

to be so generously encouraging as to make
scrupulous man hesitate on the brink of conf
dence ; but if I did hesitate it was not for long.

" He heard me out, sitting with crossed leg
Sometimes his head would disappear completely i
a great eruption of smoke, and a sympathetic grov
would come out from the cloud. When I finished l
uncrossed his legs, laid down his pipe, leaned forwar
towards me earnestly with his elbows on the arm
of his chair, the tips of his fingers together.

" ' I understand very well. He is romantic.'

" He had diagnosed the case for me, and at first
was quite startled to find how simple it was ; an
indeed our conference resembled so much a medic:
consultation—Stein, of learned aspect sitting in a
arm-chair before his desk ; I, anxious, in another
facing him, but a little to one side—that it seeme
natural to ask—

" ' What's good for it ? '

" He lifted up a long forefinger.

" ' There is only one remedy ! One thing alon
can us from being ourselves cure ! ' The finge
came down on the desk with a smart rap. Th
case which he had made to look so simple befor
became if possible still simpler—and altogethe
hopeless. There was a pause. ' Yes,' said I, ' strictl
speaking, the question is not how to get cured, bu
how to live.'

" He approved with his head, a little sadly as i
seemed. ' Ja ! ja ! In general, adapting the word
of your great poet : That is the question. . . .' H
went on nodding sympathetically. . . . ' How t
be ! Ach ! How to be.'

" He stood up with the tips of his fingers restin,
on the desk.

" ' We want in so many different ways to be,' e began again. ' This magnificent butterfly finds little heap of dirt and sits still on it ; but man he ill never on his heap of mud keep still. He want o be so, and again he want to be so.' . . . He moved his hand up, then down. . . . ' He wants o be a saint, and he wants to be a devil—and every ime he shuts his eyes he sees himself as a very fine ellow—so fine as he can never be. . . . In a ream. . . .'

" He lowered the glass lid, the automatic lock licked sharply, and taking up the case in both ands he bore it religiously away to its place, assing out of the bright circle of the lamp into he ring of fainter light—into shapeless dusk at ast. It had an odd effect—as if these few steps ad carried him out of this concrete and perplexed orld. His tall form, as though robbed of its sub-tance, hovered noiselessly over invisible things with tooping and indefinite movements ; his voice, heard a that remoteness where he could be glimpsed aysteriously busy with immaterial cares, was no onger incisive, seemed to roll voluminous and grave —mellowed by distance.

" ' And because you not always can keep your eyes hut there comes the real trouble—the heart pain —the world pain. I tell you, my friend, it is not ood for you to find you cannot make your dream ome true, for the reason that you not strong enough re, or not clever enough. *Ja!* . . . And all the ime you are such a fine fellow too ! *Wie? Was? ott in Himmel!* How can that be ? Ha ! ha ! ha ! '

" The shadow prowling amongst the graves of utterflies laughed boisterously.

" ' Yes ! Very funny this terrible thing is. A

man that is born falls into a dream like a ma
who falls into the sea. If he tries to climb o
into the air as inexperienced people endeavour t
do, he drowns—*nicht war?* . . . No! I tell you
The way is to the destructive element submit you
self, and with the exertions of your hands and fee
in the water make the deep, deep sea keep you u
So if you ask me—how to be?'

"His voice leaped up extraordinarily strong, a
though away there in the dusk he had been inspire
by some whisper of knowledge. 'I will tell you
For that too there is only one way.'

"With a hasty swish swish of his slippers h
loomed up in the ring of faint light, and suddenl
appeared in the bright circle of the lamp. Hi
extended hand aimed at my breast like a pistol
his deep-set eyes seemed to pierce through me, bu
his twitching lips uttered no word, and the auster
exaltation of a certitude seen in the dusk vanishe
from his face. The hand that had been pointing a
my breast fell, and by-and-by, coming a step nearer
he laid it gently on my shoulder. There were things
he said mournfully, that perhaps could never b
told, only he had lived so much alone that sometime
he forgot—he forgot. The light had destroyed th
assurance which had inspired him in the distan
shadows. He sat down and, with both elbows o
the desk, rubbed his forehead. 'And yet it is true—
it is true. In the destructive element immerse.' . .
He spoke in a subdued tone, without looking at me
one hand on each side of his face. 'That was th
way. To follow the dream, and again to follow th
dream—and so—*ewig—usque ad finem*. . . .' Th
whisper of his conviction seemed to open before m
a vast and uncertain expanse, as of a crepuscula

orizon on a plain at dawn—or was it, perchance, at
the coming of the night ? One had not the courage
to decide ; but it was a charming and deceptive
light, throwing the impalpable poesy of its dimness
over pitfalls—over graves. His life had begun in
sacrifice, in enthusiasm for generous ideas ; he had
travelled very far, on various ways, on strange
paths, and whatever he followed it had been without
altering, and therefore without shame and without
regret. In so far he was right. That was the way,
no doubt. Yet for all that the great plain on which
men wander amongst graves and pitfalls remained
very desolate under the impalpable poesy of its
crepuscular light, overshadowed in the centre,
circled with a bright edge as if surrounded by an
abyss full of flames. When at last I broke the silence
it was to express the opinion that no one could be
more romantic than himself.

" He shook his head slowly, and afterwards looked
at me with a patient and inquiring glance. It was
a shame, he said. There we were sitting and talking
like two boys, instead of putting our heads together
to find something practical—a practical remedy—for
the evil—for the great evil—he repeated, with a
humorous and indulgent smile. For all that, our
talk did not grow more practical. We avoided
pronouncing Jim's name as though we had tried to
keep flesh and blood out of our discussion, or he
were nothing but an erring spirit, a suffering and
nameless shade. ' Na ! ' said Stein, rising. ' To-
night you sleep here, and in the morning we shall do
something practical—practical. . . .' He lit a two-
branched candlestick and led the way. We passed
through empty dark rooms, escorted by gleams from
the lights Stein carried. They glided along the

waxed floors, sweeping here and there over the
polished surface of a table, leaped upon a fragmentary
curve of a piece of furniture, or flashed perpen
dicularly in and out of distant mirrors, while the
forms of two men and the flicker of two flames
could be seen for a moment stealing silently across
the depths of a crystalline void. He walked slowly
a pace in advance with stooping courtesy; there
was a profound, as it were a listening, quietude on
his face; the long flaxen locks mixed with white
threads were scattered thinly upon his slightly
bowed neck.

" ' He is romantic—romantic,' he repeated. ' And
that is very bad—very bad. . . . Very good, too,'
he added. ' But *is he?*' I queried.

" ' *Gewiss*,' he said, and stood still holding up the
candelabrum, but without looking at me. ' Evident
What is it that by inward pain makes him know
himself? What is it that for you and me makes
him—exist?'

" At that moment it was difficult to believe in
Jim's existence—starting from a country parsonage,
blurred by crowds of men as by clouds of dust,
silenced by the clashing claims of life and death
in a material world—but his imperishable reality
came to me with a convincing, with an irresistible
force! I saw it vividly, as though in our progress
through the lofty silent rooms amongst fleeting
gleams of light and the sudden revelations of human
figures stealing with flickering flames within un
fathomable and pellucid depths, we had approached
nearer to absolute Truth, which, like Beauty itself,
floats elusive, obscure, half submerged, in the silent
still waters of mystery. ' Perhaps he is,' I ad

mitted with a slight laugh, whose unexpectedly loud reverberation made me lower my voice directly; 'but I am sure you are.' With his head dropping on his breast and the light held high he began to walk again. 'Well—I exist too,' he said.

"He preceded me. My eyes followed his movements, but what I did see was not the head of the firm, the welcome guest at afternoon receptions, the correspondent of learned societies, the entertainer of stray naturalists; I saw only the reality of his destiny, which he had known how to follow with unfaltering footsteps, that life begun in humble surroundings, rich in generous enthusiasms, in friendship, love, war—in all the exalted elements of romance. At the door of my room he faced me. 'Yes,' I said, as though carrying on a discussion, 'and amongst other things you dreamed foolishly of a certain butterfly; but when one fine morning your dream came in your way you did not let the splendid opportunity escape. Did you? Whereas he . . .' Stein lifted his hand. 'And do you know how many opportunities I let escape; how many dreams I had lost that had come in my way?' He shook his head regretfully. 'It seems to me that some would have been very fine—if I had made them come true. Do you know how many? Perhaps I myself don't know.' 'Whether his were fine or not,' I said, 'he knows of one which he certainly did not catch.' 'Everybody knows of one or two like that,' said Stein; 'and that is the trouble—the great trouble. . . .'

"He shook hands on the threshold, peered into my room under his raised arm. 'Sleep well. And

H

to-morrow we must do something practical—
practical. . . .'

"Though his own room was beyond mine I saw
him return the way he came. He was going back
to his butterflies."

CHAPTER XXI.

"I DON'T suppose any of you had ever heard of
Patusan ? " Marlow resumed, after a silence occupied
in the careful lighting of a cigar. "It does not
matter ; there's many a heavenly body in the lot
crowding upon us of a night that mankind had
never heard of, it being outside the sphere of its
activities and of no earthly importance to anybody
but to the astronomers who are paid to talk learnedly
about its composition, weight, path—the irregularities of its conduct, the aberrations of its light,—a
sort of scientific scandal-mongering. Thus with
Patusan. It was referred to knowingly in the inner
government circles in Batavia, especially as to its
irregularities and aberrations, and it was known by
name to some few, very few, in the mercantile world.
Nobody, however, had been there, and I suspect no
one desired to go there in person, just as an astron-
omer, I should fancy, would strongly object to being
transported into a distant heavenly body, where,
parted from his earthly emoluments, he would be
bewildered by the view of an unfamiliar heavens.
However, neither heavenly bodies nor astronomers
have anything to do with Patusan. It was Jim
who went there. I only meant you to understand
that had Stein arranged to send him into a star of

the fifth magnitude the change could not have been greater. He left his earthly failings behind him and that sort of reputation he had, and there was a totally new set of conditions for his imaginative faculty to work upon. Entirely new, entirely remarkable. And he got hold of them in a remarkable way.

"Stein was the man who knew more about Patusan than anybody else. More than was known in the government circles I suspect. I have no doubt he had been there, either in his butterfly-hunting days or later on, when he tried in his incorrigible way to season with a pinch of romance the fattening dishes of his commercial kitchen. There were very few places in the Archipelago he had not seen in the original dusk of their being, before light (and even electric light) had been carried into them for the sake of better morality and—and—well—the greater profit too. It was at breakfast of the morning following our talk about Jim that he mentioned the place, after I had quoted poor Brierly's remark : 'Let him creep twenty feet underground and stay there.' He looked up at me with interested attention, as though I had been a rare insect. 'This could be done too,' he remarked, sipping his coffee. 'Bury him in some sort,' I explained. 'One doesn't like to do it of course, but it would be the best thing, seeing what he is.' 'Yes ; he is young,' Stein mused. "The youngest human being now in existence,' I affirmed. ' *Schön.* There's Patusan,' he went on in the same tone. . . . 'And the woman is dead now,' he added incomprehensibly.

"Of course I don't know that story ; I can only guess that once before Patusan had been used as a grave for some sin, trangression, or misfortune. It is impossible to suspect Stein. The only woman that had ever existed for him was the Malay girl he called 'My wife the princess,' or, more rarely, in moments of expansion, 'the mother of my Emma.' Who was the woman he had mentioned in connection with Patusan I can't say; but from his allusions I understand she had been an educated and very good-looking Dutch-Malay girl, with a tragic or perhaps only a pitiful history, whose most painful part no doubt was her marriage with a Malacca Portuguese who had been clerk in some commercial house in the Dutch colonies. I gathered from Stein that this man was an unsatisfactory person in more ways than one, all being more or less indefinite and offensive. It was solely for his wife's sake that Stein had appointed him manager of Stein & Co's trading post in Patusan; but commercially the arrangement was not a success, at any rate for the firm, and now the woman had died, Stein was disposed to try another agent there. The Portuguese, whose name was Cornelius, considered himself a very deserving but ill-used person, entitled by his abilities to a better position. This man Jim would have to relieve. 'But I don't think he will go away from the place,' remarked Stein. 'That has nothing to do with me. It was only for the sake of the woman that I . . . But as I think there is a daughter left, I shall let him, if he likes to stay, keep the old house.

"Patusan is a remote district of a native-ruled State, and the chief settlement bears the same name. At a point on the river about forty miles from the sea, where the first houses come into view, there can be seen rising above the level of the forests the summits of two steep hills very close together, and separated by what looks like a deep fissure, the cleavage of some mighty stroke. As a matter of fact, the valley between is nothing but a narrow ravine ; the appearance from the settlement is of one irregularly conical hill split in two, and with the two halves leaning slightly apart. On the third day after the full, the moon, as seen from the open space in front of Jim's house (he had a very fine house in the native style when I visited him), rose exactly behind these hills, its diffused light at first throwing the two masses into intensely black relief, and then the nearly perfect disc, glowing ruddily, appeared, gliding upwards between the sides of the chasm, till it floated away above the summits, as if escaping from a yawning grave in gentle triumph. 'Wonderful effect,' said Jim by my side. 'Worth seeing. Is it not ? '

" And this question was put with a note of personal pride that made me smile, as though he had had a hand in regulating that unique spectacle. He had regulated so many things in Patusan ! Things that would have appeared as much beyond his control as the motions of the moon and the stars.

" It was inconceivable. That was the distinctive quality of the part into which Stein and I had tumbled him unwittingly, with no other notion than to get him out of the way ; out of his own way, be it understood. That was our main purpose, though, I own, I might have had another motive which had influenced me a little. I was about to go home for a time ; and it may be I desired, more than I was aware of myself, to dispose of him—to dispose of him, you understand—before I left. I was going home, and he had come to me from there, with his miserable trouble and his shadowy claim, like a man panting under a burden in a mist. I cannot say I had ever seen him distinctly—not even to this day, after I had my last view of him; but it seemed to me that the less I understood the more I was bound to him in the name of that doubt which is the inseparable part of our knowledge. I did not know so much more about myself. And then, I repeat, I was going home—to that home distant enough for all its hearthstones to be like one hearthstone, by which the humblest of us has the right to sit. We wander in our thousands over the face of the earth, the illustrious and the obscure, earning beyond the seas our fame, our money, or only a crust of bread; but it seems to me that for each of us going home must be like going to render an account. We return to face our superiors, our kindred, our friends— those whom we obey, and those whom we love; but even they who have neither, the most free, lonely, irresponsible and bereft of ties,—even those for whom home holds no dear face, no familiar voice,—even they have to meet the spirit that dwells within the land, under its sky, in its air, in its valleys, and on its rises, in its fields, in its waters and its trees—a mute friend, judge, and inspirer. Say what you like, to get its joy, to breathe its peace, to face its truth, one must return with a clear conscience. All this may seem to you sheer sentimentalism; and indeed very few of us have the will or the capacity to look consciously under the surface of familiar emotions. There are the girls we love, the men we look up to, the tenderness, the friendships, the opportunities, the pleasures! But the fact remains that you must touch your reward with clean hands, lest it turn to dead leaves,

to thorns, in your grasp. I think it is the lonely,
without a fireside or an affection they may call
their own, those who return not to a dwelling but
to the land itself, to meet its disembodied, eternal,
and unchangeable spirit—it is those who understand
best its severity, its saving power, the grace of its
secular right to our fidelity, to our obedience. Yes !
few of us understand, but we all feel it though,
and I say *all* without exception, because those who
do not feel do not count. Each blade of grass has
its spot on earth whence it draws its life, its strength ;
and so is man rooted to the land from which he
draws his faith together with his life. I don't know
how much Jim understood ; but I know he felt,
he felt confusedly but powerfully, the demand of
some such truth or some such illusion—I don't
care how you call it, there is so little difference,
and the difference means so little. The thing is
that in virtue of his feeling he mattered. He would
never go home now. Not he. Never. Had he been
capable of picturesque manifestations he would
have shuddered at the thought and made you
shudder too. But he was not of that sort, though
he was expressive enough in his way. Before the
idea of going home he would grow desperately stiff
and immovable, with lowered chin and pouted lips,
and with those candid blue eyes of his glowering
darkly under a frown, as if before something unbearable, as if before something revolting. There
was imagination in that hard skull of his, over
which the thick clustering hair fitted like a cap.
As to me, I have no imagination (I would be more
certain about him to-day, if I had), and I do not
mean to imply that I figured to myself the spirit
of the land uprising above the white cliffs of Dover,

to ask me what I—returning with no bones broken, so to speak—had done with my very young brother. I could not make such a mistake. I knew very well he was of those about whom there is no inquiry; I had seen better men go out, disappear, vanish utterly, without provoking a sound of curiosity or sorrow. The spirit of the land, as becomes the ruler of great enterprises, is careless of innumerable lives. Woe to the stragglers! We exist only in so far as we hang together. He had straggled in a way; he had not hung on; but he was aware of it with an intensity that made him touching, just as a man's more intense life makes his death more touching than the death of a tree. I happened to be handy, and I happened to be touched. That's all there is to it. I was concerned as to the way he would go out. It would have hurt me if, for instance, he had taken to drink. The earth is so small that I was afraid of, some day, being waylaid by a blear-eyed, swollen-faced, besmirched loafer, with no soles to his canvas shoes, and with a flutter of rags about the elbows, who, on the strength of old acquaintance, would ask for a loan of five dollars. You know the awful jaunty bearing of these scarecrows coming to you from a decent past, the rasping careless voice, the half-averted impudent glances—those meetings more trying to a man who believes in the solidarity of our lives than the sight of an impenitent death-bed to a priest. That, to tell you the truth, was the only danger I could see for him and for me; but I also mistrusted my want of imagination. It might even come to something worse, in some way it was beyond my powers of fancy to foresee. He wouldn't let me forget how imaginative he was, and your imaginative people swing farther in any direction, as if given a longer scope of cable in the uneasy anchorage of life. They do. They take to drink too. It may be I was belittling him by such a fear. How could I tell? Even Stein could say no more than that he was romantic. I only knew he was one of us. And what business had he to be romantic? I am telling you so much about my own instinctive feelings and bemused reflections because there remains so little to be told of him. He existed for me, and after all it is only through me that he exists for you. I've led him out by the hand; I have paraded him before you. Were my commonplace fears unjust? I won't say—not even now. You may be able to tell better, since the proverb has it that the onlookers see most of the game. At any rate, they were superfluous He did not go out, not at all; on the contrary, he came on wonderfully, came on straight as a die and in excellent form, which showed that he could stay as well as spurt. I ought to be delighted, for it is a victory in which I had taken my part; but I am not so pleased as I would have expected to be. I ask myself whether his rush had really carried him out of that mist in which he loomed interesting if not very big, with floating outlines—a straggler yearning inconsolably for his humble place in the ranks. And besides, the last word is not said,— probably shall never be said. Are not our lives too short for that full utterance which through all our stammerings is of course our only and abiding intention? I have given up expecting those last words, whose ring, if they could only be pronounced, would shake both heaven and earth. There is never time to say our last word—the last word of our

love, of our desire, faith, remorse, submission, revolt.
The heaven and the earth must not be shaken, I
suppose—at least, not by us who know so many
truths about either. My last words about Jim shall
be few. I affirm he had achieved greatness; but
the thing would be dwarfed in the telling, or rather
in the hearing. Frankly, it is not my words that I
mistrust but your minds. I could be eloquent were
I not afraid you fellows had starved your imagina-
tions to feed your bodies. I do not mean to be
offensive; it is respectable to have no illusions—
and safe—and profitable—and dull. Yet you too
in your time must have known the intensity of life,
that light of glamour created in the shock of trifles,
as amazing as the glow of sparks struck from a
cold stone—and as short-lived, alas!"

CHAPTER XXII.

"THE conquest of love, honour, men's confidence
—the pride of it, the power of it, are fit materials
for a heroic tale; only our minds are struck by the
externals of such a success, and to Jim's successes
there were no externals. Thirty miles of forest shut
it off from the sight of an indifferent world, and the
noise of the white surf along the coast overpowered
the voice of fame. The stream of civilisation, as if
divided on a headland a hundred miles north of
Patusan, branches east and south-east, leaving its
plains and valleys, its old trees and its old mankind,
neglected and isolated, such as an insignificant and

crumbling islet between the two branches of a mighty, devouring stream. You find the name of the country pretty often in collections of old voyages. The seventeenth - century traders went there for pepper, because the passion for pepper seemed to burn like a flame of love in the breast of Dutch and English adventurers about the time of James the First. Where wouldn't they go for pepper! For a bag of pepper they would cut each other's throats without hesitation, and would forswear their souls, of which they were so careful otherwise : the bizarre obstinacy of that desire made them defy death in a thousand shapes ; the unknown seas, the loathsome and strange diseases ; wounds, captivity, hunger, pestilence, and despair. It made them great! By heavens ! it made them heroic ; and it made them pathetic too in their craving for trade with the inflexible death levying its toll on young and old. It seems impossible to believe that mere greed could hold men to such a steadfastness of purpose, to such a blind persistence in endeavour and sacrifice. And indeed those who adventured their persons and lives risked all they had for a slender reward. They left their bones to lie bleaching on distant shores, so that wealth might flow to the living at home. To us, their less tried successors, they appear magnified, not as agents of trade but as instruments of a recorded destiny, pushing out into the unknown in obedience to an inward voice, to an impulse beating in the blood, to a dream of the future. They were wonderful ; and it must be owned they were ready for the wonderful. They recorded it complacently in their sufferings, in the aspect of the seas, in the customs of strange nations, in the glory of splendid rulers.

"In Patusan they had found lots of pepper, and
had been impressed by the magnificence and the
wisdom of the Sultan; but somehow, after a century
of checkered intercourse, the country seems to drop
gradually out of the trade. Perhaps the pepper had
given out. Be it as it may, nobody cares for it now;
the glory has departed, the Sultan is an imbecile
youth with two thumbs on his left hand and an
uncertain and beggarly revenue extorted from a
miserable population and stolen from him by his
many uncles.

"This of course I have from Stein. He gave me
their names and a short sketch of life and character
of each. He was as full of information about native
States as an official report, but infinitely more
amusing. He *had* to know. He traded in so many,
and in some districts—as in Patusan, for instance—
his firm was the only one to have an agency by
special permit from the Dutch authorities. The
Government trusted his discretion, and it was
understood that he took all the risks. The men he
employed understood that too, but he made it worth
their while apparently. He was perfectly frank
with me over the breakfast-table in the morning.
As far as he was aware (the last news were thirteen
months old he stated precisely), utter insecurity for
life and property was the normal condition. There
were in Patusan antagonistic forces, and one of them
was Rajah Allang, the worst of the Sultan's uncles,
the governor of the river, who did the extorting and
the stealing, and ground down to the point of
extinction the country-born Malays, who, utterly
defenceless, had not even the resource of emigrating
—'for indeed,' as Stein remarked, 'where could they
go, and how could they get away?' No doubt they

lid not even desire to get away. The world (which
s circumscribed by lofty impassable mountains) has
been given into the hand of the high-born, and *this*
Rajah they knew : he was of their own royal house.
I had the pleasure of meeting the gentleman later
on. He was a dirty, little, used-up old man with
evil eyes and a weak mouth, who swallowed an
opium pill every two hours, and in defiance of
common decency wore his hair uncovered and falling
in wild stringy locks about his wizened grimy face.
When giving audience he would clamber upon
a sort of narrow stage erected in a hall like a ruinous
barn with a rotten bamboo floor, through the cracks
of which you could see twelve or fifteen feet below
the heaps of refuse and garbage of all kinds lying
under the house. That is where and how he received
us when, accompanied by Jim, I paid him a visit
of ceremony. There were about forty people in
the room, and perhaps three times as many in the
great courtyard below. There was constant movement, coming and going, pushing and murmuring,
at our backs. A few youths in gay silks glared
from the distance ; the majority, slaves and humble
dependants, were half naked, in ragged sarongs,
dirty with ashes and mud-stains. I had never seen
Jim look so grave, so self-possessed, in an impenetrable, impressive way. In the midst of these dark-
faced men, his stalwart figure in white apparel, the
gleaming clusters of his fair hair, seemed to catch
all the sunshine that trickled through the cracks in
the closed shutters of that dim hall, with its walls
of mats and a roof of thatch. He appeared like a
creature not only of another kind but of another
essence. Had they not seen him come up in a
canoe they might have thought he had descended

upon them from the clouds. He did, however, come
in a crazy dug-out, sitting (very still and with his
knees together, for fear of overturning the thing)—
sitting on a tin box—which I had lent him—nursing
on his lap a revolver of the navy pattern—presented
by me on parting—which, through an interposition
of Providence, or through some wrong-headed notion,
that was just like him, or else from sheer instinctive
sagacity, he had decided to carry unloaded. That's
how he ascended the Patusan river. Nothing could
have been more prosaic and more unsafe, more
extravagantly casual, more lonely. Strange, this
fatality that would cast the complexion of a flight
upon all his acts, of impulsive unreflecting desertion
—of a jump into the unknown.

"It is precisely the casualness of it that strikes
me most. Neither Stein nor I had a clear conception of what might be on the other side when we,
metaphorically speaking, took him up and hove him
over the wall with scant ceremony. At the moment
I merely wished to achieve his disappearance;
Stein characteristically enough had a sentimental
motive. He had a notion of paying off (in kind, I
suppose) the old debt he had never forgotten.
Indeed he had been all his life especially friendly to
anybody from the British Isles. His late benefactor,
it is true, was a Scot—even to the length of being
called Alexander M'Neil—and Jim came from a
long way south of the Tweed; but at the distance
of six or seven thousand miles Great Britain, though
never diminished, looks foreshortened enough even
to its own children to rob such details of their
importance. Stein was excusable, and his hinted
intentions were so generous that I begged him most
earnestly to keep them secret for a time. I felt

that no consideration of personal advantage should
be allowed to influence Jim ; that not even the risk
of such influence should be run. We had to deal
with another sort of reality. He wanted a refuge,
and a refuge at the cost of danger should be offered
him—nothing more.

" Upon every other point I was perfectly frank
with him, and I even (as I believed at the time)
exaggerated the danger of the undertaking. As a
matter of fact I did not do it justice ; his first day
in Patusan was nearly his last—would have been
his last if he had not been so reckless or so hard on
himself and had condescended to load that revolver.
I remember, as I unfolded our precious scheme
for his retreat, how his stubborn but weary resignation was gradually replaced by surprise, interest,
wonder, and by boyish eagerness. This was a
chance he had been dreaming of. He couldn't
think how he merited that I . . . He would be
shot if he could see to what he owed . . . And it
was Stein, Stein the merchant, who . . . but of
course it was me he had to . . ." I cut him short.
He was not articulate, and his gratitude caused me
inexplicable pain. I told him that if he owed this
chance to any one especially, it was to an old Scot
of whom he had never heard, who had died many
years ago, of whom little was remembered besides a
roaring voice and a rough sort of honesty. There
was really no one to receive his thanks. Stein was
passing on to a young man the help he had received
in his own young days, and I had done no more
than to mention his name. Upon this he coloured,
and, twisting a bit of paper in his fingers, he remarked
bashfully that I had always trusted him.

" I admitted that such was the case, and added

after a pause that I wished he had been able to follow my example. 'You think I don't?' he asked uneasily, and remarked in a mutter that one had to get some sort of show first; then brightening up, and in a loud voice he protested he would give me no occasion to regret my confidence, which— which . . .

"'Do not misapprehend,' I interrupted. 'It is not in your power to make me regret anything.' There would be no regrets; but if there were, it would be altogether my own affair: on the other hand, I wished him to understand clearly that this arrangement, this—this—experiment, was his own doing; he was responsible for it and no one else. 'Why? Why!' he stammered, 'this is the very thing that I' . . . I begged him not to be dense, and he looked more puzzled than ever. He was in a fair way to make life intolerable to himself. . . . 'Do you think so?' he asked disturbed; but in a moment added confidently, 'I was going on though. Was I not?' It was impossible to be angry with him: I could not help a smile, and told him that in the old days people who went on like this were on the way of becoming hermits in a wilderness. 'Hermits be hanged!' he commented with engaging impulsiveness. Of course he didn't mind a wilderness. . . . 'I was glad of it,' I said. That was where he would be going to. He would find it lively enough, I ventured to promise. 'Yes, yes,' he said keenly. He had shown a desire, I continued inflexibly, to go out and shut the door after him. . . . 'Did I?' he interrupted in a strange access of gloom that seemed to envelop him from head to foot like the shadow of a passing cloud. He was wonderfully expressive after all. Wonderfully! 'Did I?' he repeated bitterly. 'You can't say I made much noise about it. And I can keep it up too—only, confound it! you show me a door.' . . . 'Very well. Pass on,' I struck in. I could make him a solemn promise that it would be shut behind him with a vengeance. His fate, whatever it was, would be ignored, because the country, for all its rotten state, was not judged ripe for interference. Once he got in, it would be for the outside world as though he had never existed. He would have nothing but the soles of his two feet to stand upon, and he would have first to find his ground at that. 'Never existed—that's it, by Jove,' he murmured to himself. His eyes, fastened upon my lips, sparkled. If he had thoroughly understood the conditions, I concluded, he had better jump into the first gharry he could see and drive on to Stein's house for his final instructions. He flung out of the room before I had fairly finished speaking."

CHAPTER XXIII.

'He did not return till next morning. He had been kept to dinner and for the night. There never had been such a wonderful man as Mr Stein. He had in his pocket a letter for Cornelius ('the Johnnie who's going to get the sack,' he explained with a momentary drop in his elation), and he exhibited with glee a silver ring, such as natives use, worn down very thin and showing faint traces of chasing.

" This was his introduction to an old chap called
Doramin—one of the principal men out there—a
big pot—who had been Mr Stein's friend in that
country where he had all these adventures. Mr
Stein called him 'war-comrade.' War-comrade
was good. Wasn't it ? And didn't Mr Stein speak
English wonderfully well ? Said he had learned it
in Celebes—of all places ! That was awfully funny.
Was it not ? He did speak with an accent—a
twang—did I notice ? That chap Doramin had
given him the ring. They had exchanged presents
when they parted for the last time. Sort of promising eternal friendship. He called it fine—did I
not ? They had to make a dash for dear life out of
the country when that Mohammed—Mohammed—
What's-his-name had been killed. I knew the story
of course. Seemed a beastly shame, didn't it ? . .

" He ran on like this, forgetting his plate, with
a knife and fork in hand (he had found me at tiffin),
slightly flushed, and with his eyes darkened many
shades, which was with him a sign of excitement.
The ring was a sort of credential. (' It's like something you read of in books,' he threw in appreciatively), and Doramin would do his best for him.
Mr Stein had been the means of saving that chap's
life on some occasion ; purely by accident, Mr
Stein had said, but he—Jim—had his own opinion
about that. Mr Stein was just the man to look
out for such accidents. No matter. Accident or
purpose, this would serve his turn immensely.
Hoped to goodness the jolly old beggar had not
gone off the hooks meantime. Mr Stein could not
tell. There had been no news for more than a
year ; they were kicking up no end of an all-fired
row amongst themselves, and the river was closed.

Jolly awkward, this ; but, no fear ; he would manage to find a crack to get in.

" He impressed, almost frightened, me with his elated rattle. He was voluble like a youngster on the eve of a long holiday with a prospect of delightful scrapes, and such an attitude of mind in a grown man and in this connection had in it something phenomenal, a little mad, dangerous, unsafe. I was on the point of entreating him to take things seriously when he dropped his knife and fork (he had begun eating, or rather swallowing food, as it were, unconsciously), and began a search all round his plate. The ring ! The ring ! Where the devil . . . Ah ! Here it was . . . He closed his big hand on it, and tried all his pockets one after another. Jove ! wouldn't do to lose the thing. He meditated gravely over his fist. Had it ? Would hang the bally affair round his neck ! And he proceeded to do this immediately, producing a string (which looked like a bit of a cotton shoe-lace) for the purpose. There ! That would do the trick ! It would be the deuce if . . . He seemed to catch sight of my face for the first time, and it steadied him a little. I probably didn't realise, he said with a naïve gravity, how much importance he attached to that token. It meant a friend ; and it is a good thing to have a friend. He knew something about that. He nodded at me expressively, but before my disclaiming gesture he leaned his head on his hand and for a while sat silent, playing thoughtfully with the bread-crumbs on the cloth . . . ' Slam the door—that was jolly well put,' he cried, and jumping up, began to pace the room, reminding me by the set of the shoulders, the turn of his head, the headlong and uneven stride, of that night when he had paced thus, confessing, explaining—what you will—but, in the last instance, living—living before me, under his own little cloud, with all his unconscious subtlety which could draw consolation from the very source of sorrow. It was the same mood, the same and different, like a fickle companion that to-day guiding you on the true path, with the same eyes, the same step, the same impulse, to-morrow will lead you hopelessly astray. His tread was assured, his straying, darkened eyes seemed to search the room for something. One of his footfalls somehow sounded louder than the other—the fault of his boots probably—and gave a curious impression of an invisible halt in his gait. One of his hands was rammed deep into his trousers' pocket, the other waved suddenly above his head. 'Slam the door!' he shouted. 'I've been waiting for that. I'll show yet . . . I'll . . . I'm ready for any confounded thing . . . I've been dreaming of it . . . Jove! Get out of this. Jove! This is luck at last . . . You wait. I'll . . .'

"He tossed his head fearlessly, and I confess that for the first and last time in our acquaintance I perceived myself unexpectedly to be thoroughly sick of him. Why these vapourings? He was stumping about the room flourishing his arm absurdly, and now and then feeling on his breast for the ring under his clothes. Where was the sense of such exaltation in a man appointed to be a trading-clerk, and in a place where there was no trade—at that? Why hurl defiance at the universe? This was not a proper frame of mind to approach any undertaking; an improper frame of mind not only for him, I said, but for any man. He stood still over me. Did I think so? he asked,

by no means subdued, and with a smile in which
I seemed to detect suddenly something insolent.
But then I am twenty years his senior. Youth *is*
insolent; it is its right—its necessity; it has got
to assert itself, and all assertion in this world of
doubts is a defiance, is an insolence. He went off
into a far corner, and coming back, he, figuratively
speaking, turned to rend me. I spoke like that
because I—even I, who had been no end kind to
him—even I remembered—remembered—against
him—what—what had happened. And what about
others—the—the—world. Where's the wonder he
wanted to get out, meant to get out, meant to stay
out—by heavens! And I talked about proper
frames of mind!

"'It is not I or the world who remember,' I
shouted. 'It is you—you, who remember.'

"He did not flinch, and went on with heat,
'Forget everything, everybody, everybody.' . . .
His voice fell . . . 'But you,' he added.

"'Yes—me too—if it would help,' I said, also
in a low tone. After this we remained silent and
languid for a time as if exhausted. Then he began
again, composedly, and told me that Mr Stein had
instructed him to wait for a month or so, to see
whether it was possible for him to remain, before he began building a new house for himself,
so as to avoid 'vain expense.' He did make
use of funny expressions—Stein did. 'Vain expense' was good . . . Remain? Why! of course.
He would hang on. Let him only get in—
that's all; he would answer for it he would
remain. Never get out. It was easy enough to
remain.

"'Don't be foolhardy,' I said, rendered uneasy by

his threatening tone. 'If you only live long enough you will want to come back.'

" ' Come back to what ? ' he asked absently, with his eyes fixed upon the face of a clock on the wall.

"I was silent for a while. 'Is it to be never, then ? ' I said. 'Never,' he repeated dreamily without looking at me, and then flew into sudden activity. 'Jove! Two o'clock, and I sail at four ?'

"It was true. A brigantine of Stein's was leaving for the westward that afternoon, and he had been instructed to take his passage in her, only no orders to delay the sailing had been given. I suppose Stein forgot. He made a rush to get his things while I went aboard my ship, where he promised to call on his way to the outer roadstead. He turned up accordingly in a great hurry and with a small leather valise in his hand. This wouldn't do, and I offered him an old tin trunk of mine supposed to be water-tight, or at least damp-tight. He effected the transfer by the simple process of shooting out the contents of his valise as you would empty a sack of wheat. I saw three books in the tumble ; two small, in dark covers, and a thick green-and-gold volume—a half-crown complete Shakespeare. 'You read this ? ' I asked. 'Yes. Best thing to cheer up a fellow,' he said hastily. I was struck by this appreciation, but there was no time for Shakespearian talk. A heavy revolver and two small boxes of cartridges were lying on the cuddy-table. 'Pray take this,' I said. 'It may help you to remain.' No sooner were these words out of my mouth than I perceived what grim meaning they could bear. 'May help you to get in,' I corrected myself remorsefully. He however was not troubled by obscure meanings ; he

thanked me effusively and bolted out, calling Good-
bye over his shoulder. I heard his voice through
the ship's side urging his boatmen to give way, and
looking out of the stern-port I saw the boat rounding
under the counter. He sat in her leaning forward,
exciting his men with voice and gestures ; and
as he had kept the revolver in his hand and seemed
to be presenting it at their heads, I shall never
forget the scared faces of the four Javanese, and
the frantic swing of their stroke which snatched
that vision from under my eyes. Then turning
away, the first thing I saw were the two boxes
of cartridges on the cuddy-table. He had forgotten to take them.

"I ordered my gig manned at once ; but Jim's
rowers, under the impression that their lives hung
on a thread while they had that madman in the
boat, made such excellent time that before I had
traversed half the distance between the two vessels
I caught sight of him clambering over the rail, and
of his box being passed up. All the brigantine's
canvas was loose, her mainsail was set, and the
windlass was just beginning to clink as I stepped
upon her deck : her master, a dapper little half-
caste of forty or so, in a blue flannel suit, with
lively eyes, his round face the colour of lemon-peel,
and with a thin little black moustache drooping
on each side of his thick, dark lips, came forward
smirking. He turned out, notwithstanding his self-
satisfied and cheery exterior, to be of a careworn
temperament. In answer to a remark of mine
(while Jim had gone below for a moment) he said,
'Oh yes. Patusan.' He was going to carry the
gentleman to the mouth of the river, but would
'never ascend.' His flowing English seemed to be

derived from a dictionary compiled by a lunatic. Had Mr Stein desired him to 'ascend,' he would have 'reverentially'—(I think he wanted to say respectfully—but devil only knows)—'reverentially made objects for the safety of properties.' If disregarded, he would have presented 'resignation to quit.' Twelve months ago he had made his last voyage there, and though Mr Cornelius 'propitiated many offertories' to Mr Rajah Allang and the 'principal populations,' on conditions which made the trade 'a snare and ashes in the mouth,' yet his ship had been fired upon from the woods by 'irresponsive parties' all the way down the river; which causing his crew 'from exposure to limb to remain silent in hidings,' the brigantine was nearly stranded on a sandbank at the bar, where she 'would have been perishable beyond the act of man.' The angry disgust at the recollection, the pride of his fluency, to which he turned an attentive ear, struggled for the possession of his broad simple face. He scowled and beamed at me, and watched with satisfaction the undeniable effect of his phraseology. Dark frowns ran swiftly over the placid sea, and the brigantine, with her fore-topsail to the mast and her main-boom amidships, seemed bewildered amongst the cat's-paws. He told me further, gnashing his teeth, that the Rajah was a 'laughable hyæna' (can't imagine how he got hold of hyænas); while somebody else was many times falser than the 'weapons of a crocodile.' Keeping one eye on the movements of his crew forward, he let loose his volubility—comparing the place to a 'cage of beasts made ravenous by long impenitence.' I fancy he meant impunity. He had no intention, he cried, to 'exhibit

himself to be made attached purposefully to robbery.'
The long-drawn wails, giving the time for the pull
of the men catting the anchor, came to an end,
and he lowered his voice. 'Plenty too much enough
of Patusan,' he concluded, with energy.

"I heard afterwards he had been so indiscreet
as to get himself tied up by the neck with a rattan
halter to a post planted in the middle of a mud-
hole before the Rajah's house. He spent the best
part of a day and a whole night in that unwhole-
some situation, but there is every reason to believe
the thing had been meant as a sort of joke. He
brooded for a while over that horrid memory, I
suppose, and then addressed in a quarrelsome
tone the man coming aft to the helm. When he
turned to me again it was to speak judicially,
without passion. He would take the gentleman
to the mouth of the river at Batu Kring (Patusan
town 'being situated internally,' he remarked, 'thirty
miles'). But in his eyes, he continued—a tone of
bored, weary conviction replacing his previous
voluble delivery—the gentleman was already 'in the
similitude of a corpse.' 'What? What do you
say?' I asked. He assumed a startlingly ferocious
demeanour, and imitated to perfection the act of
stabbing from behind. 'Already like the body of
one deported,' he explained, with the insufferably
conceited air of his kind after what they imagine
a display of cleverness. Behind him I perceived
Jim smiling silently at me, and with a raised hand
checking the exclamation on my lips.

"Then, while the half-caste, bursting with importance, shouted his orders, while the yards swung
creaking and the heavy boom came surging over,
Jim and I, alone as it were, to leeward of the main-

sail, clasped each other's hands and exchange
the last hurried words. My heart was freed from
that dull resentment which had existed side by sid
with interest in his fate. The absurd chatter o
the half-caste had given more reality to the miserabl
dangers of his path than Stein's careful statements
On that occasion the sort of formality that ha
been always present in our intercourse vanishe
from our speech; I believe I called him ' dear boy,
and he tacked on the words ' old man ' to some half
uttered expression of gratitude, as though his ris
set off against my years had made us more equa
in age and in feeling. There was a moment o
real and profound intimacy, unexpected and short
lived like a glimpse of some everlasting, of som
saving truth. He exerted himself to soothe me a
though he had been the more mature of the two
' All right, all right,' he said rapidly and with feel
ing. ' I promise to take care of myself. Yes ;
won't take any risks. Not a single blessed risk
Of course not. I mean to hang out. Don't yo
worry; Jove! I feel as if nothing could touch me
Why! this is luck from the word Go. I wouldn'
spoil such a magnificent chance!' . . . A magni
ficent chance! Well, it *was* magnificent, but chance
are what men make them, and how was I to know
As he had said, even I—even I remembered—his—
his misfortune against him. It was true. And th
best thing for him was to go.

" My gig had dropped in the wake of the brigantine
and I saw him aft detached upon the light of th
westering sun, raising his cap high above his head
I heard an indistinct shout, ' You—shall—hear—
of—me.' Of me, or from me, I don't know which
I think it must have been *of* me. My eyes wer

too dazzled by the glitter of the sea below his feet
to see him clearly ; I am fated never to see him
clearly ; but I can assure you no man could have
appeared less 'in the similitude of a corpse,' as
that half-caste croaker had put it. I could see the
little wretch's face, the shape and colour of a ripe
pumpkin, poked out somewhere under Jim's elbow.
He too raised his arm as if for a downward
thrust. *Absit omen !* "

CHAPTER XXIV.

" THE coast of Patusan (I saw it nearly two years
afterwards) is straight and sombre, and faces a
misty ocean. Red trails are seen like cataracts of
rust streaming under the dark-green foliage of
bushes and creepers clothing the low cliffs. Swampy
plains open out at the mouth of rivers, with a view
of jagged blue peaks beyond the vast forests. In
the offing a chain of islands, dark, crumbling shapes,
stand out in the everlasting sunlit haze like the
remnants of a wall breached by the sea.

" There is a village of fisher-folk at the mouth of
the Batu Kring branch of the estuary. The river,
which had been closed so long, was open then, and
Stein's little schooner, in which I had my passage,
worked her way up in three tides without being
exposed to a fusilade from 'irresponsive parties.'
Such a state of affairs belonged already to ancient
history, if I could believe the elderly headman of
the fishing village, who came on board to act as

a sort of pilot. He talked to me (the second white man he had ever seen) with confidence, and most of his talk was about the first white man he had ever seen. He called him Tuan Jim, and the tone of his references was made remarkable by a strange mixture of familiarity and awe. They, in the village, were under that lord's special protection which showed that Jim bore no grudge. If he had warned me that I would hear of him it was perfectly true. I was hearing of him. There was already a story that the tide had turned two hours before its time to help him on his journey up the river. The talkative old man himself had steered the canoe and had marvelled at the phenomenon. Moreover, all the glory was in his family. His son and his son-in-law had paddled; but they were only youths without experience, who did not notice the speed of the canoe till he pointed out to them the amazing fact.

"Jim's coming to that fishing village was a blessing; but to them, as to many of us, the blessing came heralded by terrors. So many generations had been released since the last white man had visited the river that the very tradition had been lost. The appearance of the being that descended upon them and demanded inflexibly to be taken up to Patusan was discomposing; his insistence was alarming; his generosity more than suspicious. It was an unheard-of request. There was no precedent. What would the Rajah say to this? What would he do to them? The best part of the night was spent in consultation; but the immediate risk from the anger of that strange man seemed so great that at last a cranky dug-out was got ready. The women shrieked with grief as it put off. A fearless old hag cursed the stranger.

"He sat in it, as I've told you, on his tin box,
nursing the unloaded revolver on his lap. He sat
with precaution—than which there is nothing more
fatiguing—and thus entered the land he was destined
to fill with the fame of his virtues, from the blue
peaks inland to the white ribbon of surf on the
coast. At the first bend he lost sight of the sea
with its labouring waves for ever rising, sinking,
and vanishing to rise again—the very image of
struggling mankind,—and faced the immovable
forests rooted deep in the soil, soaring towards the
sunshine, everlasting in the shadowy might of their
tradition, like life itself. And his opportunity sat
veiled by his side like an Eastern bride waiting to
be uncovered by the hand of the master. He too
was the heir of a shadowy and mighty tradition !
He told me, however, that he had never in his life
felt so depressed and tired as in that canoe. All the
movement he dared to allow himself was to reach,
as it were by stealth, after the shell of half a cocoa-
nut floating between his shoes, and bale some of the
water out with a carefully restrained action. He
discovered how hard the lid of a block-tin case was
to sit upon. He had heroic health ; but several
times during that journey he experienced fits of
giddiness, and between whiles he speculated hazily
as to the size of the blister the sun was raising on
his back. For amusement he tried by looking ahead
to decide whether the muddy object he saw lying on
the water's edge was a log of wood or an alligator.
Only very soon he had to give that up. No fun in
it. Always alligator. One of them flopped into the
river and all but capsized the canoe. But this
excitement was over directly. Then in a long empty
reach he was very grateful to a troop of monkeys

who came right down on the bank and made an
insulting hullabaloo on his passage. Such was the
way in which he was approaching greatness as
genuine as any man ever achieved. Principally
he longed for sunset; and meantime his three
paddlers were preparing to put into execution their
plan of delivering him up to the Rajah.

"'I suppose I must have been stupid with
fatigue, or perhaps I did doze off for a time,' he said.
The first thing he knew was his canoe coming to the
bank. He became instantaneously aware of the
forest having been left behind, of the first house
being visible higher up, of a stockade on his left,
and of his boatmen leaping out together upon a
low point of land and taking to their heels. Instinctively he leaped out after them. At first he
thought himself deserted for some inconceivable
reason, but he heard excited shouts, a gate swung
open, and a lot of people poured out, making towards
him. At the same time a boat full of armed men
appeared on the river and came alongside his empty
canoe, thus shutting off his retreat.

"'I was too startled to be quite cool—don't you
know? and if that revolver had been loaded I
would have shot somebody—perhaps two, three
bodies, and that would have been the end of me.
But it wasn't. . . .' 'Why not?' I asked. 'Well,
I couldn't fight the whole population, and I wasn't
coming to them as if I were afraid of my life,' he
said, with just a faint hint of his stubborn sulkiness
in the glance he gave me. I refrained from pointing
out to him that they could not have known the
chambers were actually empty. He had to satisfy
himself in his own way. . . . 'Anyhow it wasn't,'
he repeated good-humouredly, 'and so I just stood

till and asked them what was the matter. That
seemed to strike them dumb. I saw some of these
thieves going off with my box. That long-legged
old scoundrel Kassim (I'll show him to you to-
morrow) ran out fussing to me about the Rajah
wanting to see me. I said, "All right"; I too
wanted to see the Rajah, and I simply walked in
through the gate and—and—here I am.' He
laughed, and then with unexpected emphasis, ' And
do you know what's the best in it ? ' he asked.
' I'll tell you. It's the knowledge that had I been
wiped out it is this place that would have been
the loser.'

"He spoke thus to me before his house on that
evening I've mentioned—after we had watched the
moon float away above the chasm between the hills
like an ascending spirit out of a grave ; its sheen
descended, cold and pale, like the ghost of dead
sunlight. There is something haunting in the light
of the moon ; it has all the dispassionateness of a
disembodied soul, and something of its inconceivable mystery. It is to our sunshine which—say
what you like—is all we have to live by, what the
echo is to the sound : misleading and confusing
whether the note be mocking or sad. It robs all
forms of matter—which, after all, is our domain—
of their substance, and gives a sinister reality to
shadows alone. And the shadows were very real
around us, but Jim by my side looked very stalwart, as though nothing—not even the occult power
of moonlight—could rob him of his reality in my
eyes. Perhaps, indeed, nothing could touch him
since he had survived the assault of the dark powers.
All was silent, all was still ; even on the river the
moonbeams slept as on a pool. It was the moment

of high water, a moment of immobility that accentuated the utter isolation of this lost corner of the earth. The houses crowding along the wide shining sweep without ripple or glitter, stepping into the water in a line of jostling, vague, grey, silvery forms mingled with black masses of shadow, were like a spectral herd of shapeless creatures pressing forward to drink in a spectral and lifeless stream. Here and there a red gleam twinkled within the bamboo walls, warm, like a living spark, significant of human affections, of shelter, of repose.

"He confessed to me that he often watched these tiny warm gleams go out one by one, that he loved to see people go to sleep under his eyes, confident in the security of to-morrow. 'Peaceful here, hey?' he asked. He was not eloquent, but there was a deep meaning in the words that followed. 'Look at these houses; there's not one where I am not trusted. Jove! I told you I would hang on. Ask any man, woman, or child . . .' He paused. 'Well, I am all right anyhow.'

"I observed quickly that he had found that out in the end. I had been sure of it, I added. He shook his head. 'Were you?' He pressed my arm lightly above the elbow. 'Well, then—you were right.'

"There was elation and pride, there was awe almost, in that low exclamation. 'Jove!' he cried, 'only think what it is to me.' Again he pressed my arm. 'And you asked me whether I thought of leaving. Good God! I! want to leave! Especially now after what you told me of Mr Stein's . . . Leave! Why! That's what I was afraid of. It would have been—it would have been harder than dying. No—on my word. Don't laugh. I must

feel—every day, every time I open my eyes—that
I am trusted—that nobody has a right—don't you
know? Leave! For where? What for? To get
what?'

"I had told him (indeed it was the main object
of my visit) that it was Stein's intention to present
him at once with the house and the stock of trading
goods, on certain easy conditions which would
make the transaction perfectly regular and valid.
He began to snort and plunge at first. 'Confound
your delicacy!' I shouted. 'It isn't Stein at all.
It's giving you what you had made for yourself.
And in any case keep you remarks for M'Neil—
when you meet him in the other world. I hope
it won't happen soon. . . .' He had to give in to
my arguments, because all his conquests, the trust,
the fame, the friendships, the love,—all these
things that made him master had made him a
captive too. He looked with an owner's eye at
the peace of the evening, at the river, at the houses,
at the everlasting life of the forests, at the life of
the old mankind, at the secrets of the land, at
the pride of his own heart; but it was they that
possessed him and made him their own to the
innermost thought, to the slightest stir of blood,
to his last breath.

"It was something to be proud of. I too was
proud—for him, if not so certain of the fabulous
value of the bargain. It was wonderful. It was
not so much of his fearlessness that I thought. It
is strange how little account I took of it: as if it
had been something too conventional to be at the
root of the matter. No. I was more struck by
the other gifts he had displayed. He had proved
his grasp of the unfamiliar situation, his intel-

lectual alertness in that field of thought. There
was his readiness too! Amazing. And all this had
come to him in a manner like keen scent to a well
bred hound. He was not eloquent, but there was a
dignity in this constitutional reticence, there was a
high seriousness in his stammerings. He had still
his old trick of stubborn blushing. Now and then,
though, a word, a sentence, would escape him that
showed how deeply, how solemnly, he felt about that
work which had given him the certitude of re
habilitation. That is why he seemed to love the
land and the people with a sort of fierce egoism,
with a contemptuous tenderness."

CHAPTER XXV.

" ' THIS is where I was prisoner for three days,'
he murmured to me (it was on the occasion of
our visit to the Rajah), while we were making
our way slowly through a kind of awestruck riot
of dependants across Tunku Allang's courtyard.
' Filthy place, isn't it? And I couldn't get any
thing to eat either, unless I made a row about it,
and then it was only a small plate of rice and a
fried fish not much bigger than a stickleback—
confound them! Jove! I've been hungry prowling
inside this stinking enclosure with some of these
vagabonds shoving their mugs right under my
nose. I had given up that famous revolver of
yours at the first demand. Glad to get rid of the
bally thing. Look like a fool walking about with

n empty shooting-iron in my hand.' At that
moment we came into the presence, and he became
unflinchingly grave and complimentary with his late
captor. Oh! magnificent! I want to laugh when
I think of it. But I was impressed too. The old
disreputable Tunku Allang could not help showing
his fear (he was no hero, for all the tales of his
hot youth he was fond of telling); and at the
same time there was a wistful confidence in his
manner towards his late prisoner. Note! Even
where he would be most hated he was still trusted.
Jim—as far as I could follow the conversation—
was improving the occasion by the delivery of a
lecture. Some poor villagers had been waylaid
and robbed while on their way to Doramin's house
with a few pieces of gum or bee's-wax which they
wished to exchange for rice. ' It was Doramin
who was a thief,' burst out the Rajah. A shaking
fury seemed to enter that old frail body. He
writhed weirdly on his mat, gesticulating with his
hands and feet, tossing the tangled strings of his
mop—an impotent incarnation of rage. There
were staring eyes and dropping jaws all around
us. Jim began to speak. Resolutely, coolly, and
for some time he enlarged upon the text that no
man should be prevented from getting his food and
his children's food honestly. The other sat like a
tailor at his board, one palm on each knee, his
head low, and fixing Jim through the grey hair
that fell over his very eyes. When Jim had done
there was a great stillness. Nobody seemed to
breathe even; no one made a sound till the old
Rajah sighed faintly, and looking up, with a toss
of his head, said quickly, ' You hear, my people!
No more of these little games.' This decree was

received in profound silence. A rather heavy man, evidently in a position of confidence, with intelligent eyes, a bony, broad, very dark face, and a cheerily officious manner (I learned later on he was the executioner), presented to us two cups of coffee on a brass tray, which he took from the hands of an inferior attendant. 'You needn't drink,' muttered Jim very rapidly. I didn't perceive the meaning at first, and only looked at him. He took a good sip and sat composedly, holding the saucer in his left hand. In a moment I felt excessively annoyed. 'Why the devil,' I whispered, smiling at him amiably, 'do you expose me to such a stupid risk?' I drank, of course, there was nothing for it, while he gave no sign, and almost immediately afterwards we took our leave. While we were going down the courtyard to our boat, escorted by the intelligent and cheery executioner, Jim said he was very sorry. It was the barest chance, of course. Personally he thought nothing of poison. The remotest chance. He was—he assured me—considered to be infinitely more useful than dangerous, and so . . . 'But the Rajah is afraid of you abominably. Anybody can see that,' I argued with, I own, a certain peevishness, and all the time watching anxiously for the first twist of some sort of ghastly colic. I was awfully disgusted. 'If I am to do any good here and preserve any position,' he said, taking his seat by my side in the boat, 'I must stand the risk: I take it once every month, at least. Many people trust me to do that—for them. Afraid of me. That's just it. Most likely he is afraid of me because I am not afraid of his coffee.' Then showing me a place on the north front of the stockade where the pointed tops of several stakes were broken, 'This s where I leaped over on my third day in Patusan. They haven't put new stakes there yet. Good leap, eh ?' A moment later we passed the mouth of a muddy creek. 'This is my second leap. I had a bit of a run and took this one flying, but fell short. Thought I would leave my skin there. Lost my shoes struggling. And all the time I was thinking to myself how beastly it would be to get a jab with a bally long spear while sticking in the mud like this. I remember how sick I felt wriggling in that slime. I mean really sick—as if I had bitten something rotten.'

"That's how it was—and the opportunity ran by his side, leaped over the gap, floundered in the mud . . still veiled. The unexpectedness of his coming was the only thing, you understand, that saved him from being at once despatched with krises and flung into the river. They had him, but it was like getting hold of an apparition, a wraith, a portent. What did it mean ? What to do with it ? Was it too late to conciliate him ? Hadn't he better be killed without more delay ? But what would happen then ? Wretched old Allang went nearly mad with apprehension and through the difficulty of making up his mind. Several times the council was broken up, and the advisers made a break helter-kelter for the door and out on to the verandah. One—it is said—even jumped down to the ground —fifteen feet, I should judge—and broke his leg. The royal governor of Patusan had bizarre man-nerisms, and one of them was to introduce boastful rhapsodies into every arduous discussion, when, getting gradually excited, he would end by flying off his perch with a kris in his hand. But, barring such interruptions, the deliberations upon Jim's fate went on night and day.

"Meanwhile he wandered about the courtyard shunned by some, glared at by others, but watched by all, and practically at the mercy of the first casual ragamuffin with a chopper, in there. He took possession of a small tumble-down shed to sleep in; the effluvia of filth and rotten matter incommoded him greatly: it seems he had not lost his appetite though, because—he told me—he had been hungry all the blessed time. Now and again 'some fussy ass' deputed from the council-room would come out running to him, and in honeyed tones would administer amazing interrogatories. 'Were the Dutch coming to take the country? Would the white man like to go back down the river? What was the object of coming to such a miserable country? The Rajah wanted to know whether the white man could repair a watch?' They did actually bring out to him a nickel clock of New England make, and out of sheer unbearable boredom he busied himself in trying to get the alarum to work. It was apparently when thus occupied in his shed that the true perception of his extreme peril dawned upon him. He dropped the thing—he says—'like a hot potato,' and walked out hastily, without the slightest idea of what he would, or indeed could do. He only knew that the position was intolerable. He strolled aimlessly beyond a sort of ramshackle little granary on posts, and his eyes fell on the broken stakes of the palisade; and then—he says—at once, without any mental process as it were, without any stir of emotion, he set about his escape as if executing a plan matured for a month. He walked off carelessly to give himself a good run, and when he faced about there was some dignitary with two spearmen in attendance close at his elbow ready with a

question. He started off ' from under his very nose,'
went over ' like a bird,' and landed on the other
side with a fall that jarred all his bones and seemed
to split his head. He picked himself up instantly.
He never thought of anything at the time ; all he
could remember—he said—was a great yell ; the
first houses of Patusan were before him four hundred
yards away ; he saw the creek, and as it were
mechanically put on more pace. The earth seemed
fairly to fly backwards under his feet. He took
off from the last dry spot, felt himself flying through
the air, felt himself, without any shock, planted
upright in an extremely soft and sticky mudbank. It
was only when he tried to move his legs and found he
couldn't that, in his own words, ' he came to himself.'
He began to think of the ' bally long spears.' As a
matter of fact, considering that the people inside the
stockade had to run to the gate, then get down to
the landing-place, get into boats, and pull round a
point of land, he had more advance than he imagined.
Besides, it being low water, the creek was without
water—you couldn't call it dry,—and practically he
was safe for a time from everything but a very long
shot perhaps. The higher firm ground was about
six feet in front of him. ' I thought I would have
to die there all the same,' he said. He reached and
grabbed desperately with his hands, and only
succeeded in gathering a horrible cold shiny heap of
slime against his breast—up to his very chin. It
seemed to him he was burying himself alive, and
then he struck out madly, scattering the mud with
his fists. It fell on his head, on his face, over his
eyes, into his mouth. He told me that he remembered
suddenly the courtyard, as you remember a place
where you had been very happy years ago. He

longed—so he said—to be back there again, mending
the clock. Mending the clock—that was the idea.
He made efforts, tremendous sobbing gasping efforts,
efforts that seemed to burst his eyeballs in their
sockets and make him blind, and culminating into
one mighty supreme effort in the darkness to crack
the earth asunder, to throw if off his limbs—and he
felt himself creeping feebly up the bank. He lay
full length on the firm ground and saw the light,
the sky. Then as a sort of happy thought the
notion came to him that he would go to sleep. He
will have it that he *did* actually go to sleep ; that
he slept—perhaps for a minute, perhaps for twenty
seconds, or only for one second, but he recollects
distinctly the violent convulsive start of awakening.
He remained lying still for a while, and then he
arose muddy from head to foot and stood there,
thinking he was alone of his kind for hundreds of
miles, alone, with no help, no sympathy, no pity to
expect from any one, like a hunted animal. The
first houses were not more than twenty yards from
him ; and it was the desperate screaming of a
frightened woman trying to carry off a child that
started him again. He pelted straight on in his socks,
beplastered with filth out of all semblance to a
human being. He traversed more than half the
length of the settlement. The nimbler women fled
right and left, the slower men just dropped whatever they had in their hands, and remained petrified
with dropping jaws. He was a flying terror. He
says he noticed the little children trying to run for
life, falling on their little stomachs and kicking. He
swerved between two houses up a slope, clambered
in desperation over a barricade of felled trees (there
wasn't a week without some fight in Patusan at

that time), burst through a fence into a maize-patch, where a scared boy flung a stick at him, blundered upon a path, and ran all at once into the arms of several startled men. He just had breath enough to gasp out, 'Doramin! Doramin!' He remembers being half-carried, half-rushed to the top of the slope, and in a vast enclosure with palms and fruit-trees being run up to a large man sitting massively in a chair in the midst of the greatest possible commotion and excitement. He fumbled in mud and clothes to produce the ring, and, finding himself suddenly on his back, wondered who had knocked him down. They had simply let him go—don't you know?—but he couldn't stand. At the foot of the slope random shots were fired, and above the roofs of the settlement there rose a dull roar of amazement. But he was safe. Doramin's people were barricading the gate and pouring water down his throat; Doramin's old wife, full of business and commiseration, was issuing shrill orders to her girls. 'The old woman,' he said softly, 'made a to-do over me as if I had been her own son. They put me into an immense bed—her state bed—and she ran in and out wiping her eyes to give me pats on the back. I must have been a pitiful object. I just lay there like a log for I don't know how long.'

"He seemed to have a great liking for Doramin's old wife. She on her side had taken a motherly fancy to him. She had a round, nut-brown, soft face, all fine wrinkles, large, bright red lips (she chewed betel assiduously), and screwed up, winking, benevolent eyes. She was constantly in movement, scolding busily and ordering unceasingly a troop of young women with clear brown faces and big grave eyes, her daughters, her servants, her slave-girls. You know how it is in these households : it's generally impossible to tell the difference. She was very spare, and even her ample outer garment, fastened in front with jewelled clasps, had somehow a skimpy effect. Her dark bare feet were thrust into yellow straw slippers of Chinese make. I have seen her myself flitting about with her extremely thick, long, grey hair falling about her shoulders. She uttered homely shrewd sayings, was of noble birth, and was eccentric and arbitrary. In the afternoon she would sit in a very roomy arm-chair, opposite her husband, gazing steadily through a wide opening in the wall which gave an extensive view of the settlement and the river.

"She invariably tucked up her feet under her, but old Doramin sat squarely, sat imposingly as a mountain sits on a plain. He was only of the *nakhoda* or merchant class, but the respect shown to him and the dignity of his bearing were very striking. He was the chief of the second power in Patusan. The immigrants from Celebes (about sixty families that, with dependants and so on, could muster some two hundred men 'wearing the kris') had elected him years ago for their head. The men of that race are intelligent, enterprising, revengeful, but with a more frank courage than the other Malays, and restless under oppression. They formed the party opposed to the Rajah. Of course the quarrels were for trade. This was the primary cause of faction fights, of the sudden outbreaks that would fill this or that part of the settlement with smoke, flame, the noise of shots and shrieks. Villages were burnt, men were dragged into the Rajah's stockade to be killed or tortured for the crime of trading with anybody else but himself. Only a day or two before

Jim's arrival several heads of households in the very fishing village that was afterwards taken under his special protection had been driven over the cliffs by a party of Rajah's spearmen, on suspicion of having been collecting edible birds' nests for a Celebes trader. Rajah Allang pretended to be the only trader in his country, and the penalty for the breach of the monopoly was death ; but his idea of trading was indistinguishable from the commonest forms of robbery. His cruelty and rapacity had no other bounds than his cowardice, and he was afraid of the organised power of the Celebes men, only— till Jim came—he was not afraid enough to keep quiet. He struck at them through his subjects, and thought himself pathetically in the right. The situation was complicated by a wandering stranger, an Arab half-bred, who, I believe, on purely religious grounds, had incited the tribes in the interior (the bush-folk, as Jim himself called them) to rise, and had established himself in a fortified camp on the summit of one of the twin hills. He hung over the town of Patusan like a hawk over a poultry-yard, but he devastated the open country. Whole villages, deserted, rotted on their blackened posts over the banks of clear streams, dropping piecemeal into the water the grass of their walls, the leaves of their roofs, with a curious effect of natural decay as if they had been a form of vegetation stricken by a blight at its very root. The two parties in Patusan were not sure which one this partisan most desired to plunder. The Rajah intrigued with him feebly. Some of the Bugis settlers, weary with endless insecurity, were half inclined to call him in. The younger spirits amongst them, chaffing, advised to ' get Sherif Ali with his wild men and drive the

Rajah Allang out of the country.' Doramin restrained them with difficulty. He was growing
old, and, though his influence had not diminished
the situation was getting beyond him. This was
the state of affairs when Jim, bolting from the
Rajah's stockade, appeared before the chief of the
Bugis, produced the ring, and was received, in a
manner of speaking, into the heart of the
community."

CHAPTER XXVI.

" DORAMIN was one of the most remarkable men of
his race I had ever seen. His bulk for a Malay was
immense, but he did not look merely fat ; he looked
imposing, monumental. This motionless body clad
in rich stuffs, coloured silks, gold embroideries ; this
huge head, enfolded in a red-and-gold headkerchief ;
the flat, big, round face, wrinkled, furrowed, with
two semicircular heavy folds starting on each side
of wide, fierce nostrils, and enclosing a thick-lipped
mouth ; the throat like a bull ; the vast corrugated
brow overhanging the staring proud eyes,—made a
whole that, once seen, can never be forgotten. His
impassive repose (he seldom stirred a limb when once
he sat down) was like a display of dignity. He was
never known to raise his voice. It was a hoarse and
powerful murmur, slightly veiled as if heard from a
distance. When he walked, two short, sturdy young
fellows, naked to the waist, in white sarongs and
with black skull-caps on the backs of their heads,
sustained his elbows : they would ease him down

and stand behind his chair till he wanted to rise, when he would turn his head slowly, as if with difficulty, to the right and to the left, and then they would catch him under his armpits and help him up. For all that, there was nothing of a cripple about him : on the contrary, all his ponderous movements were like manifestations of a mighty deliberate force. It was generally believed he consulted his wife as to public affairs ; but nobody, as far as I know, had ever heard them exchange a single word. When they sat in state by the wide opening it was in silence. They could see below them in the declining light the vast expanse of the forest country, a dark sleeping sea of sombre green undulating as far as the violet and purple range of mountains ; the shining sinuosity of the river like an immense letter S of beaten silver ; the brown ribbon of houses following the sweep of both banks, overtopped by the twin-hills uprising above the nearer tree-tops. They were wonderfully contrasted : she, light, delicate, spare, quick, a little witch-like, with a touch of motherly fussiness in her repose ; he, facing her, immense and heavy, like a figure of a man roughly fashioned of stone, with something magnanimous and ruthless in his immobility. The son of these old people was a most distinguished youth.

" They had him late in life. Perhaps he was not really so young as he looked. Four- or five-and-twenty is not so young when a man is already father of a family at eighteen. When he entered the large room, lined and carpeted with fine mats, and with a high ceiling of white sheeting, where the couple sat in state surrounded by a most deferential retinue, he would make his way straight to Doramin, to kiss his

hand—which the other abandoned to him, majestic
ally—and then would step across to stand by his
mother's chair. I suppose I may say they idolised
him, but I never caught them giving him an over
glance. Those, it is true, were public functions
The room was generally thronged. The solemn for
mality of greetings and leave-takings, the profound
respect expressed in gestures, on the faces, in the
low whispers, is simply indescribable. 'It's well
worth seeing,' Jim had assured me while we were
crossing the river, on our way back. 'They are
like people in a book, aren't they?' he said trium
phantly. 'And Dain Waris—their son—is the best
friend (barring you) I ever had. What Mr Stein
would call a good "war-comrade." I was in luck
Jove! I was in luck when I tumbled amongst them
at my last gasp.' He meditated with bowed head,
then rousing himself he added—

"'Of course I didn't go to sleep over it, but . . . '
He paused again. 'It seemed to come to me,' he
murmured. 'All at once I saw what I had to
do . . .'

"There was no doubt that it had come to him;
and it had come through war, too, as is natural,
since this power that came to him was the power
to make peace. It is in this sense alone that might
so often *is* right. You must not think he had seen
his way at once. When he arrived the Bugis com
munity was in a most critical position. 'They were
all afraid,' he said to me—'each man afraid for
himself; while I could see as plain as possible that
they must do something at once if they did not
want to go under one after another, what between
the Rajah and that vagabond Sherif.' But to see
that was nothing. When he got his idea he had

to drive it into reluctant minds, through the bulwarks of fear, of selfishness. He drove it in at last. And that was nothing. He had to devise the means. He devised them—an audacious plan; and his task was only half done. He had to inspire with his own confidence a lot of people who had hidden and absurd reasons to hang back; he had to conciliate imbecile jealousies, and argue away all sorts of senseless mistrusts. Without the weight of Doramin's authority, and his son's fiery enthusiasm, he would have failed. Dain Waris, the distinguished youth, was the first to believe in him; theirs was one of these strange, profound, rare friendships between brown and white, in which the very difference of race seems to draw two human beings closer by some mystic element of sympathy. Of Dain Waris, his own people said with pride that he knew how to fight like a white man. This was true; he had that sort of courage—the courage in the open, I may say,—but he had also a European mind. You meet them sometimes like that, and are surprised to discover unexpectedly a familiar turn of thought, an unobscured vision, a tenacity of purpose, a touch of altruism. Of small stature, but admirably well proportioned, Dain Waris had a proud carriage, a polished, easy bearing, a temperament like a clear flame. His dusky face, with big black eyes, was in action expressive, and in repose thoughtful. He was of a silent disposition; a firm glance, an ironic smile, a courteous deliberation of manner seemed to hint at great reserves of intelligence and power. Such beings open to the Western eye, so often concerned with mere surfaces, the hidden possibilities of races and lands over which hangs the mystery of unrecorded ages. He not

only trusted Jim, he understood him, I firmly
believe. I speak of him because he had captivated
me. His—if I may say so—his caustic placidity,
and, at the same time, his intelligent sympathy
with Jim's aspirations, appealed to me. I seemed
to behold the very origin of friendship. If Jim
took the lead, the other had captivated his leader.
In fact, Jim the leader was a captive in every sense.
The land, the people, the friendship, the love,
were like the jealous guardians of his body. Every
day added a link to the fetters of that strange
freedom. I felt convinced of it, as from day to day
I learned more of the story.

"The story! Haven't I heard the story? I've
heard it on the march, in camp (he made me scour
the country after invisible game); I've listened to a
good part of it on one of the twin-summits, after
climbing the last hundred feet or so on my hands
and knees. Our escort (we had volunteer followers
from village to village) had camped meantime on a
bit of level ground half-way up the slope, and in
the still breathless evening the smell of wood-smoke
reached our nostrils from below with the penetrating delicacy of some choice scent. Voices also
ascended, wonderful in their distinct and immaterial
clearness. Jim sat on the trunk of a felled tree,
and pulling out his pipe began to smoke. A new
growth of grass and bushes was springing up; there
were traces of an earthwork under a mass of thorny
twigs. 'It all started from here,' he said, after a
long and meditative silence. On the other hill, two
hundred yards across a sombre precipice, I saw a line
of high blackened stakes, showing here and there
ruinously—the remnants of Sherif Ali's impregnable
camp.

"But it had been taken though. That had been his idea. He had mounted Doramin's old ordnance on the top of that hill; two rusty iron 7-pounders, a lot of small brass cannon—currency cannon. But if the brass guns represent wealth, they can also, when crammed recklessly to the muzzle, send a solid shot to some little distance. The thing was to get them up there. He showed me where he had fastened the cables, explained how he had improvised a rude capstan out of a hollowed log turning upon a pointed stake, indicated with the bowl of his pipe the outline of the earthwork. The last hundred feet of the ascent had been the most difficult. He had made himself responsible for success on his own head. He had induced the war party to work hard all night. Big fires lighted at intervals blazed all down the slope, 'but up here,' he explained, 'the hoisting gang had to fly around in the dark.' From the top he saw men moving on the hillside like ants at work. He himself on that night had kept on rushing down and climbing up like a squirrel, directing, encouraging, watching all along the line. Old Doramin had himself carried up the hill in his arm-chair. They put him down on the level place upon the slope, and he sat there in the light of one of the big fires—'amazing old chap—real old chieftain,' said Jim, 'with his little fierce eyes— a pair of immense flintlock pistols on his knees. Magnificent things, ebony, silver-mounted, with beautiful locks and a calibre like an old blunderbuss. A present from Stein, it seems—in exchange for that ring, you know. Used to belong to good old M'Neil. God only knows how *he* came by them. There he sat, moving neither hand nor foot, a flame of dry brushwood behind him, and lots of people rushing about, shouting and pulling round him—the most solemn, imposing old chap you can imagine. *He* wouldn't have had much chance if Sherif Ali had let his infernal crew loose at us and stampeded my lot. Eh? Anyhow, he had come up there to die if anything went wrong. No mistake! Jove! It thrilled me to see him there—like a rock. But the Sherif must have thought us mad, and never troubled to come and see how we got on. Nobody believed it could be done. Why! I think the very chaps who pulled and shoved and sweated over it did not believe it could be done! Upon my word I don't think they did. . . .'

" He stood erect, the smouldering brier-wood in his clutch, with a smile on his lips and a sparkle in his boyish eyes. I sat on the stump of a tree at his feet, and below us stretched the land, the great expanse of the forests, sombre under the sunshine, rolling like a sea, with glints of winding rivers, the grey spots of villages, and here and there a clearing, like an islet of light amongst the dark waves of continuous tree-tops. A brooding gloom lay over this vast and monotonous landscape ; the light fell on it as if into an abyss. The land devoured the sunshine ; only far off, along the coast, the empty ocean, smooth and polished within the faint haze, seemed to rise up to the sky in a wall of steel.

" And there I was with him, high in the sunshine on the top of that historic hill of his. He dominated the forest, the secular gloom, the old mankind. He was like a figure set up on a pedestal, to represent in his persistent youth the power, and perhaps the virtues, of races that never grow old, that have emerged from the gloom. I don't know why he should always have appeared to me symbolic.

Perhaps this is the real cause of my interest in his fate. I don't know whether it was exactly fair to him to remember the incident which had given a new direction to his life, but at that very moment I remembered very distinctly. It was like a shadow in the light."

CHAPTER XXVII.

" ALREADY the legend had gifted him with supernatural powers. Yes, it was said, there had been many ropes cunningly disposed, and a strange contrivance that turned by the efforts of many men, and each gun went up tearing slowly through the bushes, like a wild pig rooting its way in the undergrowth, but, . . . and the wisest shook their heads. There was something occult in all this, no doubt; for what is the strength of ropes and of men's arms? There is a rebellious soul in things which must be overcome by powerful charms and incantations. Thus old Sura—a very respectable householder of Patusan—with whom I had a quiet chat one evening. However, Sura was a professional sorcerer also, who attended all the rice sowings and reapings for miles around for the purpose of subduing the stubborn soul of things. This occupation he seemed to think a most arduous one, and perhaps the souls of things are more stubborn than the souls of men. As to the simple folk of outlying villages, they believed and said (as the most natural thing in the world) that Jim had carried the guns up the hill on his back—two at a time.

"This would make Jim stamp his foot in vexation and exclaim with an exasperated little laugh, 'What can you do with such silly beggars? They will sit up half the night talking bally rot, and the greater the lie the more they seem to like it.' You could trace the subtle influence of his surroundings in this irritation. It was part of his captivity. The earnestness of his denials was amusing, and at last I said, 'My dear fellow, you don't suppose *I* believe this.' He looked at me quite startled. 'Well, no! I suppose not,' he said, and burst into a Homeric peal of laughter. 'Well, anyhow the guns were there, and went off all together at sunrise. Jove! You should have seen the splinters fly,' he cried. By his side Dain Waris, listening with a quiet smile, dropped his eyelids and shuffled his feet a little. It appears that the success in mounting the guns had given Jim's people such a feeling of confidence that he ventured to leave the battery under charge of two elderly Bugis who had seen some fighting in their day, and went to join Dain Waris and the storming-party who were concealed in the ravine. In the small hours they began creeping up, and when two-thirds of the way up, lay in the wet grass waiting for the appearance of the sun, which was the agreed signal. He told me with what impatient anguishing emotion he watched the swift coming of the dawn; how, heated with the work and the climbing, he felt the cold dew chilling his very bones; how afraid he was he would begin to shiver and shake like a leaf before the time came for the advance. 'It was the slowest half-hour in my life,' he declared. Gradually the silent stockade came out on the sky above him. Men scattered all down the slope were crouching amongst the dark stones and dripping bushes. Dain Waris was lying flattened by his side. 'We looked at each other,' Jim said, resting a gentle hand on his friend's shoulder. 'He smiled at me as cheery as you please, and I dared not stir my lips for fear I would break out into a shivering fit. 'Pon my word, it's true! I had been streaming with perspiration when we took cover—so you may imagine . . .' He declared, and I believe him, that he had no fears as to the result. He was only anxious as to his ability to repress these shivers. He didn't bother about the result. He was bound to get to the top of that hill and stay there, whatever might happen. There could be no going back for him. Those people had trusted him implicitly. Him alone! His bare word. . . .

"I remember how, at this point, he paused with his eyes fixed upon me. 'As far as he knew, they never had an occasion to regret it yet,' he said. 'Never. He hoped to God they never would. Meantime—worse luck!—they had got into the habit of taking his word for anything and everything. I could have no idea! Why? Only the other day an old fool he had never seen in his life came from some village miles away to find out if he should divorce his wife. Fact. Solemn word. That's the sort of thing . . . He wouldn't have believed it. Would I? Squatted on the verandah chewing betel-nut, sighing and spitting all over the place for more than an hour, and as glum as an undertaker before he came out with that dashed conundrum. That's the kind of thing that isn't so funny as it looks. What was a fellow to say?— Good wife?—Yes. Good wife—old though; started a confounded long story about some brass pots.

Been living together for fifteen years—twenty years
—could not tell. A long, long time. Good wife.
Beat her a little—not much—just a little, when she
was young. Had to—for the sake of his honour.
Suddenly in her old age she goes and lends three
brass pots to her sister's son's wife, and begins to
abuse him every day in a loud voice. His enemies
jeered at him; his face was utterly blackened. Pots
totally lost. Awfully cut up about it. Impossible
to fathom a story like that; told him to go home,
and promised to come along myself and settle it all.
It's all very well to grin, but it was the dashedest
nuisance! A day's journey through the forest,
another day lost in coaxing a lot of silly villagers
to get at the rights of the affair. There was the
making of a sanguinary shindy in the thing. Every
bally idiot took sides with one family or the other,
and one-half of the village was ready to go for the
other half with anything that came handy. Honour
bright! No joke! . . . Instead of attending to
their bally crops. Got him the infernal pots back
of course—and pacified all hands. No trouble to
settle it. Of course not. Could settle the deadliest
quarrel in the country by crooking his little finger.
The trouble was to get at the truth of anything.
Was not sure to this day whether he had been
fair to all parties. It worried him. And the talk!
Jove! There didn't seem to be any head or tail to
it. Rather storm a twenty-foot-high old stockade
any day. Much! Child's play to that other job.
Wouldn't take so long either. Well, yes; a funny
set out, upon the whole—the fool looked old enough
to be his grandfather. But from another point of
view it was no joke. His word decided everything
—ever since the smashing of Sherif Ali. An awful

responsibility,' he repeated. 'No, really—joking apart, had it been three lives instead of three rotten brass pots it would have been the same. . . .'

"Thus he illustrated the moral effect of his victory in war. It was in truth immense. It had led him from strife to peace, and through death into the innermost life of the people; but the gloom of the land spread out under the sunshine preserved its appearance of inscrutable, of secular repose. The sound of his fresh young voice (it's extraordinary how very few signs of wear he showed) floated lightly, and passed away over the unchanged face of the forests like the sound of the big guns on that cold dewy morning when he had no other concern on earth but the proper control of the chills in his body. With the first slant of sun-rays along these immovable tree-tops the summit of one hill wreathed itself, with heavy reports, in white clouds of smoke, and the other burst into an amazing noise of yells, war-cries, shouts of anger, of surprise, of dismay. Jim and Dain Waris were the first to lay their hands on the stakes. The popular story has it that Jim with a touch of one finger had thrown down the gate. He was, of course, anxious to disclaim this achievement. The whole stockade —he would insist on explaining to you—was a poor affair (Sherif Ali trusted mainly to the inaccessible position); and, anyway, the thing had been already knocked to pieces and only hung together by a miracle. He put his shoulder to it like a little fool and went in head over heels. Jove! If it hadn't been for Dain Waris, a pock-marked tattooed vagabond would have pinned him with his spear to a baulk of timber like one of Stein's beetles. The third man in, it seems, had been Tamb' Itam,

Jim's own servant. This was a Malay from the north, a stranger who had wandered into Patusan, and had been forcibly detained by Rajah Allang as paddler of one of the state boats. He had made a bolt of it at the first opportunity, and finding a precarious refuge (but very little to eat) amongst the Bugis settlers, had attached himself to Jim's person. His complexion was very dark, his face flat, his eyes prominent and injected with bile. There was something excessive, almost fanatical, in his devotion to his ' white lord.' He was inseparable from Jim like a morose shadow. On state occasions he would tread on his master's heels, one hand on the haft of his kris, keeping the common people at a distance by his truculent brooding glances. Jim had made him the headman of his establishment, and all Patusan respected and courted him as a person of much influence. At the taking of the stockade he had distinguished himself greatly by the methodical ferocity of his fighting. The storming-party had come on so quick—Jim said—that notwithstanding the panic of the garrison, there was a ' hot five minutes hand-to-hand inside that stockade, till some bally ass set fire to the shelters of boughs and dry grass, and we all had to clear out for dear life.'

" The rout, it seems, had been complete. Doramin waiting immovably in his chair on the hillside, with the smoke of the guns spreading slowly above his big head, received the news with a deep grunt. When informed that his son was safe and leading the pursuit, he, without another sound, made a mighty effort to rise ; his attendants hurried to his help, and, held up reverently, he shuffled with great dignity into a bit of shade, where he laid himself down to sleep covered entirely with a piece of white

sheeting. In Patusan the excitement was intense.
Jim told me that from the hill, turning his back on
the stockade with its embers, black ashes, and half-
consumed corpses, he could see time after time the
open spaces between the houses on both sides of the
stream fill suddenly with a seething rush of people
and get empty in a moment. His ears caught feebly
from below the tremendous din of gongs and drums ;
the wild shouts of the crowd reached him in bursts
of faint roaring. A lot of streamers made a flutter
as of little white, red, yellow birds amongst the
brown ridges of roofs. ' You must have enjoyed it,' I
murmured, feeling the stir of sympathetic emotion.

" ' It was . . . it was immense ! Immense ! ' he
cried aloud, flinging his arms open. The sudden
movement startled me as though I had seen him
bare the secrets of his breast to the sunshine, to the
brooding forests, to the steely sea. Below us the
town reposed in easy curves upon the banks of a
stream whose current seemed to sleep. ' Immense ! '
he repeated for a third time, speaking in a whisper,
for himself alone.

" Immense ! No doubt it was immense ; the seal
of success upon his words, the conquered ground for
the soles of his feet, the blind trust of men, the
belief in himself snatched from the fire, the solitude
of his achievement. All this, as I've warned you,
gets dwarfed in the telling. I can't with mere
words convey to you the impression of his total
and utter isolation. I know, of course, he was in
every sense alone of his kind there, but the unsuspected qualities of his nature had brought him
in such close touch with his surroundings that this
isolation seemed only the effect of his power. His
loneliness added to his stature. There was nothing

within sight to compare him with, as though he had been one of these exceptional men who can be only measured by the greatness of their fame; and his fame, remember, was the greatest thing around for many a day's journey. You would have to paddle, pole, or track a long weary way through the jungle before you passed beyond the reach of its voice. Its voice was not the trumpeting of the disreputable goddess we all know—not blatant—not brazen. It took its tone from the stillness and gloom of the land without a past, where his word was the one truth of every passing day. It shared something of the nature of that silence through which it accompanied you into unexplored depths, heard continuously by your side, penetrating, far-reaching—tinged with wonder and mystery on the lips of whispering men."

CHAPTER XXVIII.

" THE defeated Sherif Ali fled the country without making another stand, and when the miserable hunted villagers began to crawl out of the jungle back to their rotting houses, it was Jim who, in consultation with Dain Waris, appointed the headmen. Thus he became the virtual ruler of the land. As to old Tunku Allang, his fears at first had known no bounds. It is said that at the intelligence of the successful storming of the hill he flung himself, face down, on the bamboo floor of his audience-hall, and lay motionless for a whole night and a whole day, uttering stifled sounds of such an appalling nature that no man dared approach his prostrate form nearer than a spear's length. Already he could see himself driven ignominiously out of Patusan, wandering, abandoned, stripped, without opium, without his women, without followers, a fair game for the first comer to kill. After Sherif Ali his turn would come, and who could resist an attack led by such a devil? And indeed he owed his life and such authority as he still possessed at the time of my visit to Jim's idea of what was fair alone. The Bugis had been extremely anxious to pay off old scores, and the impassive old Doramin cherished the hope of yet seeing his son ruler of Patusan. During one of our interviews he deliberately allowed me to get a glimpse of this secret ambition. Nothing could be finer in its way than the dignified wariness of his approaches. He himself—he began by declaring—had used his strength in his young days, but now he had grown old and tired. . . . With his imposing bulk and haughty little eyes darting sagacious, inquisitive glances, he reminded one irresistibly of a cunning old elephant; the slow rise and fall of his vast breast went on powerful and regular, like the heave of a calm sea. He too, as he protested, had an unbounded confidence in Tuan Jim's wisdom. If he could only obtain a promise! One word would be enough! . . . His breathing silences, the low rumblings of his voice, recalled the last efforts of a spent thunderstorm.

"I tried to put the subject aside. It was difficult, for there could be no question that Jim had the power; in his new sphere there did not seem to be anything that was not his to hold or to give.

But that, I repeat, was nothing in comparison with the notion, which occurred to me, while I listened with a show of attention, that he seemed to have come very near at last to mastering his fate. Doramin was anxious about the future of the country, and I was struck by the turn he gave to the argument. The land remains where God had put it, but white men—he said—they come to us and in a little while they go. They go away. Those they leave behind do not know when to look for their return. They go to their own land, to their people, and so this white man too would. . . . I don't know what induced me to commit myself at this point by a vigorous 'No, no.' The whole extent of this indiscretion became apparent when Doramin, turning full upon me his face, whose expression, fixed in rugged deep folds, remained unalterable, like a huge brown mask, said that this was good news indeed, reflectively; and then wanted to know why.

"His little, motherly witch of a wife sat on my other hand, with her head covered and her feet tucked up, gazing through the great shutter-hole. I could only see a straying lock of grey hair, a high cheek-bone, the slight masticating motion of the sharp chin. Without removing her eyes from the vast prospect of forests stretching as far as the hills, she asked me in a pitying voice why was it that he so young had wandered from his home, coming so far, through so many dangers? Had he no household there, no kinsmen in his own country? Had he no old mother, who would always remember his face? . . .

"I was completely unprepared for this. I could only mutter and shake my head vaguely. Afterwards I am perfectly aware I cut a very poor figure trying to extricate myself out of this difficulty. From that moment, however, the old *nakhoda* became taciturn. He was not very pleased, I fear, and evidently I had given him food for thought. Strangely enough, on the evening of that very day (which was my last in Patusan) I was once more confronted with the same question, with the unanswerable why of Jim's fate. And this brings me to the story of his love.

" I suppose you think it is a story that you can imagine for yourselves. We have heard so many such stories, and the majority of us don't believe them to be stories of love at all. For the most part we look upon them as stories of opportunities : episodes of passion at best, or perhaps only of youth and temptation, doomed to forgetfulness in the end, even if they pass through the reality of tenderness and regret. This view mostly is right, and perhaps in this case too. . . . Yet I don't know. To tell this story is by no means so easy as it should be —were the ordinary standpoint adequate. Apparently it is a story very much like the others : for me, however, there is visible in its background the melancholy figure of a woman, the shadow of a cruel wisdom buried in a lonely grave, looking on wistfully, helplessly, with sealed lips. The grave itself, as I came upon it during an early morning stroll, was a rather shapeless brown mound, with an inlaid neat border of white lumps of coral at the base, and enclosed within a circular fence made of split saplings, with the bark left on. A garland of leaves and flowers was woven about the heads of the slender posts—and the flowers were fresh.

" Thus, whether the shadow is of my imagination

or not, I can at all events point out the significant
fact of an unforgotten grave. When I tell you
besides that Jim with his own hands had worked
at the rustic fence, you will perceive directly the
difference, the individual side of the story. There is
in his espousal of memory and affection belonging to
another human being something characteristic of his
seriousness. He had a conscience, and it was a
romantic conscience. Through her whole life the
wife of the unspeakable Cornelius had no other
companion, confidant, and friend but her daughter.
How the poor woman had come to marry the
awful little Malacca Portuguese—after the separation from the father of her girl—and how that
separation had been brought about, whether by
death, which can be sometimes merciful, or by the
merciless pressure of conventions, is a mystery to
me. From the little which Stein (who knew so many
stories) had let drop in my hearing, I am convinced
that she was no ordinary woman. Her own father
had been a white; a high official; one of the
brilliantly endowed men who are not dull enough
to nurse a success, and whose careers so often end
under a cloud. I suppose she too must have lacked
the saving dulness—and her career ended in Patusan.
Our common fate . . . for where is the man—I
mean a real sentient man—who does not remember
vaguely having been deserted in the fulness of
possession by some one or something more precious
than life ? . . . our common fate fastens upon the
women with a peculiar cruelty. It does not punish
like a master, but inflicts lingering torment, as if
to gratify a secret, unappeasable spite. One would
think that, appointed to rule on earth, it seeks to
revenge itself upon the beings that come nearest to

ising above the trammels of earthly caution ; for it
s only women who manage to put at times into
heir love an element just palpable enough to give
ne a fright—an extra-terrestrial touch. I ask myself with wonder—how the world can look to them
—whether it has the shape and substance *we* know,
he air *we* breathe ! Sometimes I fancy it must be
a region of unreasonable sublimities seething with
he excitement of their adventurous souls, lighted
by the glory of all possible risks and renunciations.
However, I suspect there are very few women in
he world, though of course I am aware of the
multitudes of mankind and of the equality of sexes
in point of numbers—that is. But I am sure that
he mother was as much of a woman as the daughter
seemed to be. I cannot help picturing to myself
hese two, at first the young woman and the child,
hen the old woman and the young girl, the awful
sameness and the swift passage of time, the barrier
of forest, the solitude and the turmoil round these
wo lonely lives, and every word spoken between
hem penetrated with sad meaning. There must
have been confidences, not so much of fact, I suppose,
as of innermost feeling—regrets—fears—warnings,
no doubt : warnings that the younger did not fully
understand till the elder was dead—and Jim came
along. Then I am sure she understood much—
not everything—the fear mostly it seems. Jim
called her by a word that means precious, in the
sense of a precious gem—jewel. Pretty, isn't it ?
But he was capable of anything. He was equal to
his fortune, as he—after all—must have been equal
to his misfortune. Jewel he called her ; and he
would say this as he might have said ' Jane,' don't
you know, with a marital, homelike, peaceful effect.

I heard the name for the first time ten minutes
after I had landed in his courtyard, when, after
nearly shaking my arm off, he darted up the steps
and began to make a joyous, boyish disturbance at
the door under the heavy eaves. 'Jewel! O
Jewel. Quick! Here's a friend come,' . . . and
suddenly peering at me in the dim verandah, he
mumbled earnestly, 'You know—this—no confounded nonsense about it—can't tell you how much
I owe to her—and so—you understand—I—exactly
as if . . .' His hurried, anxious whispers were cut
short by the flitting of a white form within the
house, a faint exclamation, and a child-like but
energetic little face with delicate features and a
profound attentive glance peeped out of the inner
gloom, like a bird out of the recess of a nest. I was
struck by the name, of course; but it was not till
later on that I connected it with an astonishing
rumour that had met me on my journey, at a little
place on the coast about 230 miles south of Patusan
river. Stein's schooner, in which I had my passage,
put in there, to collect some produce, and, going
ashore, I found to my great surprise that the
wretched locality could boast of a third-class deputy-
assistant resident, a big, fat, greasy, blinking fellow
of mixed descent, with turned out, shiny lips. I
found him lying extended on his back in a cane
chair, odiously unbuttoned, with a large green leaf
of some sort on the top of his steaming head, and
another in his hand which he used lazily as a fan. . . .
Going to Patusan? Oh yes. Stein's Trading Company. He knew. Had a permission. No business
of his. It was not so bad there now, he remarked
negligently, and, he went on drawling, 'there's some
sort of white vagabond had got in there, I hear. . . .

Eh ? What you say ? Friend of yours ? So ! . . .
Then it was true there was one of these *vordamte*—
What was he up to ? Found his way in, the rascal.
Eh ? I had not been sure. Patusan—they cut
throats there—no business of ours.' He interrupted
himself to groan. 'Phoo ! Almighty ! The heat !
The heat ! Well, then, there might be something in
the story too, after all, and . . .' He shut one of his
beastly glassy eyes (the eyelid went on quivering),
while he leered at me atrociously with the other.
Look here,' says he mysteriously, ' if—do you
understand ?—if he has really got hold of something fairly good—none of your bits of green glass—
understand ?—I am a government official—you
tell the rascal . . . Eh ? What ? Friend of
yours ? ' . . . He continued wallowing calmly in
the chair . . . 'You said so ; that's just it ; and
I am pleased to give you the hint. I suppose you
too would like to get something out of it ? Don't
interrupt. You just tell him I've heard the tale,
but to my government I have made no report.
Not yet. See ? Why make a report ? Eh ? Tell
him to come to me if they let him get alive out
of the country. He had better look out for himself.
Eh ? I promise to ask no questions. On the quiet—
you understand ? You too—you shall get something
from me. Small commission for the trouble. Don't
interrupt. I am a government official, and make
no report. That's business. Understand ? I know
some good people that will buy anything worth
having, and can give him more money than the
scoundrel ever saw in his life. I know his sort.' He
fixed me steadfastly with both his eyes open, while I
stood over him utterly amazed, and asking myself
whether he was mad or drunk. He perspired, puffed,

K

moaning feebly, and scratching himself with suc
horrible composure that I could not bear the sigh
long enough to find out. Next day, talking casuall
with the people of the little native court of th
place, I discovered that a story was travellin
slowly down the coast about a mysterious whit
man in Patusan who had got hold of an extraor
dinary gem—namely, an emerald of an enormou
size, and altogether priceless. The emerald seem
to appeal more to the Eastern imagination tha
any other precious stone. The white man ha
obtained it, I was told, partly by the exercise o
his wonderful strength and partly by cunning
from the ruler of a distant country, whence he ha
fled instantly, arriving in Patusan in utmost distress
but frightening the people by his extreme ferocity
which nothing seemed able to subdue. Most of m
informants were of the opinion that the stone wa
probably unlucky,—like the famous stone of th
Sultan of Succadana, which in the old times ha
brought wars and untold calamities upon tha
country. Perhaps it was the same stone—on
couldn't say. Indeed the story of a fabulousl
large emerald is as old as the arrival of the firs
white men in the Archipelago ; and the belief i
it is so persistent that less than forty years ag
there had been an official Dutch inquiry into th
truth of it. Such a jewel—it was explained t
me by the old fellow from whom I heard most o
this amazing Jim-myth—a sort of scribe to th
wretched little Rajah of the place ;—such a jewe
he said, cocking his poor purblind eyes up at m
(he was sitting on the cabin floor out of respect)
is best preserved by being concealed about the per
son of a woman. Yet it is not every woman tha

would do. She must be young—he sighed deeply—
and insensible to the seductions of love. He shook
his head sceptically. But such a woman seemed to
be actually in existence. He had been told of a tall
girl, whom the white man treated with great respect
and care, and who never went forth from the house
unattended. People said the white man could be
seen with her almost any day ; they walked side by
side, openly, he holding her arm under his—pressed
to his side—thus—in a most extraordinary way.
This might be a lie, he conceded, for it was indeed
a strange thing for any one to do : on the other
hand, there could be no doubt she wore the white
man's jewel concealed upon her bosom.''

CHAPTER XXIX.

" THIS was the theory of Jim's marital evening
walks. I made a third on more than one occasion,
unpleasantly aware every time of Cornelius, who
nursed the aggrieved sense of his legal paternity,
slinking in the neighbourhood with that peculiar
twist of his mouth as if he were perpetually on
the point of gnashing his teeth. But do you notice
how, three hundred miles beyond the end of tele-
graph cables and mail-boat lines, the haggard
utilitarian lies of our civilisation wither and die,
to be replaced by pure exercises of imagination,
that have the futility, often the charm, and sometimes the deep hidden truthfulness, of works of
art ? Romance had singled Jim for its own—

and that was the true part of the story, which
otherwise was all wrong. He did not hide his
jewel. In fact, he was extremely proud of it.

"It comes to me now that I had, on the whole,
seen very little of her. What I remember best is
the even, olive pallor of her complexion, and the
intense blue-black gleams of her hair, flowing abun-
dantly from under a small crimson cap she wore
far back on her shapely head. Her movements were
free, assured, and she blushed a dusky red. While
Jim and I were talking, she would come and go with
rapid glances at us, leaving on her passage an impression of grace and charm and a distinct suggestion
of watchfulness. Her manner presented a curious
combination of shyness and audacity. Every pretty
smile was succeeded swiftly by a look of silent, repressed anxiety, as if put to flight by the recollection of some abiding danger. At times she would
sit down with us and, with her soft cheek dimpled
by the knuckles of her little hand, she would listen
to our talk ; her big clear eyes would remain fastened
to our lips, as though each pronounced word had a
visible shape. Her mother had taught her to read
and write ; she had learned a good bit of English
from Jim, and she spoke it most amusingly, with
his own clipping, boyish intonation. Her tenderness hovered over him like a flutter of wings. She
lived so completely in his contemplation that she
had acquired something of his outward aspect,
something that recalled him in her movements,
in the way she stretched her arm, turned her head,
directed her glances. Her vigilant affection had
an intensity that made it almost perceptible to
the senses ; it seemed actually to exist in the
ambient matter of space, to envelop him like a

peculiar fragrance, to dwell in the sunshine like a tremulous, subdued, and impassioned note. I suppose you think that I too am romantic, but it is a mistake. I am relating to you the sober impressions of a bit of youth, of a strange uneasy romance that had come in my way. I observed with interest the work of his—well—good fortune. He was jealously loved, but why she should be jealous, and of what, I could not tell. The land, the people, the forests were her accomplices, guarding him with vigilant accord, with an air of seclusion, of mystery, of invincible possession. There was no appeal, as it were; he was imprisoned within the very freedom of his power, and she, though ready to make a footstool of her head for his feet, guarded her conquest inflexibly—as though he were hard to keep. The very Tamb' Itam, marching on our journeys upon the heels of his white lord, with his head thrown back, truculent and be-weaponed like a janissary, with kris, chopper, and lance (besides carrying Jim's gun); even Tamb' Itam allowed himself to put on the airs of uncompromising guardianship, like a surly devoted jailer ready to lay down his life for his captive. On the evenings when we sat up late his silent, indistinct form would pass and repass under the verandah, with noiseless footsteps, or lifting my head I would unexpectedly make him out standing rigidly erect in the shadow. As a general rule he would vanish after a time, without a sound; but when we rose he would spring up close to us as if from the ground, ready for any orders Jim might wish to give. The girl too, I believe, never went to sleep till we had separated for the night. More than once I saw her and Jim through the

window of my room come out together quietly
and lean on the rough balustrade—two white
forms very close, his arm about her waist, her head
on his shoulder. Their soft murmurs reached me,
penetrating, tender, with a calm sad note in the
stillness of the night, like a self-communion of
one being carried on in two tones. Later on, tossing
on my bed under the mosquito-net, I was sure to
hear slight creakings, faint breathing, a throat
cleared cautiously—and I would know that Tamb'
Itam was still on the prowl. Though he had (by
the favour of the white lord) a house in the compound, had 'taken wife,' and had lately been
blessed with a child, I believe that, during my
stay at all events, he slept on the verandah every
night. It was very difficult to make this faithful
and grim retainer talk. Even Jim himself was
answered in jerky short sentences, under protest
as it were. Talking, he seemed to imply, was no
business of his. The longest speech I heard him
volunteer was one morning when, suddenly extending
his hand towards the courtyard, he pointed at
Cornelius and said, 'Here comes the Nazarene.'
I don't think he was addressing me, though I stood
at his side; his object seemed rather to awaken
the indignant attention of the universe. Some
muttered allusions, which followed, to dogs and
the smell of roast-meat, struck me as singularly
felicitous. The courtyard, a large square space, was
one torrid blaze of sunshine, and, bathed in intense
light, Cornelius was creeping across in full view
with an inexpressible effect of stealthiness, of dark
and secret slinking. He reminded one of everything
that is unsavoury. His slow laborious walk resembled the creeping of a repulsive beetle, the legs

alone moving with horrid industry while the body glided evenly. I suppose he made straight enough for the place where he wanted to get to, but his progress with one shoulder carried forward seemed oblique. He was often seen circling slowly amongst the sheds, as if following a scent; passing before the verandah with upward stealthy glances; disappearing without haste round the corner of some hut. That he seemed free of the place demonstrated Jim's absurd carelessness or else his infinite disdain, for Cornelius had played a very dubious part (to say the least of it) in a certain episode which might have ended fatally for Jim. As a matter of fact, it had redounded to his glory. But everything redounded to his glory; and it was the irony of his good fortune that he, who had been too careful of it once, seemed to bear a charmed life.

"You must know he had left Doramin's place very soon after his arrival—much too soon, in fact, for his safety, and of course a long time before the war. In this he was actuated by a sense of duty; he had to look after Stein's business, he said. Hadn't he? To that end, with an utter disregard of his personal safety, he crossed the river and took up his quarters with Cornelius. How the latter had managed to exist through the troubled times I can't say. As Stein's agent, after all, he must have had Doramin's protection in a measure; and in one way or another he had managed to wriggle through all the deadly complications, while I have no doubt that his conduct, whatever line he was forced to take, was marked by that abjectness which was like the stamp of the man. That was his characteristic; he was fundamentally and outwardly abject, as other men are markedly of a generous, distinguished, or venerable appearance. It was the element of his nature which permeated all his acts and passions and emotions ; he raged abjectly, smiled abjectly, was abjectly sad ; his civilities and his indignations were alike abject. I am sure his love would have been the most abject of sentiments—but can one imagine a loathsome insect in love ? And his loathsomeness too was abject, so that a simply disgusting person would have appeared noble by his side. He has his place neither in the background nor in the foreground of the story ; he is simply seen skulking on its outskirts, enigmatical and unclean, tainting the fragrance of its youth and of its naïveness.

"His position in any case could not have been other than extremely miserable, yet it may very well be that he found some advantages in it. Jim told me he had been received at first with an abject display of the most amicable sentiments. 'The fellow apparently couldn't contain himself for joy,' said Jim with disgust. 'He flew at me every morning to shake both my hands—confound him ! but I could never tell whether there would be any breakfast. If I got three meals in two days I considered myself jolly lucky, and he made me sign a chit for ten dollars every week. Said he was sure Mr Stein did not mean him to keep me for nothing. Well—he kept me on nothing as near as possible. Put it down to the unsettled state of the country, and made as if to tear his hair out, begging my pardon twenty times a-day, so that I had at last to entreat him not to worry. It made me sick. Half the roof of his house had fallen in, and the whole place had a mangy look, with wisps of dry grass sticking out and the corners of broken mats flapping on every wall. He did his best to make out that Mr Stein owed him money on the last three years' trading, but his books were all torn, and some were missing. He tried to hint it was his late wife's fault. Disgusting scoundrel! At last I had to forbid him to mention his late wife at all. It made Jewel cry. I couldn't discover what became of all the trade-goods; there was nothing in the store but rats, having a high old time amongst a litter of brown paper and old sacking. I was assured on every hand that he had a lot of money buried somewhere, but of course could get nothing out of him. It was the most miserable existence I led there in that wretched house. I tried to do my duty by Stein, but I had also other matters to think of. When I escaped to Doramin old Tunku Allang got frightened and returned all my things. It was done in a roundabout way, and with no end of mystery, through a Chinaman who keeps a small shop here; but as soon as I left the Bugis quarter and went to live with Cornelius it began to be said openly that the Rajah had made up his mind to have me killed before long. Pleasant, wasn't it? And I couldn't see what was there to prevent him if he really *had* made up his mind. The worst of it was, I couldn't help feeling I wasn't doing any good either for Stein or for myself. Oh! it was beastly—the whole six weeks of it.'"

CHAPTER XXX.

"He told me further that he didn't know what made him hang on—but of course we may guess. He sympathised deeply with the defenceless girl, at the mercy of that 'mean, cowardly scoundrel.' It appears Cornelius led her an awful life, stopping only short of actual ill-usage, for which he had not the pluck, I suppose. He insisted upon her calling him father—'and with respect too—with respect,' he would scream, shaking a little yellow fist in her face. 'I am a respectable man, and what are you? Tell me—what are you? You think I am going to bring up somebody else's child and not be treated with respect? You ought to be glad I let you. Come—say Yes, father. . . . No? . . . You wait a bit.' Thereupon he would begin to abuse the dead woman, till the girl would run off with her hands to her head. He pursued her, dashing in and out and round the house and amongst the sheds, would drive her into some corner, where she would fall on her knees stopping her ears, and then he would stand at a distance and declaim filthy denunciations at her back for half an hour at a stretch. 'Your mother was a devil, a deceitful devil—and you too are a devil,' he would shriek in a final outburst, pick up a bit of dry earth or a handful of mud (there was plenty of mud around the house), and fling it into her hair. Sometimes, though, she would hold out full of scorn, confronting him in silence, her face sombre and contracted, and only now and then uttering a word or two that would make the other jump and writhe with the sting. Jim told me these scenes were terrible. It was indeed a strange thing to come upon in a wilderness. The endlessness of such a subtly cruel situation was appalling—if you think of it. The respectable Cornelius (Inchi 'Nelyus the Malays called him, with a grimace that meant many things) was a much-disappointed man. I don't know what he had expected would be done for him in consideration of his marriage; but evidently the liberty to steal, and embezzle, and appropriate to himself for many years and in any way that suited him best, the goods of Stein's Trading Co. (Stein kept the supply up unfalteringly as long as he could get his skippers to take it there) did not seem to him a fair equivalent for the sacrifice of his honourable name. Jim would have enjoyed exceedingly thrashing Cornelius within an inch of his life; on the other hand, the scenes were of so painful a character, so abominable, that his impulse would be to get out of earshot, in order to spare the girl's feelings. They left her agitated, speechless, clutching her bosom now and then with a stony, desperate face, and then Jim would lounge up and say unhappily, 'Now—come—really—what's the use— you must try to eat a bit,' or give some such mark of sympathy. Cornelius would keep on slinking through the doorways, across the verandah and back again, as mute as a fish, and with malevolent, mistrustful, underhand glances. 'I can stop his game,' Jim said to her once. 'Just say the word.' And do you know what she answered? She said— Jim told me impressively—that if she had not been sure he was intensely wretched himself, she would have found the courage to kill him with her own hands. 'Just fancy that! The poor devil of a girl, almost a child, being driven to talk like that,' he

exclaimed in horror. It seemed impossible to save
her not only from that mean rascal but even from
herself! It wasn't that he pitied her so much, he
affirmed; it was more than pity; it was as if he had
something on his conscience, while that life went on.
To leave the house would have appeared a base
desertion. He had understood at last that there
was nothing to expect from a longer stay, neither
accounts nor money, nor truth of any sort, but he
stayed on, exasperating Cornelius to the verge, I
won't say of insanity, but almost of courage. Meantime he felt all sorts of dangers gathering obscurely
about him. Doramin had sent over twice a trusty
servant to tell him seriously that he could do nothing
for his safety unless he would recross the river again
and live amongst the Bugis as at first. People of
every condition used to call, often in the dead of
night, in order to disclose to him plots for his
assassination. He was to be poisoned. He was to
be stabbed in the bath-house. Arrangements were
being made to have him shot from a boat on the
river. Each of these informants professed himself
to be his very good friend. It was enough—he
told me—to spoil a fellow's rest for ever. Something of the kind was extremely possible—nay,
probable—but the lying warnings gave him only
the sense of deadly scheming going on all around
him, on all sides, in the dark. Nothing more calculated to shake the best of nerve. Finally, one
night, Cornelius himself, with a great apparatus of
alarm and secrecy, unfolded in solemn wheedling
tones a little plan wherein for one hundred dollars—
or even for eighty; let's say eighty—he, Cornelius,
would procure a trustworthy man to smuggle Jim
out of the river, all safe. There was nothing else

for it now—if Jim cared a pin for his life. What's eighty dollars? A trifle. An insignificant sum. While he, Cornelius, who had to remain behind, was absolutely courting death by this proof of devotion to Mr Stein's young friend. The sight of his abject grimacing was—Jim told me—very hard to bear: he clutched at his hair, beat his breast, rocked himself to and fro with his hands pressed to his stomach, and actually pretended to shed tears. 'Your blood be on your own head,' he squeaked at last, and rushed out. It is a curious question how far Cornelius was sincere in that performance. Jim confessed to me that he did not sleep a wink after the fellow had gone. He lay on his back on a thin mat spread over the bamboo flooring, trying idly to make out the bare rafters, and listening to the rustlings in the thorn thatch. A star suddenly twinkled through a hole in the roof. His brain was in a whirl; but, nevertheless, it was on that very night that he matured his plan for overcoming Sherif Ali. It had been the thought of all the moments he could spare from the hopeless investigation into Stein's affairs, but the notion—he says—came to him then all at once. He could see, as it were, the guns mounted on the top of the hill. He got very hot and excited lying there; sleep was out of the question more than ever. He jumped up, and went out barefooted on the verandah. Walking silently, he came upon the girl, motionless against the wall, as if on the watch. In his then state of mind it did not surprise him to see her up, nor yet to hear her ask in an anxious whisper where Cornelius could be. He simply said he did not know. She moaned a little, and peered into the *campong*. Everything was very quiet. He was possessed by his new idea, and so full of it that he could not help telling the girl all about it at once. She listened, clapped her hands lightly, whispered softly her admiration, but was evidently on the alert all the time. It seems he had been used to make a confidant of her all along—and that she on her part could and did give him a lot of useful hints as to Patusan affairs there is no doubt. He assured me more than once that he had never found himself the worse for her advice. At any rate, he was proceeding to explain his plan fully to her there and then, when she pressed his arm once, and vanished from his side. Then Cornelius appeared from somewhere, and, perceiving Jim, ducked sideways, as though he had been shot at, and afterwards stood very still in the dusk. At last he came forward prudently, like a suspicious cat. 'There were some fishermen there—with fish,' he said in a shaky voice. 'To sell fish—you understand.' . . . It must have been then two o'clock in the morning—a likely time for anybody to hawk fish about !

"Jim, however, let the statement pass, and did not give it a single thought. Other matters occupied his mind, and besides he had neither seen nor heard anything. He contented himself by saying, 'Oh !' absently, got a drink of water out of a pitcher standing there, and leaving Cornelius a prey to some inexplicable emotion—that made him embrace with both arms the worm-eaten rail of the verandah as if his legs had failed—went in again and lay down on his mat to think. By-and-by he heard stealthy footsteps. They stopped. A voice whispered tremulously through the wall, 'Are you asleep ?' 'No ! What is it ?' he answered briskly, and there was an abrupt movement out-

side, and then all was still, as if the whisperer had
been startled. Extremely annoyed at this, Jim
came out impetuously, and Cornelius with a faint
shriek fled along the verandah as far as the steps,
where he hung on to the broken banister. Very
puzzled, Jim called out to him from the distance
to know what the devil he meant. 'Have you
given your consideration to what I spoke to you
about?' asked Cornelius, pronouncing the words
with difficulty, like a man in the cold fit of a fever.
'No!' shouted Jim in a passion. 'I did not, and
I don't intend to. I am going to live here, in
Patusan.' 'You shall d-d-die h-h-here,' answered
Cornelius, still shaking violently, and in a sort of
expiring voice. The whole performance was so absurd and provoking that Jim didn't know whether
he ought to be amused or angry. 'Not till I had
seen you tucked away, you bet,' he called out, exasperated yet ready to laugh. Half seriously (being
excited with his own thoughts, you know) he went
on shouting, 'Nothing can touch me! You can do
your damnedest.' Somehow the shadowy Cornelius
far off there seemed to be the hateful embodiment
of all the annoyances and difficulties he had found
in his path. He let himself go—his nerves had
been over-wrought for days—and called him many
pretty names,—swindler, liar, sorry rascal: in fact,
carried on in an extraordinary way. He admits
he passed all bounds, that he was quite beside
himself—defied all Patusan to scare him away—
declared he would make them all dance to his own
tune yet, and so on, in a menacing, boasting strain.
Perfectly bombastic and ridiculous, he said. His
ears burned at the bare recollection. Must have
been off his chump in some way. . . . The girl,

who was sitting with us, nodded her little head at me quickly, frowned faintly, and said, 'I heard him,' with childlike solemnity. He laughed and blushed. What stopped him at last, he said, was the silence, the complete deathlike silence, of the indistinct figure far over there, that seemed to hang collapsed, doubled over the rail in a weird immobility. He came to his senses, and ceasing suddenly, wondered greatly at himself. He watched for a while. Not a stir, not a sound. 'Exactly as if the chap had died while I had been making all that noise,' he said. He was so ashamed of himself that he went indoors in a hurry without another word, and flung himself down again. The row seemed to have done him good though, because he went to sleep for the rest of the night like a baby. Hadn't slept like that for weeks. 'But *I* didn't sleep,' struck in the girl, one elbow on the table and nursing her cheek. 'I watched.' Her big eyes flashed, rolling a little, and then she fixed them on my face intently."

CHAPTER XXXI.

"You may imagine with what interest I listened. All these details were perceived to have some significance twenty-four hours later. In the morning Cornelius made no allusion to the events of the night. 'I suppose you will come back to my poor house,' he muttered surlily, slinking up just as Jim was entering the canoe to go over to Doramin's

campong. Jim only nodded, without looking at
him. ' You find it good fun, no doubt,' muttered
the other in a sour tone. Jim spent the day with
the old *nakhoda*, preaching the necessity of vigorous
action to the principal men of the Bugis community,
who had been summoned for a big talk. He remembered with pleasure how very eloquent and
persuasive he had been. ' I managed to put some
backbone into them that time, and no mistake,' he
said. Sherif Ali's last raid had swept the outskirts of the settlement, and some women belonging to the town had been carried off to the stockade.
Sherif Ali's emissaries had been seen in the market-
place the day before, strutting about haughtily in
white cloaks, and boasting of the Rajah's friendship for their master. One of them stood forward
in the shade of a tree, and, leaning on the long
barrel of a rifle, exhorted the people to prayer and
repentance, advising them to kill all the strangers
in their midst, some of whom, he said, were in-
fidels and others even worse—children of Satan in
the guise of Moslems. It was reported that several
of the Rajah's people amongst the listeners had
loudly expressed their approbation. The terror
amongst the common people was intense. Jim,
immensely pleased with his day's work, crossed the
river again before sunset.

" As he had got the Bugis irretrievably committed
to action, and had made himself responsible for success on his own head, he was so elated that in the
lightness of his heart he absolutely tried to be civil
with Cornelius. But Cornelius became wildly jovial
in response, and it was almost more than he could
stand, he says, to hear his little squeaks of false
laughter, to see him wriggle and blink, and sud-

denly catch hold of his chin and crouch low over
the table with a distracted stare. The girl did not
show herself, and Jim retired early. When he rose
to say good-night, Cornelius jumped up, knocking
his chair over, and ducked out of sight as if to pick
up something he had dropped. His good-night
came huskily from under the table. Jim was
amazed to see him emerge out with a dropping
jaw, and staring, stupidly frightened eyes. He
clutched the edge of the table. 'What's the matter? Are you unwell?' asked Jim. 'Yes, yes, yes.
A great colic in my stomach,' says the other; and
it is Jim's opinion that it was perfectly true. If
so, it was, in view of his contemplated action, an
abject sign of a still imperfect callousness for which
he must be given all due credit.

"Be it as it may, Jim's slumbers were disturbed
by a dream of heavens like brass resounding with
a great voice, which called upon him to Awake!
Awake! so loud that, notwithstanding his desperate determination to sleep on, he did wake up in
reality. The glare of a red spluttering conflagration going on in mid-air fell on his eyes. Coils
of black thick smoke curved round the head of
some apparition, some unearthly being, all in white,
with a severe, drawn, anxious face. After a second
or so he recognised the girl. She was holding a
dammar torch at arm's-length aloft, and in a persistent, urgent monotone she was repeating, 'Get
up! Get up! Get up!'

"Suddenly he leaped to his feet; at once she
put into his hand a revolver, his own revolver,
which had been hanging on a nail, but loaded this
time. He gripped it in silence, bewildered, blinking
in the light. He wondered what he could do for her.

"She asked rapidly and very low, 'Can you face four men with this?' He laughed while narrating this part at the recollection of his polite alacrity. It seems he made a great display of it. 'Certainly —of course—certainly—command me.' He was not properly awake, and had a notion of being very civil in these extraordinary circumstances, of showing his unquestioning, devoted readiness. She left the room, and he followed her; in the passage they disturbed an old hag who did the casual cooking of the household, though she was so decrepit as to be hardly able to understand human speech. She got up and hobbled behind them, mumbling toothlessly. On the verandah a hammock of sail-cloth, belonging to Cornelius, swayed lightly to the touch of Jim's elbow. It was empty.

"The Patusan establishment, like all the posts of Stein's Trading Company, had originally consisted of four buildings. Two of them were represented by two heaps of sticks, broken bamboos, rotten thatch, over which the four corner-posts of hardwood leaned sadly at different angles: the principal storeroom, however, stood yet, facing the agent's house. It was an oblong hut, built of mud and clay: it had at one end a wide door of stout planking, which so far had not come off the hinges, and in one of the side walls there was a square aperture, a sort of window, with three wooden bars. Before descending the few steps the girl turned her face over her shoulder and said quickly, 'You were to be set upon while you slept.' Jim tells me he experienced a sense of deception. It was the old story. He was weary of these attempts upon his life. He had had his fill of these alarms. He was sick of them. He assured me he was **angry** with the girl for deceiving him. He had followed her under the impression that it was she who wanted his help, and now he had half a mind to turn on his heel and go back in disgust. 'Do you know,' he commented profoundly, 'I rather think I was not quite myself for whole weeks on end about that time ? ' ' Oh yes. You were though,' I couldn't help contradicting.

"But she moved on swiftly, and he followed her into the courtyard. All its fences had fallen in a long time ago ; the neighbours' buffaloes would pace in the morning across the open space, snorting profoundly, without haste ; the very jungle was invading it already. Jim and the girl stopped in the rank grass. The light in which they stood made a dense blackness all round, and only above their heads there was an opulent glitter of stars. He told me it was a beautiful night —quite cool, with a little stir of breeze from the river. It seems he noticed its friendly beauty. Remember this is a love-story I am telling you now. A lovely night that seemed to breathe on them a soft caress. The flame of the torch streamed now and then with a fluttering noise like a flag, and for a time this was the only sound. ' They are in the storeroom waiting,' whispered the girl ; ' they are waiting for the signal.' ' Who's to give it ? ' he asked. She shook the torch, which blazed up after a shower of sparks. ' Only you have been sleeping so restlessly,' she continued in a murmur. ' I watched your sleep, too.' ' You ! ' he exclaimed, craning his neck to look about him. ' You think I watched on this night only ! ' she said, with a sort of despairing indignation.

"He says it was as if he had received a blow on

the chest. He gasped. He thought he had been an awful brute somehow, and he felt remorseful, touched, happy, elated. This, let me remind you again, is a love-story; you can see it by the imbecility, not a repulsive imbecility, the exalted imbecility of these proceedings, this station in torchlight, as if they had come there on purpose to have it out for the edification of concealed murderers. If Sherif Ali's emissaries had been possessed—as Jim remarked—of a pennyworth of spunk, this was the time to make a rush. His heart was thumping—not with fear—but he seemed to hear the grass rustle, and he stepped smartly out of the light. Something dark, imperfectly seen, flitted rapidly out of sight. He called out in a strong voice, 'Cornelius! O Cornelius!' A profound silence succeeded: his voice did not seem to have carried twenty feet. Again the girl was by his side. 'Fly!' she said. The old woman was coming up; her broken figure hovered in crippled little jumps on the edge of the light; they heard her mumbling, and a light, moaning sigh. 'Fly!' repeated the girl excitedly. 'They are frightened now—this light—the voices. They know you are awake now—they know you are big, strong, fearless . . .' 'If I am all that,' he began, but she interrupted him. 'Yes—to-night! But what of to-morrow night? Of the next night? Of the night after—of all the many, many nights? Can I be always watching?' A sobbing catch of her breath affected him beyond the power of words.

"He told me that he had never felt so small, so powerless—and as to courage, what was the good of it, he thought. He was so helpless that even flight seemed of no use; and though she kept on whispering, 'Go to Doramin, go to Doramin,' with feverish insistence, he realised that for him there was no refuge from that loneliness which centupled all his dangers except—in her. 'I thought,' he said to me, 'that if I went away from her it would be the end of everything some-how.' Only as they couldn't stop there for ever in the middle of that courtyard, he made up his mind to go and look into the storehouse. He let her follow him without thinking of any protest, as if they had been indissolubly united. 'I am fearless—am I?' he muttered through his teeth. She restrained his arm. 'Wait till you hear my voice,' she said, and, torch in hand, ran lightly round the corner. He remained alone in the dark-ness, his face to the door : not a sound, not a breath came from the other side. The old hag let out a dreary groan somewhere behind his back. He heard a high-pitched almost screaming call from the girl. 'Now! Push!' He pushed violently ; the door swung with a creak and a clatter, dis-closing to his intense astonishment the low dungeon-like interior illuminated by a lurid, wavering glare. A turmoil of smoke eddied down upon an empty wooden crate in the middle of the floor, a litter of rags and straw tried to soar, but only stirred feebly in the draught. She had thrust the light through the bars of the window. He saw her bare round arm extended and rigid, holding up the torch with the steadiness of an iron bracket. A conical ragged heap of old mats cumbered a distant corner almost to the ceiling, and that was all.

"He explained to me that he was bitterly dis-appointed at this. His fortitude had been tried by so many warnings, he had been for weeks sur-

rounded by so many hints of danger, that he
wanted the relief of some reality, of something
tangible that he could meet. 'It would have
cleared the air for a couple of hours at least, if
you know what I mean,' he said to me. 'Jove!
I had been living for days with a stone on my
chest.' Now at last he had thought he would
get hold of something, and—nothing! Not a
trace, not a sign of anybody. He had raised his
weapon as the door flew open, but now his arm
fell. 'Fire! Defend yourself,' the girl outside
cried in an agonising voice. She, being in the
dark and with her arm thrust in to the shoulder
through the small hole, couldn't see what was going
on, and she dared not withdraw the torch now to
run round. 'There's nobody here!' yelled Jim contemptuously, but his impulse to burst into a resent-
ful exasperated laugh died without a sound: he had
perceived in the very act of turning away that he
was exchanging glances with a pair of eyes in the
heap of mats. He saw a shifting gleam of whites.
'Come out!' he cried in a fury, a little doubtful,
and a dark-faced head, a head without a body,
shaped itself in the rubbish, a strangely detached
head, that looked at him with a steady scowl.
Next moment the whole mound stirred, and with
a low grunt a man emerged swiftly, and bounded
towards Jim. Behind him the mats as it were
jumped and flew, his right arm was raised with
a crooked elbow, and the dull blade of a *kriss*
protruded from his fist held off, a little above his
head. A cloth wound tight round his loins seemed
dazzlingly white on his bronze skin; his naked body
glistened as if wet.

"Jim noted all this. He told me he was experi-

encing a feeling of unutterable relief, of vengeful
elation. He held his shot, he says, deliberately.
He held it for the tenth part of a second, for three
strides of the man—an unconscionable time. He
held it for the pleasure of saying to himself, That's
a dead man! He was absolutely positive and certain. He let him come on because it did not matter.
A dead man, anyhow. He noticed the dilated
nostrils, the wide eyes, the intent, eager stillness of
the face, and then he fired.

"The explosion in that confined space was stun-
ning. He stepped back a pace. He saw the man
jerk his head up, fling his arms forward, and drop
the *kriss*. He ascertained afterwards that he had
shot him through the mouth, a little upwards, the
bullet coming out high at the back of the skull.
With the impetus of his rush the man drove straight
on, his face suddenly gaping disfigured, with his
hands open before him gropingly, as though blinded,
and landed with terrific violence on his forehead,
just short of Jim's bare toes. Jim says he didn't
lose the smallest detail of all this. He found himself calm, appeased, without rancour, without un-
easiness, as if the death of that man had atoned
for everything. The place was getting very full
of sooty smoke from the torch, in which the un-
swaying flame burned blood-red without a flicker.
He walked in resolutely, striding over the dead
body, and covered with his revolver another naked
figure outlined vaguely at the other end. As he
was about to pull the trigger, the man threw away
with force a short heavy spear, and squatted sub-
missively on his hams, his back to the wall and
his clasped hands between his legs. 'You want
your life?' Jim said. The other made no sound.

'How many more of you?' asked Jim again. 'Two more, Tuan,' said the man very softly, looking with big fascinated eyes into the muzzle of the revolver. Accordingly two more crawled from under the mats, holding out ostentatiously their empty hands."

CHAPTER XXXII.

"JIM took up an advantageous position and shepherded them out in a bunch through the doorway: all that time the torch had remained vertical in the grip of a little hand, without so much as a tremble. The three men obeyed him, perfectly mute, moving automatically. He ranged them in a row. 'Link arms!' he ordered. They did so. 'The first who withdraws his arm or turns his head is a dead man,' he said. 'March!' They stepped out together, rigidly; he followed, and at the side the girl, in a trailing white gown, her black hair falling as low as her waist, bore the light. Erect and swaying, she seemed to glide without touching the earth; the only sound was the silky swish and rustle of the long grass. 'Stop!' cried Jim.

"The river-bank was steep; a great freshness ascended, the light fell on the edge of smooth dark water frothing without a ripple; right and left the shapes of the houses ran together below the sharp outlines of the roofs. 'Take my greetings to Sherif Ali—till I come myself,' said Jim. Not one head of the three budged. 'Jump!' he thundered. The three splashes made one splash, a shower flew up, black heads bobbed convulsively, and disappeared; but a great blowing and spluttering went on, growing faint, for they were diving industriously, in great fear of a parting shot. Jim turned to the girl, who had been a silent and attentive observer. His heart seemed suddenly to grow too big for his breast and choke him in the hollow of his throat. This probably made him speechless for so long, and after returning his gaze she flung the burning torch with a wide sweep of the arm into the river. The ruddy fiery glare, taking a long flight through the night, sank with a vicious hiss, and the calm soft starlight descended upon them, unchecked.

"He did not tell me what it was he said when at last he recovered his voice. I don't suppose he could be very eloquent. The world was still, the night breathed on them, one of those nights that seem created for the sheltering of tenderness, and there are moments when our souls, as if freed from their dark envelope, glow with an exquisite sensibility that makes certain silences more lucid than speeches. As to the girl, he told me, 'She broke down a bit. Excitement—don't you know. Reaction. Deucedly tired she must have been—and all that kind of thing. And—and—hang it all—she was fond of me, don't you see. . . . I too . . . didn't know, of course . . . never entered my head . . .'

"There he got up and began to walk about in some agitation. 'I—I love her dearly. More than I could tell. Of course one cannot tell. You take a different view of your actions when you come to understand, when you are *made* to understand every day that your existence is necessary—you see, absolutely necessary—to another person. I am made

to feel that. Wonderful. But only try to think
what her life had been. It is too extravagantly
awful! Isn't it? And me finding her here like
this—as you may go out for a stroll and come
suddenly upon somebody drowning in a lonely dark
place. Jove! No time to lose. Well, it is a trust
too . . . I believe I am equal to it . . .'

"I must tell you the girl had left us to ourselves
some time before. He slapped his chest. ' Yes!
I feel that, but I believe I am equal to all my luck!'
He had the gift of finding a special meaning in
everything that happened to him. This was the
view he took of his love-affair; it was idyllic, a
little solemn, and also true, since his belief had
all the unshakable seriousness of youth. Some
time after, on another occasion, he said to me,
' I've been only two years here, and now, upon
my word, I can't conceive being able to live anywhere else. The very thought of the world outside
is enough to give me a fright; because, don't you
see,' he continued, with downcast eyes watching the
action of his boot busied in squashing thoroughly
a tiny bit of dried mud (we were strolling on the
river-bank)—' Because I have not forgotten why I
came here. Not yet!'

"I refrained from looking at him, but I think I
heard a short sigh; we took a turn or two in silence.
' Upon my soul and conscience,' he began again,
' if such a thing can be forgotten, then I think I
have a right to dismiss it from my mind. Ask
any man here ' . . . his voice changed. ' Is it
not strange,' he went on in a gentle, almost yearning
tone, ' that all these people, all these people who
would do anything for me, can never be made
to understand? Never! If you disbelieved me

I could not call them up. It seems hard, somehow.
I am stupid, am I not? What more can I want?
If you ask them who is brave—who is true—who
is just—who is it they would trust with their lives?
—they would say, Tuan Jim. And yet they can
never know the real, real truth . . .'

"That's what he said to me on my last day
with him. I did not let a murmur escape me: I
felt he was going to say more, and come no nearer
to the root of the matter. The sun, whose concentrated glare dwarfs the earth into a restless
mote of dust, had sunk behind the forest, and the
diffused light from an opal sky seemed to cast
upon a world without shadows and without brilliance the illusion of a calm and pensive greatness.
I don't know why, listening to him, I should have
noted so distinctly the gradual darkening of the
river, of the air; the irresistible slow work of the
night settling silently on all the visible forms,
effacing the outlines, burying the shapes deeper
and deeper, like a steady fall of impalpable black
dust.

"'Jove!' he began abruptly, 'there are days
when a fellow is too absurd for anything; only I
know I can tell you what I like. I talk about
being done with it—with the bally thing at the
back of my head . . . Forgetting . . . Hang me
if I know! I can think of it quietly. After all,
what has it proved? Nothing. I suppose you
don't think so . . .'

"I made a protesting murmur.

"'No matter,' he said. 'I am satisfied . . .
nearly. I've got to look only at the face of the
first man that comes along, to regain my confidence.
They can't be made to understand what is going on

n me. What of that? Come! I haven't done so
badly.'

" ' Not so badly,' I said.

" ' But all the same, you wouldn't like to have me
aboard your own ship—hey?'

" ' Confound you!' I cried. ' Stop this.'

" ' Aha! You see,' he said, crowing, as it were,
over me placidly. ' Only,' he went on, ' you just
try to tell this to any of them here. They would
think you a fool, a liar, or worse. And so I can
stand it. I've done a thing or two for them, but
this is what they have done for me.'

" ' My dear chap,' I cried, ' you shall always remain
for them an insoluble mystery.' Thereupon we
were silent.

" ' Mystery,' he repeated, before looking up. ' Well,
then let me always remain here.'

" After the sun had set, the darkness seemed to
drive upon us, borne in every faint puff of the
breeze. In the middle of a hedged path I saw
the arrested, gaunt, watchful, and apparently one-
legged silhouette of Tamb' Itam; and across the
dusky space my eye detected something white
moving to and fro behind the supports of the roof.
As soon as Jim, with Tamb' Itam at his heels, had
started upon his evening rounds, I went up to the
house alone, and, unexpectedly, found myself waylaid by the girl, who had been clearly waiting for
this opportunity.

" It is hard to tell you what it was precisely she
wanted to wrest from me. Obviously it would be
something very simple—the simplest impossibility
in the world; as, for instance, the exact description
of the form of a cloud. She wanted an assurance,
a statement, a promise, an explanation—I don't

know how to call it : the thing has no name. I
was dark under the projecting roof, and all I could
see were the flowing lines of her gown, the pale
small oval of her face, with the white flash of her
teeth, and, turned towards me, the big sombre orbits
of her eyes, where there seemed to be a faint stir,
such as you may fancy you can detect when you
plunge your gaze to the bottom of an immensely
deep well. What is it that moves there ? you ask
yourself. Is it a blind monster or only a lost gleam
from the universe ? It occurred to me—don't
laugh—that all things being dissimilar, she was
more inscrutable in her childish ignorance than the
sphinx propounding childish riddles to wayfarers.
She had been carried off to Patusan before her
eyes were open. She had grown up there ; she
had seen nothing, she had known nothing, she
had no conception of anything. I ask myself
whether she were sure that anything else existed.
What notions she may have formed of the outside
world is to me inconceivable : all that she knew
of its inhabitants were a betrayed woman and a
sinister pantaloon. Her lover also came to her
from there, gifted with irresistible seductions ;
but what would become of her if he should return
to these inconceivable regions that seemed always
to claim back their own ? Her mother had warned
her of this with tears, before she died . . .

"She had caught hold of my arm firmly, and
as soon as I had stopped she had withdrawn her
hand in haste. She was audacious and shrinking.
She feared nothing, but she was checked by the
profound incertitude and the extreme strangeness
—a brave person groping in the dark. I belonged
to this Unknown that might claim Jim for its

own at any moment. I was, as it were, in the
secret of its nature and of its intentions;—the
confidant of a threatening mystery;—armed with
its power perhaps! I believe she supposed I could
with a word whisk Jim away out of her very arms :
it is my sober conviction she went through agonies
of apprehension during my long talks with Jim ;
through a real and intolerable anguish that might
have conceivably driven her into plotting my murder,
had the fierceness of her soul been equal to the
tremendous situation it had created. This is my
impression, and it is all I can give you : the whole
thing dawned gradually upon me, and as it got
clearer and clearer I was overwhelmed by a slow
incredulous amazement. She made me believe her,
but there is no word that on my lips could render
the effect of the headlong and vehement whisper,
of the soft, passionate tones, of the sudden breathless pause and the appealing movement of the
white arms extended swiftly. They fell ; the
ghostly figure swayed like a slender tree in the
wind, the pale oval of the face drooped ; it was
impossible to distinguish her features, the darkness of the eyes was unfathomable ; two wide
sleeves uprose in the dark like unfolding wings,
and she stood silent, holding her head in her
hands."

CHAPTER XXXIII.

"I was immensely touched : her youth, her ignorance, her pretty beauty, which had the simple charm and the delicate vigour of a wild-flower, her pathetic pleading, her helplessness, appealed to me with almost the strength of her own unreasonable and natural fear. She feared the unknown as we all do, and her ignorance made the unknown infinitely vast. I stood for it, for myself, for you fellows, for all the world that neither cared for Jim nor needed him in the least. I would have been ready enough to answer for the indifference of the teeming earth but for the reflection that he too belonged to this mysterious unknown of her fears, and that, however much I stood for, I did not stand for him. This made me hesitate. A murmur of hopeless pain unsealed my lips. I began by protesting that I at least had come with no intention to take Jim away.

"Why did I come, then ? After a slight movement she was as still as a marble statue in the night. I tried to explain briefly : friendship, business ; if I had any wish in the matter it was rather to see him stay. . . . 'They always leave us,' she murmured. The breath of sad wisdom from the grave which her piety wreathed with flowers seemed to pass in a faint sigh. . . . Nothing, I said, could separate Jim from her.

"It is my firm conviction now ; it was my conviction at the time ; it was the only possible conclusion from the facts of the case. It was not made more certain by her whispering in a tone in which one speaks to oneself, ' He swore this to me.' 'Did you ask him ? ' I said.

" She made a step nearer. ' No. Never ! ' She had asked him only to go away. It was that night on the river-bank, after he had killed the man—after she had flung the torch in the water because he was looking at her so. There was too much light, and the danger was over then—for a little time—for a little time. He said then he would not abandon her to Cornelius. She had insisted. She wanted him to leave her. He said that he could not—that it was impossible. He trembled while he said this. She had felt him tremble. . . . One does not require much imagination to see the scene, almost to hear their whispers. She was afraid for him too. I believe that then she saw in him only a predestined victim of dangers which she understood better than himself. Though by nothing but his mere presence he had mastered her heart, had filled all her thoughts, and had possessed himself of all her affections, she under-estimated his chances of success. It is obvious that at about that time everybody was inclined to under-estimate his chances. Strictly speaking he didn't seem to have any. I know this was Cornelius's view. He confessed that much to me in extenua-tion of the shady part he had played in Sherif Ali's plot to do away with the infidel. Even Sherif Ali himself, as it seems certain now, had nothing but contempt for the white man. Jim was to be murdered mainly on religious grounds, I believe. A simple act of piety (and so far infinitely meri-torious), but otherwise without much importance. In the last part of this opinion Cornelius concurred. 'Honourable sir,' he argued abjectly on the only

occasion he managed to have me to himself—
' Honourable sir, how was I to know ? Who was he ?
What could he do to make people believe him ?
What did Mr Stein mean sending a boy like that
to talk big to an old servant ? I was ready to save
him for eighty dollars. Only eighty dollars. Why
didn't the fool go ? Was I to get stabbed myself
for the sake of a stranger ? ' He grovelled in spirit
before me, with his body doubled up insinuatingly
and his hands hovering about my knees, as though
he were ready to embrace my legs. ' What's eighty
dollars ? An insignificant sum to give to a defence-
less old man ruined for life by a deceased she-devil.'
Here he wept. But I anticipate. I didn't that night
chance upon Cornelius till I had had it out with the
girl.

"She was unselfish when she urged Jim to leave
her, and even to leave the country. It was his
danger that was foremost in her thoughts—even
if she wanted to save herself too—perhaps unconsciously : but then look at the warning she had,
look at the lesson that could be drawn from every
moment of the recently ended life in which all her
memories were centred. She fell at his feet—she
told me so—there by the river, in the discreet light
of stars which showed nothing except great masses
of silent shadows, indefinite open spaces, and trembling faintly upon the broad stream made it appear
as wide as the sea. He had lifted her up. He
lifted her up, and then she would struggle no more.
Of course not. Strong arms, a tender voice, a
stalwart shoulder to rest her poor lonely little
head upon. The need—the infinite need—of all
this for the aching heart, for the bewildered mind ;
—the promptings of youth—the necessity of the

moment. What would you have? One understands—unless one is incapable of understanding anything under the sun. And so she was content to be lifted up—and held. 'You know—Jove! this is serious—no nonsense in it!' as Jim had whispered hurriedly with a troubled concerned face on the threshold of his house. I don't know so much about nonsense, but there was nothing light-hearted in their romance: they came together under the shadow of a life's disaster, like knight and maiden meeting to exchange vows amongst haunted ruins. The starlight was good enough for that story, a light so faint and remote that it cannot resolve shadows into shapes, and show the other shore of a stream. I did look upon the stream that night and from the very place; it rolled silent and as black as Styx: the next day I went away, but I am not likely to forget what it was she wanted to be saved from when she entreated him to leave her while there was time. She told me what it was, calmed—she was now too passionately interested for mere excitement—in a voice as quiet in the obscurity as her white half-lost figure. She told me, 'I didn't want to die weeping.' I thought I had not heard aright.

" 'You did not want to die weeping?' I repeated after her. 'Like my mother,' she added readily. The outlines of her white shape did not stir in the least. 'My mother had wept bitterly before she died,' she explained. An inconceivable calmness seemed to have risen from the ground around us, imperceptibly, like the still rise of a flood in the night, obliterating the familiar landmarks of emotions. There came upon me, as though I had felt myself losing my footing in the midst of waters, a sudden dread, the dread of the unknown depths. She went on explaining that, during the last moments, being alone with her mother, she had to leave the side of the couch to go and set her back against the door, in order to keep Cornelius out. He desired to get in, and kept on drumming with both fists, only desisting now and again to shout huskily, 'Let me in! Let me in! Let me in!' In a far corner upon a few mats the moribund woman, already speechless and unable to lift her arm, rolled her head over, and with a feeble movement of her hand seemed to command—No! No! and the obedient daughter, setting her shoulders with all her strength against the door, was looking on. 'The tears fell from her eyes—and then she died,' concluded the girl in an imperturbable monotone, which more than anything else, more than the white statuesque immobility of her person, more than mere words could do, troubled my mind profoundly with the passive, irremediable horror of the scene. It had the power to drive me out of my conception of existence, out of that shelter each of us makes for himself to creep under in moments of danger, as a tortoise withdraws within its shell. For a moment I had a view of a world that seemed to wear a vast and dismal aspect of disorder, while, in truth, thanks to our unwearied efforts, it is as sunny an arrangement of small conveniences as the mind of man can conceive. But still—it was only a moment: I went back into my shell directly. One *must*— don't you know?—though I seemed to have lost all my words in the chaos of dark thoughts I had contemplated for a second or two beyond the pale. These came back too very soon, for words

also belong to the sheltering conception of light
and order which is our refuge. I had them ready
at my disposal before she whispered softly, ' He
swore he would never leave me, when we stood
there alone! He swore to me!' . . . 'And is
it possible that you—you! do not believe him?'
I asked, sincerely reproachful, genuinely shocked.
Why couldn't she believe? Wherefore this craving
for incertitude, this clinging to fear, as if incertitude
and fear had been the safeguards of her love. It
was monstrous. She should have made for herself
a shelter of inexpugnable peace out of that honest
affection. She had not the knowledge—not the
skill perhaps. The night had come on apace; it
had grown pitch-dark where we were, so that
without stirring she had faded like the intangible
form of a wistful and perverse spirit. And suddenly
I heard her quiet whisper again, ' Other men had
sworn the same thing.' It was like a meditative
comment on some thoughts full of sadness, of awe.
And she added, still lower if possible, ' My father
did.' She paused the time to draw an inaudible
breath. ' Her father too.' . . . These were the
things she knew! At once I said, ' Ah! but he is
not like that.' This, it seemed, she did not intend
to dispute; but after a time the strange still whisper
wandering dreamily in the air stole into my ears.
' Why is he different? Is he better? Is he . . .'
' Upon my word of honour,' I broke in, ' I believe
he is.' We subdued our tones to a mysterious
pitch. Amongst the huts of Jim's workmen (they
were mostly liberated slaves from the Sherif's
stockade) somebody started a shrill, drawling song.
Across the river a big fire (at Doramin's, I think)
made a glowing ball, completely isolated in the

night. 'Is he more true?' she murmured. 'Yes,' I said.

"'More true than any other man,' she repeated in lingering accents. 'Nobody here,' I said, 'would dream of doubting his word—nobody would dare —except you.'

"I think she made a movement at this. 'More brave,' she went on in a changed tone. 'Fear shall never drive him away from you,' I said a little nervously. The song stopped short on a shrill note, and was succeeded by several voices talking in the distance. Jim's voice too. I was struck by her silence. 'What has he been telling you? He has been telling you something?' I asked. There was no answer. 'What is it he told you?' I insisted.

"'Do you think I can tell you? How am I to know? How am I to understand?' she cried at last. There was a stir. I believe she was wringing her hands. 'There is something he can never forget.'

"'So much the better for you,' I said gloomily.

"'What is it? What is it?' She put an extraordinary force of appeal into her supplicating tone. 'He says he had been afraid. How can I believe this? Am I a mad woman to believe this? You all remember something! You all go back to it. What is it? You tell me! What is this thing? Is it alive?—is it dead? I hate it. It is cruel. Has it got a face and a voice—this calamity? Will he see it—will he hear it? In his sleep perhaps when he cannot see me—and then arise and go. Ah! I shall never forgive him. My mother had forgiven — but I, never! Will it be a sign— a call . . .'

"It was a wonderful experience. She mistrusted

his very slumbers—and she seemed to think I could tell her why! Thus a poor mortal seduced by the charm of an apparition might have tried to wring from another ghost the tremendous secret of the claim the other world holds over a disembodied soul astray amongst the passions of this earth. The very ground on which I stood seemed to melt under my feet. And it was so simple too; but if the spirits evoked by our fears and our unrest have ever to vouch for each other's constancy before the forlorn magicians that we are, then I—I alone of us dwellers in the flesh—have shuddered in the hopeless chill of such a task. A sign, a call! How telling in its expression was her ignorance. A few words! How she came to know them, how she came to pronounce them, I can't imagine. Women find their inspiration in the stress of moments that for us are merely awful, absurd, or futile. To discover that she had a voice at all was enough to strike awe into the heart. Had a spurned stone cried out in pain it could not have appeared a greater and more pitiful miracle. These few sounds wandering in the dark had made their two be-nighted lives tragic to my mind. It was impossible to make her understand. I chafed silently at my impotence. And Jim, too—poor devil! Who would need him? Who would remember him? He had what he wanted. His very existence probably had been forgotten by this time. They had mastered their fates. They were tragic.

" Her immobility before me was clearly expectant, and my part was to speak for my brother from the realm of forgetful shades. I was deeply moved at my responsibility and at her distress. I would have given anything for the power to soothe her frail

soul, tormenting itself in its invincible ignorance
like a small bird beating about the cruel wires of
a cage. Nothing easier than to say, Have no fear!
Nothing more difficult. How does one kill fear, I
wonder? How do you shoot a spectre through
the heart, slash off its spectral head, take it by
its spectral throat? It is an enterprise you rush
into while you dream, and are glad to make your
escape with wet hair and every limb shaking. The
bullet is not run, the blade not forged, the man
not born; even the winged words of truth drop
at your feet like lumps of lead. You require for
such a desperate encounter an enchanted and
poisoned shaft dipped in a lie too subtle to be
found on earth. An enterprise for a dream, my
masters!

"I began my exorcism with a heavy heart, with a
sort of sullen anger in it too. Jim's voice, suddenly
raised with a stern intonation, carried across the
courtyard, reproving the carelessness of some dumb
sinner by the river-side. Nothing—I said, speaking
in a distinct murmur—there could be nothing, in
that unknown world she fancied so eager to rob her
of her happiness, there was nothing neither living nor
dead, there was no face, no voice, no power, that
could tear Jim from her side. I drew breath and
she whispered softly, 'He told me so.' 'He told
you the truth,' I said. 'Nothing,' she sighed out,
and abruptly turned upon me with a barely audible
intensity of tone. 'Why did you come to us from
out there? He speaks of you too often. You make
me afraid. Do you—do you want him?' A sort
of stealthy fierceness had crept into our hurried
mutters. 'I shall never come again,' I said bitterly.
'And I don't want him. No one wants him.' 'No

one,' she repeated in a tone of doubt. 'No one,' I affirmed feeling myself swayed by some strange excitement. 'You think him strong, wise, courageous, great—why not believe him to be true too? I shall go to-morrow—and that is the end. You shall never be troubled by a voice from there again. This world you don't know is too big to miss him. You understand? Too big. You've got his heart in your hand. You must feel that. You must know that.' 'Yes, I know that,' she breathed out, hard and still, as a statue might whisper.

"I felt I had done nothing. And what is it that I had wished to do? I am not sure now. At the time I was animated by an inexplicable ardour, as if before some great and necessary task—the influence of the moment upon my mental and emotional state. There are in all our lives such moments, such influences, coming from the outside, as it were, irresistible, incomprehensible—as if brought about by the mysterious conjunctions of the planets. She owned, as I had put it to her, his heart. She had that and everything else—if she could only believe it. What I had to tell her was that in the whole world there was no one who ever would need his heart, his mind, his hand. It was a common fate, and yet it seemed an awful thing to say of any man. She listened without a word, and her stillness now was like the protest of an invincible unbelief. What need she care for the world beyond the forests? I asked. From all the multitudes that peopled the vastness of that unknown there would come, I assured her, as long as he lived, neither a call nor a sign for him. Never. I was carried away. Never! Never! I remember with wonder the sort of dogged fierceness I displayed. I had the illusion of having got the spectre by the throat at last. Indeed the whole real thing has left behind the detailed and amazing impression of a dream. Why should she fear? She knew him to be strong, true, wise, brave. He was all that. Certainly. He was more. He was great—invincible—and the world did not want him, it had forgotten him, it would not even know him.

"I stopped; the silence over Patusan was profound, and the feeble dry sound of a paddle striking the side of a canoe somewhere in the middle of the river seemed to make it infinite. 'Why?' she murmured. I felt that sort of rage one feels during a hard tussle. The spectre was trying to slip out of my grasp. 'Why?' she repeated louder; 'tell me!' And as I remained confounded, she stamped with her foot like a spoilt child. 'Why? Speak.' 'You want to know,' I asked in a fury. 'Yes!' she cried. 'Because he is not good enough,' I said brutally. During the moment's pause I noticed the fire on the other shore blaze up, dilating the circle of its glow like an amazed stare, and contract suddenly to a red pin-point. I only knew how close to me she had been when I felt the clutch of her fingers on my forearm. Without raising her voice, she threw into it an infinity of scathing contempt, bitterness, and despair.

"'This is the very thing he said. . . . You lie!'

"The last two words she cried at me in the native dialect. 'Hear me out!' I entreated; she caught her breath tremulously, flung my arm away. 'Nobody, nobody is good enough,' I began with the greatest earnestness. I could hear the sobbing labour of her breath frightfully quickened. I hung my head. What was the use? Footsteps were approaching; I slipped away without another word. . . .'"

CHAPTER XXXIV.

MARLOW swung his legs out, got up quickly, and
staggered a little, as though he had been set down
after a rush through space. He leaned his back
against the balustrade and faced a disordered array
of long cane-chairs. The bodies prone in them
seemed startled out of their torpor by his movement. One or two sat up as if alarmed; here and
there a cigar glowed yet; Marlow looked at them
all with the eyes of a man returning from the excessive remoteness of a dream. A throat was
cleared; a calm voice encouraged negligently,
" Well."

" Nothing," said Marlow with a slight start. " He
had told her—that's all. She did not believe him—
nothing more. As to myself, I do not know whether
it be just, proper, decent for me to rejoice or to be
sorry. For my part, I cannot say what I believed
—indeed I don't know to this day, and never shall
probably. But what did the poor devil believe
himself? Truth shall prevail—don't you know.
Magna est veritas et . . . Yes, when it gets a chance.
There is a law, no doubt—and likewise a law regul-
ates your luck in the throwing of dice. It is not
Justice the servant of men, but accident, hazard,
Fortune—the ally of patient Time—that holds an
even and scrupulous balance. Both of us had said
the very same thing. Did we both speak the truth—
or one of us did—or neither? . . ."

Marlow paused, crossed his arms on his breast,
and in a changed tone—

" She said we lied. Poor soul. Well—let's leave

it to chance, whose ally is Time, that cannot be hurried, and whose enemy is Death, that will not wait. I had retreated—a little cowed, I must own. I had tried a fall with fear itself and got thrown—of course. I had only succeeded in adding to her anguish the hint of some mysterious collusion, of an inexplicable and incomprehensible conspiracy to keep her for ever in the dark. And it had come easily, naturally, unavoidably, by his act, by her own act! It was as though I had been shown the working of the implacable destiny of which we are the victims—and the tools. It was appalling to think of the girl whom I had left standing there motionless; Jim's footsteps had a fateful sound as he tramped by, without seeing me, in his heavy laced boots. 'What? No lights!' he said in a loud, surprised voice. 'What are you doing in the dark—you two?' Next moment he caught sight of her, I suppose. 'Hallo, girl!' he cried cheerily. 'Hallo boy!' she answered at once, with amazing pluck.

"This was their usual greeting to each other, and the bit of swagger she would put into her rather high but sweet voice was very droll, pretty, and childlike. It delighted Jim greatly. This was the last occasion on which I heard them exchange this familiar hail, and it struck a chill into my heart. There was the high sweet voice, the pretty effort, the swagger; but it all seemed to die out prematurely, and the playful call sounded like a moan. It was too confoundedly awful. 'What have you done with Marlow?' Jim was asking; and then, 'Gone down—has he? Funny I didn't meet him. . . . You there, Marlow?'

"I didn't answer. I wasn't going in—not yet at

any rate. I really couldn't. While he was calling
me I was engaged in making my escape through
a little gate leading out upon a stretch of newly
cleared ground. No; I couldn't face them yet. I
walked hastily with lowered head along a trodden
path. The ground rose gently, the few big trees
had been felled, the undergrowth had been cut
down and the grass fired. He had a mind to try
a coffee-plantation there. The big hill, rearing its
double summit coal-black in the clear yellow glow
of the rising moon, seemed to cast its shadow upon
the ground prepared for that experiment. He was
going to try ever so many experiments; I had admired his energy, his enterprise, and his shrewdness.
Nothing on earth seemed less real now than his
plans, his energy, and his enthusiasm; and raising
my eyes, I saw part of the moon glittering through
the bushes at the bottom of the chasm. For a
moment it looked as though the smooth disc, falling
from its place in the sky upon the earth, had rolled
to the bottom of that precipice: its ascending
movement was like a leisurely rebound; it dis-
engaged itself from the tangle of twigs; the bare
contorted limb of some tree, growing on the slope,
made a black crack right across its face. It threw
its level rays afar as if from a cavern, and in this
mournful eclipse-like light the stumps of felled trees
uprose very dark, the heavy shadows fell at my feet
on all sides, my own moving shadow, and across my
path the shadow of the solitary grave perpetually
garlanded with flowers. In the darkened moonlight
the interlaced blossoms took on shapes foreign to
one's memory and colours indefinable to the eye, as
though they had been special flowers gathered by
no man, grown not in this world, and destined for

the use of the dead alone. Their powerful scent hung in the warm air, making it thick and heavy like the fumes of incense. The lumps of white coral shone round the dark mound like a chaplet of bleached skulls, and everything around was so quiet that when I stood still all sound and all movement in the world seemed to come to an end.

"It was a great peace, as if the earth had been one grave, and for a time I stood there thinking mostly of the living who, buried in remote places out of the knowledge of mankind, still are fated to share in its tragic or grotesque miseries. In its noble struggles too—who knows? The human heart is vast enough to contain all the world. It is valiant enough to bear the burden, but where is the courage that would cast it off?

"I suppose I must have fallen into a sentimental mood; I only know that I stood there long enough for the sense of utter solitude to get hold of me so completely that all I had lately seen, all I had heard, and the very human speech itself, seemed to have passed away out of existence, living only for a while longer in my memory, as though I had been the last of mankind. It was a strange and melancholy illusion, evolved half-consciously like all our illusions, which I suspect only to be visions of remote unattainable truth, seen dimly. This was, indeed, one of the lost, forgotten, unknown places of the earth; I had looked under its obscure surface; and I felt that when to-morrow I had left it for ever, it would slip out of existence, to live only in my memory till I myself passed into oblivion. I have that feeling about me now; perhaps it is that feeling which had incited me to tell you the story, to try to hand over to you, as it were, its very existence, its reality—the truth disclosed in a moment of illusion.

"Cornelius broke upon it. He bolted out, vermin-like, from the long grass growing in a depression of the ground. I believe his house was rotting somewhere near by, though I've never seen it, not having been far enough in that direction. He ran towards me upon the path; his feet, shod in dirty white shoes, twinkled on the dark earth; he pulled himself up, and began to whine and cringe under a tall stove-pipe hat. His dried-up little carcass was swallowed up, totally lost, in a suit of black broadcloth. That was his costume for holidays and ceremonies, and it reminded me that this was the fourth Sunday I had spent in Patusan. All the time of my stay I had been vaguely aware of his desire to confide in me, if he only could get me all to himself. He hung about with an eager craving look on his sour yellow little face; but his timidity had kept him back as much as my natural reluctance to have anything to do with such an unsavoury creature. He would have succeeded, nevertheless, had he not been so ready to slink off as soon as you looked at him. He would slink off before Jim's severe gaze, before my own, which I tried to make indifferent, even before Tamb' Itam's surly, superior glance. He was perpetually slinking away; whenever seen he was seen moving off deviously, his face over his shoulder, with either a mistrustful snarl or a woe-begone, piteous, mute aspect; but no assumed expression could conceal this innate irremediable abjectness of his nature, any more than an arrangement of clothing can conceal some monstrous deformity of the body.

"I don't know whether it was the demoralisation

of my utter defeat in my encounter with a spectre of fear less than an hour ago, but I let him capture me without even a show of resistance. I was doomed to be the recipient of confidences, and to be confronted with unanswerable questions. It was trying; but the contempt, the unreasoned contempt, the man's appearance provoked, made it easier to bear. He couldn't possibly matter. Nothing mattered, since I had made up my mind that Jim, for whom alone I cared, had at last mastered his fate. He had told me he was satisfied . . . nearly. This is going further than most of us dare. I—who have the right to think myself good enough —dare not. Neither does any of you here, I suppose? . . .''

Marlow paused, as if expecting an answer. Nobody spoke.

"Quite right," he began again. "Let no soul know, since the truth can be wrung out of us only by some cruel, little, awful catastrophe. But he is one of us, and he could say he was satisfied . . . nearly. Just fancy this! Nearly satisfied. One could almost envy him his catastrophe. Nearly satisfied. After this nothing could matter. It did not matter who suspected him, who trusted him, who loved him, who hated him—especially as it was Cornelius who hated him.

"Yet after all this was a kind of recognition. You shall judge of a man by his foes as well as by his friends, and this enemy of Jim was such as no decent man would be ashamed to own, without, however, making too much of him. This was the view Jim took, and in which I shared; but Jim disregarded him on general grounds. 'My dear Marlow,' he said, 'I feel that if I go straight nothing can touch me. Indeed I do. Now you have been long enough here to have a good look round—and, frankly, don't you think I am pretty safe. It all depends upon me, and, by Jove! I have lots of confidence in myself. The worst thing he could do would be to kill me, I suppose. I don't think for a moment he would. He couldn't, you know—not if I were myself to hand him a loaded rifle for the purpose, and then turn my back on him. That's the sort of thing he is. And suppose he would—suppose he could? Well—what of that? I didn't come here flying for my life—did I? I came here to set my back against the wall, and I am going to stay here . . .'

" ' Till you are *quite* satisfied,' I struck in.

" We were sitting at the time under the roof in the stern of his boat; twenty paddles flashed like one, ten on a side, striking the water with a single splash, while behind our backs Tamb' Itam dipped silently right and left, and stared right down the river, attentive to keep the long canoe in the greatest strength of the current. Jim bowed his head, and our last talk seemed to flicker out for good. He was seeing me off as far as the mouth of the river. The schooner had left the day before, working down and drifting on the ebb, while I had prolonged my stay overnight. And now he was seeing me off.

" Jim had been a little angry with me for mentioning Cornelius at all. I had not, in truth, said much. The man was too insignificant to be dangerous, though he was as full of hate as he could hold. He had called me ' honourable sir ' at every second sentence, and had whined at my elbow as he followed me from the grave of his ' late wife ' to the gate of Jim's compound. He declared himself the most

unhappy of men, a victim, crushed like a worm;
he entreated me to look at him. I wouldn't turn
my head to do so; but I could see out of the corner
of my eye his obsequious shadow gliding after mine,
while the moon, suspended on our right hand,
seemed to gloat serenely upon the spectacle. He
tried to explain—as I've told you—his share in
the events of the memorable night. It was a matter
of expediency. How could he know who was going
to get the upper hand? 'I would have saved him,
honourable sir! I would have saved him for eighty
dollars', he protested in dulcet tones, keeping a
pace behind me. 'He has saved himself,' I said,
'and he has forgiven you.' I heard a sort of tittering,
and turned upon him; at once he appeared ready
to take to his heels. 'What are you laughing
at?' I asked, standing still. 'Don't be deceived,
honourable sir!' he shrieked, seemingly losing all
control over his feelings. '*He* save himself! He
knows nothing, honourable sir—nothing whatever.
Who is he? What does he want here—the big
thief? What does he want here? He throws
dust into everybody's eyes; he throws dust into
your eyes, honourable sir; but he can't throw
dust into my eyes. He is a big fool, honourable
sir.' I laughed contemptuously, and, turning on
my heel, began to walk on again. He ran up to
my elbow and whispered forcibly, 'He's no more
than a little child here—like a little child—a little
child.' Of course I didn't take the slightest notice,
and seeing the time pressed, because we were
approaching the bamboo fence that glittered over
the blackened ground of the clearing, he came to
the point. He commenced by being abjectly lachry-
mose. His great misfortune had affected his head.

He hoped I would kindly forget what nothing but
his troubles made him say. He didn't mean anything by it ; only the honourable sir did not know
what it was to be ruined, broken down, trampled
upon. After this introduction he approached the
matter near his heart, but in such a rambling,
ejaculatory, craven fashion, that for a long time
I couldn't make out what he was driving at. He
wanted me to intercede with Jim in his favour. It
seemed, too, to be some sort of money affair. I
heard time and again the words, 'Moderate provision—suitable present.' He seemed to be claiming
value for something, and he even went the length
of saying with some warmth that life was not
worth having if a man were to be robbed of everything. I did not breathe a word, of course, but
neither did I stop my ears. The gist of the affair,
which became clear to me gradually, was in this,
that he regarded himself as entitled to some money
in exchange for the girl. He had brought her up.
Somebody else's child. Great trouble and pains—
old man now—suitable present. If the honourable
sir would say a word. . . . I stood still to look
at him with curiosity, and fearful lest I should
think him extortionate, I suppose, he hastily brought
himself to make a concession. In consideration
of a 'suitable present' given at once, he would,
he declared, be willing to undertake the charge
of the girl, 'without any other provision—when
the time came for the gentleman to go home.' His
little yellow face, all crumpled as though it had been
squeezed together, expressed the most anxious,
eager avarice. His voice whined coaxingly, 'No
more trouble — natural guardian — a sum of
money . . .'

"I stood there and marvelled. That kind of thing, with him, was evidently a vocation. I discovered suddenly in his cringing attitude a sort of assurance, as though he had been all his life dealing in certitudes. He must have thought I was dispassionately considering his proposal, because he became as sweet as honey. 'Every gentleman made a provision when the time came to go home,' he began insinuatingly. I slammed the little gate. 'In this case, Mr Cornelius,' I said, 'the time shall never come.' He took a few seconds to gather this in. 'What!' he fairly squealed. 'Why,' I continued from my side of the gate, 'haven't you heard him say so himself? He will never go home.' 'Oh! this is too much,' he shouted. He would not address me as 'honoured sir' any more. He was very still for a time, and then without a trace of humility began very low. 'Never go—ah! He—he—he comes here devil knows from where —comes here—devil knows why—to trample on me till I die—ah—trample' (he stamped softly with both feet), 'trample like this—nobody knows why—till I die. . . .' His voice became quite extinct; he was bothered by a little cough; he came up close to the fence and told me, dropping into a confidential and piteous tone, that he would *not* be trampled upon. 'Patience—patience,' he muttered, striking his breast. I had done laughing at him, but unexpectedly he treated me to a wild cracked burst of it. 'Ha! ha! ha! We shall see! We shall see! What? Steal from me? Steal from me everything. Everything! Everything!' His head drooped on one shoulder, his hands were hanging before him lightly clasped. One would have thought he had cherished the girl with surpassing love, that his spirit had been crushed and his heart broken by the most cruel of spoliations. Suddenly he lifted his head and shot out an infamous word. 'Like her mother—she is like her deceitful mother. Exactly. In her face too. In her face. The devil!' He leaned his forehead against the fence, and in that position uttered threats and horrible blasphemies in Portuguese in very weak ejaculations, mingled with miserable plaints and groans, coming out with a heave of the shoulders as though he had been overtaken by a deadly fit of sickness. It was an inexpressibly grotesque and vile performance, and I hastened away. He tried to shout something after me. Some disparagement of Jim, I believe—not too loud though, we were too near the house. All I heard distinctly was, ' No more than a little child—a little child.' "

CHAPTER XXXV.

"But next morning, at the first bend of the river shutting off the houses of Patusan, all this dropped out of my sight bodily, with its colour, its design, and its meaning, like a picture created by fancy on a canvas, upon which, after long contemplation, you turn your back for the last time. It remains in the memory motionless, unfaded, with its life arrested, in an unchanging light. There are the ambitions, the fears, the hate, the hopes, and they remain in my mind just as I had seen them— intense and as if for ever suspended in their expression. I had turned away from the picture and was going back to the world where events move, men change, light flickers, life flows in a clear stream, no matter whether over mud or over stones. I wasn't going to dive into it; I would have enough to do to keep my head above the surface. But as to what I was leaving behind, I cannot imagine any alteration. The immense and magnanimous Doramin and his little motherly witch of a wife, gazing together upon the land and nursing secretly their dreams of parental ambition; Tunku Allang, wizened and greatly perplexed; Dain Waris, intelligent and brave, with his faith in Jim, with his firm glance and his ironic friendliness; the girl, absorbed in her frightened, suspicious adoration; Tamb' Itam, surly and faithful; Cornelius, leaning his forehead against the fence under the moonlight —I am certain of them. They exist as if under an enchanter's wand. But the figure round which all these are grouped—that one lives, and I am not certain of him. No magician's wand can immobilise him under my eyes. He is one of us.

"Jim, as I've told you, accompanied me on the first stage of my journey back to the world he had renounced, and the way at times seemed to lead through the very heart of untouched wilderness. The empty reaches sparkled under the high sun; between the high walls of vegetation the heat drowsed upon the water, and the boat, impelled vigorously, cut her way through the air that seemed to have settled dense and warm under the shelter of lofty trees.

"The shadow of the impending separation had already put an immense space between us, and when we spoke it was with an effort, as if to force

our low voices across a vast and increasing distance.
The boat fairly flew; we sweltered side by side in
the stagnant superheated air; the smell of mud,
of marsh, the primeval smell of fecund earth, seemed
to sting our faces; till suddenly at a bend it was as
if a great hand far away had lifted a heavy curtain,
had flung open an immense portal. The light itself
seemed to stir, the sky above our heads widened,
a far off murmur reached our ears, a freshness enveloped us, filled our lungs, quickened our thoughts,
our blood, our regrets—and, straight ahead, the
forests sank down against the dark-blue ridge of
the sea.

"I breathed deeply, I revelled in the vastness of
the opened horizon, in the different atmosphere that
seemed to vibrate with the toil of life, with the
energy of an impeccable world. This sky and this
sea were open to me. The girl was right—there
was a sign, a call in them—something to which I
responded with every fibre of my being. I let my
eyes roam through space, like a man released from
bonds who stretches his cramped limbs, runs, leaps,
responds to the inspiring elation of freedom. 'This
is glorious!' I cried, and then I looked at the sinner
by my side. He sat with his head sunk on his
breast and said 'Yes,' without raising his eyes, as
if afraid to see writ large on the clear sky of the
offing the reproach of his romantic conscience.

"I remember the smallest details of that afternoon. We landed on a bit of white beach. It was
backed by a low cliff wooded on the brow, draped
in creepers to the very foot. Below us the plain
of the sea, of a serene and intense blue, stretched
with a slight upward tilt to the thread-like horizon
drawn at the height of our eyes. Great waves of

glitter blew lightly along the pitted dark surface, as swift as feathers chased by the breeze. A chain of islands sat broken and massive facing the wide estuary, displayed in a sheet of pale glassy water reflecting faithfully the contour of the shore. High in the colourless sunshine a solitary bird, all black, hovered, dropping and soaring above the same spot with a slight rocking motion of the wings. A ragged, sooty bunch of flimsy mat hovels was perched over its own inverted image upon a crooked multitude of high piles the colour of ebony. A tiny black canoe put off from amongst them with two tiny men, all black, who toiled exceedingly, striking down at the pale water : and the canoe seemed to slide painfully on a mirror. This bunch of miserable hovels was the fishing village that boasted of the white lord's especial protection, and the two men crossing over were the old headman and his son-in-law. They landed and walked up to us on the white sand, lean, dark-brown as if dried in smoke, with ashy patches on the skin of their naked shoulders and breasts. Their heads were bound in dirty but carefully folded headkerchiefs, and the old man began at once to state a complaint, voluble, stretching a lank arm, screwing up at Jim his old bleared eyes confidently. The Rajah's people would not leave them alone ; there had been some trouble about a lot of turtles' eggs his people had collected on the islets there—and leaning at arm's-length upon his paddle, he pointed with a brown skinny hand over the sea. Jim listened for a time without looking up, and at last told him gently to wait. He would hear him by-and-by. They withdrew obediently to some little distance, and sat on their heels, with their paddles lying before them on the

sand ; the silvery gleams in their eyes followed our
movements patiently : and the immensity of the
outspread sea, the stillness of the coast, passing
north and south beyond the limits of my vision,
made up one colossal Presence watching us four
dwarfs isolated on a strip of glistening sand.

" ' The trouble is,' remarked Jim moodily, ' that
for generations these beggars of fishermen in that
village there had been considered as the Rajah's
personal slaves—and the old rip can't get it into
his head that . . .'

" He paused. ' That you have changed all that,'
I said.

" ' Yes. I've changed all that,' he muttered in a
gloomy voice.

" ' You have had your opportunity,' I pursued.

" ' Had I ? ' he said. ' Well, yes. I suppose so.
Yes. I have got back my confidence in myself
—a good name—yet sometimes I wish . . . No !
I shall hold what I've got. Can't expect anything
more.' He flung his arm out towards the sea.
' Not out there anyhow.' He stamped his foot
upon the sand. ' This is my limit, because nothing
less will do.'

" We continued pacing the beach. ' Yes, I've
changed all that,' he went on, with a sidelong
glance at the two patient squatting fishermen ;
' but only try to think what it would be if I went
away. Jove ! can't you see it ? Hell loose. No !
To-morrow I shall go and take my chance of drinking that silly old Tunku Allang's coffee, and I shall
make no end of fuss over these rotten turtles' eggs.
No. I can't say—enough. Never. I must go on,
go on for ever holding up my end, to feel sure
that nothing can touch me. I must stick to their

belief in me to feel safe and to—to ' . . . He cast
about for a word, seemed to look for it on the
sea . . . 'to keep in touch with ' . . . His voice
sank suddenly to a murmur . . . 'with those whom
perhaps, I shall never see any more. With—with
—you, for instance.'

"I was profoundly humbled by his words. 'For
God's sake,' I said, 'don't set me up, my dear
fellow; just look to yourself.' I felt a gratitude,
an affection, for that straggler whose eyes had
singled me out, keeping my place in the ranks of
an insignificant multitude. How little that was to
boast of, after all! I turned my burning face
away; under the low sun, glowing, darkened and
crimson, like an ember snatched from the fire, the
sea lay outspread, offering all its immense stillness
to the approach of the fiery orb. Twice he was
going to speak, but checked himself: at last, as if
he had found a formula—

"'I shall be faithful,' he said quietly. 'I shall
be faithful,' he repeated, without looking at me,
but for the first time letting his eyes wander upon
the waters, whose blueness had changed to a gloomy
purple under the fires of sunset. Ah! he was romantic, romantic. I recalled some words of Stein's.
. . . 'In the destructive element immerse! . . .
To follow the dream, and again to follow the dream
—and so—always—*usque ad finem* . . .' He was
romantic, but none the less true. Who could tell
what forms, what visions, what faces, what forgiveness he could see in the glow of the west! . . . A
small boat, leaving the schooner, moved slowly, with
a regular beat of two oars, towards the sandbank
to take me off. 'And then there's Jewel,' he said,
out of the great silence of earth, sky, and sea, which

had mastered my very thoughts so that his voice made me start. 'There's Jewel.' 'Yes,' I murmured. 'I need not tell you what she is to me,' he pursued. 'You've seen. In time she will come to understand . . .' 'I hope so,' I interrupted. 'She trusts me, too,' he mused, and then changed his tone. 'When shall we meet next, I wonder?' he said.

"'Never—unless you come out,' I answered, avoiding his glance. He didn't seem to be surprised; he kept very quiet for a while.

"'Good-bye, then,' he said, after a pause. 'Perhaps it's just as well.'

"We shook hands, and I walked to the boat, which waited with her nose on the beach. The schooner, her mainsail set and jib-sheet to windward, curveted on the purple sea; there was a rosy tinge on her sails. 'Will you be going home again soon?' asked Jim, just as I swung my leg over the gunwale. 'In a year or so if I live,' I said. The forefoot grated on the sand, the boat floated, the wet oars flashed and dipped once, twice. Jim, at the water's edge, raised his voice, 'Tell them . . .' he began. I signed to the men to cease rowing, and waited in wonder. Tell who? The half-submerged sun faced him; I could see its red gleam in his eyes that looked dumbly at me. . . . 'No—nothing,' he said, and with a slight wave of his hand motioned the boat away. I did not look again at the shore till I had clambered on board the schooner.

"By that time the sun had set. The twilight lay over the east, and the coast, turned black, extended infinitely its sombre wall that seemed the very stronghold of the night; the western horizon

was one great blaze of gold and crimson in which
a big detached cloud floated dark and still, casting
a slaty shadow on the water beneath, and I saw
Jim on the beach watching the schooner fall off
and gather headway.

"The two half-naked fishermen had arisen as
soon as I had gone ; they were no doubt pouring
the plaint of their trifling, miserable, oppressed lives
into the ears of the white lord, and no doubt he
was listening to it, making it his own, for was it
not a part of his luck—the luck 'from the word
Go '—the luck to which he had assured me he was
so completely equal. They too, I should think,
were in luck, and I was sure their pertinacity
would be equal to it. Their dark-skinned bodies
vanished on the dark background long before I
had lost sight of their protector. He was white
from head to foot, and remained persistently visible
with the stronghold of the night at his back, the
sea at his feet, the opportunity by his side—still
veiled. What do you say ? Was it still veiled ?
I don't know. For me that white figure in the
stillness of coast and sea seemed to stand at the
heart of a vast enigma. The twilight was ebbing
fast from the sky above his head, the strip of sand
had sunk already under his feet, he himself appeared
no bigger than a child—then only a speck, a tiny
white speck, that seemed to catch all the light left
in a darkened world. . . . And, suddenly, I lost
him. . . ."

CHAPTER XXXVI.

WITH these words Marlow had ended his narrative, and his audience had broken up forthwith, under his abstract, pensive gaze. Men drifted off the verandah in pairs or alone without loss of time, without offering a remark, as if the last image of that incomplete story, its incompleteness itself, and the very tone of the speaker, had made discussion vain and comment impossible. Each of them seemed to carry away his own impression, to carry it away with him like a secret; but there was only one man of all these listeners who was ever to hear the last word of the story. It came to him at home, more than two years later, and it came contained in a thick packet addressed in Marlow's upright and angular handwriting.

The privileged man opened the packet, looked in, then, laying it down, went to the window. His rooms were in the highest flat of a lofty building, and his glance could travel afar beyond the clear panes of glass, as though he were looking out of the lantern of a lighthouse. The slopes of the roofs glistened, the dark broken ridges succeeded each other without end like sombre, uncrested waves, and from the depths of the town under his feet ascended a confused and unceasing mutter. The spires of churches, numerous, scattered haphazard, uprose like beacons on a maze of shoals without a channel; the driving rain mingled with the falling dusk of a winter's evening; and the booming of a big clock on a tower striking the hour, rolled past in voluminous, austere bursts of sound, with a shrill

vibrating cry at the core. He drew the heavy
curtains.

The light of his shaded reading-lamp slept like
a sheltered pool, his footfalls made no sound on
the carpet, his wandering days were over. No more
horizons as boundless as hope, no more twilights
within the forests as solemn as temples, in the hot
quest for the Ever-undiscovered Country over the
hill, across the stream, beyond the wave. The hour
was striking! No more! No more!—but the
opened packet under the lamp brought back the
sounds, the visions, the very savour of the past—
a multitude of fading faces, a tumult of low voices
dying away upon the shores of distant seas under
a passionate and unconsoling sunshine. He sighed
and sat down to read.

At first he saw three distinct enclosures. A good
many pages closely blackened and pinned together,
a loose square sheet of greyish paper with a few
words traced in a handwriting he had never seen
before, and an explanatory letter from Marlow.
From this last fell another letter, yellowed by time
and frayed on the folds. He picked it up and,
laying it aside, turned to Marlow's message, ran
swiftly over the opening lines, and, checking himself,
thereafter read on deliberately, like one approaching
with slow feet and alert eyes the glimpse of an un-
discovered country.

" . . . I don't suppose you've forgotten," went on
the letter. " You alone have showed an interest in
him that survived the telling of his story, though
I remember well you would not admit he had mastered his fate. You prophesied for him the disaster
of weariness and of disgust with acquired honour,
with the self-appointed task, with the love sprung

rom pity and youth. You had said you knew so
well 'that kind of thing,' its illusory satisfaction,
ts unavoidable deception. You said also—I call
o mind—that 'giving your life up to them' (*them*
meaning all of mankind with skins brown, yellow,
r black in colour) 'was like selling your soul to a
brute.' You contended that 'that kind of thing'
was only endurable and enduring when based on
firm conviction in the truth of ideas racially our
own, in whose name are established the order, the
morality of an ethical progress. 'We want its
strength at our backs,' you had said. 'We want
belief in its necessity and its justice, to make a
worthy and conscious sacrifice of our lives. Without
t the sacrifice is only forgetfulness, the way of
ffering is no better than the way to perdition.'
n other words, you maintained that we must fight
n the ranks or our lives don't count. Possibly!
You ought to know—be it said without malice—
ou who have rushed into one or two places single-
handed and came out cleverly, without singeing
our wings. The point, however, is that of all
mankind Jim had no dealings but with himself,
nd the question is whether at the last he had
not confessed to a faith mightier than the laws
f order and progress.

"I affirm nothing. Perhaps you may pronounce
—after you've read. There is much truth—after
all—in the common expression 'under a cloud.' It
s impossible to see him clearly—especially as it is
through the eyes of others that we take our last
ook at him. I have no hesitation in imparting to
ou all I know of the last episode that, as he used
o say, had 'come to him.' One wonders whether
his was perhaps that supreme opportunity, that

last and satisfying test for which I had alway
suspected him to be waiting, before he could fram
a message to the impeccable world. You remembe
that when I was leaving him for the last time h
had asked whether I would be going home soor
and suddenly cried after me, ' Tell them ! ' . . .
had waited—curious I'll own, and hopeful too—
only to hear him shout, ' No. Nothing.' Tha
was all then—and there shall be nothing more
there shall be no message, unless such as each o
us can interpret for himself from the language o
facts, that are so often more enigmatic than th
craftiest arrangement of words. He made, it i
true, one more attempt to deliver himself ; but tha
too failed, as you may perceive if you look at th
sheet of greyish foolscap enclosed here. He ha
tried to write ; do you notice the commonplac
hand ? It is headed ' The Fort, Patusan.' I sup
pose he had carried out his intention of making ou
of his house a place of defence. It was an excellen
plan : a deep ditch, an earth wall topped by a palis
ade, and at the angles guns mounted on platforms t
sweep each side of the square. Doramin had agree
to furnish him the guns ; and so each man of hi
party would know there was a place of safety, upo
which every faithful partisan could rally in case o
some sudden danger. All this showed his judiciou
foresight, his faith in the future. What he calle
' my own people '—the liberated captives of th
Sherif—were to make a distinct quarter of Patusan
with their huts and little plots of ground under th
walls of the stronghold. Within he would be ai
invincible host in himself. ' The Fort, Patusan.' N
date, as you observe. What is a number and a nam
to a day of days ? It is also impossible to say whom

he had in his mind when he seized the pen : Stein—myself—the world at large—or was this only the aimless startled cry of a solitary man confronted by his fate ? 'An awful thing has happened,' he wrote before he flung the pen down for the first time ; look at the ink blot resembling the head of an arrow under these words. After a while he had tried again, scrawling heavily, as if with a hand of lead, another line. 'I must now at once . . .' The pen had spluttered, and that time he gave it up. There's nothing more ; he had seen a broad gulf that neither eye nor voice could span. I can understand this. He was overwhelmed by the inexplicable ; he was overwhelmed by his own personality—the gift of that destiny which he had done his best to master.

"I send you also an old letter—a very old letter. It was found carefully preserved in his writing-case. It is from his father, and by the date you can see he must have received it a few days before he joined the *Patna*. Thus it must be the last letter he ever had from home. He had treasured it all these years. The good old parson fancied his sailor-son. I've looked in at a sentence here and there. There is nothing in it except just affection. He tells his 'dear James' that the last long letter from him was very 'honest and entertaining.' He would not have him 'judge men harshly or hastily.' There are four pages of it, easy morality and family news. Tom had 'taken orders.' Carrie's husband had 'money losses.' The old chap goes on equably trusting Providence and the established order of the universe, but alive to its small dangers and its small mercies. One can almost see him, grey-haired and serene in the inviolable shelter of his book-lined,

faded, and comfortable study, where for forty years
he had conscientiously gone over and over again
the round of his little thoughts about faith and
virtue, about the conduct of life and the only proper
manner of dying; where he had written so many
sermons, where he sits talking to his boy, over
there, on the other side of the earth. But what
of the distance. Virtue is one all over the world,
and there is only one faith, one conceivable conduct
of life, one manner of dying. He hopes his 'dear
James' will never forget that 'who once gives way
to temptation, in the very instant hazards his total
depravity and everlasting ruin. Therefore resolve
fixedly never, through any possible motives, to do
anything which you believe to be wrong.' There
is also some news of a favourite dog; and a pony,
'which all you boys used to ride,' had gone blind
from old age and had to be shot. The old chap
invokes Heaven's blessing; the mother and all the
girls then at home send their love. . . . No, there
is nothing much in that yellow frayed letter fluttering out of his cherishing grasp after so many years.
It was never answered, but who can say what converse he may have held with all these placid, colourless forms of men and women peopling that quiet
corner of the world as free of danger or strife as
a tomb, and breathing equably the air of undisturbed rectitude. It seems amazing that he should
belong to it, he to whom so many things 'had come.'
Nothing ever came to them; they would never be
taken unawares, and never be called upon to grapple
with fate. Here they all are, evoked by the mild
gossip of the father, all these brothers and sisters,
bone of his bone and flesh of his flesh, gazing with
clear unconscious eyes, while I seem to see him, re-

turned at last, no longer a mere white speck at the heart of an immense mystery, but of full stature, standing disregarded amongst their untroubled shapes, with a stern and romantic aspect, but always mute, dark—under a cloud.

" The story of the last events you shall find in the few pages enclosed here. You must admit that it is romantic beyond the wildest dreams of his boyhood, and yet there is to my mind a sort of profound and terrifying logic in it, as if it were our imagination alone that could set loose upon us the might of an overwhelming destiny. The imprudence of our thoughts recoils upon our heads ; who toys with the sword shall perish by the sword. This astounding adventure, of which the most astounding part is that it is true, comes on as an unavoidable consequence. Something of the sort had to happen. You repeat this to yourself while you marvel that such a thing could happen in the year of grace before last. But it has happened—and there is no disputing its logic.

" I put it down here for you as though I had been an eyewitness. My information was fragmentary, but I've fitted the pieces together, and there is enough of them to make an intelligible picture. I wonder how he would have related it himself. He has confided so much in me that at times it seems as though he must come in presently and tell the story in his own words, in his careless yet feeling voice, with his offhand manner, a little puzzled, a little bothered, a little hurt, but now and then by a word or a phrase giving one of these glimpses of his very own self that were never any good for purposes of orientation. It's difficult to believe he will never come. I shall never hear his voice again, nor shall I see his smooth tan-and-pink face with a white line on the forehead, and the youthful eyes darkened by excitement to a profound, unfathomable blue.''

CHAPTER XXXVII.

''It all begins with a remarkable exploit of a man called Brown, who stole with complete success a Spanish schooner out of a small bay near Zamboanga. Till I discovered the fellow my information was incomplete, but most unexpectedly I did come upon him a few hours before he gave up his arrogant ghost. Fortunately he was willing and able to talk between the choking fits of asthma, and his racked body writhed with malicious exultation at the bare thought of Jim. He exulted thus at the idea that he had ' paid out the stuck-up beggar after all.' He gloated over his action. I had to bear the sunken glare of his fierce crow-footed eyes if I wanted to know ; and so I bore it, reflecting how much certain forms of evil are akin to madness, derived from intense egoism, inflamed by resistance, tearing the soul to pieces, and giving factitious vigour to the body. The story also reveals unsuspected depths of cunning in the wretched Cornelius, whose abject and intense hate acts like a subtle inspiration, pointing out an unerring way towards revenge.

'' ' I could see directly I set my eyes on him what sort of a fool he was,' gasped the dying Brown.

'He a man! Hell! He was a hollow sham. As if he couldn't have said straight out, "Hands off my plunder!" blast him! That would have been like a man! Rot his superior soul! He had me there—but he hadn't devil enough in him to make an end of me. Not he! A thing like that letting me off as if I wasn't worth a kick! . . .' Brown struggled desperately for breath. . . . 'Fraud. . . . Letting me off. . . . And so I did make an end of him after all. . . .' He choked again. . . . 'I expect this thing'll kill me, but I shall die easy now. You . . . you here. . . . I don't know your name—I would give you a five-pound note if—if I had it—for the news—or my name's not Brown. . . .' He grinned horribly. . . . 'Gentleman Brown.'

"He said all these things in profound gasps, staring at me with his yellow eyes out of a long, ravaged brown face; he jerked his left arm; a pepper-and-salt matted beard hung almost into his lap; a dirty ragged blanket covered his legs. I had found him out in Bankok through that busy-body Schomberg, the hotelkeeper, who had, confidentially, directed me where to look. It appears that a sort of loafing, fuddled vagabond—a white man living amongst the natives with a Siamese woman—had considered it a great privilege to give a shelter to the last days of the famous Gentleman Brown. While he was talking to me in the wretched hovel, and, as it were, fighting for every minute of his life, the Siamese woman, with big bare legs and a stupid coarse face, sat in a dark corner chewing betel stolidly. Now and then she would get up for the purpose of shooing a chicken away from the door. The whole hut shook when she walked. An ugly yellow child, naked and potbellied like a little heathen god, stood at the foot of the couch, finger in mouth, lost in a profound and calm contemplation of the dying man.

"He talked feverishly; but in the middle of a word, perhaps, an invisible hand would take him by the throat, and he would look at me dumbly with an expression of doubt and anguish. He seemed to fear that I would get tired of waiting and go away, leaving him with his tale untold, with his exultation unexpressed. He died during the night, I believe, but by that time I had nothing more to learn.

"So much as to Brown, for the present.

"Eight months before this, coming into Samarang, I went as usual to see Stein. On the garden side of the house a Malay on the verandah greeted me shyly, and I remembered that I had seen him in Patusan, in Jim's house, amongst other Bugis men who used to come in the evening to talk interminably over their war reminiscences and to discuss State affairs. Jim had pointed him out to me once as a respectable petty trader owning a small seagoing native craft, who had showed himself 'one of the best at the taking of the stockade.' I was not very surprised to see him, since any Patusan trader venturing as far as Samarang would naturally find his way to Stein's house. I returned his greeting and passed on. At the door of Stein's room I came upon another Malay in whom I recognised Tamb' Itam.

"I asked him at once what he was doing there; it occurred to me that Jim might have come on a visit. I own I was pleased and excited at the thought. Tamb' Itam looked as if he did not know what to say. 'Is Tuan Jim inside?' I asked impatiently. 'No,' he mumbled, hanging his head for a moment, and then with sudden earnestness, 'He would not fight. He would not fight,' he repeated twice. As he seemed unable to say anything else, I pushed him aside and went in.

"Stein, tall and stooping, stood alone in the middle of the room between the rows of butterfly cases. 'Ach! is it you, my friend?' he said sadly, peering through his glasses. A drab sack-coat of alpaca hung, unbuttoned, down to his knees. He had a Panama hat on his head, and there were deep furrows on his pale cheeks. 'What's the matter now?' I asked nervously. 'There's Tamb' Itam there. . . .' 'Come and see the girl. Come and see the girl. She is here,' he said, with a half-hearted show of activity. I tried to detain him, but with gentle obstinacy he would take no notice of my eager questions. 'She is here, she is here,' he repeated, in great perturbation. 'They came here two days ago. An old man like me, a stranger—*sehen sie*—can not do much. . . . Come this way. . . . Young hearts are unforgiving. . . .' I could see he was in utmost distress. . . . 'The strength of life in them, the cruel strength of life. . . .' He mumbled, leading me round the house; I followed him, lost in dismal and angry conjectures. At the door of the drawing-room he barred my way. 'He loved her very much,' he said interrogatively, and I only nodded, feeling so bitterly disappointed that I would not trust myself to speak. 'Very frightful,' he murmured. 'She can't understand me. I am only a strange old man. Perhaps you . . . she knows you. Talk to her. We can't leave it like this. Tell her to forgive him. It was very frightful.' 'No doubt,' I said, exasperated at being in the

dark; 'but have *you* forgiven him?' He looked
at me queerly. 'You shall hear,' he said, and opening the door, absolutely pushed me in.

"You know Stein's big house and the two immense reception-rooms, uninhabited and uninhabit-
able, clean, full of solitude and of shining things
that look as if never beheld by the eye of man?
They are cool on the hottest days, and you enter
them as you would a scrubbed cave underground.
I passed through one, and in the other I saw the
girl sitting at the end of a big mahogany table, on
which she rested her head, the face hidden in her
arms. The waxed floor reflected her dimly as though
it had been a sheet of frozen water. The rattan
screens were down, and through the strange greenish
gloom made by the foliage of the trees outside, a
strong wind blew in gusts, swaying the long draperies
of windows and doorways. Her white figure seemed
shaped in snow; the pendent crystals of a great
chandelier clicked above her head like glittering
icicles. She looked up and watched my approach.
I was chilled as if these vast apartments had been
the cold abode of despair.

"She recognised me at once, and as soon as I had
stopped looking down at her: 'He has left me,' she
said quietly; 'you always leave us—for your own
ends.' Her face was set. All the heat of life seemed
withdrawn within some inaccessible spot in her
breast. 'It would have been easy to die with him,'
she went on, and made a slight weary gesture as
if giving up the incomprehensible. 'He would
not! It was like a blindness—and yet it was I
who was speaking to him; it was I who stood
before his eyes; it was at me that he looked all the
time! Ah! you are hard, treacherous, without

truth, without compassion. What makes you so
wicked? Or is it that you are all mad?'

"I took her hand; it did not respond, and when
I dropped it, it hung down to the floor. That
indifference, more awful than tears, cries, and
reproaches, seemed to defy time and consolation.
You felt that nothing you could say would reach
the seat of the still and benumbing pain.

"Stein had said, 'You shall hear.' I did hear.
I heard it all, listening with amazement, with awe,
to the tones of her inflexible weariness. She could
not grasp the real sense of what she was telling
me, and her resentment filled me with pity for her
—for him too. I stood rooted to the spot after she
had finished. Leaning on her arm, she stared with
hard eyes, and the wind passed in gusts, the crystals
kept on clicking in the greenish gloom. She went
on whispering to herself: 'And yet he was looking
at me! He could see my face, hear my voice, hear
my grief! When I used to sit at his feet, with my
cheek against his knee and his hand on my head, the
curse of cruelty and madness was already within
him, waiting for the day. The day came! . . . and
before the sun had set he could not see me any
more—he was made blind and deaf and without
pity, as you all are. He shall have no tears from
me. Never, never. Not one tear. I will not! He
went away from me as if I had been worse than
death. He fled as if driven by some accursed thing
he had heard or seen in his sleep. . . .'

"Her steady eyes seemed to strain after the shape
of a man torn out of her arms by the strength of a
dream. She made no sign to my silent bow. I was
glad to escape.

"I saw her once again, the same afternoon. On

leaving her I had gone in search of Stein, whom I could not find indoors; and I wandered out, pursued by distressful thoughts, into the gardens, these famous gardens of Stein, in which you can find every plant and tree of tropical lowlands. I followed the course of the canalised stream, and sat for a long time on a shaded bench near the ornamental pond, where some waterfowl with clipped wings were diving and splashing noisily. The branches of casuarina-trees behind me swayed lightly, incessantly, reminding me of the soughing of fir-trees at home.

"This mournful and restless sound was a fit accompaniment to my meditations. She had said he had been driven away from her by a dream,—and there was no answer one could make her—there seemed to be no forgiveness for such a transgression. And yet is not mankind itself, pushing on its blind way, driven by a dream of its greatness and its power upon the dark paths of excessive cruelty and of excessive devotion? And what is the pursuit of truth—after all?

"When I rose to get back to the house I caught sight of Stein's drab coat through a gap in the foliage, and very soon at a turn of the path I came upon him walking with the girl. Her little hand rested on his forearm, and under the broad, flat rim of his Panama hat he bent over her, greyhaired, paternal, with compassionate and chivalrous deference. I stood aside, but they stopped, facing me. His gaze was bent on the ground at his feet; the girl, erect and slight on his arm, stared sombrely beyond my shoulder with black, clear, motionless eyes. '*Schrecklich*,' he murmured. 'Terrible! Terrible! What can one do?' He seemed to be appealing to me, but her youth, the length of the days suspended over her head, appealed to me more ; and suddenly, even as I realised that nothing could be said, I found myself pleading his cause for her sake. ' You must forgive him.' I concluded, and my own voice seemed to me muffled, lost in an irresponsive deaf immensity. ' We all want to be forgiven,' I added after a while.

" ' What have I done ? ' she asked with her lips only.

" ' You always mistrusted him,' I said.

" ' He was like the others,' she pronounced slowly.

" ' Not like the others,' I protested, but she continued evenly, without any feeling—

" ' He was false.' And suddenly Stein broke in. ' No ! no ! no ! My poor child ! . . .' He patted her hand lying passively on his sleeve. ' No ! no ! Not false ! True ! true ! true ! ' He tried to look into her stony face. ' You don't understand. Ach ! Why you do not understand ? . . . Terrible,' he said to me. ' Some day she *shall* understand.'

" ' Will *you* explain ? ' I asked, looking hard at him. They moved on.

" I watched them. Her gown trailed on the path, her black hair fell loose. She walked upright and light by the side of the tall man, whose long shapeless coat hung in perpendicular folds from the stooping shoulders, whose feet moved slowly. They disappeared beyond that spinney (you may remember) where sixteen different kinds of bamboo grow together, all distinguishable to the learned eye. For my part, I was fascinated by the exquisite grace and beauty of that fluted grove, crowned with pointed leaves and feathery heads, the lightness, the vigour, the charm as distinct as a voice of that unperplexed

luxuriating life. I remember staying to look at it
for a long time, as one would linger within reach
of a consoling whisper. The sky was pearly grey
It was one of these overcast days so rare in the
tropics, in which memories crowd upon one, memories of other shores, of other faces.

"I drove back to town the same afternoon, taking
with me Tamb' Itam and the other Malay, in whose
seagoing craft they had escaped in the bewilderment,
fear, and gloom of the disaster. The shock of it
seemed to have changed their natures. It had
turned her passion into stone, and it made the
surly taciturn Tamb' Itam almost loquacious. His
surliness, too, was subdued into puzzled humility,
as though he had seen the failure of a potent charm
in a supreme moment. The Bugis trader, a shy
hesitating man, was very clear in the little he had
to say. Both were evidently overawed by a sense
of deep inexpressible wonder, by the touch of an
inscrutable mystery."

There with Marlow's signature the letter proper
ended. The privileged reader screwed up his lamp,
and solitary above the billowy roofs of the town, like
a lighthouse-keeper above the sea, he turned to the
pages of the story.

CHAPTER XXXVIII.

"It all begins, as I've told you, with the man
called Brown," ran the opening sentence of Marlow's narrative. "You who have knocked about
the Western Pacific must have heard of him. He

was the show ruffian on the Australian coast—
not that he was often to be seen there, but because he was always trotted out in the stories of
lawless life a visitor from home is treated to ; and
the mildest of these stories which were told about
him from Cape York to Eden Bay was more than
enough to hang a man if told in the right place.
They never failed to let you know, too, that he was
supposed to be the son of a baronet. Be it as it
may, it is certain he had deserted from a home ship
in the early gold-digging days, and in a few years
became talked about as the terror of this or that
group of islands in Polynesia. He would kidnap
natives, he would strip some lonely white trader
to the very pyjamas he stood in, and after he
had robbed the poor devil, he would as likely as
not invite him to fight a duel with shot-guns on
the beach—which would have been fair enough as
these things go, if the other man hadn't been by
that time already half-dead with fright. Brown
was a latter-day buccaneer, sorry enough, like his
more celebrated prototypes ; but what distinguished
him from his contemporary brother ruffians, like
Bully Hayes or the mellifluous Pease, or that per-
fumed, Dundreary-whiskered, dandified scoundrel
known as Dirty Dick, was the arrogant temper
of his misdeeds and a vehement scorn for mankind
at large and for his victims in particular. The
others were merely vulgar and greedy brutes, but
he seemed moved by some complex intention. He
would rob a man as if only to demonstrate his
poor opinion of the creature, and he would bring
to the shooting or maiming of some quiet, unoffending stranger a savage and vengeful earnestness fit to terrify the most reckless of desperadoes.

In the days of his greatest glory he owned an
armed barque, manned by a mixed crew of Kanakas
and runaway whalers, and boasted, I don't know
with what truth, of being financed on the quiet by
a most respectable firm of copra merchants. Later
on he ran off—it was reported—with the wife of
a missionary, a very young girl from Clapham
way, who had married the mild, flat-footed fellow
in a moment of enthusiasm, and suddenly trans-
planted to Melanesia, lost her bearings somehow.
It was a dark story. She was ill at the time he
carried her off, and died on board his ship. It is
said—as the most wonderful part of the tale—that
over her body he gave way to an outburst of sombre
and violent grief. His luck left him, too, very soon
after. He lost his ship on some rocks off Malaita,
and disappeared for a time as though he had gone
down with her. He is heard of next at Nuka-Hiva,
where he bought an old French schooner out of
Government service. What creditable enterprise he
might have had in view when he made that pur-
chase I can't say, but it is evident that what with
High Commissioners, consuls, men-of-war, and international control, the South Seas were getting too
hot to hold gentlemen of his kidney. Clearly he
must have shifted the scene of his operations farther
west, because a year later he plays an incredibly
audacious, but not a very profitable part, in a
serio-comic business in Manila Bay, in which a
peculating governor and an absconding treasurer
are the principal figures ; thereafter he seems to
have hung around the Philippines in his rotten
schooner, battling with an adverse fortune, till at
last, running his appointed course, he sails into Jim's
history, a blind accomplice of the Dark Powers.

" His tale goes that when a Spanish patrol cutter
captured him he was simply trying to run a few
guns for the insurgents. If so, then I can't understand what he was doing off the south coast of
Mindanao. My belief, however, is that he was
blackmailing the native villages along the coast.
The principal thing is that the cutter, throwing a
guard on board, made him sail in company towards
Zamboanga. On the way, for some reason or other,
both vessels had to call at one of these new Spanish
settlements—which never came to anything in the
end—where there was not only a civil official in
charge on shore, but a good stout coasting schooner
lying at anchor in the little bay ; and this craft, in
every way much better than his own, Brown made
up his mind to steal.

" He was down on his luck—as he told me himself.
The world he had bullied for twenty years with
fierce, aggressive disdain, had yielded him nothing in
the way of material advantage except a small bag of
silver dollars, which was concealed in his cabin so
that ' the devil himself couldn't smell it out.' And
that was all—absolutely all. He was tired of his
life, and not afraid of death. But this man, who
would stake his existence on a whim with a bitter
and jeering recklessness, stood in mortal fear of
imprisonment. He had an unreasoning cold-sweat,
nerve-shaking, blood-to-water-turning sort of horror
at the bare possibility of being locked up—the sort of
terror a superstitious man would feel at the thought
of being embraced by a spectre. Therefore the civil
official who came on board to make a preliminary
investigation into the capture, investigated ardu-
ously all day long, and only went ashore after dark,
muffled up in a cloak, and taking great care not to

let Brown's little all clink in its bag. Afterwards, being a man of his word, he contrived (the very next evening, I believe) to send off the Government cutter on some urgent bit of special service. As her commander could not spare a prize crew, he contented himself by taking away before he left all the sails of Brown's schooner to the very last rag, and took good care to tow his two boats on to the beach a couple of miles off.

"But in Brown's crew there was a Solomon Islander, kidnapped in his youth and devoted to Brown, who was the best man of the whole gang. That fellow swam off to the coaster—five hundred yards or so—with the end of a warp made up of all the running gear unrove for the purpose. The water was smooth, and the bay dark, 'like the inside of a cow,' as Brown described it. The Solomon Islander clambered over the bulwarks with the end of the rope in his teeth. The crew of the coaster —all Tagals—were ashore having a jollification in the native village. The two shipkeepers left on board woke up suddenly and saw the devil. It had glittering eyes and leaped quick as lightning about the deck. They fell on their knees, paralysed with fear, crossing themselves and mumbling prayers. With a long knife he found in the caboose the Solomon Islander, without interrupting their orisons, stabbed first one, then the other ; with the same knife he set to sawing patiently at the coir cable till suddenly it parted under the blade with a splash. Then in the silence of the bay he let out a cautious shout, and Brown's gang, who meantime had been peering and straining their hopeful ears in the darkness, began to pull gently at their end of the warp. In less than five minutes the two schooners came together with a slight shock and a creak of spars.

"Brown's crowd transferred themselves without losing an instant, taking with them their firearms and a large supply of ammunition. They were sixteen in all : two runaway blue-jackets, a lanky deserter from a Yankee man-of-war, a couple of simple, blond Scandinavians, a mulatto of sorts, one bland Chinaman who cooked—and the rest of the nondescript spawn of the South Seas. None of them cared ; Brown bent them to his will, and Brown, indifferent to gallows, was running away from the spectre of a Spanish prison He didn't give them the time to trans-ship enough provisions ; the weather was calm, the air was charged with dew, and when they cast off the ropes and set sail to a faint off-shore draught there was no flutter in the damp canvas ; their old schooner seemed to detach itself gently from the stolen craft and slip away silently, together with the black mass of the coast, into the night.

"They got clear away. Brown related to me in detail their passage down the Straits of Macassar. It is a harrowing and desperate story. They were short of food and water ; they boarded several native craft and got a little from each. With a stolen ship Brown did not dare to put into any port, of course. He had no money to buy anything, no papers to show, and no lie plausible enough to get him out again. An Arab barque, under the Dutch flag, surprised one night at anchor off Poulo Laut, yielded a little dirty rice, a bunch of bananas, and a cask of water ; three days of squally, misty weather from the north-east shot the schooner across the Java Sea. The yellow muddy waves drenched that collection of hungry ruffians. They sighted mail-boats moving on their appointed routes ; passed well-found home ships with rusty iron sides anchored in the shallow sea waiting for a change of weather or the turn of the tide ; an English gunboat, white and trim, with two slim masts, crossed their bows one day in the distance ; and on another occasion a Dutch corvette, black and heavily sparred, loomed up on their quarter, steaming dead slow in the mist. They slipped through unseen or disregarded, a wan, sallow-faced band of utter outcasts, enraged with hunger and hunted by fear. Brown's idea was to make for Madagascar, where he expected, on grounds not altogether illusory, to sell the schooner in Tama-tave, and no questions asked, or perhaps obtain some more or less forged papers for her. Yet before he could face the long passage across the Indian Ocean food was wanted—water too.

" Perhaps he had heard of Patusan—or perhaps he just only happened to see the name written in small letters on the chart—probably that of a largish village up a river in a native state, perfectly defence-less, far from the beaten tracks of the sea and from the ends of submarine cables. He had done that kind of thing before—in the way of business ; and this now was an absolute necessity, a question of life and death—or rather of liberty. Of liberty ! He was sure to get provisions—bullocks—rice—sweet-potatoes. The sorry gang licked their chops. A cargo of produce for the schooner perhaps could be extorted—and, who knows—some real ringing coined money ! Some of these chiefs and village headmen can be made to part freely. He told me he would have roasted their toes rather than be baulked. I believe him. His men believed him too.

They didn't cheer aloud, being a dumb pack, but made ready wolfishly.

"Luck served him as to weather. A few days of calm would have brought unmentionable horrors on board that schooner, but with the help of land and sea breezes, in less than a week after clearing the Sunda Straits, he anchored off the Batu Kring mouth within a pistol-shot of the fishing village.

"Fourteen of them packed into the schooner's long-boat (which was big, having been used for cargo-work) and started up the river, while two remained in charge of the schooner with food enough to keep starvation off for ten days. The tide and wind helped, and early one afternoon the big white boat under a ragged sail shouldered its way before the sea breeze into Patusan Reach, manned by fourteen assorted scarecrows glaring hungrily ahead, and fingering the breach-blocks of cheap rifles. Brown calculated upon the terrifying surprise of his appearance. They sailed in with the last of the flood; the Rajah's stockade gave no sign; the first houses on both sides of the stream seemed deserted. A few canoes were seen up the reach in full flight. Brown was astonished at the size of the place. A profound silence reigned. The wind dropped between the houses; two oars were got out and the boat held on upstream, the idea being to effect a lodgment in the centre of the town before the inhabitants could think of resistance.

"It seems, however, that the headman of the fishing village at Batu Kring had managed to send off a timely warning. When the long-boat came abreast of the mosque (which Doramin had built: a structure with gables and roof finials of carved

coral) the open space before it was full of people.
A shout went up, and was followed by a clash of
gongs all up the river. From a point above two
little brass 6-pounders were discharged, and the
round-shot came skipping down the empty reach,
spirting glittering jets of water in the sunshine.
In front of the mosque a shouting lot of men
began firing in volleys that whipped athwart the
current of the river; an irregular, rolling fusilade
was opened on the boat from both banks, and
Brown's men replied with a wild, rapid fire. The
oars had been got in.

"The turn of the tide at high water comes on
very quick in that river, and the boat in mid-
stream, nearly hidden in smoke, began to drift
back stern foremost. Along both shores the smoke
thickened also, lying below the roofs in a level
streak as you may see a long cloud cutting the
slope of a mountain. A tumult of war-cries, the
vibrating clang of gongs, the deep snoring of drums,
yells of rage, crashes of volley-firing, made an awful
din, in which Brown sat confounded but steady at
the tiller, working himself into a fury of hate and
rage against those people who dared to defend
themselves. Two of his men had been wounded,
and he saw his retreat cut off below the town by
some boats that had put off from Tunku Allang's
stockade. There were six of them full of men.
While he was thus beset he perceived the entrance
of the narrow creek (the same which Jim had
jumped at low water). It was then brim full.
Steering the long-boat in, they landed, and, to
make a long story short, they established themselves on a little knoll about 900 yards from the
stockade, which, in fact, they commanded from that

position. The slopes of the knoll were bare, but there were a few trees on the summit. They went to work cutting these down for a breastwork, and were fairly intrenched before dark; meantime the Rajah's boats remained in the river with curious neutrality. When the sun set the glare of many brushwood blazes lighted on the river-front, and between the double line of houses on the land side threw into black relief the roofs, the groups of slender palms, the heavy clumps of fruit-trees. Brown ordered the grass round his position to be fired; a low ring of thin flames under the slow ascending smoke wriggled rapidly down the slopes of the knoll; here and there a dry bush caught with a tall, vicious roar. The conflagration made a clear zone of fire for the rifles of the small party, and expired smouldering on the edge of the forests and along the muddy bank of the creek. A strip of jungle luxuriating in a damp hollow between the knoll and the Rajah's stockade stopped it on that side with a great crackling and detonations of bursting bamboo stems. The sky was sombre, velvety, and swarming with stars. The blackened ground smoked quietly with low creeping wisps, till a little breeze came on and blew everything away. Brown expected an attack to be delivered as soon as the tide had flowed enough again to enable the war-boats which had cut off his retreat to enter the creek. At any rate he was sure there would be an attempt to carry off his long-boat, which lay below the hill, a dark high lump on the feeble sheen of a wet mud-flat. But no move of any sort was made by the boats in the river. Over the stockade and the Rajah's buildings Brown saw their lights on the water. They seemed to be anchored across the stream. Other lights afloat were moving in the reach, crossing and recrossing from side to side. There were also lights twinkling motionless upon the long walls of houses up the reach, as far as the bend, and more still beyond, others isolated inland. The loom of the big fires disclosed buildings, roofs, black piles as far as he could see. It was an immense place. The fourteen desperate invaders lying flat behind the felled trees raised their chins to look over at the stir of that town that seemed to extend up-river for miles and swarm with thousands of angry men. They did not speak to each other. Now and then they would hear a loud yell, or a single shot rang out, fired very far somewhere. But round their position everything was still, dark, silent. They seemed to be forgotten, as if the excitement keeping awake all the population had nothing to do with them, as if they had been dead already."

CHAPTER XXXIX.

"ALL the events of that night have a great importance, since they brought about a situation which remained unchanged till Jim's return. Jim had been away in the interior for more than a week, and it was Dain Waris who had directed the first repulse. That brave and intelligent youth (' who knew how to fight after the manner of white men ') wished to settle the business off-hand, but his

people were too much for him. He had not Jim's
racial prestige and the reputation of invincible,
supernatural power. He was not the visible, tangible incarnation of unfailing truth and of unfailing
victory. Beloved, trusted, and admired as he was,
he was still one of *them*, while Jim was one of *us*.
Moreover, the white man, a tower of strength in
himself, was invulnerable, while Dain Waris could
be killed. Those unexpressed thoughts guided the
opinions of the chief men of the town who elected
to assemble in Jim's fort for deliberation upon the
emergency as if expecting to find wisdom and
courage in the dwelling of the absent white man.
The shooting of Brown's ruffians was so far good
or lucky that there had been half-a-dozen casualties
amongst the defenders. The wounded were lying
on the verandah tended by their womenfolk. The
women and children from the lower part of the town
had been sent into the fort at the first alarm. There
Jewel was in command, very efficient and high-
spirited, obeyed by Jim's 'own people,' who, quitting
in a body their little settlement under the stockade,
had gone in to form the garrison. The refugees
crowded round her ; and through the whole affair,
to the very disastrous last, she showed an extraordinary martial ardour. It was to her that Dain Waris
had gone at once at the first intelligence of danger,
for you must know that Jim was the only one in
Patusan who possessed a store of gunpowder.
Stein, with whom he had kept up intimate relations
by letters, had obtained from the Dutch Government
a special authorisation to export five hundred kegs
of it to Patusan. The powder-magazine was a
small hut of rough logs covered entirely with earth,
and in Jim's absence the girl had the key. In the

council, held at eleven o'clock in the evening in Jim's
dining-room, she backed up Waris's advice for
immediate and vigorous action. I am told that she
stood up by the side of Jim's empty chair at the head
of the long table and made a warlike impassioned
speech, which for the moment extorted murmurs
of approbation from the assembled headmen. Old
Doramin, who had not showed himself outside his
own gate for more than a year, had been brought
across with great difficulty. He was, of course,
the chief man there. The temper of the council
was very unforgiving, and the old man's word
would have been decisive ; but it is my opinion
that, well aware of his son's fiery courage, he dared
not pronounce the word. More dilatory counsels
prevailed. A certain Haji Saman pointed out at
great length that ' these tyrannical and ferocious
men had delivered themselves to a certain death
in any case. They would stand fast on their hill
and starve, or they would try to regain their boat
and be shot from ambushes across the creek, or they
would break and fly into the forest and perish
singly there.' He argued that by the use of proper
stratagems these evil-minded strangers could be
destroyed without the risk of a battle, and his
words had a great weight, especially with the
Patusan men proper. What unsettled the minds
of the townfolk was the failure of the Rajah's
boats to act at the decisive moment. It was the
diplomatic Kassim who represented the Rajah at
the council. He spoke very little, listened smil-
ingly, very friendly and impenetrable. During the
sitting messengers kept arriving every few minutes
almost, with reports of the invaders' proceedings.
Wild and exaggerated rumours were flying : there

was a large ship at the mouth of the river with big guns and many more men—some white, others with black skins and of bloodthirsty appearance. They were coming with many more boats to exterminate every living thing. A sense of near, incomprehensible danger affected the common people. At one moment there was a panic in the courtyard amongst the women ; shrieking ; a rush ; children crying—Haji Saman went out to quiet them. Then a fort sentry fired at something moving on the river, and nearly killed a villager bringing in his women-folk in a canoe together with the best of his domestic utensils and a dozen fowls. This caused more confusion. Meantime the palaver inside Jim's house went on in the presence of the girl. Doramin sat fierce-faced, heavy, looking at the speakers in turn, and breathing slow like a bull. He didn't speak till the last, after Kassim had declared that the Rajah's boats would be called in because the men were required to defend his master's stockade. Dain Waris in his father's presence would offer no opinion, though the girl entreated him in Jim's name to speak out. She offered him Jim's own men in her anxiety to have these intruders driven out at once. He only shook his head, after a glance or two at Doramin. Finally, when the council broke up it had been decided that the houses nearest the creek should be strongly occupied to obtain the command of the enemy's boat. The boat itself was not to be interfered with openly, so that the robbers on the hill should be tempted to embark, when a well-directed fire would kill most of them, no doubt. To cut the escape of those who might survive, and to prevent more of them coming up, Dain Waris was ordered

by Doramin to take an armed party of Bugis down
the river to a certain spot ten miles below Patusan,
and there form a camp on the shore and blockade
the stream with the canoes. I don't believe for a
moment that Doramin feared the arrival of fresh
forces. My opinion is that his conduct was guided
solely by his wish to keep his son out of harm's
way. To prevent a rush being made into the town
the construction of a stockade was to be commenced at daylight at the end of the street on
the left bank. The old Nakhoda declared his intention to command there himself. A distribution
of powder, bullets, and percussion-caps was made
immediately under the girl's supervision. Several
messengers were to be despatched in different
directions after Jim, whose exact whereabouts
were unknown. These men started at dawn, but
before that time Kassim had managed to open
communications with the besieged Brown.

"That accomplished diplomatist and confidant of
the Rajah, on leaving the fort to go back to his
master, took into his boat Cornelius, whom he found
slinking mutely amongst the people in the courtyard.
Kassim had a little plan of his own and wanted him
for an interpreter. Thus it came about that towards
morning Brown, reflecting upon the desperate
nature of his position, heard from the marshy
overgrown hollow an amicable, quavering, strained
voice crying—in English—for permission to come up,
under a promise of personal safety and on a very
important errand. He was overjoyed. If he was
spoken to he was no longer a hunted wild beast.
These friendly sounds took off at once the awful
stress of vigilant watchfulness as of so many blind
men not knowing whence the deathblow might

come. He pretended a great reluctance. The voice declared itself 'a white man. A poor, ruined, old man who had been living here for years.' A mist, wet and chilly, lay on the slopes of the hill, and after some more shouting from one to the other, Brown called out, 'Come on, then, but alone, mind!' As a matter of fact—he told me, writhing with rage at the recollection of his helplessness—it made no difference. They couldn't see more than a few yards before them, and no treachery could make their position worse. By-and-by Cornelius, in his week-day attire of a ragged dirty shirt and pants, bare-footed, with a broken-rimmed pith hat on his head, was made out vaguely, sidling up to the defences, hesitating, stopping to listen in a peering posture. 'Come along! You are safe,' yelled Brown, while his men stared. All their hopes of life became suddenly centred in that dilapidated, mean new-comer, who in profound silence clambered clumsily over a felled tree-trunk, and shivering, with his sour mistrustful face, looked about at the knot of bearded, anxious, sleepless desperadoes.

"Half an hour's confidential talk with Cornelius opened Brown's eyes as to the home affairs of Patusan. He was on the alert at once. There were possibilities, immense possibilities; but before he would talk over Cornelius's proposals he de-manded that some food should be sent up as a guarantee of good faith. Cornelius went off, creeping sluggishly down the hill on the side of the Rajah's place, and after some delay a few of Tunku Allang's men came up, bringing a scanty supply of rice, chillies, and dried fish. This was immeasurably better than nothing. Later on Cornelius returned accompanying Kassim, who stepped out with an air

of perfect good-humoured trustfulness, in sandals
and muffled up from neck to ankles in dark-blue
sheeting. He shook hands with Brown discreetly
and the three drew aside for a conference. Brown's
men, recovering their confidence, were slapping each
other on the back, and cast knowing glances at their
captain while they busied themselves with preparations for cooking.

"Kassim disliked Doramin and his Bugis very
much, but he hated the new order of things still
more. It had occurred to him that these whites
together with the Rajah's followers, could attack
and defeat the Bugis before Jim's return. Then, he
reasoned, general defection of the townfolk was sure
to follow, and the reign of the white man who
protected poor people would be over. Afterwards
the new allies could be dealt with. They would have
no friends. The fellow was perfectly able to perceive
the difference of character, and had seen enough of
white men to know that these new-comers were
outcasts, men without country. Brown preserved a
stern and inscrutable demeanour. When he first
heard Cornelius's voice demanding admittance, it
brought merely the hope of a loophole for escape.
In less than an hour other thoughts were seething
in his head. Urged by an extreme necessity, he had
come there to steal food, a few tons of rubber or
gum may be, perhaps a handful of dollars, and had
found himself enmeshed by deadly dangers. Now
in consequence of these overtures from Kassim he
began to think of stealing the whole country. Some
confounded fellow had apparently accomplished
something of the kind—single-handed at that.
Couldn't have done it very well though. Perhaps

they could work together—squeeze everything dry
and then go out quietly. In the course of his negotiations with Kassim he became aware that he was
supposed to have a big ship with plenty of men
outside. Kassim begged him earnestly to have this
big ship with his many guns and men brought up
the river without delay for the Rajah's service.
Brown professed himself willing, and on this basis
the negotiation was carried on with mutual distrust.
Three times in the course of the morning the courteous
and active Kassim went down to consult the Rajah
and came up busily with his long stride. Brown,
while bargaining, had a sort of grim enjoyment
in thinking of his wretched schooner, with nothing
but a heap of dirt in her hold, that stood for an
armed ship, and a Chinaman and a lame ex-beach-
comber of Levuka on board, who represented all his
many men. In the afternoon he obtained further
doles of food, a promise of some money, and a supply
of mats for his men to make shelters for themselves.
They lay down and snored, protected from the burning sunshine; but Brown, sitting fully exposed on
one of the felled trees, feasted his eyes upon the
view of the town and the river. There was much
loot there. Cornelius, who had made himself at
home in the camp, talked at his elbow, pointing
out the localities, imparting advice, giving his own
version of Jim's character, and commenting in his
own fashion upon the events of the last three years.
Brown, who, apparently indifferent and gazing away,
listened with attention to every word, could not
make out clearly what sort of man this Jim could
be. 'What's his name? Jim! Jim! That's not
enough for a man's name.' 'They call him,' said

Cornelius scornfully, 'Tuan Jim here. As you may
say Lord Jim.' 'What is he? Where does he come
from?' inquired Brown. 'What sort of man is he?
Is he an Englishman?' 'Yes, yes, he's an Englishman. I am an Englishman too. From Malacca.
He is a fool. All you have to do is to kill him and
then you are king here. Everything belongs to
him,' explained Cornelius. 'It strikes me he may
be made to share with somebody before very long,'
commented Brown half aloud. 'No, no. The
proper way is to kill him the first chance you get,
and then you can do what you like,' Cornelius
would insist earnestly. 'I have lived for many
years here, and I am giving you a friend's
advice.'

"In such converse and in gloating over the view
of Patusan, which he had determined in his mind
should become his prey, Brown whiled away most of
the afternoon, his men, meantime, resting. On that
day Dain Waris's fleet of canoes stole one by one
under the shore farthest from the creek, and went
down to close the river against his retreat. Of this
Brown was not aware, and Kassim, who came up the
knoll an hour before sunset, took good care not to
enlighten him. He wanted the white man's ship to
come up the river, and this news, he feared, would
be discouraging. He was very pressing with Brown
to send the 'order,' offering at the same time a
trusty messenger, who for greater secrecy (as he
explained) would make his way by land to the mouth
of the river and deliver the 'order' on board. After
some reflection Brown judged it expedient to tear
a page out of his pocket-book, on which he simply
wrote, 'We are getting on. Big job. Detain the
man.' The stolid youth selected by Kassim for that

service performed it faithfully, and was rewarded by
being suddenly tipped, head first, into the schooner's
empty hold by the ex-beach-comber and the Chinaman, who thereupon hastened to put on the hatches.
What became of him afterwards Brown did not say."

CHAPTER XL.

"Brown's object was to gain time by fooling
with Kassim's diplomacy. For doing a real stroke
of business he could not help thinking the white
man was the person to work with. He could not
imagine such a chap (who must be confoundedly
clever after all to get hold of the natives like that)
refusing a help that would do away with the necessity
for slow, cautious, risky cheating, that imposed
itself as the only possible line of conduct for a
single-handed man. He, Brown, would offer him the
power. No man could hesitate. Everything was
in coming to a clear understanding. Of course
they would share. The idea of there being a fort—
all ready to his hand—a real fort, with artillery
(he knew this from Cornelius), excited him. Let
him only once get in and . . . He would impose
modest conditions. Not too low, though. The man
was no fool, it seemed. They would work like
brothers till, . . . till the time came for a quarrel
and a shot that would settle all accounts. With
grim impatience of plunder he wished himself to
be talking with the man now. The land already
seemed to be his to tear to pieces, squeeze, and

throw away. Meantime Kassim had to be fooled
for the sake of food first—and for a second string.
But the principal thing was to get something to
eat from day to day. Besides, he was not averse
to begin fighting on that Rajah's account, and
teach a lesson to those people who had received
him with shots. The lust of battle was upon him.

"I am sorry that I can't give you this part of
the story, which of course I have mainly from
Brown, in Brown's own words. There was in the
broken, violent speech of that man, unveiling before
me his thoughts with the very hand of Death upon
his throat, an undisguised ruthlessness of purpose,
a strange vengeful attitude towards his own past,
and a blind belief in the righteousness of his will
against all mankind, something of that feeling which
could induce the leader of a horde of wandering
cut-throats to call himself proudly the Scourge of
God. No doubt the natural senseless ferocity which
is the basis of such a character was exasperated by
failure, ill-luck, and the recent privations, as well
as by the desperate position in which he found
himself; but what was most remarkable of all was
this, that while he planned treacherous alliances,
had already settled in his own mind the fate of
the white man, and intrigued in an overbearing
offhand manner with Kassim, one could perceive
that what he had really desired, almost in spite of
himself, was to play havoc with that jungle town
which had defied him, to see it strewn over with
corpses and enveloped in flames. Listening to his
pitiless, panting voice, I could imagine how he
must have looked at it from the hillock, peopling
it with images of murder and rapine. The part
nearest to the creek wore an abandoned aspect,

though as a matter of fact every house concealed
a few armed men on the alert. Suddenly beyond
the stretch of waste ground, interspersed with small
patches of low dense bush, excavations, heaps of
rubbish, with trodden paths between, a man, solitary
and looking very small, strolled out into the deserted
opening of the street between the shut-up, dark,
lifeless buildings at the end. Perhaps one of the
inhabitants, who had fled to the other bank of
the river, coming back for some object of domestic
use. Evidently he supposed himself quite safe at
that distance from the hill on the other side of
the creek. A light stockade, set up hastily, was
just round the turn of the street, full of his friends.
He moved leisurely. Brown saw him, and instantly
called to his side the Yankee deserter, who acted
as a sort of second in command. This lanky, loose-
jointed fellow came forward, wooden-faced, trailing
his rifle lazily. When he understood what was
wanted from him a homicidal and conceited smile
uncovered his teeth, making two deep folds down
his sallow, leathery cheeks. He prided himself
on being a dead shot. He dropped on one knee,
and taking aim from a steady rest through the un-
lopped branches of a felled tree, fired, and at once
stood up to look. The man, far away, turned his
head to the report, made another step forward,
seemed to hesitate, and abruptly got down on his
hands and knees. In the silence that fell upon
the sharp crack of the rifle, the dead shot, keeping
his eyes fixed upon the quarry, guessed that ' this
there coon's health would never be a source of
anxiety to his friends any more.' The man's limbs
were seen to move rapidly under his body in an
endeavour to run on all-fours. In that empty

space arose a multitudinous shout of dismay and surprise. The man sank flat, face down, and moved no more. 'That showed them what we could do,' said Brown to me. 'Struck the fear of sudden death into them. That was what we wanted. They were two hundred to one, and this gave them something to think over for the night. Not one of them had an idea of such a long shot before. That beggar belonging to the Rajah scouted downhill with his eyes hanging out of his head.'

" As he was telling me this he tried with a shaking hand to wipe the thin foam on his blue lips. 'Two hundred to one. Two hundred to one . . . strike terror, . . . terror, terror, I tell you. . . .' His own eyes were starting out of their sockets. He fell back, clawing the air with skinny fingers, sat up again, bowed and hairy, glared at me sideways like some man-beast of folk-lore, with open mouth in his miserable and awful agony before he got his speech back after that fit. There are sights one never forgets.

" Furthermore, to draw the enemy's fire and locate such parties as might have been hiding in the bushes along the creek, Brown ordered the Solomon Islander to go down to the boat and bring an oar, as you send a spaniel after a stick into the water. This failed, and the fellow came back without a single shot having been fired at him from anywhere. 'There's nobody,' opined some of the men. It is 'onnatural,' remarked the Yankee. Kassim had gone, by that time, very much impressed, pleased too, and also uneasy. Pursuing his tortuous policy, he had despatched à message to Dain Waris warning him to look out for the white men's ship, which, he had had information, was about to come up the river. He

minimised its strength and exhorted him to oppose
its passage. This double-dealing answered his
purpose, which was to keep the Bugis forces divided
and to weaken them by fighting. On the other
hand, he had in the course of that day sent word
to the assembled Bugis chiefs in town, assuring
them that he was trying to induce the invaders to
retire ; his messages to the fort asked earnestly for
powder for the Rajah's men. It was a long time
since Tunku Allang had had ammunition for the
score or so of old muskets rusting in their arm-
racks in the audience-hall. The open intercourse
between the hill and the palace unsettled all the
minds. It was already time for men to take sides,
it began to be said. There would soon be much
bloodshed, and thereafter great trouble for many
people. The social fabric of orderly, peaceful life,
when every man was sure of to-morrow, the edifice
raised by Jim's hands, seemed on that evening ready
to collapse into a ruin reeking with blood. The
poorer folk were already taking to the bush or
flying up the river. A good many of the upper class
judged it necessary to go and pay their court to the
Rajah. The Rajah's youths jostled them rudely.
Old Tunku Allang, almost out of his mind with
fear and indecision, either kept a sullen silence or
abused them violently for daring to come with empty
hands : they departed very much frightened ; only
old Doramin kept his countrymen together and
pursued his tactics inflexibly. Enthroned in a big
chair behind the improvised stockade, he issued his
orders in a deep veiled rumble, unmoved, like a deaf
man, in the flying rumours.

" Dusk fell, hiding first the body of the dead man,
which had been left lying with arms outstretched

as if nailed to the ground, and then the revolving
sphere of the night rolled smoothly over Patusan
and came to a rest, showering the glitter of countless
worlds upon the earth. Again, in the exposed part
of the town big fires blazed along the only street,
revealing from distance to distance upon their glares
the falling straight lines of roofs, the fragments of
wattled walls jumbled in confusion, here and there
a whole hut elevated in the glow upon the vertical
black stripes of a group of high piles ; and all this
line of dwellings, revealed in patches by the swaying
flames, seemed to flicker tortuously away up-river
into the gloom at the heart of the land. A great
silence, in which the looms of successive fires played
without noise, extended into the darkness at the foot
of the hill ; but the other bank of the river, all dark
save for a solitary bonfire at the river-front before
the fort, sent out into the air an increasing tremor
that might have been the stamping of a multitude
of feet, the hum of many voices, or the fall of an
immensely distant waterfall. It was then, Brown
confessed to me, while, turning his back on his
men, he sat looking at it all, that notwithstanding
his disdain, his ruthless faith in himself, a feeling
came over him that at last he had run his head
against a stone wall. Had his boat been afloat at
the time, he believed he would have tried to steal
away, taking his chances of a long chase down the
river and of starvation at sea. It is very doubtful
whether he would have succeeded in getting away,
However he didn't try this. For another moment
he had a passing thought of trying to rush the
town, but he perceived very well that in the end
he would find himself in the lighted street, where
they would be shot down like dogs from the houses.

They were two hundred to one—he thought, while
his men, huddling round two heaps of smouldering
embers, munched the last of the bananas and roasted
the few yams they owed to Kassim's diplomacy.
Cornelius sat amongst them dozing sulkily.

"Then one of the whites remembered that some
tobacco had been left in the boat, and, encouraged
by the impunity of the Solomon Islander, said he
would go to fetch it. At this all the others shook
off their despondency. Brown applied to, said, 'Go,
and be d—d to you,' scornfully. He didn't think
there was any danger in going to the creek in the
dark. The man threw a leg over the tree-trunk
and disappeared. A moment later he was heard
clambering into the boat and then clambering out.
'I've got it,' he cried. A flash and a report at
the very foot of the hill followed. 'I am hit,'
yelled the man. 'Look out, look out—I am hit,'
and instantly all the rifles went off. The hill
squirted fire and noise into the night like a little
volcano, and when Brown and the Yankee with
curses and cuffs stopped the panic-stricken firing,
a profound, weary groan floated up from the creek,
succeeded by a plaint whose heartrending sadness
was like some poison turning the blood cold in the
veins. Then a strong voice pronounced several distinct incomprehensible words somewhere beyond the
creek. 'Let no one fire,' shouted Brown. 'What
does it mean?' . . . 'Do you hear on the hill? Do
you hear? Do you hear?' repeated the voice three
times. Cornelius translated, and then prompted the
answer. 'Speak,' cried Brown, 'we hear.' Then
the voice, declaiming in the sonorous inflated tone
of a herald, and shifting continually on the edge
of the vague waste-land, proclaimed that between

the men of the Bugis nation living in Patusan and
the white men on the hill and those with them,
there would be no faith, no compassion, no speech,
no peace. A bush rustled; a haphazard volley
rang out. 'Dam' foolishness,' muttered the Yankee,
vexedly grounding the butt. Cornelius translated.
The wounded man below the hill, after crying out
twice, 'Take me up! take me up!' went on complaining in moans. While he had kept on the
blackened earth of the slope, and afterwards crouching in the boat, he had been safe enough. It seems
that in his joy at finding the tobacco he forgot himself and jumped out on her off-side, as it were. The
white boat, lying high and dry, showed him up; the
creek was no more than seven yards wide in that
place, and there happened to be a man crouching in
the bush on the other bank.

"He was a Bugis of Tondano only lately come
to Patusan, and a relation of the man shot in the
afternoon. That famous long shot had indeed
appalled the beholders. The man in utter security
had been struck down, in full view of his friends,
dropping with a joke on his lips, and they seemed
to see in the act an atrocity which had stirred a
bitter rage. That relation of his, Si-Lapa by name,
was then with Doramin in the stockade only a few
feet away. You who know these chaps must admit
that the fellow showed an unusual pluck by volun-
teering to carry the message, alone, in the dark.
Creeping across the open ground, he had deviated
to the left and found himself opposite the boat.
He was startled when Brown's man shouted. He
came to a sitting position with his gun to his shoulder,
and when the other jumped out, exposing himself,
he pulled the trigger and lodged three jagged

slugs point-blank into the poor wretch's stomach. Then, lying flat on his face, he gave himself up for dead, while a thin hail of lead chopped and swished the bushes close on his right hand ; afterwards he delivered his speech shouting, bent double, dodging all the time in cover. With the last word he leaped sideways, lay close for a while, and afterwards got back to the houses unharmed, having achieved on that night such a renown as his children will not willingly allow to die.

" And on the hill the forlorn band let the two little heaps of embers go out under their bowed heads. They sat dejected on the ground with compressed lips and downcast eyes, listening to their comrade below. He was a strong man and died hard, with moans now loud, now sinking to a strange confidential note of pain. Sometimes he shrieked, and again, after a period of silence, he could be heard muttering deliriously a long and unintelligible complaint. Never for a moment did he cease.

" ' What's the good ? ' Brown had said unmoved once, seeing the Yankee, who had been swearing under his breath, prepare to go down. ' That's so,' assented the deserter, reluctantly desisting. ' There's no encouragement for wounded men here. Only his noise is calculated to make all the others think too much of the hereafter, cap'n.' ' Water ! ' cried the wounded man in an extraordinary clear vigorous voice, and then went off moaning feebly. ' Ay, water. Water will do it,' muttered the other to himself, resignedly. ' Plenty by-and-by. The tide is flowing.'

" At last the tide flowed, silencing the plaint and the cries of pain, and the dawn was near when

Brown, sitting with his chin in the palm of his hand before Patusan, as one might stare at the unscalable side of a mountain, heard the brief ringing bark of a brass 6-pounder far away in town somewhere. 'What's this?' he asked of Cornelius, who hung about him. Cornelius listened. A muffled roaring shout rolled down-river over the town; a big drum began to throb, and others responded, pulsating and droning. Tiny scattered lights began to twinkle in the dark half of the town, while the part lighted by the loom of fires hummed with a deep and prolonged murmur. 'He has come,' said Cornelius. 'What? Already? Are you sure?' Brown asked. 'Yes! yes! Sure. Listen to the noise.' 'What are they making that row about?' pursued Brown. 'For joy,' snorted Cornelius; 'he is a very great man, but all the same, he knows no more than a child, and so they make a great noise to please him, because they know no better.' 'Look here,' said Brown, 'How is one to get at him?' 'He shall come to talk to you,' Cornelius declared. 'What do you mean? Come down here strolling as it were?' Cornelius nodded vigorously in the dark. 'Yes. He will come straight here and talk to you. He is just like a fool. You shall see what a fool he is.' Brown was incredulous. 'You shall see; you shall see,' repeated Cornelius. 'He is not afraid—not afraid of anything. He will come and order you to leave his people alone. Everybody must leave his people alone. He is like a little child. He will come to you straight.' Alas! he knew Jim well—that 'mean little skunk,' as Brown called him to me. 'Yes, certainly,' he pursued with ardour, 'and then, captain, you tell that tall man with a gun to shoot

him. Just you kill him, and you shall frighten
everybody so much that you can do anything you
like with them afterwards—get what you like—go
away when you like. Ha! ha! ha! Fine . . .'
He almost danced with impatience and eagerness;
and Brown, looking over his shoulder at him, could
see, shown up by the pitiless dawn, his men drenched
with dew, sitting amongst the cold ashes and the
litter of the camp, haggard, cowed, and in rags."

CHAPTER XLI.

" To the very last moment, till the full day came
upon them with a spring, the fires on the west
bank blazed bright and clear; and then Brown saw
in a knot of coloured figures motionless between
the advanced houses a man in European clothes, in
a helmet, all white. 'That's him; look! look!'
Cornelius said excitedly. All Brown's men had
sprung up and crowded at his back with lustreless eyes. The group of vivid colours and dark
faces with the white figure in their midst were
observing the knoll. Brown could see naked arms
being raised to shade the eyes and other brown
arms pointing. What should he do? He looked
around, and the forests that faced him on all sides
walled the cock-pit of an unequal contest. He
looked once more at his men. A contempt, a weariness, the desire of life, the wish to try for one
more chance—for some other grave—struggled in
his breast. From the outline the figure presented

it seemed to him that the white man there, backed
up by all the power of the land, was examining
his position through binoculars. Brown jumped up
on the log, throwing his arms up, the palms out-
wards. The coloured group closed round the white
man, and fell back twice before he got clear of
them, walking slowly alone. Brown remained standing on the log till Jim, appearing and disappearing
between the patches of thorny scrub, had nearly
reached the creek; then Brown jumped off and
went down to meet him on his side.

"They met, I should think, not very far from
the place, perhaps on the very spot, where Jim
took the second desperate leap of his life—the leap
that landed him into the life of Patusan, into the
trust, the love, the confidence of the people. They
faced each other across the creek, and with steady
eyes tried to understand each other before they
opened their lips. Their antagonism must have
been expressed in their glances; I know that Brown
hated Jim at first sight. Whatever hopes he might
have had vanished at once. This was not the man
he had expected to see. He hated him for this—
and in a checked flannel shirt with sleeves cut off
at the elbows, grey bearded, with a sunken, sun-
blackened face—he cursed in his heart the other's
youth and assurance, his clear eyes and his untroubled bearing. That fellow had got in a long
way before him! He did not look like a man who
would be willing to give anything for assistance.
He had all the advantages on his side—possession,
security, power; he was on the side of an overwhelming force! He was not hungry and desperate,
and he did not seem in the least afraid. And
there was something in the very neatness of Jim's

clothes, from the white helmet to the canvas leg-
gings and the pipeclayed shoes, which in Brown's
sombre irritated eyes seemed to belong to things
he had in the very shaping of his life contemned
and flouted.

" ' Who are you ? ' asked Jim at last, speaking in
his usual voice. ' My name's Brown,' answered the
other loudly. ' Captain Brown. What's yours ? '
and Jim after a little pause went on quietly, as if
he had not heard : ' What made you come here ? '
' You want to know,' said Brown bitterly. ' It's
easy to tell. Hunger. And what made you ? '

" ' The fellow started at this,' said Brown, relating to me the opening of this strange conversation between those two men, separated only by
the muddy bed of a creek, but standing on the
opposite poles of that conception of life which in-
cludes all mankind—' The fellow started at this and
got very red in the face. Too big to be questioned,
I suppose. I told him that if he looked upon me
as a dead man with whom you may take liberties,
he himself was not a whit better off really. I had
a fellow up there who had a bead drawn on him
all the time, and only waited for a sign from me.
There was nothing to be shocked at in this. He
had come down of his own freewill. " Let us
agree," said I, " that we are both dead men, and
let us talk on that basis, as equals. We are all
equal before death," I said. I admitted I was
there like a rat in a trap, but we had been driven
to it, and even a trapped rat can give a bite. He
caught me up in a moment. " Not if you don't
go near the trap till the rat is dead." I told him
that sort of game was good enough for these native
friends of his, but I would have thought him too

white to serve even a rat so. Yes, I had wanted
to talk with him. Not to beg for my life, though.
My fellows were—well—what they were—men like
himself, anyhow. All we wanted from him was
to come on in the devil's name and have it out.
"God d—n it," said I, while he stood there as
still as a wooden post, "you don't want to come
out here every day with your glasses to count how
many of us are left on our feet. Come. Either
bring your infernal crowd along or let us go out
and starve in the open sea, by God! You have
been white once, for all your tall talk of this being
your own people and you being one with them.
Are you? And what the devil do you get for
it; what is it you've found here that is so d—d
precious? Hey? You don't want us to come down
here perhaps—do you? You are two hundred to
one. You don't want us to come down into the
open. Ah! I promise you we shall give you some
sport before you've done. You talk about me
making a cowardly set upon unoffending people.
What's that to me that they are unoffending when
I am starving for next to no offence? But I am
not a coward. Don't you be one. Bring them
along, or by all the fiends, we shall yet manage
to send half of your unoffending town to heaven
with us in smoke!"'

"He was terrible—relating this to me—this tortured skeleton of a man drawn up together with
his face over his knees, upon a miserable bed in
that wretched hovel, and lifting his head to look
at me with malignant triumph.

"'That's what I told him—I knew what to say,'
he began again, feebly at first, but working himself
up with incredible speed into a fiery utterance of

his scorn. 'We aren't going into the forest to wander like a string of living skeletons dropping one after another for ants to go to work upon us before we are fairly dead. Oh no! . . . "You don't deserve a better fate," he said. "And what do you deserve," I shouted at him, "you that I find skulking here with your mouth full of your responsibility, of innocent lives, of your infernal duty? What do you know more of me than I know of you? I came here for food. D'ye hear? —food to fill our bellies. And what did *you* come for? What did you ask for when you came here? We don't ask you for anything but to give us a fight or a clear road to go back whence we came. . . ." "I would fight with you now," says he, pulling at his little moustache. "And I would let you shoot me, and welcome," I said. "This is as good a jumping-off place for me as another. I am sick of my infernal luck. But it would be too easy. There are my men in the same boat—and, by God, I am not the sort to jump out of trouble and leave them in a d—d lurch," I said. He stood thinking for a while and then wanted to know what I had done ("out there" he says, tossing his head down-stream) to be hazed about so. "Have we met to tell each other the story of our lives?" I asked him. "Suppose you begin. No? Well, I am sure I don't want to hear. Keep it to yourself. I know it is no better than mine. I've lived—and so did you, though you talk as if you were one of those people that should have wings so as to go about without touching the dirty earth. Well—it is dirty. I haven't got any wings. I am here because I was afraid once in my life. Want to know what of? Of a prison. That scares me, and you may know

it—if it's any good to you. I won't ask you what
scared you into this infernal hole, where you seem
to have found pretty pickings. That's your luck
and this is mine—the privilege to beg for the favour
of being shot quickly, or else kicked out to go free
and starve in my own way." . . .'

'"His debilitated body shook with an exultation
so vehement, so assured, and so malicious that it
seemed to have driven off the death waiting for him
in that hut. The corpse of his mad self-love uprose
from rags and destitution as from the dark horrors
of a tomb. It is impossible to say how much he lied
to Jim then, how much he lied to me now—and to
himself always. Vanity plays lurid tricks with our
memory, and the truth of every passion wants some
pretence to make it live. Standing at the gate of
the other world in the guise of a beggar, he had
slapped this world's face, he had spat on it, he had
thrown upon it an immensity of scorn and revolt
at the bottom of his misdeeds. He had overcome
them all—men, women, savages, traders, ruffians,
missionaries—and Jim—that beefy-faced beggar. I
did not begrudge him this triumph in *articulo mortis*,
this almost posthumous illusion of having trampled
all the earth under his feet. While he was boasting
to me, in his sordid and repulsive agony, I couldn't
help thinking of the chuckling talk relating to the
time of his greatest splendour when, during a year
or more, Gentleman Brown's ship was to be seen,
for many days on end, hovering off an islet be-
fringed with green upon azure, with the dark dot
of the mission-house on a white beach; while
Gentleman Brown, ashore, was casting his spells
over a romantic girl for whom Melanesia had been
too much, and giving hopes of a remarkable con-

version to her husband. The poor man, some time
or other, had been heard to express the intention
of winning 'Captain Brown to a better way of
life.' . . . 'Bag Gentleman Brown for Glory '—as
a leery-eyed loafer expressed it once—' just to let
them see up above what a Western Pacific trading
skipper looks like.' And this was the man, too,
who had run off with a dying woman, and had
shed tears over her body. 'Carried on like a big
baby,' his then mate was never tired of telling, 'and
where the fun came in may I be kicked to death
by diseased Kanakas if *I* know. Why, gents! She
was too far gone when he brought her aboard to
know him; she just lay there on her back in his
bunk staring at the beam with awful shining eyes—
and then she died. Dam' bad sort of fever, I
guess. . . .' I remembered all these stories while,
wiping his matted lump of a beard with a livid hand,
he was telling me from his noisome couch how he got
round, got in, got home, on that confounded, immaculate, don't-you-touch-me sort of fellow. He admitted
that he couldn't be scared, but there was a way, 'as
broad as a turnpike, to get in and shake his two-
penny soul around and inside out and upside down—
by God!'"

CHAPTER XLII.

"I DON'T think he could do more than perhaps
look upon that straight path. He seemed to have
been puzzled by what he saw, for he interrupted
himself in his narrative more than once to exclaim,

'He nearly slipped from me there. I could not make him out. Who was he?' And after glaring at me wildly he would go on, jubilating and sneering. To me the conversation of these two across the creek appears now as the deadliest kind of duel on which Fate looked on with her cold-eyed knowledge of the end. No, he didn't turn Jim's soul inside out, but I am much mistaken if the spirit so utterly out of his reach had not been made to taste to the full the bitterness of that contest. These were the emissaries with whom the world he had renounced was pursuing him in his retreat. White men from 'out there' where he did not think himself good enough to live. This was all that came to him—a menace, a shock, a danger to his work. I suppose it is this sad, half-resentful, half-resigned feeling, piercing through the few words Jim said now and then, that puzzled Brown so much in the reading of his character. Some great men owe most of their greatness to the ability of detecting in those they destine for their tools the exact quality of strength that matters for their work; and Brown, as though he had been really great, had a satanic gift of finding out the best and the weakest spot in his victims. He admitted to me that Jim wasn't of the sort that can be got over by truckling, and accordingly he took care to show himself as a man confronting without dismay ill-luck, censure, and disaster. The smuggling of a few guns was no great crime, he pointed out. As to coming to Patusan, who had the right to say he hadn't come to beg? The infernal people here let loose at him from both banks without staying to ask questions. He made the point brazenly, for, in truth, Dain Waris's energetic action has prevented the greatest calamities; because Brown told me distinctly that, perceiving the size of the place, he had resolved instantly in his mind that as soon as he had gained a footing he would set fire right and left, and begin by shooting down everything living in sight, in order to cow and terrify the population. The disproportion of forces was so great that this was the only way giving him the slightest chance of attaining his ends—he argued in a fit of coughing. But he didn't tell Jim this. As to the hardships and starvation they had gone through, these had been very real; it was enough to look at his band. He made, at the sound of a shrill whistle, all his men appear standing in a row on the logs in full view, so that Jim could see them. For the killing of the man, it had been done—well, it had—but was not this war, bloody war—in a corner? and the fellow had been killed cleanly, shot through the chest, not like that poor devil of his lying now in the creek. They had to listen to him dying for six hours, with his entrails torn with slugs. At any rate this was a life for a life. . . . And all this was said with the weariness, with the recklessness of a man spurred on and on by ill-luck till he cares not where he runs. When he asked Jim, with a sort of brusque despairing frankness, whether he himself—straight now—didn't understand that when 'it came to saving one's life in the dark, one didn't care who else went—three, thirty, three hundred people'—it was as if a demon had been whispering advice in his ear. 'I made him wince,' boasted Brown to me. 'He very soon left off coming the righteous over me. He just stood there with nothing to say, and looking as black as thunder—not at me—on the ground.' He asked Jim whether he had nothing fishy in his life to remember that he was so damnedly hard upon a man trying to get out of a deadly hole by the first means that came to hand—and so on, and so on. And there ran through the rough talk a vein of subtle reference to their common blood, an assumption of common experience ; a sickening suggestion of common guilt, of secret knowledge that was like a bond of their minds and of their hearts.

"At last Brown threw himself down full length and watched Jim out of the corners of his eyes. Jim on his side of the creek stood thinking and switching his leg. The houses in view were silent as if a pestilence had swept them clean of every breath of life ; but many invisible eyes were turned, from within, upon the two men with the creek between them, a stranded white boat, and the body of the third man half sunk in the mud. On the river canoes were moving again, for Patusan was recovering its belief in the stability of earthly institutions since the return of the white lord. The right bank, the platforms of the houses, the rafts moored along the shores, even the roofs of bathing-huts, were covered with people that, far away out of earshot and almost out of sight, were straining their eyes towards the knoll beyond the Rajah's stockade. Within the wide irregular ring of forests, broken in two places by the sheen of the river, there was a silence. 'Will you promise to leave the coast ?' Jim asked. Brown lifted and let fall his hand, giving everything up as it were—accepting the inevitable. 'And surrender your arms ?' Jim went on. Brown sat up and glared across. 'Sur-

render our arms! Not till you come to take them
out of our stiff hands. You think I am gone crazy
with funk? Oh no! That and the rags I stand
in is all I have got in the world, besides a few more
breech-loaders on board; and I expect to sell
the lot in Madagascar, if I ever get so far,—begging
my way from ship to ship.'

"Jim said nothing to this. At last, throwing
away the switch he held in his hand, he said, as
if speaking to himself, 'I don't know whether I
have the power. . . .' 'You don't know! And
you wanted me just now to give up my arms!
That's good, too,' cried Brown. 'Suppose they say
one thing to you, and do the other thing to me.'
He calmed down markedly. 'I daresay you have
the power, or what's the meaning of all this talk?'
he continued. 'What did you come down here for?
To pass the time of day?'

"'Very well,' said Jim, lifting his head suddenly
after a long silence. 'You shall have a clear road
or else a clear fight.' He turned on his heel and
walked away.

"Brown got up at once, but he did not go up
the hill till he had seen Jim disappear between the
first houses. He never set his eyes on him again.
On his way back he met Cornelius slouching down
with his head between his shoulders. He stopped
before Brown. 'Why didn't you kill him?' he
demanded in a sour, discontented voice. 'Because I
could do better than that,' Brown said with an
amused smile. 'Never! never!' protested Cornelius
with energy. 'Couldn't. I have lived here for
many years.' Brown looked up at him curiously.
There were many sides to the life of that place in
arms against him; things he would never find out.

Cornelius slunk past dejectedly in the direction of
the river. He was now leaving his new friends ;
he accepted the disappointing course of events with
a sulky obstinacy which seemed to draw more together his little yellow old face ; and as he went
down he glanced askant here and there, never giving
up his fixed idea.

"Henceforth events move fast without a check,
flowing from the very hearts of men like a stream
from a dark source, and we see Jim amongst them,
mostly through Tamb' Itam's eyes. The girl's eyes
had watched him too, but her life is too much
entwined with his : there is her passion, her wonder,
her anger, and, above all, her fear and her unforgiving love. Of the faithful servant, uncomprehending as the rest of them, it is the fidelity alone
that comes into play ; a fidelity and a belief in
his lord so strong that even amazement is subdued
to a sort of saddened acceptance of a mysterious
failure. He has eyes only for one figure, and through
all the mazes of bewilderment he preserves his air
of guardianship, of obedience, of care.

"His master came back from his talk with the
white men, walking slowly towards the stockade
in the street. Everybody was rejoiced to see him
return, for while he was away every man had been
afraid not only of him being killed, but also of
what would come after. Jim went into one of the
houses, where old Doramin had retired, and remained alone for a long time with the head of the
Bugis settlers. No doubt he discussed the course to
follow with him then, but no man was present at the
conversation. Only Tamb' Itam, keeping as close
to the door as he could, heard his master say, ' Yes.
I shall let all the people know that such is my

wish; but I spoke to you, O Doramin, before all the others, and alone; for you know my heart as well as I know yours and its greatest desire. And you know well also that I have no thought but for the people's good.' Then his master, lifting the sheeting in the doorway, went out, and he, Tamb' Itam, had a glimpse of old Doramin within, sitting in the chair with his hands on his knees, and looking between his feet. Afterwards he followed his master to the fort, where all the principal Bugis and Patusan inhabitants had been summoned for a talk. Tamb' Itam himself hoped there would be some fighting. 'What was it but the taking of another hill?' he exclaimed regretfully. However, in the town many hoped that the rapacious strangers would be induced, by the sight of so many brave men making ready to fight, to go away. It would be a good thing if they went away. Since Jim's arrival had been made known before daylight by the gun fired from the fort and the beating of the big drum there, the fear that had hung over Patusan had broken and subsided like a wave on a rock, leaving the seething foam of excitement, curiosity, and endless speculation. Half of the population had been ousted out of their homes for purposes of defence, and were living in the street on the left side of the river, crowding round the fort, and in momentary expectation of seeing their abandoned dwellings on the threatened bank burst into flames. The general anxiety was to see the matter settled quickly. Food, through Jewel's care, had been served out to the refugees. Nobody knew what their white man would do. Some remarked that it was worse than in Sherif Ali's war. Then many people did not care; now everybody had something to lose. The movements of canoes passing to and fro between the two parts of the town were watched with interest. A couple of Bugis war-boats lay anchored in the middle of the stream to protect the river, and a thread of smoke stood at the bow of each ; the men in them were cooking their mid-day rice when Jim, after his interviews with Brown and Doramin, crossed the river and entered by the water-gate of his fort. The people inside crowded round him so that he could hardly make his way to the house. They had not seen him before, because on his arrival during the night he had only ex-changed a few words with the girl, who had come down to the landing-stage for the purpose, and had then gone on at once to join the chiefs and the fighting men on the other bank. People shouted greetings after him. One old woman raised a laugh by pushing her way to the front madly and enjoining him in a scolding voice to see to it that her two sons who were with Doramin did not come to harm at the hands of the robbers. Several of the bystanders tried to pull her away, but she struggled and cried, ' Let me go. What is this, O Muslims ? This laughter is unseemly. Are they not cruel, bloodthirsty robbers bent on killing ? ' ' Let her be,' said Jim, and as a silence fell suddenly, he said slowly, ' Everybody shall be safe.' He entered the house before the great sigh, and the loud murmurs of satisfaction, had died out.

" There's no doubt his mind was made up that Brown should have his way clear back to the sea. His fate, revolted, was forcing his hand. He had for the first time to affirm his will in the face of outspoken opposition. ' There was much talk, and at first my master was silent,' Tamb' Itam said.

' Darkness came, and then I lit the candles on the long table. The chiefs sat on each side, and the lady remained by my master's right hand.'

" When he began to speak the unaccustomed difficulty seemed only to fix his resolve more immovably. The white men were now waiting for his answer on the hill. Their chief had spoken to him in the language of his own people, making clear many things difficult to explain in any other speech. They were erring men whom suffering had made blind to right and wrong. It is true that lives had been lost already, but why lose more ? He declared to his hearers, the assembled heads of the people, that their welfare was his welfare, their losses his losses, their mourning his mourning. He looked round at the grave listening faces and told them to remember that they had fought and worked side by side. They knew his courage . . . Here a murmur interrupted him . . . And that he had never deceived them. For many years they had dwelt together. He loved the land and the people living in it with a very great love. He was ready to answer with his life for any harm that should come to them if the white men with beards were allowed to retire. They were evil-doers, but their destiny had been evil too. Had he ever advised them ill ? Had his words ever brought suffering to the people ? he asked. He believed that it would be best to let these whites and their followers go with their lives. It would be a small gift. ' I whom you have tried and found always true ask you to let them go.' He turned to Doramin. The old Nakhoda made no movement. ' Then,' said Jim, ' call in Dain Waris, your son, my friend, for in this business I shall not lead.' "

CHAPTER XLIII.

" TAMB' ITAM behind his chair was thunderstruck.
The declaration produced an immense sensation.
' Let them go because this is best in my knowledge, which has never deceived you,' Jim insisted.
There was a silence. In the darkness of the courtyard
could be heard the subdued whispering, shuffling
noise of many people. Doramin raised his heavy
head and said that there was no more reading of
hearts than touching the sky with the hand, but—
he consented. The others gave their opinion in turn.
' It is best,' ' Let them go,' and so on. But most
of them simply said that they ' believed Tuan Jim.'

" In this simple form of assent to his will lies the
whose gist of the situation ; their creed, his truth ;
and the testimony to that faithfulness which made
him in his own eyes the equal of the impeccable
men who never fall out of the ranks. Stein's words,
' Romantic !—Romantic ! ' seem to ring over those
distances that will never give him up now to a
world indifferent to his failing and his virtues, and
to that ardent and clinging affection that refuses
him the dole of tears in the bewilderment of a great
grief and of eternal separation. From the moment
the sheer truthfulness of his last three years of life
carries the day against the ignorance, the fear, and
the anger of men, he appears no longer to me as I
saw him last—a white speck catching all the dim
light left upon a sombre coast and the darkened
sea—but greater and more pitiful in the loneliness
of his soul, that remains even for her who loved
him best a cruel and insoluble mystery.

"It is evident that he did not mistrust Brown; there was no reason to doubt the story, whose truth seemed warranted by the rough frankness, by a sort of virile sincerity in accepting the morality and the consequences of his acts. But Jim did not know the almost inconceivable egotism of the man which made him, when resisted and foiled in his will, mad with the indignant and revengeful rage of a thwarted autocrat. But if Jim did not mistrust Brown, he was evidently anxious that some misunderstanding should not occur, ending perhaps in collision and bloodshed. It was for this reason that directly the Malay chiefs had gone he asked Jewel to get him something to eat, as he was going out of the fort to take command in the town. On her remonstrating against this on the score of his fatigue, he said that something might happen for which he would never forgive himself. 'I am responsible for every life in the land,' he said. He was moody at first; she served him with her own hands, taking the plates and dishes (of the dinner-service presented him by Stein) from Tamb' Itam. He brightened up after a while; told her she would be again in command of the fort for another night. 'There's no sleep for us, old girl,' he said, 'while our people are in danger.' Later on he said jokingly that she was the best man of them all. 'If you and Dain Waris had done what you wanted, not one of these poor devils would be alive to-day.' 'Are they very bad?' she asked, leaning over his chair. 'Men act badly sometimes without being much worse than others,' he said after some hesitation.

"Tamb' Itam followed his master to the landing-stage outside the fort. The night was clear but without a moon, and the middle of the river was

dark, while the water under each bank reflected
the light of many fires 'as on a night of Ramadan,'
Tamb' Itam said. War-boats drifted silently in the
dark lane or, anchored, floated motionless with a
loud ripple. That night there was much paddling
in a canoe and walking at his master's heels for
Tamb' Itam : up and down the street they tramped,
where the fires were burning, inland on the outskirts
of the town where small parties of men kept guard
in the fields. Tuan Jim gave his orders and was
obeyed. Last of all they went to the Rajah's
stockade, which a detachment of Jim's people
manned on that night. The old Rajah had fled early
in the morning with most of his women to a small
house he had near a jungle village on a tributary
stream. Kassim, left behind, had attended the
council with his air of diligent activity to explain
away the diplomacy of the day before. He was
considerably cold-shouldered, but managed to preserve his smiling, quiet alertness, and professed
himself highly delighted when Jim told him sternly
that he proposed to occupy the stockade on that
night with his own men. After the council broke
up he was heard outside accosting this and that
departing chief, and speaking in a loud, gratified
tone of the Rajah's property being protected in the
Rajah's absence.

"About ten or so Jim's men marched in. The
stockade commanded the mouth of the creek, and
Jim meant to remain there till Brown had passed
below. A small fire was lit on the flat, grassy
point outside the wall of stakes, and Tamb' Itam
placed a little folding-stool for his master. Jim
told him to try and sleep. Tamb' Itam got a mat
and lay down a little way off ; but he could not

sleep, though he knew he had to go on an important journey before the night was out. His master walked to and fro before the fire with bowed head and with his hands behind his back. His face was sad. Whenever his master approached him Tamb' Itam pretended to sleep, not wishing his master to know he had been watched. At last his master stood still, looking down on him as he lay, and said softly, ' It is time.'

"Tamb' Itam arose directly and made his preparations. His mission was to go down the river, preceding Brown's boat by an hour or more, to tell Dain Waris finally and formally that the whites were to be allowed to pass out unmolested. Jim would not trust anybody else with that service. Before starting Tamb' Itam, more as a matter of form (since his position about Jim made him perfectly known), asked for a token. ' Because, Tuan,' he said, ' the message is important, and these are thy very words I carry.' His master first put his hand into one pocket, then into another, and finally took off his forefinger Stein's silver ring, which he habitually wore, and gave it to Tamb' Itam. When Tamb' Itam left on his mission, Brown's camp on the knoll was dark but for a single small glow shining through the branches of one of the trees the white men had cut down.

"Early in the evening Brown had received from Jim a folded piece of paper on which was written, ' You get the clear road. Start as soon as your boat floats on the morning tide. Let your men be careful. The bushes on both sides of the creek and the stockade at the mouth are full of well-armed men. You would have no chance, but I don't believe you want bloodshed.' Brown read it,

tore the paper into small pieces, and, turning to
Cornelius, who had brought it, said jeeringly, 'Good-
bye, my excellent friend.' Cornelius had been in
the fort, and had been sneaking around Jim's house
during the afternoon. Jim chose him to carry the
note because he could speak English, was known
to Brown, and was not likely to be shot by some
nervous mistake of one of the men as a Malay,
approaching in the dusk, perhaps might have been.

"Cornelius didn't go away after delivering the
paper. Brown was sitting up over a tiny fire; all
the others were lying down. 'I could tell you
something you would like to know,' Cornelius
mumbled crossly. Brown paid no attention. 'You
did not kill him,' went on the other, 'and what
do you get for it? You might have had money
from the Rajah, besides the loot of all the Bugis
houses, and now you get nothing.' 'You had
better clear out from here,' growled Brown, without even looking at him. But Cornelius let himself
drop by his side and began to whisper very fast,
touching his elbow from time to time. What he
had to say made Brown sit up at first, with a curse.
He had simply informed him of Dain Waris's armed
party down the river. At first Brown saw himself
completely sold and betrayed, but a moment's
reflection convinced him that there could be no
treachery intended. He said nothing, and after a
while Cornelius remarked, in a tone of complete
indifference, that there was another way out of the
river which he knew very well. 'A good thing
to know, too,' said Brown, pricking up his ears;
and Cornelius began to talk of what went on in
town and repeated all that had been said in council,
gossiping in an even undertone at Brown's ear as

you talk amongst sleeping men you do not wish
to wake. 'He thinks he has made me harmless,
does he?' mumbled Brown very low. . . . 'Yes.
He is a fool. A little child. He came here and robbed
me,' droned on Cornelius, 'and he made all the people
believe him. But if something happened that they
did not believe him any more, where would he be?
And the Bugis Dain who is waiting for you down
the river there, captain, is the very man who chased
you up here when you first came.' Brown observed
nonchalantly that it would be just as well to avoid
him, and with the same detached, musing air Cornelius declared himself acquainted with a backwater
broad enough to take Brown's boat past Waris's
camp. 'You will have to be quiet,' he said as
an afterthought, 'for in one place we pass close
behind his camp. Very close. They are camped
ashore with their boats hauled up.' 'Oh, we know
how to be as quiet as mice. Never fear,' said Brown.
Cornelius stipulated that in case he were to pilot
Brown out, his canoe should be towed. 'I'll have
to get back quick,' he explained.

"It was two hours before the dawn when word
was passed to the stockade from outlying watchers
that the white robbers were coming down to their
boat. In a very short time every armed man from
one end of Patusan to the other was on the alert,
yet the banks of the river remained so silent that
but for the fires burning with sudden blurred flares
the town might have been asleep as if in peace-time.
A heavy mist lay very low on the water, making
a sort of illusive grey light that showed nothing.
When Brown's long-boat glided out of the creek
into the river, Jim was standing on the low point
of land before the Rajah's stockade—on the very

spot where for the first time he put his foot on Patusan shore. A shadow loomed up, moving in the greyness, solitary, very bulky, and yet constantly eluding the eye. A murmur of low talking came out of it. Brown at the tiller heard Jim speak calmly : ' A clear road. You had better trust to the current while the fog lasts ; but this will lift presently.' ' Yes, presently we shall see clear,' replied Brown.

" The thirty or forty men standing with muskets at ready outside the stockade held their breath. The Bugis owner of the prau, whom I saw on Stein's verandah, and who was amongst them, told me that the boat, shaving the low point close, seemed for a moment to grow big and hang over it like a mountain. ' If you think it worth your while to wait a day outside,' called out Jim, ' I'll try to send you down something—a bullock, some yams—what I can.' The shadow went on moving. ' Yes. Do,' said a voice, blank and muffled out of the fog. Not one of the many attentive listeners understood what the words meant ; and then Brown and his men in their boat floated away, fading spectrally without the slightest sound.

" Thus Brown, invisible in the mist, goes out of Patusan elbow to elbow with Cornelius in the stern-sheets of the long-boat. ' Perhaps you shall get a small bullock,' said Cornelius. ' Oh yes. Bullock. Yam. You'll get it if *he* said so. He always speaks the truth. He stole everything I had. I suppose you like a small bullock better than the loot of many houses.' ' I would advise you to hold your tongue, or somebody here may fling you overboard into this damned fog,' said Brown. The boat seemed to be standing still ; nothing could be seen,

not even the river alongside, only the water-dust
flew and trickled, condensed, down their beards and
faces. It was weird, Brown told me. Every individual man of them felt as though he were adrift
alone in a boat, haunted by an almost imperceptible
suspicion of sighing, muttering ghosts. 'Throw me
out, would you? But I would know where I was,'
mumbled Cornelius surlily. 'I've lived many years
here.' 'Not long enough to see through a fog
like this,' Brown said, lolling back with his arm
swinging to and fro on the useless tiller. 'Yes.
Long enough for that,' snarled Cornelius. 'That's
very useful,' commented Brown. 'Am I to believe
you could find that backway you spoke of blind-
fold, like this?' Cornelius grunted. 'Are you too
tired to row?' he asked after a silence. 'No, by
God!' shouted Brown suddenly. 'Out with your
oars there.' There was a great knocking in the
fog, which after a while settled into a regular grind
of invisible sweeps against invisible tholepins.
Otherwise nothing was changed, and but for the
slight splash of a dipped blade it was like rowing
a balloon car in a cloud, said Brown. Thereafter
Cornelius did not open his lips except to ask querul-
ously for somebody to bale out his canoe, which
was towing behind the long-boat. Gradually the
fog whitened and became luminous ahead. To
the left Brown saw a darkness as though he had
been looking at the back of the departing night.
All at once a big bough covered with leaves appeared
above his head, and ends of twigs, dripping and
still, curved slenderly close alongside. Cornelius,
without a word, took the tiller from his hand."

CHAPTER XLIV.

"I DON'T think they spoke together again. The boat entered a narrow by-channel, where it was pushed by the oar-blades set into crumbling banks, and there was a gloom as if enormous black wings had been outspread above the mist that filled its depth to the summits of the trees. The branches overhead showered big drops through the gloomy fog. At a mutter from Cornelius, Brown ordered his men to load. 'I'll give you a chance to get even with them before we're done, you dismal cripples, you,' he said to his gang. 'Mind you don't throw it away—you hounds.' Low growls answered that speech. Cornelius showed much fussy concern for the safety of his canoe.

"Meantime Tamb' Itam had reached the end of his journey. The fog had delayed him a little, but he had paddled steadily, keeping in touch with the south bank. By-and-by daylight came like a glow in a ground glass globe. The shores made on each side of the river a dark smudge, in which one could detect hints of columnar forms and shadows of twisted branches high up. The mist was still thick on the water, but a good watch was being kept, for as Tamb' Itam approached the camp the figures of two men emerged out of the white vapour, and voices spoke to him boisterously. He answered, and presently a canoe lay alongside, and he exchanged news with the paddlers. All was well. The trouble was over. Then the men in the canoe let go their grip on the side of his dug-out and incontinently fell out of sight. He pursued his

way till he heard voices coming to him quietly
over the water, and saw, under the now lifting,
swirling mist, the glow of many little fires burning
on a sandy stretch, backed by lofty thin timber
and bushes. There again a look-out was kept,
for he was challenged. He shouted his name as
the two last sweeps of his paddle ran his canoe
up on the strand. It was a big camp. Men crouched
in many little knots under a subdued murmur
of early morning talk. Many thin threads of smoke
curled slowly on the white mist. Little shelters,
elevated above the ground, had been built for
the chiefs. Muskets were stacked in small pyramids,
and long spears were stuck singly into the sand
near the fires.

"Tamb' Itam, assuming an air of importance,
demanded to be led to Dain Waris. He found the
friend of his white lord lying on a raised couch
made of bamboo, and sheltered by a sort of shed
of sticks covered with mats. Dain Waris was
awake, and a bright fire was burning before his
sleeping place, which resembled a rude shrine. The
only son of Nakhoda Doramin answered his greeting
kindly. Tamb' Itam began by handing him the
ring which vouched for the truth of the messenger's
words. Dain Waris, reclining on his elbow, bade
him speak and tell all the news. Beginning with
the consecrated formula, 'The news is good,' Tamb'
Itam delivered Jim's own words. The white men,
departing with the consent of all the chiefs, were
to be allowed to pass down the river. In answer
to a question or two Tamb' Itam then reported
the proceedings of the last council. Dain Waris
listened attentively to the end, toying with the
ring which ultimately he slipped on the forefinger

of his right hand. After hearing all he had to say he dismissed Tamb' Itam to have food and rest. Orders for the return in the afternoon were given immediately. Afterwards Dain Waris lay down again, open-eyed, while his personal attendants were preparing his food at the fire, by which Tamb' Itam also sat talking to the men who lounged up to hear the latest intelligence from the town. The sun was eating up the mist. A good watch was kept upon the reach of the main stream where the boat of the whites was expected to appear every moment.

" It was then that Brown took his revenge upon the world which, after twenty years of contemptuous and reckless bullying, refused him the tribute of a common robber's success. It was an act of cold-blooded ferocity, and it consoled him on his death-bed like a memory of an indomitable defiance. Stealthily he landed his men on the other side of the island opposite to the Bugis camp, and led them across. After a short but quite silent scuffle Cornelius, who had tried to slink away at the moment of landing, resigned himself to show the way where the undergrowth was most sparse. Brown held both his skinny hands together behind his back in the grip of one vast fist, and now and then impelled him forward with a fierce push. Cornelius remained as mute as a fish, abject but faithful to his purpose, whose accomplishment loomed before him dimly. At the edge of the patch of forest Brown's men spread themselves out in cover and waited. The camp was plain from end to end before their eyes, and no one looked their way. Nobody even dreamed that the white men could have any knowledge of the narrow channel at the back of the island. When he judged the moment come, Brown yelled, ' Let them have it,' and fourteen shots rang out like one.

"Tamb' Itam told me the surprise was so great that, except for those who fell dead or wounded, not a soul of them moved for quite an appreciable time after the first discharge. Then a man screamed, and after that scream a great yell of amazement and fear went up from all the throats. A blind panic drove these men in a surging swaying mob to and fro along the shore like a herd of cattle afraid of the water. Some few jumped into the river then, but most of them did so only after the last discharge. Three times Brown's men fired into the ruck, Brown, the only one in view, cursing and yelling, ' Aim low ! aim low ! '

"Tamb' Itam says that, as for him, he understood at the first volley what had happened. Though untouched he fell down and lay as if dead, but with his eyes open. At the sound of the first shots Dain Waris, reclining on the couch, jumped up and ran out upon the open shore, just in time to receive a bullet in his forehead at the second discharge. Tamb' Itam saw him fling his arms wide open before he fell. Then, he says, a great fear came upon him—not before. The white men retired as they had come—unseen.

"Thus Brown balanced his account with the evil fortune. Notice that even in this awful outbreak there is a superiority as of a man who carries right —the abstract thing—within the envelope of his common desires. It was not a vulgar and treacherous massacre ; it was a lesson, a retribution—a demonstration of some obscure and awful attribute of our nature which, I am afraid, is not so very far under the surface as we like to think.

"Afterwards the whites depart unseen by Tamb' Itam, and seem to vanish from before men's eyes altogether; and the schooner, too, vanishes after the manner of stolen goods. But a story is told of a white long-boat picked up a month later in the Indian Ocean by a cargo-steamer. Two parched, yellow, glassy-eyed, whispering skeletons in her recognised the authority of a third, who declared that his name was Brown. His schooner, he reported, bound south with a cargo of Java sugar, had sprung a bad leak and sank under his feet. He and his companions were the survivors of a crew of six. The two died on board the steamer which rescued them. Brown lived to be seen by me, and I can testify that he had played his part to the last.

"It seems, however, that in going away they had neglected to cast off Cornelius's canoe. Cornelius himself Brown had let go at the beginning of the shooting, with a kick for a parting benediction. Tamb' Itam, after arising from amongst the dead, saw the Nazarene running up and down the shore amongst the corpses and the expiring fires. He uttered little cries. Suddenly he rushed to the water, and made frantic efforts to get one of the Bugis boats into the water. 'Afterwards, till he had seen me,' related Tamb' Itam, 'he stood looking at the heavy canoe and scratching his head.' 'What became of him?' I asked. Tamb' Itam, staring hard at me, made an expressive gesture with his right arm. 'Twice I struck, Tuan,' he said. 'When he beheld me approaching he cast himself violently on the ground and made a great outcry, kicking. He screeched like a frightened hen till he felt the point; then he was still, and lay staring at me while his life went out of his eyes.'

"This done, Tamb' Itam did not tarry. He understood the importance of being the first with the awful news at the fort. There were, of course many survivors of Dain Waris's party; but in the extremity of panic some had swam across the river, others had bolted into the bush. The fact is that they did not know really who struck that blow—whether more white robbers were not coming, whether they had not already got hold of the whole land. They imagined themselves to be the victims of a vast treachery, and utterly doomed to destruction. It is said that some small parties did not come in till three days afterwards. However, a few tried to make their way back to Patusan at once, and one of the canoes that were patrolling the river that morning was in sight of the camp at the very moment of the attack. It is true that at first the men in her leaped overboard and swam to the opposite bank, but afterwards they returned to their boat and started fearfully up-stream. Of these Tamb' Itam had an hour's advance."

CHAPTER XLV.

"WHEN Tamb' Itam, paddling madly, came into the town-reach, the women, thronging the platforms before the houses, were looking out for the return of Dain Waris's little fleet of boats. The town had a festive air; here and there men, still with spears or guns in their hands, could be seen moving or standing on the shore in groups. Chinamen's shops had been opened early; but the market-place was empty, and a sentry, still posted at the corner of the fort, made out Tamb' Itam, and shouted to those within. The gate was wide open. Tamb' Itam jumped ashore and ran in headlong. The first person he met was the girl coming down from the house.

"Tamb' Itam, disordered, panting, with trembling lips and wild eyes, stood for a time before her as if a sudden spell had been laid on him. Then he broke out very quickly: 'They have killed Dain Waris and many more.' She clapped her hands, and her first words were, 'Shut the gates.' Most of the fortmen had gone back to their houses, but Tamb' Itam hurried on the few who remained for their turn of duty within. The girl stood in the middle of the courtyard while the others ran about. 'Doramin,' she cried despairingly as Tamb' Itam passed her. Next time he went by he answered her thought rapidly, 'Yes. But we have all the powder in Patusan.' She caught him by the arm, and, pointing at the house, 'Call him out,' she whispered, trembling.

"Tamb' Itam ran up the steps. His master was sleeping. 'It is I, Tamb' Itam,' he cried at the door, 'with tidings that cannot wait.' He saw Jim turn over on the pillow and open his eyes, and he burst out at once. 'This, Tuan, is a day of evil, an accursed day.' His master raised himself on his elbow to listen—just as Dain Waris had done. And then Tamb' Itam began his tale, trying to relate the story in order, calling Dain Waris Panglima, and saying, 'The Panglima then called out to the chief of his own boatmen, "Give Tamb' Itam something to eat"'—when his master put his feet to the ground and looked at him with

such a discomposed face that the words remained
in his throat.

"'Speak out,' said Jim. 'Is he dead?' 'May
you live long,' cried Tamb' Itam. 'It was a most
cruel treachery. He ran out at the first shots and
fell.' . . . His master walked to the window and
with his fist struck at the shutter. The room was
made light; and then in a steady voice, but speaking fast, he began to give him orders to assemble
a fleet of boats for immediate pursuit, go to this
man, to the other—send messengers; and as he
talked he sat down on the bed, stooping to lace
his boots hurriedly, and suddenly looked up. 'Why
do you stand here?' he asked, very red-faced.
'Waste no time.' Tamb' Itam did not move. 'Forgive me, Tuan, but . . . but,' he began to stammer.
'What?' cried his master aloud, looking terrible,
leaning forward with his hands gripping the edge
of the bed. 'It is not safe for thy servant to go
out amongst the people,' said Tamb' Itam, after
hesitating a moment.

"Then Jim understood. He had retreated from
one world, for a small matter of an impulsive jump,
and now the other, the work of his own hands,
had fallen in ruins upon his head. It was not
safe for his servant to go out amongst his own
people! I believe that in that very moment he had
decided to defy the disaster in the only way it
occurred to him such a disaster could be defied;
but all I know is that without a word he came out
of his room and sat before the long table, at the
head of which he was accustomed to regulate the
affairs of his world, proclaiming daily the truth that
surely lived in his heart. The dark powers should
not rob him twice of his peace. He sat like a stone

figure. Tamb' Itam, deferential, hinted at preparations for defence. The girl he loved came in
and spoke to him, but he made a sign with his hand,
and she was awed by the dumb appeal for silence
in it. She went out on the verandah and sat on
the threshold, as if to guard him with her body
from dangers outside.

"What thoughts passed through his head—what
memories? Who can tell. Everything was gone,
and he who had been once unfaithful to his trust
had lost again all men's confidence. It was then,
I believe, he tried to write—to somebody—and
gave it up. Loneliness was closing on him. People
had trusted him with their lives—only for that;
and yet they could never, as he had said, never be
made to understand him. Those without did not
hear him make a sound. Later, towards the evening,
he came to the door and called for Tamb' Itam.
'Well,' he asked. 'There is much weeping. Much
anger too,' said Tamb' Itam. Jim looked up at
him, 'You know,' he murmured. 'Yes, Tuan,'
said Tamb' Itam. 'Thy servant does know, and
the gates are closed. We shall have to fight.'
'Fight! What for?' he asked. 'For our lives.'
'I have no life,' he said. Tamb' Itam heard a
cry from the girl at the door. 'Who knows?'
said Tamb' Itam. 'By audacity and cunning we
may even escape. There is much fear in men's
hearts too.' He went out, thinking vaguely of
boats and of open sea, leaving Jim and the girl
together.

"I haven't the heart to set down here such
glimpses as she had given me of the hour or more
she has passed in there wrestling with him for
the possession of her happiness. Whether he had

any hope—what he expected, what he imagined—
it is impossible to say. He was inflexible, and
with the growing loneliness of his obstinacy his
spirit seemed to rise above the ruins of his existence.
She cried ' Fight ! ' into his ear. She could not
understand. There was nothing to fight for. He
was going to prove his power in another way and
conquer the fatal destiny itself. He came out
into the courtyard, and behind him, with streaming
hair, wild of face, breathless, she staggered out
and leaned on the side of the doorway. ' Open the
gates,' he ordered. Afterwards turning to those of
his men who were inside, he gave them leave to
depart to their homes. ' For how long, Tuan ? '
asked one of them timidly. ' For all life,' he said,
in a sombre tone.

" A hush had fallen upon the town after the
outburst of wailing and lamentation that had swept
over the river, like a gust of wind from the opened
abode of sorrow. But rumours flew in whispers,
filling the hearts with consternation and horrible
doubts. The robbers were coming back, bringing
many others with them, in a great ship, and there
would be no refuge in the land for any one. A
sense of utter insecurity as during an earthquake
pervaded the minds of men, who whispered their
suspicions, looking at each other as if in the presence
of some awful portent.

" The sun was sinking towards the forests when
Dain Waris's body was brought into Doramin's
campong. Four men carried it in, covered decently
with a white sheet which the old mother had sent
out down to the gate to meet her son on his return.
They laid him at Doramin's feet, and the old man
sat still for a long time, one hand on each knee,

looking down. The fronds of palms swayed gently, and the foliage of fruit-trees stirred above his head. Every single man of his people was there, fully armed, when the old Nakhoda at last raised his eyes. He moved them slowly over the crowd, as if seeking for a missing face. Again his chin sank on his breast. The whisper of many men mingled with the slight rustling of the leaves.

"The Malay who had brought Tamb' Itam and the girl to Samarang was there too. 'Not so angry as many,' he said to me, but struck with a great awe and wonder at the 'suddenness of men's fate, which hangs over their heads like a cloud charged with thunder.' He told me that when Dain Waris's body was uncovered at a sign of Doramin's, he whom they often called the white lord's friend was disclosed lying unchanged with his eyelids a little open as if about to wake. Doramin leaned forward a little more, like one looking for something fallen on the ground. His eyes searched the body from its feet to its head, for the wound maybe. It was in the forehead and small ; and there was no word spoken while one of the bystanders, stooping, took off the silver ring from the cold stiff hand. In silence he held it up before Doramin. A murmur of dismay and horror ran through the crowd at the sight of that familiar token. The old Nakhoda stared at it, and suddenly let out one great fierce cry, deep from the chest, a roar of pain and fury, as mighty as the bellow of a wounded bull, bringing great fear into men's hearts, by the magnitude of his anger and his sorrow that could be plainly discerned without words. There was a great stillness afterwards for a space, while the body was being borne aside by four men. They laid it down under a tree, and on the instant, with one long shriek, all the women of the household began to wail together; they mourned with shrill cries; the sun was setting, and in the intervals of screamed lamentations the high sing-song voices of two old men intoning the Koran chanted alone.

"About this time Jim, leaning on a gun-carriage, looked at the river, and turned his back on the house; and the girl, in the doorway, panting as if she had run herself to a standstill, was looking at him across the yard. Tamb' Itam stood not far from his master, waiting patiently for what might happen. All at once Jim, who seemed to be lost in quiet thought, turned to him and said, 'Time to finish this.'

"'Tuan?' said Tamb' Itam, advancing with alacrity. He did not know what his master meant, but as soon as Jim made a movement the girl started too and walked down into the open space. It seems that no one else of the people of the house was in sight. She tottered slightly, and about half-way down called out to Jim, who had apparently re-sumed his peaceful contemplation of the river. He turned round, setting his back against the gun. 'Will you fight?' she cried. 'There is nothing to fight for,' he said; 'nothing is lost.' Saying this he made a step towards her. 'Will you fly?' she cried again. 'There is no escape,' he said, stopping short, and she stood still also, silent, devouring him with her eyes. 'And you shall go?' she said slowly. He bent his head. 'Ah!' she exclaimed, peering at him as it were, 'you are mad or false. Do you remember the night I prayed you to leave me, and you said that you could not? That it was impossible! Impossible! Do you remember you said you would never leave me? Why? I asked you for no promise. You promised unasked—remember.' 'Enough, poor girl,' he said. 'I should not be worth having.'

"Tamb' Itam said that while they were talking she would laugh loud and senselessly like one under the visitation of God. His master put his hands to his head. He was fully dressed as for every day, but without a hat. She stopped laughing suddenly. 'For the last time,' she cried menacingly, 'will you defend yourself?' 'Nothing can touch me,' he said in a last flicker of superb egoism. Tamb' Itam saw her lean forward where she stood, open her arms, and run at him swiftly. She flung herself upon his breast and clasped him round the neck.

"'Ah! but I shall hold thee thus,' she cried. . . . 'Thou art mine!'

"She sobbed on his shoulder. The sky over Patusan was blood-red, immense, streaming like an open vein. An enormous sun nestled crimson amongst the tree-tops, and the forest below had a black and forbidding face.

"Tamb' Itam tells me that on that evening the aspect of the heavens was angry and frightful. I may well believe it, for I know that on that very day a cyclone passed within sixty miles of the coast, though there was hardly more than a languid stir of air in the place.

"Suddenly Tamb' Itam saw Jim catch her arms, trying to unclasp her hands. She hung on them with her head fallen back; her hair touched the ground. 'Come here!' his master called, and Tamb' Itam helped to ease her down. It was difficult to separate her fingers. Jim, bending over her, looked earnestly upon her face, and all at once ran to the landing-stage. Tamb' Itam followed him, but turning his head, he saw that she had struggled up to her feet. She ran after them a few steps, then fell down heavily on her knees. ' Tuan ! Tuan ! ' called Tamb' Itam, ' look back ; ' but Jim was already in a canoe, standing up paddle in hand. He did not look back. Tamb' Itam had just time to scramble in after him when the canoe floated clear. The girl was then on her knees, with clasped hands, at the water-gate. She remained thus for a time in a supplicating attitude before she sprang up. ' You are false ! ' she screamed out after Jim. ' Forgive me,' he cried. ' Never ! Never ! ' she called back.

" Tamb' Itam took the paddle from Jim's hands, it being unseemly that he should sit while his lord paddled. When they reached the other shore his master forbade him to come any farther ; but Tamb' Itam did follow him at a distance, walking up the slope to Doramin's *campong*.

" It was beginning to grow dark. Torches twinkled here and there. Those they met seemed awestruck, and stood aside hastily to let Jim pass. The wailing of women came from above. The court-yard was full of armed Bugis with their followers, and of Patusan people.

" I do not know what this gathering really meant. Were these preparations for war, or for vengeance, or to repulse a threatened invasion ? Many days elapsed before the people had ceased to look out, quaking, for the return of the white men with long beards and in rags, whose exact relation to their own white man they could never understand. Even for those simple minds poor Jim remains under a cloud.

" Doramin, alone, immense and desolate, sat in

his armchair with the pair of flintlock pistols on his knees, faced by an armed throng. When Jim appeared, at somebody's exclamation, all the heads turned round together, and then the mass opened right and left, and he walked up a lane of averted glances. Whispers followed him ; murmurs : ' He has worked all the evil.' ' He hath a charm.' . . . He heard them—perhaps !

"When he came up into the light of torches the wailing of the women ceased suddenly. Doramin did not lift his head, and Jim stood silent before him for a time. Then he looked to the left, and moved in that direction with measured steps. Dain Waris's mother crouched at the head of the body, and the grey dishevelled hair concealed her face. Jim came up slowly, looked at his dead friend, lifting the sheet, then dropped it without a word. Slowly he walked back.

"'He came ! He came,' was running from lip to lip, making a murmur to which he moved. ' He hath taken it upon his own head,' a voice said aloud. He heard this and turned to the crowd. ' Yes. Upon my head.' A few people recoiled. Jim waited awhile before Doramin, and then said gently, ' I am come in sorrow.' He waited again. ' I am come ready and unarmed,' he repeated.

"The unwieldy old man, lowering his big forehead like an ox under a yoke, made an effort to rise, clutching at the flintlock pistols on his knees. From his throat came gurgling, choking, inhuman sounds, and his two attendants helped him from behind. People remarked that the ring which he had dropped on his lap fell and rolled against the foot of the white man, and that poor Jim glanced down at the talisman that had opened for him the door of fame, love, and success within the wall of forests fringed with white foam, within the coast that under the western sun looks like the very stronghold of the night. Doramin, struggling to keep his feet, made with his two supporters a swaying, tottering group; his little eyes stared with an expression of mad pain, of rage, with a ferocious glitter, which the bystanders noticed, and then, while Jim stood stiffened and with bared head in the light of torches, looking him straight in the face, he clung heavily with his left arm round the neck of a bowed youth, and lifting deliberately his right, shot his son's friend through the chest.

"The crowd, which had fallen apart behind Jim as soon as Doramin had raised his hand, rushed tumultuously forward after the shot. They say that the white man sent right and left at all those faces a proud and unflinching glance. Then with his hand over his lips he fell forward, dead.

"And that's the end. He passes away under a cloud, inscrutable at heart, forgotten, unforgiven, and excessively romantic. Not in the wildest days of his boyish visions could he have seen the alluring shape of such an extraordinary success! For it may very well be that in the short moment of his last proud and unflinching glance, he had beheld the face of that opportunity which, like an Eastern bride, had come veiled to his side.

"But we can see him, an obscure conqueror of fame, tearing himself out of the arms of a jealous love at the sign, at the call of his exalted egoism. He goes away from a living woman to celebrate his pitiless wedding with a shadowy ideal of conduct. Is he satisfied—quite, now, I wonder? We ought to know. He is one of us—and have I not stood up once, like an evoked ghost, to answer for his eternal constancy? Was I so very wrong after all? Now, he is no more, there are days when the reality of his existence comes to me with an immense, with an overwhelming force; and yet upon my honour there are moments too when he passes from my eyes like a disembodied spirit astray amongst the passions of this earth, ready to surrender himself faithfully to the claim of his own world of shades.

"Who knows? He is gone, inscrutable at heart, and the poor girl is leading a sort of soundless, inert life in Stein's house. Stein has aged greatly of late. He feels it himself, and says often that he is 'preparing to leave all this; preparing to leave, . . .' while he waves his hand sadly at his butterflies."

September 1899–July 1900.

Printed in Great Britain by
WILLIAM BLACKWOOD & SONS LTD.